Long Memories and Other Writings

Also by Peter Cannon

The Chronology out of Time: Dates in the Fiction of H. P. Lovecraft (1986)

H. P. Lovecraft (1989)

Sunset Terrace Imagery in Lovecraft and Other Essays (1990)

Scream for Jeeves: A Parody (1994)

The Early Cannon (1997)

Lovecraft Remembered (editor, 1998)

Forever Azathoth (1999)

More Annotated Lovecraft (coeditor with S. T. Joshi, 1999)

The Lovecraft Chronicles (2004)

Long Memories

and Other Writings

Peter Cannon

Hippocampus Press

New York

Published by Hippocampus Press
P.O. Box 641, New York, NY 10156.
www.hippocampuspress.com

Cover design by Dan Sauer, dansauerdesign.com
Hippocampus Press logo by Anastasia Damianakos.

First Edition
1 3 5 7 9 8 6 4 2

978-1-61498-371-2 (paperback)
978-1-61498-380-4 (ebook)

Contents

Introduction

In the spring of 1996, when my wife, Nan Hawley, and I moved from New York City to London, where Nan was starting a banking job that would allow me to devote myself full-time to writing, I brought with me a dozen or so diaries. In these diaries I had been recording since 1980 anything Lovecraft related, such as my meetings with Frank Belknap Long, HPL's old friend and fellow *Weird Tales* contributor. The entries contained bits of conversations jotted down from memory shortly after they occurred, along with other information that would form the basis of the memoir I completed that summer. I have Ramsey Campbell to thank for persuading the British Fantasy Society to publish *Long Memories: Recollections of Frank Belknap Long* the following year as a chapbook.

After returning to New York in the fall of 1999, I intended to get *Long Memories* published in the U.S., but it was a low priority. Derrick Hussey and S. T. Joshi of Hippocampus Press have been extremely patient over the years while I've taken my time preparing a new edition of the memoir, which I've supplemented with essays and other nonfiction as well as fiction featuring Frank or his various avatars, most notably my novella *Pulptime,* narrated by a young Frank Belknap Long, who plays Dr. Watson to H. P. Lovecraft and Sherlock Holmes. Hence the present volume—so nicely designed and laid out by David E. Schultz—is divided into two sections, Fact and Fiction.

For the American edition, I've made minor corrections and changes. I've added last names for most of the people I called by only their first names in the British edition and dates for the time span of each chapter. At one point, I came across a note I'd made to myself years before that indicated a gathering of Long fans in New York I described was out of sequence. The note provided no specifics. I decided to let it remain as was, not feeling up to the task of rereading my diaries to figure out where I'd erred. I confess to only once having fudged the facts for the sake of economy, combining two meetings after Frank's death with his wife, Lyda, into one. I owe thanks to my friend Ted Klein for the corrected account of his efforts to ensure the *New York Times* ran an obituary of Frank as well as for a telling detail about the evening my first wife and I entertained Frank and Lyda at our Manhattan apartment.

I haven't included every piece in which I use Frank and Lyda. Frank has a cameo role as aged Atal in "Tender Is the Night-Gaunt," and Lyda is the model for the demented copyeditor in "The Undercliffe Sentences," both available in the various editions of my story collection *Forever Azathoth*. And, of course, the Longs play a key role as themselves in the final section of my alternate history novel, *The Lovecraft Chronicles*.

In the summer of 2019, on a trip to the Adirondacks, Nan and I made a stop at the home of rare book dealer Lloyd Currey, from whom I was considering buying two related items. On Lloyd's website the year before, I'd spotted a listing for a copy of *Pulptime* inscribed by Frank to a friend of his, Richard Fawcett, cofounder of the August Derleth Society. Included was a letter dated February 17, 1985, from Frank to Fawcett, the contents of which I didn't read until Lloyd showed me the one-page handwritten letter in his Elizabethtown office. I was hoping Frank would have a lot of good things to say about me and my book, but I was disappointed. Instead, Frank remarks on how much strain he's been under lately, advises Fawcett not to worry about arthritis attacks, and mentions his own bouts with arthritis. Below his signature, in a sort of P.S., Frank refers in passing, albeit favorably, to *Pulptime,* then comments on how he hoped to benefit financially from its modest success. But all he got was the fifty dollars I paid him for the introduction, plus a few bucks in royalties. For Frank, my making him the hero of my story mattered far less than the chance to make money from the potential publicity. I wrote a check to Lloyd anyway.

—*Peter Cannon*

New York City, 2021

Fact

Long Memories

Introduction

I suspect not every Frank Long fan who reads this memoir will like it. Surely Frank himself, an intensely private individual, would not have approved. On the other hand, his wife Lyda, never one to shy from embarrassing personal revelations, may not have minded. They left no immediate survivors with feelings to consider. As only children who married too late in life to produce offspring of their own, Frank and Lyda had to rely largely on friends to look after their needs in old age. I was one of those friends. In the absence of a son or nephew or grandson I played the part I did—and accumulated the experiences that form the basis of this memoir.

I originally thought I should first describe at some scholarly length the friendship between Frank Belknap Long and H. P. Lovecraft back in the 1920s and '30s. Then I imagined skipping across some four decades—those mysterious middle years that Frank neglected to cover in his *Autobiographical Memoir*—to the point where I myself enter the story. I would start out distant and detached, but as I became more and more personally involved lose my emotional grip, until I finally disintegrated, like one of Poe's mad narrators or Delapore at the climax of Lovecraft's "The Rats in the Walls." As a fictional technique this has a lot to recommend it, but in the end I decided it was unsuitable for a memoir, however gothic. A formal essay on FBL and HPL's relationship must await publication elsewhere.

In drawing on my memories of the Longs I have done some selecting and shaping, a bit of dramatizing if you will, but I have invented nothing. I have done my best to quote Frank and Lyda accurately. And despite my many fraught encounters with Frank, I did enjoy his company at times and could see the boyish charm that so impressed Lovecraft.

As the epigraph for *Ackerley,* his biography of the British author J. R. Ackerley, Peter Parker quotes his subject from a letter to Stephen Spender: "To speak the truth, I think that people ought to be upset, and if I had a paper I would upset them all the time; I think that life is so important and, in its workings, so upsetting, that nobody should be spared." In the text Parker cites this passage in discussing *My Dog Tulip,* Ackerley's book about his Alsatian bitch, whose real name was

Queenie. Ackerley acquired Queenie from her original owners through a fluke, and, while she was a difficult and demanding animal, a trial to everyone who had to deal with her, not least Ackerley himself, he remained devoted to her to the end. Parker notes: "In celebrating Queenie Ackerley is celebrating life, in all its mess and muddle." So I like to think in these pages I'm celebrating the lives of Frank and Lyda Long, both of whom incidentally were fond of dogs, in all their mess and muddle.

Prologue

July 2, 1985

"They're here! It's too late I tell you!"

It was a little past seven on a pleasant summer evening, and my fiancée, Julie Glass, and I were waiting, flowers and bottles of wine in hand, outside the apartment of legendary horror and science fiction writer Frank Belknap Long. It was his frail old man's voice we could hear through the door. That morning he and his wife, Lyda (pronounced LEE-da, like the swan of Greek myth), had phoned to invite us to dinner. Just two weeks earlier I'd proposed to Julie. We'd recently returned from Massachusetts, where we'd announced our engagement to our respective parents. Now we were about to make another leap into the unknown. I'd considered not bringing my bride-to-be, but had decided it best to introduce her sooner rather than later to a side of my life that could be difficult. Having known Frank for years, I stood on the verge of entering the Longs' apartment as well as meeting Lyda in the flesh for the first time.

After further muffled bumpings and mutterings, the door finally opened. Lyda, in her wheelchair, welcomed us into a narrow hallway. A single overhead bulb illuminated blood-red walls. Frank took the flowers and wine and disappeared into the darkness beyond. The rest of the apartment would remain in mystery, for it soon became clear that the party would be limited to the hall.

Despite her bad legs and her bulk, Lyda could maneuver well enough, using her arms like an ape. At her bidding we sat down—she in a chair by the door, Julie in a chair next to her, and I in Lyda's wheelchair facing the ladies. Frank stood behind the wheelchair, hovering like Igor, as Julie later put it. From her vantage point she could observe him retreat at intervals, not always to apparent purpose, into the nether regions.

We declined a partly filled glass of vodka proffered by Lyda, instead accepting from Frank an empty, less than sanitary-looking glass, in which we poured vodka and orange juice. (Lyda's comment that neither of them was mechanical when we'd presented the wine suggested it was pointless to ask for a corkscrew.) Julie and I agreed to share the glass, counting on the alcohol to kill any germs. Frank mixed his vodka with Diet Coke, while Lyda swigged hers straight from the bottle. It was plain they'd been drinking before our arrival.

"What can I tell you?" Lyda began. But first she reached over and lifted Julie's turquoise-rimmed sunglasses off her forehead and put them on. After all, she was the star that evening. "I'm being interviewed for *Interview*, Andy Warhol's magazine, you know," she said. "Photographers have been over to take pictures of me, one in the bathtub."

What our hostess proceeded to tell us, with occasional prompting when she wearied or lost the thread, was the life story of Lyda Arco Long. Her parents were famous actors in the Yiddish theater in Russia. She caught polio when she was five, so no stage career for Lydasha. From Russia they made their way to Shanghai, where she lived in a Catholic convent. At age fourteen or sixteen or twenty-one (her statements varied), she and her parents came to America. The family traveled through Canada in vaudeville. Her tone betrayed a certain disdain for Americans and, conversely, an elevated regard for Europeans.

"Don't take anything she says seriously," said Frank. "She's more American than I am, despite her criticisms of Americans." A native New Yorker, Frank owned that he spoke with a Brooklyn accent, though it struck me as being an old-fashioned, educated Brooklyn accent.

As a grown woman, Lyda continued, she had worked as an agent in New York. She had represented many prominent singers and musicians, including Myra Hess. She mentioned other names that were unfamiliar to me, though I had no reason to doubt the essential truth of her account, that she'd been active in the cultural life of New York from about the 1940s on and had known important people in the performing arts. Perhaps she'd been married to a number of them.

To substantiate her claim of past glory there was, screwed into the wall above us, a murallike oil painting done in a flat, cartoon style. I was reminded of *New Yorker* magazine drawings of an earlier era. Several small isolated human figures stood out against a murky background, one of whom, a woman in elegant black dress and elaborately coifed red hair, was strangling a swan.

The Lyda Long of today was dressed in a two-toned pastel summer dress. "I made it myself," she said. "I never wear a bra." Her long gray hair was done up in an untidy bun.

As further proof of her cultured background, she sang for us—snatches of Russian folk songs and operatic airs. Hers was not only a strong but a trained voice. When she asked for requests, we suggested Cole Porter.

"Cole Porter? Who is this Cole Porter? Bah!" Cole Porter was evidently not part of her repertoire.

Lyda did allow "Frankele," whom she ordered about like a servant, to share the stage briefly. He recited a couple of his own poems, most memorably the one with that portentous opening line, "The gods are dead, the earth has covered them." In addition, Frank produced a pen-and-ink drawing used as a logo for one of the World Fantasy Conventions. The design featured cameo portraits of those four giants of the genre: Edgar Allan Poe, H. P. Lovecraft, Stephen King, and Frank Belknap Long.

On one of his forays, after a few unsuccessful attempts to find them, Frank returned with Lyda's dark glasses. These flared at the tips in a pattern of black-and-white checks. Julie retrieved her less exotic pair.

With the business of the glasses sorted out, Frank could now serve dinner—deli food in plastic containers. We the guests ate tuna-fish salad with plastic forks while our hosts watched. They had already eaten, they explained. A dog that resembled a midget German shepherd wandered in, wearing a plastic necklace. The Hound of Tindalos? I had to lift the ice bucket off the floor to let the animal squeeze past the wheelchair. Cockroaches crawled on the painting of Lyda and the swan.

When Lyda resumed her narrative it was to hold forth on Frank.

"Don't take anything she says seriously," Frank piped up.

Lyda sounded serious enough on the subject of his "orthopedist" father (in fact Frank Long, Sr., had been an orthodontist, a dental surgeon) and the decline of the Long family fortunes.

"For forty years Frank didn't have to do anything because of his family's wealth," she boomed. "He wrote a story only when he felt like it. Then somehow he found himself on welfare. Get it?"

Surely Frank had not been quite such a dilettante.

"When I first met Frank at a party, at the National Arts Club I think it was, I wasn't impressed. He was drunk and when he's drunk he drools. Then one Saturday night when I was lonely I called him up—I was one of those popular people everyone assumed had plenty of friends—and he was by himself too. That's where everything started. Get it?"

The time between their meeting and their wedding appeared to be only a matter of weeks.

"Once, when I first knew him, I was kissing him passionately and one of his teeth came out. Can you imagine, the son of a rich orthopedist, and he doesn't have a tooth to call his own in his head!"

"Are you happy, dear!" Frank shrieked from his post behind the wheelchair.

"He has to put gum in his mouth to simulate teeth!"

"Are you happy, dear, humiliating me in front of these people!"

"Frank is a child—that's why I married him," Lyda proclaimed triumphantly.

It may have been at this point that Lyda admitted she suffered from spells of manic depression. "It's genetic, so drugs like lithium don't work," she said. "My mother had a lobotomy."

To our relief Lyda shifted her focus to me. She was impressed that I'd dedicated *Pulptime,* my novella narrated by the young Frank Belknap Long, to my grandparents. That's why she'd wanted to meet me. I must be a nice boy. When I told her my age—thirty-three—she couldn't believe it. I looked twenty-one. She herself was seventy-seven. She would get me on Joe Franklin to promote my book. Since Franklin was based in Secaucus I'd have to arrange for travel to New Jersey. She'd tried to phone me the night before and early that morning but had gotten no answer. When I confessed I'd spent the night at Julie's in Brooklyn, she smiled and exclaimed, "How un-Lovecraftian of you!" (She evidently knew Lovecraft had been a prude.)

Then it was my turn for a taste of the lash. "For a nice boy you're a cheapskate," Lyda declared. "You paid Frankele a measly twenty-five dollars for his introduction to your book."

I protested that I had paid him fifty dollars, then realized Frank may well have underestimated the sum deliberately when he told her about my offer. I defended my actions further by saying he was receiving a percentage of the royalties.

As if it were not already obvious, she admitted they had little money.

They couldn't afford a maid. One problem was that Frank was such an innocent. Once she gave him a Russian brooch to go sell that was worth hundreds, but he came home with only sixty dollars for it. Frank was so easily taken advantage of. He was like the title character of Dostoevsky's *The Idiot.*

Finally, around nine o'clock, Lyda wound down. "I've said all I have to say. Get it?" she announced. Our audience was over. Julie gave Lyda a kiss on the cheek and I kissed her hand in what I imagined might have been the Russian manner. We waved good-bye to Frank behind the wheelchair. I may have had a momentary pang about abandoning good wine they couldn't open (I'd had the foresight to bring red rather than white, in case refrigeration proved a problem), but decided not to delay our escape.

On the street, though we joked it was lucky neither of us had had to ask to use the bathroom, our mood was somber. So this was what married life could be like.

I
Fall 1975–Fall 1980

That memorable dinner proved to be the turning point in my relationship with the Longs. Before that night I considered Frank a casual friend. Afterwards, like it or not, I realized I had a bond with them both as demanding as any blood tie. Indeed, they were to occupy far more of my attention than my dedicatees, my two grandparents then living out their last years in California. Ten years earlier, I'd observed Frank and Lyda at the fabled First World Fantasy Convention, two among a host of colorful characters who'd come to Providence, Rhode Island, H. P. Lovecraft's beloved hometown, to honor the life and work of the great American horror writer. Ten years later, at Woodlawn Cemetery in the Bronx, I would scatter Lyda's ashes over Frank's grave.

To return to the beginning: I first set eyes on Frank around noon Saturday of Halloween weekend 1975. We were both registering late for the convention, in the lobby of the Providence Holiday Inn. The short, slight older man with wispy goatee picking up his program materials, if not immediately recognizable from youthful photographs I'd studied in Arkham House books, could be none other than—his name badge confirmed it—Frank Belknap Long. While I may not have felt exactly like the lady in that twenties song who danced with a man who danced with a woman who danced with the Prince of Wales, for a fan like myself to be standing inches from the person reputed to have been Lovecraft's best friend was no small thrill. Later that day and the next I lurked at the fringes while others paid court to this gentleman and a corpulent red-haired woman in a wheelchair by his side who I surmised was Mrs. Long. Only once did I overcome my diffidence. In the dealers' room I'd picked up a copy of a fan magazine called *Xenophile*, a special Lovecraft issue filled with contributions from many of the writers present. "Mr. Long," as I'm sure I addressed him, was kind enough to sign the page featuring his poem "Innsmouth Revisited." (I also got a friendly, self-deprecating fellow a generation older than myself named Ben Indick to sign his *Xenophile* article, "Lovecraft's Ladies.")

Sunday morning I was in the audience for the convention's final panel, "Lovecraft the Man," whose participants included L. Sprague de Camp, author of the controversial *Lovecraft: A Biography;* Dirk Mosig, a psychology professor acclaimed as the father of modern Lovecraft criticism; and Frank Belknap Long. Supported vigorously by Mosig, Frank did his best to rebut de Camp's image of the Providence Gentleman as impractical misfit and rabid racist. Most of us watching silently cheered these efforts. We felt de Camp had been too harsh, and in fact under pressure he would back down some—if not in front of his opponents on the panel, then in print a year or so later. (What had provoked his undue severity, de Camp confessed, was impatience with weaknesses in Lovecraft he saw in himself.) More than once in his remarks Frank sorely regretted that his own book on HPL, *Howard Phillips Lovecraft: Dreamer on the Nightside,* which presented his case far better than he could in person, had not been ready by convention time.

A few months later, as soon as the order from Arkham House arrived, I devoured *Dreamer on the Nightside* as eagerly as I had de Camp's biography. Again, I was left dissatisfied, if for different reasons. De Camp at least presented a coherent, detailed account, however unsympathetic toward Lovecraft. While having a better understanding of his subject, Long was short on substance. After some charming vignettes in the early chapters, especially of HPL's courtship of his future wife, the memoir trailed off into rambling speculations and hypothetical conversations of little interest. Of course, Frank was writing forty to fifty years after events of which he'd kept no record. He'd simply forgotten much of the past and was too old and too tired to produce the kind of meaty reminiscence fans like me wanted, despite his keenness to correct de Camp.

In addition, Frank temperamentally was no biographer, either of himself or others. In "Some Random Memories of HPL," his brief contribution to *Marginalia,* one of the early Arkham House volumes of Lovecraft miscellany, he warned his readers: "Being in all respects the exact opposite of a Boswell, the most I can hope to do is put down for the record now, while my memories of Howard are still green, a few random impressions." And a few random impressions they are indeed, among the poorest of the several personal tributes written by close friends in the decade following Lovecraft's death in 1937. (Without benefit of letters or other papers, W. Paul Cook served HPL best in the Boswell role. His *In Memoriam* is a magnificent effort, a model of its type.)

Here, too, I should admit that I was unimpressed by what of Frank's fiction I'd read, chiefly in the Arkham House collections of his stories and assorted paperback reprints. In my view Long was simply not in the same league as Lovecraft. How curious that his two most famous stories, "The Space-Eaters" and "The Hounds of Tindalos," both written in the twenties, each used Lovecraft as their protagonist. (In the first tale, the narrator and his friend are called "Frank" and "Howard." In the sequel, "Frank" is still the narrator but, because he was killed off in "The Space-Eaters," the Lovecraft character returns as "Halpin Chalmers"—who as before resides in "Partridgeville," a name I always thought a bad choice for a New England town until I recognized it as a parody of "Providence.") Today these stories are notable as good-humored spoofs, not as sterling examples of weird fiction.

To be fair, Frank in his prime eschewed the weird or supernatural horror tale in favor of science fiction, a genre with a wider market. During the so-called Golden Age of Science Fiction, he shone as a star of the second or third magnitude—before fading with the pulp magazines that were fast becoming obsolete with the rise of the paperback. Not that he was without admirers among his peers. Ray Bradbury, to cite one distinguished name whose opinions deserve respect, has praised Frank's fiction for its gentle childlike wonder. Some readers still respond to this quality in his work, and no doubt future fans will be so affected. Alas, I cannot count myself among this elite. For me Frank's fiction remains at best competent, on average pedestrian, and at worst hilariously awful. I find him more naturally gifted as a poet than a prose stylist. In old age his reputation rested principally on his very survival, on his dedication for most of the century to a profession that paid him few rewards.

If unenthusiastic about the work, I was nonetheless interested in striking up an acquaintance with the man Lovecraft had regarded as his favorite "adopted grandson." In the summer of '75 I had moved from Massachusetts to Manhattan, to seek a career in book publishing. I was living on the Upper West Side, about a dozen blocks south of the West End Avenue address where Frank and his parents had made their home in the early and mid-twenties, when HPL had been a frequent caller. I was walking the same streets that Lovecraft and Long and others of their informal literary circle, the Kalem Club (so called because the original members all had last names starting with K, L, or M), had walked some fifty years before.

Dreamer on the Nightside, to its credit, did convey some sense of that magical era, with its long hours of carefree male companionship and genial conversation. Most of the Kalems were unhampered by regular jobs or wives. For Frank this must have been one of the happiest periods of his life. A slow recovery from an appendicitis, which had cut short his undergraduate studies at NYU, allowed him to read and write at his leisure. Encouraged by his mentor, who'd noticed his promise as an amateur journalist, he made his first story sales to *Weird Tales* magazine. For his older friend Howard, however, this period was a disaster. It had opened on high hopes with his move from Providence to Brooklyn in March of '24, to wed Sonia Greene, a fellow amateur who'd been pursuing him romantically since their meeting in July of '21 at a Boston convention. Economic and emotional difficulties soon put an intolerable strain on the marriage. It effectively ended in the spring of '26 when Lovecraft retreated home to New England, to spend his all too few remaining years, as he told one correspondent, in "a dour celibate dignity." In sum, Frank Long, last of the original Kalems, stood as a sort of living shrine that no Lovecraftian pilgrim to New York could afford to miss.

Finally, finding myself in Greenwich Village one lovely spring afternoon within easy walking distance of Frank's place on West 21st Street, I decided to pay him an unannounced call. I knew that he was at least aware of my existence, thanks to Dirk Mosig, who appeared to be in touch with everyone of consequence in the Lovecraft world. (At the Providence convention timidity hadn't prevented me from chatting with Mosig, with whom I'd since developed a steady correspondence.) Earlier in the day, at the Science Fiction Shop, then located on Eighth Avenue, I'd bought a less than pristine copy of *Marginalia*—for eighty dollars. A hefty price perhaps, but the rare and long out-of-print *Marginalia* was an essential volume for one's Lovecraft library and, it occurred to me as I left the SF Shop, potentially something of interest to Lovecraft's best friend.

Frank lived in Chelsea, a neighborhood north of the Village that had seen better days but was starting to revive. His block, between Ninth and Tenth Avenues, was a pleasant tree-lined street, occupied for much of its southern length by General Theological Seminary (Episcopal). His address, 421, proved to be a brick building six stories high, with flower beds at either side of the entrance, a pair of heavy glass doors. Inside a short flight of steps led up to a glass-fronted door. A lace curtain hid the lobby area beyond. I pressed the buzzer for 1-A, "Long-Arco." It appeared the Longs lived on the ground floor. Arco, I later learned, was Lyda's maiden name.

I identified myself over the intercom, and after a minute or two Frank appeared at the curtained door, dressed in a plain brown bathrobe. I don't remember whether we shook hands. Probably not. If so, it was the first and last time. Frank was not a person who invited such physical familiarity. While I explained how Dirk Mosig had suggested I look him up, Frank nodded. As a conversation starter, I showed him my recent purchase. "Oh, yes," he said, perking up, "one of Howard's first Arkham House books." (He quaintly pronounced it "Awkum.") "I paid three-fifty or thereabouts for it when it came out. Now I'd say a copy without the jacket like yours there would fetch as high as thirty-five or forty dollars . . ." After a pause Frank explained that he was halfway through writing a novel to order for a paperback house, and since it was due in thirty-six hours he had to get back to it. In any case, his wife wasn't feeling well. We parted with assurances we'd meet again soon.

After this encounter I was in no mood to take any further initiative to get together with Frank. A shy man with important work to do, he didn't need yet another stranger pestering him about the past. What, after all, did I have to offer in return? Over the next few years I saw him only on occasion, in the company of other fans, most of whom like myself belonged to the Esoteric Order of Dagon or EOD, an amateur press association whose members self-published "zines" devoted in theory to matters Lovecraftian. These outings afforded little chance for increased intimacy because Frank's voice was so hard to hear. (No doubt a set of false teeth would have helped.) In a group of any size you had to be sitting right next to him to catch everything he said, and somehow I never was. Conversation could be awkward in any event, with long pauses while Frank puffed on his ubiquitous pipe. During one such gathering, in the fall of '79, though, I did manage to get him to inscribe my copy of *Dreamer on the Nightside*.

At this time I had only a dim notion of Frank's financial situation. That he might be truly short of funds finally came home to me in a little incident a year later at the Sixth World Fantasy Convention, held outside Baltimore, Maryland. That Sunday morning of the convention weekend, after discovering the hotel dining room offered only a pricey brunch, I decided to opt instead for breakfast in the snack bar. There I was surprised to pass Frank on his way out, carrying a hot dog.

II
Fall 1980–Fall 1982

Then again, maybe Frank always ate hot dogs for breakfast. At any rate, for him I'm sure I was just another vaguely familiar face in the convention crowd, while for me there were other senior figures on hand of fresher appeal. Most memorably I stood in a decaying Baltimore graveyard at midnight while Fritz Leiber, who'd corresponded with Lovecraft in the final months of his life, recited Poe's "Conqueror Worm" and "The City in the Sea." Earlier in the day I listened to a panel of such younger heavyweights as Stephen King and Peter Straub discuss trends in fantasy and horror in the eighties. I pricked up my ears when the conversation turned to the use of H. P. Lovecraft as a fictional character. Rumor had it that a novel about HPL was in the works.

This was both exciting and unsettling news. For some time I'd been contemplating writing an extended story with Lovecraft as hero, and I feared that another person had already thought of my particular twist—juxtaposing him with Sherlock Holmes. Since the success of Nicholas Meyer's *The Seven-Per-Cent Solution* in 1974, there'd been a spate of novels wherein the great fictional detective dueled with this or that historical personage (or other fictional character, like Dracula). As far as I knew no one yet had thought of linking him to Lovecraft, but I felt that I'd better get cracking before somebody else did.

On the other hand, Lovecraft was not as obvious a candidate for such treatment as, say, Oscar Wilde or Lewis Carroll, given his birth date of 1890. To have Holmes enlist HPL's aid in a case the detective would have to be on the elderly side—and, if I was to retain some vestige of verisimilitude, he would have to be the one to cross the Atlantic, since the horror writer never set foot outside North America. ("I must see London, Child, before I die," Lovecraft once wrote Frank, but he was too poor ever to afford the trip.) I also had to think of a strong motive to bring Holmes to the US after he'd long retired to the Sussex Downs to raise bees. And what of Watson? Well, the good doctor wasn't indispensable. For the role of narrator I had in mind a character who was as close a friend and disciple to Lovecraft as Watson was to

Holmes—the young Frank Belknap Long. The rest of the Kalems—for it was in the heyday of the Kalem Club that I decided to set my apocryphal adventure—could lend background support, like the Baker Street Irregulars whose services the detective from time to time employed.

The following February I began the first draft. About a year later I had a finished manuscript of short-novel length. My friend Ted Klein, editor of *Twilight Zone* magazine, suggested I call it *Pulptime,* to echo E. L. Doctorow's *Ragtime,* which likewise mixed fictional with real people, among them Harry Houdini. The famed escape artist and anti-spiritualist campaigner had a key part in my story as well. Before starting the search for a publisher, I knew I had to secure Frank's permission to proceed. As a book editor I was aware that as a rule you avoided putting living people into a work of fiction, unless thoroughly disguised. I was hopeful, however, that Frank would find nothing offensive in my portrait of him as a young man, indeed might even give the project his blessing. I considered requesting permission through Frank's agent, Kirby McCauley, but on Ted's advice I simply sent him the manuscript directly and waited nervously for his reaction. I agreed with Ted it was better not to raise the permissions issue immediately.

A couple of weeks later Frank called, from the street. Evidently he had no phone. It appeared he liked the story, but I'd gotten a few things wrong. Morton and Leeds, for example, two of the Kalems, never used slang in their speech as I had them do. It was his mother who had been the oversolicitous one, not both parents. And so on. I promised to amend the narrative accordingly. Furthermore, I assured him I hadn't submitted the manuscript anywhere, nor was I trying to pass it off as his work. Frank was especially concerned that he not be credited as author. Then he spoke of his personal situation:

"It's been a terrible year for me. My wife's had an operation, I'm behind in my work, I haven't had time to socialize, not even with Tom." Tom Collins, a fellow EOD member, lived in Frank's neighborhood and was, I gathered, his closest friend. "But I do want to go over the manuscript with you. I'll call you again in two weeks. We can meet at a local bar."

When in closing I said I was willing to let him have a share of any income from the sale of *Pulptime,* he replied, "Don't worry about that."

I waited a month for Frank to phone back before initiating a get-together of the New York area gang. I hesitated to be too direct. In the end the only EODer available was Tom. A few days before the June date Tom and I had set, I mailed Frank a postcard inviting him to join us for dinner, our treat. Tom later confirmed that Frank could make it but only for the early part of the evening. His wife was too ill to leave alone for long. Later that night Tom and I would attend an off-off-Broadway play with a plot inspired by Poe.

When at six o'clock that Saturday I arrived at our designated rendezvous spot, a Blimpie's on Eighth Avenue, the two of them were already seated. "I was just telling Tom about your story," said Frank. "How you got the slang all wrong." He went on to say he didn't think Arkham House would be a good place to submit *Pulptime*. He didn't explain why, or else his remarks were lost in the background noise.

At Tom's suggestion we left the Blimpie's for a bar a couple of blocks away. It was drizzling and Frank walked slowly, though for a man of around eighty he seemed in pretty good shape, both physically and mentally. The only obvious sign of decay was his tobacco-stained fingers. We stopped briefly at Tom's so Frank could use the bathroom. I remained in the hall outside the apartment—Tom hoped I wouldn't mind but it was too much of a mess. "My place isn't fit for visitors either," Frank added.

We passed Frank's building on West 21st, and again I noted that he lived on an attractive block. At a trendy restaurant on Tenth Avenue we got a table in the bar area and ordered drinks—beers for Frank and myself, a Scotch for Tom. While Tom did most of the talking, I did get a chance, for the first time, to ask Frank about himself. He'd spent all his life in New York, his first home having been in Harlem, where he was born. He didn't especially care for the city, though. In fact, like Lovecraft, he preferred New England. During the summer he and his wife got away to the country. (Perhaps they weren't so badly off, I thought.) He was pleased with Tom's interview of himself in *Twilight Zone*, which I'd read in a recent issue. Tom smiled. Unlike myself, he was at ease with Frank, to the point of engaging him in a little playful kidding.

HPL had been a tremendous letter-writer, Frank resumed, but he less so. "I'm very careful about what I say in letters," he said, confessing that he'd been burned by being too candid in writing to Donald Wan-

drei, one of the founders of Arkham House, concerning a certain notorious figure in the Lovecraft world. As for the volume of mail he received, "I have more correspondents than I can possibly handle—
professors and fans asking about Lovecraft and so forth. I don't have
time to answer them."

Frank appeared to take a more balanced view of his late friend's literary stature than the run of his correspondents. "Joshi exaggerates
HPL's greatness," he said. "He's not Henry James." Frank was referring
to leading Lovecraft scholar S. T. Joshi, whose last name he pronounced "Jaw-shi" instead of "Joe-shi." Though he would hear others
say it correctly, he never would get it right. Back in the thirties Frank
had called a new member of their circle, Herman C. Koenig, "*Co*-nig"
instead of the proper "*Kay*-nig." In a letter from this period Lovecraft
remarked, "Belknap—who is slow to learn new ways—still says Co'nig
quite unashamedly!"

A little before eight Tom and I announced we had to go if we were
to get any dinner before our play started. Tom picked up the tab—one
beer for Frank, two beers for me, and two Scotches for himself. On the
sidewalk we said good-bye. For the moment the rain had stopped. "I'll
write you with my comments and suggestions for your story," Frank assured me before heading home.

Tom and I grabbed a hurried bite at a Chinese restaurant across the
street. *Extraordinary Histories,* a mishmash of various poems and stories, turned out to be enjoyable enough, though the non-Poe fan would
have been mystified. I parted from Tom afterwards with promises of
trying to arrange an EOD expedition to the Bronx to visit the Poe Cottage, which HPL and Frank and others of the Kalems had toured some
sixty years before. But Tom was soon to leave New York for a job on the
West Coast, and no trip to the Poe Cottage materialized that summer.

Neither did any communication from Frank. I sent *Pulptime* to Jim
Turner, editor of Arkham House, who in rejecting it confided that they
already had a novel with Lovecraft as a major character under contract.
So the rumors were true. At least this other book, judging from Jim's
remarks, didn't also feature Sherlock Holmes.

At the World Fantasy Convention that fall, held in New Haven, I
spotted Frank and Lyda but made no approach. Three weeks later a group
of us made one of our Saturday tours of the Village bookstores, from the

Strand and Forbidden Planet in the east to Foul Play and the Science Fiction Shop in the west. Though no one had tried to alert him in advance, a tentative part of our itinerary included dropping in on Frank.

Since I'd forgotten to check his address before leaving in the morning, it took us some searching to find his building that afternoon. Lyda responded to the buzzer, and after a bit of a wait Frank appeared at the door. He seemed quite pleased to see us, indeed went on to say how disappointed he'd been to see no EOD people in New Haven. He'd been taking a nap and could join us in twenty minutes. "I was going to call you," he said to me.

At my suggestion we wandered over to the Blimpie's on Eighth. The gang was content to pass on visiting the Nicholas Roerich Museum, which housed a collection of paintings that had deeply impressed Lovecraft half a century before. Once settled, fellow EODer Bob Price and I returned at a leisurely pace to West 21st Street to retrieve Frank. Back at the Blimpie's I bought him a cup of coffee. Again, because there were five of us in addition to Frank, it was a challenge to catch his every word. He'd brought a number of items to show us—Spanish and Italian editions of his tales, translations of the usual Long classics, as well as copies of a new story in chapbook form, *Rehearsal Night.* I accepted Frank's offer to purchase one of these, with its tobacco-smudged cover, for the bargain price of twelve bucks. It regularly cost fifteen.

"I'd like to see a 'best of' collection of my stories. No one's done it yet," Frank said. He admitted Lester Del Rey had been an enemy since some long-ago dispute, so there was no hope for the Del Rey paperback line. "I've written some of my best stories in recent years, yet *Twilight Zone* keeps rejecting them. Not cheerful enough, I suppose." In fact, Ted had published a new tale of his to accompany Tom's interview, but I could see how from his perspective that didn't really count.

Bob solicited Frank to contribute to his zine, *Crypt of Cthulhu* (subtitled "A Pulp Thriller and Theological Journal"), which was beginning to circulate outside the EOD. A Baptist minister as well as community college teacher, Bob was an enterprising fellow with a good sense of humor. In particular he hoped Frank would be willing to compose a passage from the *Necronomicon,* Lovecraft's mythical tome. Evidently there was more demand for new Long fiction at the fan than at the professional level.

Frank wrote S. T. Joshi a check for ten dollars, payment for some obscure item or service S. T. had provided. "My bank is closed," he said. Using the cash I'd given him for the chapbook didn't seem to be an option. When someone asked whether the accent on the word *Tindalos* fell on the first or second syllable, he chuckled and said he didn't know. Either pronunciation was correct.

Finally, Frank expressed astonishment at the sexual explicitness of *Penthouse* and other skin magazines of the modern era. "Such things would've been unimaginable when I was growing up. Absolutely unimaginable." Where had Frank seen *Penthouse*, I wondered. Courtesy of some obliging fan?

A few days later I read *Rehearsal Night*. A total muddle. If it was representative of his recent work then, as Ted had suggested, the "early Long" was synonymous with the "best of Long."

III
Winter 1983–Winter 1984

In early February of '83 Frank called from a pay phone—in the rain, no doubt. He had several questions to ask me. Had I heard from Tom? Not since Christmas, I replied. Was I in touch with Marc? Marc Michaud, publisher of Necronomicon Press, had given him an advance to write an autobiography and he was late delivering the manuscript. Based in Rhode Island, Necronomicon specialized in Lovecraft-related books and magazines, including the scholarly journal *Lovecraft Studies,* edited by S. T. Joshi. I told Frank not to worry, Marc could wait a little longer. Finally, who were those other two guys, besides Bob and Joshi, at the Blimpie's last fall? I could remember the name of only one of them myself. Frank stopped talking once his three minutes were up.

Clearly, our visit had meant a lot to him. Feeling guilty, I phoned Ted and said I thought Frank would appreciate having some company. Ted confessed he hadn't gotten in touch as he'd mentioned he would, but would drop him a line the next day. A month later the two of us and Alice Turner, an editor friend of Ted's, had dinner with Frank at Harvey's, an old-fashioned, wood-paneled restaurant that was a Chelsea landmark and a nice change from Blimpie's. Beforehand, I met Frank at his building. On the walk over he launched into his litany about how many letters he received from fans and scholars and how he regretted having time only to answer a few. He was amazed at how much money some horror writers were being paid. Over dinner I sat at the opposite end of the table, next to Alice. Ted had the task of making conversation with Frank. Afterwards Ted and I agreed that for someone billed as Lovecraft's "best friend" Frank simply wasn't that interesting. What had Lovecraft found so fascinating? (In fact, when I studied HPL's *Selected Letters* carefully, I saw that he grew progressively disillusioned with his young protégé.)

In June Frank phoned me to say he'd enjoyed my "interview" with Lovecraft in the latest *Twilight Zone.* "You got HPL's speech just right." No great feat, as I'd constructed the text from passages in Lovecraft's letters. As usual he hadn't heard in a while from Tom. He had a story appearing in an anthology, *Whispers 4* (actually *Weird Tales 4*, I later learned, a less prestigious venue), and was working on a novel. "It's gratifying to receive all the kind letters from people, especially in the last year or two," he said, "but unfortunately that doesn't translate into increased income."

Early one morning toward the end of July, Frank called to ask to borrow twenty dollars. He needed it to get through the weekend. Normally his agent took care of tiding him over, but Kirby was out of town. He met me later at my office, which, located at Park and 32nd, wasn't too far to come from Chelsea. Frank gave me a check. I promised not to cash it until the following week, presumably after the deposit of his monthly Social Security check. "My wife is difficult," he explained. "She thinks I have a much larger income than I do."

Two weeks later, I had lined up Bob and Sam Gafford (one of the guys at the Blimpie's Frank had been curious about) for another social outing. Frank was ready for us when we arrived at his door. At his suggestion we walked over to a diner on the corner of Ninth and 23rd, the Chelsea Square. He'd had another place in mind that might have been a little nicer, but the Chelsea Square turned out to be perfectly decent.

Frank said he was pleased with the ten dollars Bob had paid him for his three-hundred-word extract from the *Necronomicon*. "I put in two hours work on it." Five dollars an hour didn't strike me as a very good rate. Bob offered to pay him forty dollars for a sequel to "The Hounds of Tindalos." Frank said he'd do it right away, since he needed the money. "In the past couple of years I've received all sorts of awards," he added. "Isaac Asimov gave me a silver cup. But they don't translate into cash." Frank then got going on Stephen King, who was fast becoming the most commercially successful horror author of all time. Frank just couldn't understand it. Why was Stephen King, also a client of Kirby's, raking in the millions while he wasn't?

Frank admitted to writing a couple of pornographic novels in the past. These apparently hadn't been any more of a goldmine than his legitimate fiction. (I later identified them as *Woman from Another Planet* and *The Mating Center*.)

Frank tended to repeat the same themes. Now and then, though, he'd come up with a new Lovecraft anecdote. This time he mentioned that the two of them once climbed up on a New York lightboat where

Howard recited his narrative poem "Psychopompos." This was the sort of detail we fans wished he'd put more of into *Dreamer on the Nightside.*

When Frank complained that the publisher of *Weird Tales 4* hadn't sent him his contributor's copies, Sam gave him his copy, which he'd bought earlier in the day. (I later read Frank's story, "Homecoming," in which Lin Carter, the series editor, had let pass the howler, "The letter had clearly been written before his uncle's death," the letter's author being the uncle.) At parting Frank told me he'd like to get together again with "Twilight Zone," meaning Ted. I said I'd see what I could arrange, but their meeting at Harvey's proved to be their last before Ted resigned the magazine's editorship in 1985.

In early December, I received a rejection letter from Pinnacle, the one professional house where I felt I had a prayer. The editor had held *Pulptime* for months, but in the end decided it was aimed at too specialized a market. That same day, however, a letter came from W. Paul Ganley, editor of Weirdbook Press, a specialty publisher I'd queried, asking to see the complete manuscript. By New Year's Ganley had sent me his acceptance. I had agreed to change the ending—and to try to persuade Frank to provide a foreword.

In late January, I met Frank after work at his building. This time he let me into the lobby area, while he returned inside his apartment. Ten minutes later we were on our way to the Chelsea Square, where we had dinner. "My wife doesn't like it here. Not fancy enough for her." In fact, the food was good and reasonably priced. "She gives me a hard time sometimes," he added. As usual Frank lamented his not making any money from the attention he'd been getting. "I'd like to see a collection of my later stories published, my best stories, but there doesn't seem to be much of a chance of that. I've been able to place nearly all my stories in the past couple of years, through Kirby, and there may be a television sale in the offing. The money, though, is in novels. I'm working on two of them now." The vagaries of literary reputation concerned him. He was astonished that Joseph Hergesheimer, a well-known writer in the twenties, could be so utterly forgotten today.

At last I broached the subject of his writing a foreword to *Pulptime.* I said I could get him fifty dollars, apparently his minimum rate, plus a one-percent royalty. Ganley had given me a hundred-dollar advance— *Pulptime* was not going to make either my fortune or Frank's. I said I'd changed the story so that now it was his mother, not both his parents, who worried overly much about his health. To my relief, Frank was agreeable. He'd do it right away. His main concern was that he be paid up front. As for content: "Maybe I'll have some news about hearing from Sherlock Holmes."

Frank had recently heard from another one of Lovecraft's "grandsons," Alfred Galpin, who was in Paris. Galpin had just sold his Lovecraft letters. Frank had sold his Lovecraft letters long ago to Samuel Loveman, another friend of HPL's, for hundreds of dollars when his mother was sick and he needed money to pay her hospital bills. "If I'd held on to them they'd now be worth tens of thousands." It irked him that old letters of his were being sold and he got nothing. Some years after HPL's death, Loveman had turned against Lovecraft after reading anti-Semitic comments in letters to others. In his friend's defense, Frank said Howard got along well with Sonia's Jewish friends, including a noted columnist named Isaacson. On the other hand, Mosig went too far, was too fanatical in trying to clear Lovecraft of the racist charge.

When I commented on the bond between himself and HPL, Frank confirmed it: "Howard very much saw a younger version of himself in me. We both came from similar old American families, we both had coddling mothers." In his youth Frank was an agnostic, much to his mother's distress. Mrs. Long had been a regular churchgoer.

On the walk back to his door Frank said he'd had a letter recently from Joseph Payne Brennan, another *Weird Tales* veteran. Brennan had a heart condition, while his wife had suffered a nervous breakdown. His latest short story collection, even with the Stephen King introduction, evidently didn't sell much. "So relative to others, I'm not doing so badly," he said.

As soon as I got home I wrote Frank a note thanking him for his cooperation and enclosed a check for fifty dollars. A few days later he phoned to thank me. "Fifty dollars is fine," he said. "You needn't bother about a royalty or a contract."

IV
Winter 1984–Fall 1984

As a junior editor at a major New York publishing house, however, I did care about such formalities. In due course, Paul prepared a letter of agreement for Frank that permitted me to use the persona of his younger self as *Pulptime*'s narrator in return for a fifty-dollar flat fee and a one-percent royalty on any reprint.

In late February Frank phoned to tell me he'd almost finished his foreword, or introduction as he called it, to my book. "I want to read it over another time before mailing it to you." It sounded as if I'd have it shortly. He was still anxious about the status of his autobiography. He was supposed to get $150 on delivery of the manuscript, having already received three hundred dollars. This struck me as big money for Necronomicon Press. He hoped to take a week off to clean up the apartment so he and Lyda could have friends over. He indicated he'd enjoyed the most recent New Kalem gathering, which I'd missed.

For about a year, in emulation of the original Kalem Club, some of us Lovecraft devotees had been meeting regularly at the East Side apartment of Lin Carter, another senior horror-fantasy figure. With his slight build, thick-lensed glasses, gray mane of hair and goatee, Carter could have been taken for Frank's younger brother (a more worldly and profane younger brother, I hasten to add, for our bachelor host, who liked to boast of his male prowess, favored the erotic in his decor—most memorably cartoon drawings in his bathroom of sexually active aliens). Frank was always welcome to join the group, but because it was a long way to go and Lyda was ill he invariably failed to appear, until the one time I happened not to be present.

A few days after our phone conversation, at the next New Kalem meeting, I asked how the previous one had gone with Frank there. Bob said Frank had had a good time but had nodded off after one glass of wine. Bob was contemplating a special Long issue of *Crypt*, to include a couple of unreprinted stories from the twenties, "The Eye Above the Mantel" and "The Desert Lich." On the question of the early versus the late Long, Lin was blunt: "Frank's a terrible writer. Always has been. He's a sweet old guy, though."

Three weeks later, en route to another gathering of the New Kalems, I decided to swing through Frank's neighborhood and was lucky enough to run into him on West 21st Street.

"I was just on my way to the phone booth on the corner to call you," he said. Lyda had been sick, with edema, and might have to go into the hospital again. "The past two months I've never been under such pressure." They hoped she was healthy enough to make it to the forthcoming Lunacon in New Jersey, where they could see friends. He hadn't had a chance to straighten up the apartment. As for the introduction to my story, he had revised it and made it much stronger since he'd promised he almost had it ready. He had only the last paragraph to work on. He'd mail it to me soon. "I doubt I'll make it this afternoon, but please give everyone my greetings." At the New Kalem meeting, Lin did a wicked imitation of Frank mumbling then falling asleep on the couch.

More than a week later, Frank called: "I've just put my introduction for you in the mail. It runs to five pages, part of it handwritten because one of my typewriters broke down." He had both a pica and an elite, he explained. He'd tried to keep the piece light as befitted the tone of the story, which he recognized was basically a comedy with some serious bits. Lyda was still in the hospital, but was doing okay and might be out by the end of the week. He didn't get to the Lunacon—too far to go, especially on St. Patrick's Day and with uncertain travel arrangements at the other end.

Two days later the foreword came—four untidy sheets, mostly typed, with the final page in blue ink. Notwithstanding the agonizing wait, I had no reason to complain. How often does an author get his narrator to supply a foreword? The spirit was appropriately tongue-in-cheek, though Frank couldn't resist a pessimistic aside when touching on the subject of Lovecraft's fame enduring well into the twenty-first century: "always remembering, of course, that there may not be a twenty-first century for Man."

After sending him a note thanking him for his foreword, he phoned to say he was glad I liked it. He'd sent the letter of agreement back to Ganley. At the next gang gathering I got everyone to sign a birthday card to Frank. In my note I suggested we meet soon for dinner.

He called on his birthday, April 27. "Have you heard from Crawford?" he asked. By Crawford he meant Ganley. (He probably was confusing Paul Ganley with William Crawford, a small press publisher who'd issued HPL's *The Shadow over Innsmouth* in book form in the thirties.) I gave him an update on the status of *Pulptime*, which was scheduled to come out in the summer. Lyda was again in the hospital. "This year has been terrible," he said. "I've never been under such pressure." The usual refrain. He was curious to find out how I knew it was his birthday. I said I'd seen it in a who's who of fantasy. He promised to call another time to schedule a get-together.

As the publication date neared, I had a scare when I discovered that Sherlock Holmes was not in the public domain and I would need permission from the estate. I was fortunate that the estate's U.S. representative, Otto Penzler, and I were quickly able to come to an understanding.

Frank and I spoke again in June. Lyda was in and out of the hospital. He hadn't finished his novel, which Kirby was sure he could sell, despite the field not being in very good shape for the past couple of years. I informed Frank that the New Kalems were no more, since Lin Carter had been evicted from his apartment. (Serious financial and health problems would take their toll on Lin, who was to die in 1988.) In another conversation he reported he was under too much pressure to set a date to get together. Lyda had been difficult. "When she's feeling well she gets angry and takes it out on me," he confided. He worried about the cost of a phone call going up to twenty-five cents. "Lyda makes a lot of them." In discussing *Pulptime*, he continued to refer to Ganley as "Crawford."

The last week of July, he called to borrow thirty dollars. For unspecified reasons he didn't want to bother Kirby. When he came by my office to give me the check, dated August 1, he had an issue of *Pulpsmith* to show me. It included a reprint of "The Hounds of Tindalos." The editor was a fan. Next issue there would be an interview. He was expecting several checks from foreign sales in August. The final day of the month he phoned to request that I hold off a few more days before depositing his check. Again, he promised to get together soon.

Soon turned out to be the last day of September, when I lugged a box of twenty-four copies of *Pulptime* down to Frank's for his signature. After the customary wait, he came out and we walked over to a new place on West 23rd near Seventh he knew of, a cafeteria. But it turned out it had discontinued its cafeteria service—it was now just a bar. We ordered beer and sandwiches. Frank signed all twenty-four copies, laboriously printing his name. He had the usual items to share—somebody's EOD zine with a reprint of "The Space-Eaters," the summer issue of *Pulpsmith* with the interview of him, and a new Berkeley paperback edition of *The Hounds of Tindalos*. Bob had asked him to write another story, had even supplied an outline, but for fifty dollars he wasn't sure it was worth it. "You have to write a novel to make real money. I hope I can come up with a strong one." The following week he'd be meeting Kirby to discuss his novel-in-progress.

On rereading *Pulptime* Frank said he had enjoyed it all the more. "Of course, you got a few things wrong—not that they matter. Having a lively story is the important thing." He then proceeded to enumerate my faults. HPL had three or four ways of speaking, but he would never have used slang at that period, only in his letters. James Morton never used slang, and he would never have mentioned sex in conversation as I had him do at one point. The line, "And when they dragged your weary flesh through Baltimore—did you betray the ticket, Poe?" I had his younger self quote from Hart Crane's *The Bridge* had a very clear meaning to him—genius abused. (One theory has it that, shortly before his death, Poe fell victim on election day to partisans who got citizens drunk so they could vote several times.) Speaking of politics, Frank admitted he'd been on the left in the past and despaired of Reagan. The current mixing of religion and politics would have been unimaginable in another era. His parents had been Baptists, religious but not overly so. Finally, it was time to get back home to Lyda, who hadn't been feeling well and had been sort of depressed for the past week. "Good luck with your book," he said. "You ought to sell three thousand of them."

At the World Fantasy Convention that fall, held in Ottawa, I did my best to push *Pulptime,* which had a first printing of fifteen hundred copies, both paper and cloth. Friday evening, before the hordes were let in for the traditional author signing, Stephen King himself approached where I was sitting at the tables reserved for us mere mortals, seemingly attracted by the promotional poster an artist friend of mine had created for *Pulptime*. He peered from a distance for a moment or two, then went back to his special table, set aside to accommodate the army of book-laden fans who would soon be descending on him.

After my return to New York, Frank called. "This may sound egotistical," he said, "but I'm curious to know if anyone talked about me at the convention." I replied that I remembered hearing his name in passing, even though I hadn't. To my relief the three-minute warning cut us off before I could elaborate further.

V
December 1984–July 1985

The day after Christmas Frank called. From the lack of background noise other than a television it appeared the Longs now had a phone. Frank confirmed this and gave me the number. He was curious to hear about the recent group gathering in Marblehead, inspired by Lovecraft's "The Festival," his Yule yarn celebrating the old Massachusetts seaport. I informed him that Bob was getting married in a few days and would be moving back to the South, where he'd grown up. Frank had a story to pass on to him for *Crypt*. He was sorry to see him go, since Bob had been the driving force behind the local gang.

In the background Lyda shouted something. Frank said he worried about her running up a big phone bill, then put her on the line. Feeling I needed to justify my use of her husband in *Pulptime*, I told her Frank would be getting royalty money, since it had just been reprinted. After a minute Frank got back on. He confessed he hadn't done a good job getting out Christmas cards. After New Year's we'd get together.

Later that night, to my surprise, Lyda called. It seemed she hadn't focused on who I was during our earlier chat. "I wanted to tell you how original your book was," she said. "How much better than the usual science fiction-fantasy crap. It's beautifully produced, too." From my voice she took me to be in my twenties. I said I was thirty-three but looked younger. She liked the fact that I'd dedicated the book to my grandparents. She spoke of her own family, who had been in the Yiddish theater under the czars. She'd written an account of her grandfather and was planning to do her own life though she was no writer. When she asked if I'd read Dostoevsky's *The Idiot*, I said no. "There's a character in it who's just like Frank—smart, talented, modest, but easily taken advantage of." Then she asked, "Did you know we eloped?" Again I said no. "Frank proposed to me an hour after we met. Twenty-five years we've been married and it's still like the first day!" She closed by promising to have some of us over soon.

Early in the new year, I phoned Frank to schedule a get-together. Eager to discuss his autobiography with S. T., the editor of Necronomicon Press, he suggested we go out to dinner in the neighborhood. Then Lyda got on. She had in mind making a social occasion of it at their apartment, not going out. When I said a Lovecraft scholar would be along, referring to S. T., she said, "I'm not a great fan of Lovecraft's. He stole my thunder by marrying someone like me, a Russian Jew, and Frank had to follow his example!" When Frank got back on, I reassured him Bob was going ahead with the special Long issue of *Crypt*. He'd just written Bob a long letter saying he was ready with a new story.

In the event we did go out, for a "business" meeting, but not before Frank called to accuse me of misinforming him that Bob had moved to Mississippi. I had in truth told him that Bob was originally from Mississippi and had recently moved to North Carolina. (I could identify with HPL when he complained in his letters about Frank's tendency to mix things up. "These Yankees think Southern states are all the same" was Bob's comment.) Dinner, at the Chelsea Square, proved an awkward affair, with Frank admitting he didn't really have much to discuss with S. T. about his autobiography. He brought a couple of items to show us—a Spanish edition of his tales and a book of black-and-white photographs of SF authors. The one of himself was excellent.

At the end of February, Lyda called. "I'm still planning to send you my memoir," she said, "but I've been under pressure of a deadline." She was aware of the second printing of *Pulptime*. "You see Frank's name does count for something."

In April, Frank called to say he could have his autobiography ready in two weeks if Marc could give him a check for the remaining advance immediately on delivery of the manuscript. "I could be paid better if I did other sorts of writing," he said, "but this is important." I alerted S. T., who promised he'd call Marc to let him know. I phoned Frank back to tell him that he should soon be hearing from Marc. Frank asked me about *Pulptime*. He said he continued to plug it to his correspondents. Since things were somewhat confused at his place that evening, we left it that I'd call him the next day at around the same time. Twenty-four hours later, Lyda answered the phone after about ten rings and put Frank on. Marc had reached him the previous night and all was well. He thanked me for my efforts.

By the middle of May, S. T. let me know he had Frank's manuscript in hand. The two of them had met for a drink recently at the

Chelsea Square, where Frank had griped about Stephen King's good fortune. A week later, Marc phoned to ask if I'd like to write a foreword to Frank's memoir. I said I wouldn't have thought one was necessary, but Marc explained that Frank had said little about himself (he mentioned Lyda only once in passing, and not by name). I agreed to do it. After all, he had done me a similar favor.

A few days later, as I was making some notes for the foreword, the man himself called. He was anxious about the status of his autobiography. I told him it had reached Necronomicon Press and was scheduled to come out in July. I declined to mention my own role in the project. Frank was also concerned that the new Arkham House novel with Lovecraft as a character would portray HPL as a racist. *Lovecraft's Book*, by the science fiction author Richard Lupoff, had been out a couple of weeks and was dedicated to him. He hadn't seen a copy yet. (I shortly acquired a copy of *Lovecraft's Book*. Lupoff's view of Lovecraft was certainly no more damning than that of de Camp's biography. *Pulptime* had underlined his racist side as well.)

At the end of May, I received a photocopy of Frank's *Autobiographical Memoir*, as it was to be called, from Marc, who now suggested I do an "afterword" instead. Frank had already written an introduction. It was only about fifty pages, much of it handwritten. A superficial glance indicated that it was a lot of hot air, low on substance. A close reading confirmed my initial impression. With few specific anecdotes of interest, it was far worse than *Dreamer on the Nightside*. The style was particularly wordy, the opening sentence epitomizing the whole: "It is often taken for granted—I've always felt quite unjustifiably—that a fiction writer's characters are thinly disguised aspects of himself wearing multiple-personality type costumes." The final paragraph of my afterword opened, "Champion of the florid, extravagant poetry and prose that flourished in the decadent era just before his birth . . . ," an awkward attempt to put the best face on his clumsy prose.

When I met S. T. a week later to deliver the finished afterword, we agreed that Frank's forte was as a poet or prose-poet. He had never been able to sustain any longer piece, fiction or nonfiction, with any coherence. S. T. remarked that Frank had received a total of six hundred dollars for the memoir from Necronomicon, a sizeable advance for a small press.

Toward the end of June, Lyda phoned, from the intensive care unit of the hospital, she claimed, sounding hale and hearty. She was full of plans for Frank's enemies. First and foremost was Kirby, whom she resented for failing to get any of Frank's stories adapted for the new *Twilight Zone* television series. "Even though Kirby gives Frank a hundred dollars from time to time, I feel he has his worst interests at heart," she said. "Why did Stephen King choose Kirby as his agent? Because King admired Frank so much and Kirby, then a nobody, was Frank's agent." Tom was next on the list, though he hadn't been on the scene for years. She was sure he had moved next door in order to exploit Frank, whom he used to ask to look after his cats when he was away. Furthermore, Tom had spread the rumor that she was manic-depressive. "My 'idiot' would die if he knew I was telling you all this, so mum's the word."

Lyda admitted she was seventy-seven years old, "three times your age." It was their twenty-fifth anniversary, but they hadn't had much of a celebration. "It kills me when Frank has to borrow money from you." She indicated she had a press conference in the works about her book on the Yiddish theater in czarist Russia. She would promote my book as well. "I'd like to meet you," she said. "I'll call again." Which she did a short time later, to suggest I phone them at four the next day so she could invite me to dinner.

At a quarter past three the following day, Frank called to tell me not to phone at four. "Lyda and I have had a big fight," he said, "and I fear we're breaking up." He wanted to talk to me, but it would have to wait. That night Lyda called. "We're having guests for dinner tomorrow and you're invited," she said. I had to decline. "Anyway, we need to borrow fifteen dollars—no, better make it twenty-five—to pay for it, so you and Frank have to get together." She had a few choice words on how she was going to get Kirby before abruptly hanging up.

When Frank stopped by my office to give me a check, he seemed in reasonably good spirits. He'd recently heard from Tom, who wasn't happy with his job. "I'd like to do a collection of my short stories, ten old and ten new," he said, "but everyone tells me I have to do a novel first." He was upset by *Lovecraft's Book,* which he felt portrayed HPL inaccurately. Naive fans would get the wrong idea. Why hadn't Arkham House consulted him? "But as I have no wish to offend Lupoff," he said, "there's not much I can do." He appreciated the dedication.

When he said he'd heard nothing about his memoir, I told him it would be out soon. "I could've written some more if I'd had another couple of days."

Three days later, Lyda called at seven in the morning to invite me to dinner at seven that night. When I arrived at their building, bottle of wine in hand, no one answered the buzzer. Then Frank showed up from the street. "I was expecting you at eight," he said. "In any event, Lyda's asleep and we have nothing to feed you." After some debate whether I should just go home, Frank decided he should wake her. I waited. When he came back he said her first impulse was to see me, then she felt she just couldn't.

Frank walked me to the corner, emphasizing again what a mess it all was and how he might have to leave her. "Maybe next week you can visit," he said, "or at least you and she can talk on the phone." He wasn't keen on their going on TV, which for some reason seemed to be a possibility. "She'll just say I'm the greatest science fiction writer in the world, which won't do me any good."

The following day I spoke with both of them in the morning. We arranged that I would come that night for dinner with my "girlfriend" (I wasn't ready to introduce Julie to the Longs as my fiancée).

VI
July 1985–September 1985

About a week after that unforgettable night, Lyda phoned—to invite us back for dinner that evening. Either she or Frank, it was unclear who, was going into the hospital soon for "internal bleeding" and she wanted to have a party beforehand. I hemmed and hawed, saying I'd phone later. When we spoke that evening, she said she was exhausted and we'd better call it off. It was she who was going into the hospital the next day. In the meantime, she'd arranged with a bookstore in Woodstock, where she once lived, for an autographing party (for *Pulptime? Autobiographical Memoir?* both books?).

The following Friday Frank called. He wished to see me in the evening, but since I was leaving that afternoon for New England to attend a local convention, he was willing simply to talk on the phone. Lyda was in the hospital for tests on a growth similar to Reagan's. She had wanted me to visit her, but he would explain how I wasn't available. "Don't take anything she said the other evening seriously," he reiterated. On the other hand, things were now relatively serene in the Long household. He was once again "wonderful" in Lyda's eyes. He'd recently gotten a check from "Crawford" for fifteen dollars.

In mid-July, Frank called to report he'd received copies of his *Autobiographical Memoir,* which pleased him immensely on rereading. He liked my afterword, except for the last paragraph characterizing him as a champion of florid prose. "I once wrote that way," he admitted, "but not anymore. I'm afraid this comment could wreck my chances to get my novel published. Editors will think I'm old-fashioned." He and Lyda would both like to see a correction made, say, a new paragraph pasted over the old mentioning his Life Achievement Award and First Fandom Hall of Fame Award. I said I'd consult Marc and see what could be done. Frank was surprised when I told him four or five hundred copies had been published. He'd been expecting a figure more like two thousand. Afterwards I regretted not having run the manuscript by Frank before publication, but I was confident Marc could come up with a solution.

When later that day I reached Marc, we agreed to deceive Frank. I would write a new paragraph and he would have it typeset and a patch put over the offending text in a few copies. (To atone further, I would write a review praising the memoir for *Lovecraft Studies,* under a pseudonym.) The following day Lyda called from St. Vincent's Hospital, where she was recuperating. "I'm very European," she said, "I expect flowers." After work I stopped by a florist and ordered the cheapest arrangement they had. The day after that, she phoned to thank me. "How did you know red was my favorite color?" I sent Frank a copy of the new paragraph for his approval.

When Frank next called he wanted to know if I'd heard from Lyda recently. "She's in a down mood again." Everything seemed to be okay, but the doctors were somewhat vague. "I'm to have a long talk with a doctor tomorrow and hopefully get the straight story." As for the substitute paragraph, he mentioned it only briefly before raising a new complaint—a typo on the first page, where the word *mandatory* had been misspelled *manditory.* I told him not to worry about it. "You could write over the wrong letter with a pen and put 'p.e.' in the margin," he suggested. "Maybe there'll be a paperback sale." As usual I wasn't about to disillusion him. Publishers on occasion do provide errata sheets, but no self-respecting press would ever mark a "printer's error" in a finished book— or as here in a thin stapled booklet, the modest format of all Necronomicon Press publications of that period. In whatever form, the memoir was an extremely unlikely candidate for mass-market paperback.

At the end of the month, Frank called to borrow fifty dollars. Lyda got on the phone to say she was about to take off for China. She invited the whole gang to visit soon. "Just name the day!" I explained I was leaving for Massachusetts shortly. Frank appeared early that afternoon with his check. All his friends were out of town, he didn't want to bother Kirby, so once again he'd come to me for help. "This is the very last time," he vowed. He asked me to tell Marc to call him to discuss the memoir. He was less troubled by my closing paragraph (in fact, he appreciated it all the more on rereading) than by the "manditory" typo. He confessed he was growing a full beard, was in his sixth day, hence his seedy appearance.

Before leaving, Frank gave me a pair of envelopes from Lyda. The larger one included, among other odd items, a sheet of parchment-like floral stationery, evidently the paper used to announce their wedding (on one side she'd written "Lyda Arco & Frank Belknap Long became one August 13, 1960"). The other, a perfumed pink envelope, contained a short letter, which read in part: "Have just again reread the afterword—even shed a tear. My Frankele so truthfully presented—thank you!" She closed, "Best to Janet. Lydasha." An hour later Lyda phoned. "Frank's going to be on ABC's *Good Morning America* in two weeks," she crowed. She'd been in touch with Joe Franklin. "One good turn deserves another!"

While on vacation I sent Frank a postcard with the news of my engagement. Soon after returning to New York I got a call from Lyda. Joe Franklin was coming by the next morning to pick up copies of both *Pulptime* and Frank's memoir. "Frank doesn't want to go on the show," she said. "I think you should fill in."

A week later, while I was out of the office, Lyda came by to pick up copies of *Pulptime* and *Autobiographical Memoir* for delivery to Joe Franklin. At the reception desk she'd left two packages. One contained a peasant shirt for "Jennie," the other an assortment of photocopied newspaper clippings and collage-like notes all to do with herself. The next day she called to make sure I'd gotten everything. "Joe Franklin likes to help young writers and artists," she said. "His son is a big fan of Frank's." She promised to have me scheduled as a guest on the show by the following week.

I showed Julie the peasant shirt. It was a size fit for a child and scarcely her style. Julie wrote Lyda a gracious thank-you note. A few days later, Lyda called to tell me she'd set a date with Joe Franklin. She asked me to return her "autobiography," the materials she'd left off the other day. "Please thank Jennie for her note," she added.

Further calls from Lyda finally fixed a date with Franklin in early September, at his studio in Times Square. She wasn't sure if she would make it, but if she did, we could all meet afterwards at the Algonquin. At one point Frank got on the line to bitch about the "manditory" typo. "I'd like it corrected in time for the World Fantasy Convention." I mailed Lyda's "autobiography" back to her.

At the appointed hour, I showed up at the WOR studio just as one taping session of *The Joe Franklin Show* was ending and another beginning. There was no sign of Lyda, who had telephoned the night before to assure me she'd be there at five. I took a seat in the waiting area, where I signed a disclaimer and nervously waited my turn. I had slept badly. From talking to friends I was aware that just about anybody who wanted to could and did appear on Joe Franklin, the more off-beat or even crazy the better. I was unlikely to sell many extra copies of my book as a result. Nonetheless, the opportunity to be on television, any television, was one I felt I shouldn't pass up.

Suddenly the taping was over. I was not going to get on, not that day at any rate. Someone on the staff called my name. I had a visitor. It was Frank. After telling me Lyda was in terrible shape and couldn't make it, he led me over to the stage to introduce me to Joe Franklin. Evidently, Lyda had failed to confirm my appearance earlier in the day as she was supposed to, but Franklin was happy to reschedule me for the following week. He suggested I bring a couple of copies of my book, plus whatever promotional materials I had. He didn't know anything really about science fiction, he admitted, but his son was a fan of Frank's. "One of the greats," he said, "one of the greats." Maybe Frank could take a bow, assuming he'd be there too. Frank said he and Lyda had been on the show eight years earlier.

The two of us left together. On the walk to the subway Frank went on about how pleased he was with my afterword, except for the last paragraph. For what seemed like the thousandth time I heard how his style was in fact quite modern, how editors might be misled by my statement, how— I welcomed the din of the 42nd Street station.

That night Julie told me Lyda had called her at home in Brooklyn. She'd put her return address on the envelope of her thank-you note, allowing Lyda to get her number from information. Lyda had repeated the whole rambling story of her and Frank. Now she wanted to have lunch, just the two of them. Julie dreaded the prospect.

On the next attempt, I appeared on Joe Franklin without a hitch, better prepared and more relaxed than I'm sure I would have been had the previous try not ended in anticlimax. Though reluctant to part with it, I gave Franklin the copy of *Autobiographical Memoir* Marc had sent me with the new last paragraph. It was for his son. (Marc had also sent Frank the "corrected" text, the only other copy.) Lyda and Frank didn't show. When I talked with them that evening, I learned they had arrived two hours late. "Never mind," said Lyda. "We got double exposure—

even better than if we'd been on the same program." Frank had spoken on camera for a few minutes and signed his memoir for Franklin's son.

A few days later, Lyda called. She asked me to send her a New Year's card, that is, a Jewish New Year's card. "All my friends are dead or out of the country," she said. She reiterated how much she liked Julie (finally she had the name right). They were planning a twenty-fifth wedding anniversary party in October. She confessed that when she got high she phoned all her friends.

A few days after that, she called again. "Where's my New Year's card?" she asked. (Lyda rarely bothered to say hello or identify herself at the start of a phone conversation.) I said I'd only mailed it that morning. She and Frank had been strolling in the Village earlier. "He pins up his trousers rather than go to a tailor," she said. "What can you expect of a man who didn't get married until his late fifties? His full beard is very becoming. He's quite vain."

The next night, Julie and I stayed up late to watch my TV debut. "*Pulptime,* it's sure to be a good time," quipped Franklin as he introduced me. Despite a shiny forehead and a certain nervousness evident at the start, I thought I did okay. In context I saw that I had received, understandably enough, much less air time than the guests paired with me, Kit McClure and another member of her all-girl swing band. Afterwards—it was a quarter of two in the morning—Lyda called to congratulate me on my sensational performance.

The next night I stayed up even later, to catch Frank's performance, which came at the end of the show, right after a rap group did their thing. Frank was utterly unselfconscious in what amounted to a Bob and Ray routine. "Just in the last four or five months—no, no, I mean ten or fifteen years—there's been a tremendous upsurge of interest in science fiction and supernatural horror," he began. Joe Franklin described the show as a kind of time capsule. When he asked what Frank thought people would make of it in ten thousand years, Frank expressed his usual pessimism about the future of mankind. As the credits rolled, Franklin pressed him about his most important early literary influence—"It was H. P. Lovecraft, right?" In a soft but firm voice, Frank replied no, it was primarily sea and adventure stories. As deadpan comedy it was brilliant.

VII
September 1985–March 1986

A day or two later, Lyda phoned. "Guess what?" she said. "When Frank went into the grocery store and the liquor store today, everyone recognized him! Now we don't have to worry about our grocery bills!" Frank had been reluctant to go on TV, she conceded, but it had all worked out happily.

At the end of September, Frank came by to borrow thirty dollars. He looked better dressed than usual, may even have been wearing new clothes. His mood was cheerful. He wanted to get together soon. "I have a lot to talk with you about." He had a present from Lyda, this time for both me and Julie, a collection of prose-poems printed in brown ink by a woman named Nina Balaban. Later I looked at this little self-published booklet carefully. Entitled *In Earth's Bondage* and published by "Lydacia Press" in 1966, it contained sixteen rather mystical prose-poems in Russian with English translations on facing pages. It opened with a two-page "In Appreciation" by Frank that impressed me as being as fine as his best poetry. Lyda had inscribed it to us with the message "Eternal Bliss!" She had signed it from Lydasha, Frankele, and Shim Sham (their dog), and dated it August 13, 1985.

A couple of weeks later, Frank phoned. He had several things on his mind, foremost the essay on himself in the new Scribner's *Supernatural Fiction Writers* encyclopedia. Written by Les Daniels, a horror writer and pulp culture historian, it was I saw—when I read it later that fall—a sympathetic and intelligent critical appraisal of which Frank had every reason to be proud. As usual, he was under a lot of pressure, but he promised to call again in a few days.

More than a week later, we spoke. Frank more or less repeated what he told me our last conversation, except this time he complained about editors who put too many semicolons in his work. In particular Joshi, the editor of his memoir, had been guilty of this sin. "Semicolons are old-fashioned or else academic," he said. "I don't use them these days."

We were finally able to arrange a get-together for a Saturday afternoon in mid-November. S. T. and I met him at his door and we walked over to the Chelsea Square. We stopped at a drugstore so Frank could pick up a prescription for Lyda, who he said hadn't been well lately. At the restaurant, Frank had a briefcase full of items to show us, including a copy of the favorable piece from the Scribner's volume. S. T. gave him a copy of a booklet put out in England devoted to the Welsh fantasist Arthur Machen—which included Frank's sonnet "On Reading Arthur Machen." Frank was both surprised and pleased. According to S. T., his contact in England had gotten Frank's permission to reprint the poem, but Frank had no recollection of this transaction. (HPL had cited it in full in his survey "Supernatural Horror in Literature," probably without asking Frank either.)

From his briefcase, Frank produced one unexpected item—a letter from an official committee planning to celebrate the Statue of Liberty's centennial in '87. He was going to meet with some people from this group on Tuesday. He seemed to think somebody at my office would know whether they were legitimate or not. "I hope they're important enough to want to pay a lot of money for this signed book I have." Frank's grandfather, Charles O. Long, had been the contractor who built the pedestal for the Statue of Liberty and later served as its first superintendent. Frank told me once that his family had possessed the American flag used in the dedication ceremony, so it was entirely possible he had a valuable relic or two preserved from that era. I said I'd see what I could do.

Another potential big money-maker was his uncompleted novel. "Kirby told me he could get me a two-hundred-thousand-dollar advance on a really strong one." He confessed he had to keep working to pay for the basics of life. "At my age I'd gladly give up writing if I had enough to live on." Apropos of Lovecraft, he mentioned that once, provoked by a museum Civil War exhibit, Howard had called General Sherman a barbarian.

A few days later, Frank phoned to report that he'd had a good meeting with the Statue of Liberty people, at the Chelsea Square. He would have to lend them his souvenir book, though. If he wanted to get any money for it, he'd have to sell it elsewhere. I said nobody at my office knew the organization. Frank meant to write Marc to thank him for correcting the last paragraph of my afterword, and to ask for more copies of the memoir. "I'm curious to know how it sold at the World

Fantasy Convention. Do you know?" Since I hadn't attended that year, I couldn't enlighten him.

The last day of December, Lyda phoned to wish me Happy New Year. She'd been calling up all her friends by way of celebration. When she offered to be my agent, I said I'd be honored but had done no work in which an agent would be interested. Full of good cheer, she announced that she was going to open a Russian restaurant in 1986. "The Russian Tea Room's a fake!" She claimed she had a backer with money. It would be called Lydasha's. In the new year she expected to get to Boston, where she hoped to meet my grandparents. When I explained my grandparents lived in California, she said she meant my parents. She was planning to agent a Ray Bradbury play in Boston. I wished her and Frank a Happy New Year from Julie and myself.

In January I received a series of calls, some of them no more than a few seconds long, from Lyda. Frank's *Dreamer* was a bad book because he was so harassed when he wrote it. She was plotting her revenge on Kirby for the World Fantasy Convention that fall. President Reagan was sending her to Russia as a cultural envoy. Frank, incidentally, was deathly afraid of the Soviets. She needed help with the materials she'd been collecting for her various "books." Would one of my sisters be interested in doing the necessary errands? "Money's no object!" (I'd revealed that I had two younger sisters, both living in New York.) Later she called back to say she'd found a student at the seminary across the street to take care of her work. My sisters were spared, but not my fiancée, who objected to Lyda's phoning so early in the morning.

One morning Lyda called three times in a row. "I'd like you to order a hundred copies of Frank's memoir for me," she said. "I'm planning a big party." I promised to get in touch with Marc. "Of course, I want the corrected version." She also asked me to order a hundred copies of *Pulptime* for placement in various stores in Chelsea, "run by those homo sapiens" (homosexuals?). In the neighborhood everyone knew and loved Frank. I said I'd send her some flyers with ordering information to distribute. Later I wrote Marc warning him Lyda might be placing a large order for Frank's memoir.

The next day I sent Lyda some flyers for *Pulptime*, along with a note requesting that she not call me before noon on the weekends. A few days later she phoned, full of apologies for having called too early. I heard how in October they'd traveled by bus to Texas to attend the World Fantasy Convention, after cashing in the plane tickets the organizers had sent Frank. He had received the Life Achievement Award.

Finally, one night Frank called—from the street, as in the old days. He didn't want Lyda to know he was phoning me. He was concerned about her ordering hundreds of copies of our books. I said I'd alerted Marc to the situation. Again Frank said he was going to write Marc soon to thank him for the splendid job he'd done on the memoir. He wanted to get together with me for a long talk.

In February, Lyda called with ideas of bargain Valentine's Day presents for me to give Julie. "I'm very pleased with Frank's memoir, the look of it and all," she said, "but is there any chance of doing it in hardcover?" Not unless he rewrote and expanded it, I answered. She had read the interview with Stephen King in the current *Interview*. "I assume he uses four-letter words because that's the custom these days." (In general, Lyda regarded King favorably, since he once serenaded her at a convention with his guitar.)

Lyda phoned the day after Valentine's. "Frank never gets me a present," she said. "He scrambles around at the last minute. So I called up my favorite stationery store and ordered them to send me their best card signed 'Frankele.'" They'd had their kitchen redone. Frank apparently wanted to save a cockroach to mount. In his youth he used to collect insects as a hobby. She confessed their phone bill for the past month had been $350. She also said she was drunk—on vodka. This led to a discussion of the likes of Yevteshenko and Pasternak, the last whom she claimed to have known or at least met. Yevteshenko's new movie had no plot, but was excellent on showing the Russian character. On the other hand, the recent *Peter the Great* on TV was garbage.

In March, both Lyda and Frank phoned one night after eleven. Lyda ranted about Kirby, while Frank said he'd like to have lunch soon with me and Joshi. He was worried about the forthcoming special Long issue of *Crypt*. "People will get the impression that I haven't changed my style any," he said, "when in fact I'm now writing in a very different fashion." Lyda said we could all have lunch in their new kitchen.

When S. T. and I showed up a few days later, Frank came to the door and informed us Lyda wasn't well, the plumbers had been in, the place was a mess—he'd meet us at the Chelsea Square in ten minutes.

S. T. and I had started our lunch by the time he joined us. Frank ordered soup and a vodka on the rocks, straight up. When the drink came he complained it was too strong.

Frank first groused about Bob's decision to drop one of the stories he'd written for the Long issue of *Crypt*, relegating it to a new magazine devoted to spaceship fiction or some such that he feared wouldn't be as well-known as *Crypt*. "I wanted to write Bob a three-page letter explaining what a mistake that would be," he said, "but I just don't have the time." He lamented the passing of a number of his friends and associates, including Wilfred B. Talman, who had been a later recruit to the Kalems. Lester Del Rey still bore him a grudge since a long-ago feud divided the science fiction writers of the time. He was sure Del Rey had avoided the World Fantasy Convention because of his receipt of the Life Achievement Award.

Frank Herbert had taken the worm image for *Dune* from a short story of his in *Weird Tales*, he asserted, while Stephen King had gotten the idea for "the shining" from a story of his about a boy drifting down the Mississippi on a raft. He didn't resent either author. In fact, he was grateful, presumably for the satisfaction of having inspired them. Frank admitted he'd left out the whole middle part of his memoir—an account of his relationships with writers and editors for the past several decades. S. T. and I suggested the possibility of his writing an article to supplement the memoir, without the burden of a deadline. Marc could maybe pay him a hundred dollars.

Thanks to the vodka, which had become more and more drinkable as the ice melted, Frank was more candid on personal matters than usual. "Loveman was never an active homosexual," he said. "He would never have had sex with Hart Crane, his boyhood friend. Crane, on the other hand, was always picking up sailors." (To that degree my cameo of Crane in *Pulptime* was accurate, I noted smugly.) "Howard and the rest knew of it, but that didn't affect their friendship with Crane." HPL and James Morton, another Kalem, had had very different tastes and views, yet were great pals. When I mentioned that Jill Fein, an EOD member and fan of his, had recently divorced and remarried, he said, "It always amazes me how quickly people marry and divorce these days." Finally, Frank asked S. T. for the address of Les Daniels, whom he wished to write to thank for his essay.

VIII
May 1986–April 1987

In May I tried to phone Frank, to arrange a get-together with Jill and her new husband Richard, but discovered their number had been disconnected. In early June a call from Lyda confirmed this was the case. "We want to give you a wedding present," she said. "An oak side-table." I wrote Frank and Lyda a card thanking them for their kind offer and saying we hoped to see them after our wedding, scheduled for Saturday the 14th. (Since we were to leave the following day for two weeks in Sicily, with any luck it would be well into the summer before we saw the Longs again.)

We saw them the Tuesday before the wedding. Despite all Julie and I still had to do to get ready for the big event, we accepted their invitation—for dinner on their roof, which proved a far more appealing locale, with its open views, than their hall. This time we came better prepared, bringing a bottle of champagne and plastic champagne glasses. The Longs provided chairs. The weather was sunny and clear. Frank went out to shop, returning with nuts and a selection of deli salads. He forgot to buy orange juice for the vodka, but at least there were enough glasses to go around. They both stayed sober. Lyda held forth but she said nothing overly embarrassing. Frank had written a new story, for an anthology edited by Dennis Etchison, which he needed typed. Evidently, he no longer had a working typewriter. Maybe Joshi could do it. They presented us with their wedding gift—a collapsible TV tray, on wheels no less. Very practical. While they did ask why we'd chosen Sicily for our honeymoon, they didn't otherwise show much interest in our lives. We left before it got dark. I sent them a postcard from Sicily.

Late in July, the Longs called. They needed twenty or twenty-five bucks. No, we weren't free to join them for dinner tomorrow, but I said when I stopped by we'd try to arrange something. In February I'd joined S. T. on the staff of Chelsea House, a reference book publisher in the Village. It was easy to get to their place on my lunch hour. When I arrived, Lyda was in her wheelchair on the sidewalk in front of 421, their dog beside her. She didn't recognize me at first. "So young," she muttered. Frank appeared. "Better make it thirty," he said as I reached for my wallet. We set Friday evening for dinner, to include S. T. I later sent them a card telling them also to expect Jill and her husband. Everyone would bring something to eat or drink. Julie and I agreed there was strength in numbers.

After work S. T. and I walked over to the Longs', where again we found Lyda sitting out front. We took a seat on a neighboring stoop while we waited for Frank, who was buying groceries. Lyda worried about him. He'd been mugged three times over the years. "Once, in the hallway outside the apartment, thieves stripped him of his pants," she said. "They thought the truss he was wearing for his hernia was a money belt." When, questioned about himself, S. T. replied "What's there to say?," she continued with her monologue.

We were about to leave a note at the entrance saying we'd gone to the roof when Frank toddled into view. He led us to the roof while Lyda stayed below. For a summer evening in New York it wasn't too humid. Frank disappeared, but it wasn't long before he returned with Julie, Jill, and Richard. We helped Lyda up the final flight of stairs to the roof. Our hosts provided the usual selection of deli treats, including whole scallions. As the first item of business, Julie, Jill, and Richard excused themselves to go use the Longs' bathroom. They took a key downstairs. I was dying to know what they'd discovered in the inner sanctum, but had to be patient until the party was over. Before we could pour the wine, Frank had to return to the apartment to get a corkscrew. (So they did have one after all.)

Lyda didn't zero in on Julie the way she had in the past, though at one point she declared, "You don't look as *zaftig* as I remember." It was not the sort of personal remark Julie appreciated. The rest of us chuckled nervously. Lyda did virtually all the talking until Frank, apropos of nothing, launched into a sententious speech about the greatest minds being those who were the greatest innovators. By this standard Shakespeare didn't make the list, but one of the early Greek philosophers did (I forget which). A sudden cloudburst put an end to our picnic. We hastened inside and regrouped in the apartment below.

At last my curiosity was satisfied to learn what lay beyond the first ten feet of the hall. First came a closed door on the left, to the bedroom, then another door, to the bathroom. The hall widened into an alcove and at the end was a tiny kitchen, which we shunned. To the right was a sunken living room. It was dark, but there was enough light from the hall to tell it was filled with debris, while festoons of paint hung from the ceiling. "The man on the floor above has a clubfoot," said Lyda, as if that explained the ceiling problem. (I was reminded that earlier she'd told S. T. and me that Frank had recently trod by accident on their marriage certificate—I could now see why that was easy to do.) The bathroom was the neatest room in the place, decorated with posters that Lyda said she changed every week. "Some of them anyway," she added.

"I want to get out of here," Julie said to me under her breath. We didn't linger.

Jill and Richard gave us a ride in their car to the subway. "An interesting evening," said Richard. Indeed, visiting the Longs' was definitely a novelty, but as Julie noted the experience soon began to wear thin. Jill said she thought at first there were bats hanging from the living-room ceiling. Julie said the bedroom was as foul as the living room. She had no idea where they slept. We speculated that the bathtub was Lyda's bed.

More than a week later, I came home to find a message from Frank on our answering machine. He complained that a lot of valuable stuff was lost in the aftermath of the party, including Lyda's pipe. He seemed to want some sort of restitution, but he hesitated to ask for it outright.

In September, I received the contract for my next major book project—a critical study of Lovecraft for Twayne's United States Authors Series. Various others had been under contract, but, since the publisher paid only a modest royalty and no advance, I gathered my predecessors had lacked motivation. Writing a scholarly survey of HPL's fiction soon became a higher priority than looking after his aging best friend. Julie and I went to Providence for the World Fantasy Convention, where Paul Ganley gave me a copy of Frank's Arkham House poetry collection, *In Mayan Splendor*, for Frank's signature. The Longs did not go, rumor having it that Lyda was sick. Afterwards, I wrote Frank a postcard saying he was missed.

The third week of December Frank called. He was under the usual terrible pressures, but there was one bright spot—he'd received a contract for his novel. Kirby had clearly come through on his behalf, though I wouldn't have been surprised to learn that the editor had done it as an act of charity. I congratulated him, promising we'd get together after Christmas.

In the new year, we were blessed to hear nothing from the Longs for months. Finally, I felt it was time to check up on them. In April, a few days before leaving New York on a six-week leave of absence to work full-time on my Twayne study, I stopped by their building and pushed the buzzer for 1-A. Frank came to the door, then went back inside to get his hat. Since it was a warm day, he took off his hat, along with the lightweight blue blazer he was wearing. As it happened, I was wearing an almost identical blue blazer. At some point, while we stood chatting on the sidewalk, I may have removed my blazer too and hung it over my arm.

The advance for the novel was allowing them to live more comfortably of late, he indicated, though "another ten or fifteen hundred dollars would be a big help." Lyda was apparently in need of a cataract operation. He was hoping for a television or even a movie sale. He was annoyed that he'd heard nothing from Marc since his memoir came out. He'd be willing to write up the part he left out—that is, an account of HPL's Brooklyn days. (Evidently he'd forgotten that he'd theoretically covered that subject in *Dreamer*.)

Frank regretted not having been in touch recently. "I was going to write you a card asking the best times to reach you," he said. About forty unanswered fan letters had piled up. When he said he wished to have lunch with me and S. T. soon, I explained I wasn't going to be around for the next six weeks. "I know Joshi doesn't think much of my *Dreamer*, but I've gotten many favorable responses to it," he said. "Including a couple from filmmakers in Providence."

Frank was keen to hear what went on at the World Fantasy Convention, as well as at the recent fiftieth-anniversary observance in Providence of HPL's death. Due to Lyda's ill health, he'd been unable to attend these events, even with the promise of all expenses paid. Two recent tributes especially pleased him—an appreciation in the Long issue of *Crypt*, by Ben Indick, and inclusion in the *Penguin Encyclopedia of Horror and the Supernatural*. It was particularly gratifying that he'd received a longer entry than Jack London, one of his boyhood idols. (When I later compared them, I saw that he'd gotten fifty lines to his boyhood idol's forty-nine. Ben had written the one on him, Ted the one on London.) He criticized the author of the London entry for not mentioning *The Sea Wolf,* though he also referred to it as *The Sea Rover.* "Probably never even read it," he muttered. I told him of my contract with Twayne. It astounded him that I'd been given no advance for it. "No wonder they can't get anybody," he said. He signed Paul's copy of *In Mayan Splendor* while I held his hat. As I left he said, "Please send my greetings to your wife."

The next day Frank left a message on our machine accusing me of walking off with his jacket. That he might have misplaced it in the jungle of their apartment didn't seem to have occurred to him. "I hope you and Joshi can join me for lunch either Thursday or Friday," he added. I relayed this invitation to S. T., who promised to get in touch with Frank somehow. He would run the idea of Frank's doing another memoir past Marc. The day before Julie and I left for Massachusetts, I wrote Frank a card saying I was sorry I wouldn't be able to see him for lunch.

IX
October 1987–June 1988

Again all was quiet on the Long front for months. (When, after returning to the city, I'd asked S. T. if he'd seen Frank in my absence, he said he hadn't, because he never heard from Frank.) Then Lyda called the first week of October. She'd just gotten out of the hospital. "Have you received the jacket of my forthcoming book?" she asked. I gathered she meant her history of the Yiddish theater in Russia. I hadn't. She was hoping to make a lot of money for Frank, "the idiot." She was planning a twenty-seventh anniversary party. "I've invited King and Fritz Leiber. I'll keep you posted." Minutes later she phoned again. "I'm hoping to get Frank to a doctor tomorrow," she said. "He has four hernias but refuses to do anything about them." Claiming she was feeling tired, she hung up. Apparently, their phone had been reconnected.

The day before Halloween, I ran into Lyda sitting in her wheelchair in front of B. Altman's, the department store then at Madison and 34th. She was wearing a seasonal orange and black coat. She recognized me, but I had to tell her my name. "Are you wearing a wig?" she asked. "You don't look like you." Maybe I was having a bad hair day. "Frank calls you a pig because you haven't been in touch," she continued in a nastier tone. I protested that I'd made the effort but Frank hadn't responded. As she wheeled off down the sidewalk, I called after her to let me know their new phone number. This chance meeting didn't make me feel good.

Happily, that evening Lyda left a friendly message on our machine with their new number. Another message a couple of days later said Frank was very sick. She was taking him away for a week to get him out of Kirby's clutches. I decided I ought to try to arrange a lunch with Frank soon. But I was busy working on my critical study, and I didn't feel like it. From New Mexico, where Julie and I spent Thanksgiving with her uncle and aunt, I mailed Frank a postcard. In mid-December I sent a Christmas card. When we returned from visiting our families in Massachusetts after Christmas, we found Lyda had left a brief acknowledging message.

We heard nothing more until the end of February, when Lyda phoned. "Guess what?" she said. "I'm going to Israel next week. My book's selling well." She put Frank on. As usual, he'd been under quite a lot of pressure, trying to finish up his novel. When I told him I'd been working hard on my critical study, he asked to see the manuscript. "Joshi had quite a few errors in his book," he said, referring to a Lovecraft guide S. T. had done for a specialty press. "I want to make sure you don't make mistakes." Since Lyda was jabbering in the background, he couldn't talk long. In fact, she was trying to get him to tell me it was her birthday that day, I could hear. I promised we'd meet soon for lunch. A short time later Lyda phoned again—to tell me it was her eightieth birthday, but mainly to berate me for not inviting them over. I said we were having our kitchen redone. "That's no excuse," she said, "when we've had you here so often." I confessed I'd been neglectful. "Frank is very fond of you," she said. "You should have him over, feed him, talk to him."

About two weeks later, shortly after speaking to Lyda from a pay phone on 21st Street, I ran into Frank. He'd been out doing errands. Again he asked to check my Twayne book for errors. "Joshi doesn't always get it right," he said. I waited in the hallway outside the apartment while he went inside. The place was being repainted. A few minutes later he called me in to see Lyda, who was making collages in her bathtub. She was lucid and pleasant enough, though she did harp on the ignorance of "Lousecrattians." Frank showed me a French translation of *Dreamer,* which was beautifully produced, with a photograph section at the back. Evidently, he had a new French translation of his fiction, but he couldn't find it. I'd have to come back another time. As for his financial situation, "I'm afraid I may have to beg soon on the street with a sign around my neck," he said. "Or maybe Kirby will work some sort of deal that will get me half a million dollars." Then he started to harangue me for having called him a florid writer. "Yes," he admitted, "I did go through a 'yellow nineties' period once, but that was long ago. Others have written pointing out how clear my prose is." And so on. I departed with promises of having a proper get-together soon.

In mid-April, Lyda phoned about dinner plans. Since we were still reluctant to entertain the Longs at our apartment, we compromised by offering to take them out to dinner in honor of Frank's birthday. The upshot was that Julie and I showed up the evening of the 27th with tulips and cheap champagne for a surprise party chez Long. We were met at the door by an older black gentleman, whom Lyda introduced as an actor named Giles. Years before Giles had performed in a production of *The Cherry Orchard* that Lyda had staged in their living room—which, in contrast to our first visit, was now open to guests. It had been painted, and the clutter seemed somewhat organized.

On a shawl-covered trunk Lyda had set out paper plates suitable for a child's birthday and plastic glasses. When Julie suggested we put the champagne on ice, Lyda said they had no refrigerator. I poured a glass of cranberry juice and vodka for each of us. Frank, who'd been out buying orange juice, arrived after a few minutes. Since he'd had a fall earlier in the day and had trouble getting up (Giles had had to help him), he was in no mood for a surprise party, though he seemed pleased enough to see us.

Lyda and Julie sat on the single bed, covered by a thin Indian blanket, that occupied the near corner of the living room. Giles took a seat on the bench in front of the upright piano next to the bed. After opening and pouring the champagne, I joined Frank on the couch at the far end of the room, under the window. Or rather I should say I variously stood and squatted near him, since the junk on the couch allowed room for only one person to sit. Giles showed us some snapshots he'd taken of Lyda holding court in her tub. He had his camera with him and took pictures. Lyda exhibited her latest collage, which included the illustration from the back of *Pulptime* showing Long, Lovecraft, and Holmes. One poignant relic was a fragmentary black-and-white photograph of Frank's father. The face, what was left of it, strongly resembled that of the son.

Frank and I ended up holding our own conversation. He lamented how he couldn't answer any of his fan mail or autograph books people sent him, how he had yet to finish his novel, how he was the last of the Lovecraft circle, how his fame hadn't brought him any money. Then he started talking about his *Autobiographical Memoir.* "*Biographical Memoir* it's called," he said. "Only seven dollars. You should buy a copy." Then he remembered—and took me to task for calling his style old-fashioned.

For dinner we ordered from the Chelsea Square, our treat—moussaka for Julie and me, chicken à la king for Lyda. Unfortunately,

Giles left before the meal was delivered, pleading other engagements. Frank shuffled into the kitchen to heat up some Chinese food someone had given them that morning. He complained it was too spicy. Frank cooked on a hot plate, not liking to use the stove. I peeked in the kitchen—litter covered the floor, cockroaches the walls. There was indeed no refrigerator.

During dinner Lyda droned on, dropping names. Julie ceased to show the animated interest she'd displayed earlier. It was time to go. As we headed for the door, Frank asked, "Have you heard from Tom?" No, not in a few years, I told him. Frank looked cheerful as he waved us out. On the street Julie reported that at one point during cocktails she'd brushed a cockroach off her eyebrow.

A few weeks later Lyda called, all excited by the recent closing of the musical *Carrie*, based on the Stephen King novel, after opening night. Frank got on briefly to thank us for attending his surprise birthday—and to apologize for not having been in a good mood at the time. Lyda phoned again the next night. Encouraged by Gorbachev's reforms, she was hopeful she could get her history of the Yiddish theater published in Russia. "Now that Heinlein's gone, Frank's the only one left," she said, speaking of the late science fiction author. "He will get his due." In her next call, a week later, she read a letter to Frank from Charles Grant, head of the Horror Writers of America. Frank was to receive a special award at their upcoming annual meeting in New York. Included were free accommodations at the Warwick Hotel. "Frank is finally getting his due!" she crowed. The only ominous note was that he'd been failing down a lot lately.

In early June I phoned Frank to invite him to lunch. He was under great pressure; Lyda was depressed. "I can't get over all the terrible things going on in the city," he said. "Eighteen eighty-four is near!" (Presumably he was referring to Orwell's *Nineteen Eighty-four*.) With the Reagan-Gorbachev summit in progress, he had time only to read the newspaper headlines. The next day, on Lyda's advice, I arrived at the apartment a half hour later than planned. I still had to wait fifteen minutes, and even then Frank had to go back inside to get his hat and to exchange Lyda's cane for his own sturdier model, which he couldn't find at first.

At the Chelsea Square Frank ordered a bowl of pea soup and a

Rum Collins. He especially recommended the Rum Collins. This time he had fewer complaints than usual, though they'd had a wild three days staying with friends of Lyda's in Brooklyn over the Memorial Day weekend. I told him about one fan-scholar's recent discovery that Lovecraft's paternal grandparents were buried in Woodlawn Cemetery in the Bronx. Frank suspected HPL was unaware of this fact when he was living in New York. "My family has a plot in Woodlawn," he added. "That's where I'll be buried."

When I asked if Lovecraft had ever gone swimming in the ocean, Frank responded with the familiar story of how his friend had taken his one and only airplane ride in a seaplane off Onset, on Cape Cod. "The memory of Howard being carried by two men through the surf is still clear as day to me," he said. "I was too scared to go." He knew Joshi didn't believe his accounts of Lovecraft were all that reliable.

Frank spoke of his *Mayflower* ancestor, Edward Doty, who'd been the first English servant in America. "The Pilgrims were religious fanatics," he said. "The evangelicals of their day."

When I asked if he'd had any uncles or aunts, he said he had uncles on his father's side. A "niece," that is, a granddaughter of one of these uncles, lived in Florida, but he hadn't been in touch with her in a few years. He mentioned his connection to Lord Mansfield. (All the aristocratic ancestors appeared to be on his mother's side.) He grumbled a bit about the whole Statue of Liberty business falling through, though he did identify his grandparents in an old photograph taken at the site, presumably provided by one of the committee members who met with him.

Of the assorted items Frank had brought, the most interesting was a request from the French publishers of *Dreamer* for sample letters or manuscript material to include in their edition. "I regret not even having replied," he said, "but I couldn't have honored the request anyway." Another item he had to show me was the jacket from *Lovecraft's Book*. "Howard hated Viereck," he said, speaking of the Fascist propagandist with whom HPL collaborates in the novel. And he had a photocopy of his entry from the *Penguin Encyclopedia*. "More space than Jack London," he murmured. I promised to let him review the manuscript of my Twayne study, then nearly finished.

"Bob has accepted a number of my recent stories," he said. "He even sent me an extra fifty dollars. It was supposedly anonymous, but I knew who it was." Frank could use more friends like Bob, I thought. "I'd like to see a new story collection of mine published, with ten or fifteen of the old and ten or fifteen of the new," Frank continued. "But it would have to be coordinated with the new novel." He hadn't been able to get ahold of Kirby of late and was worried about the status of his novel. Since he hadn't heard from Marc in several years, he assumed the memoir had not been a big hit. While I didn't say so, I knew through S. T. that Marc was in no mood to issue any sort of sequel given his losses on *Autobiographical Memoir*.

X
July 1988–October 1988

In midsummer Lyda phoned—to say they were nearly raped and murdered by intruders Frank had accidentally buzzed in. They'd pretended to be painters come to measure the living room. "The next time you go to Massachusetts you must bring me along," she said, prompted perhaps by the postcard I'd recently sent while visiting my parents. "I'm planning a big gala for our anniversary this year," she added.

About a week later she left a message on our machine. "Pick up the July issue of *Interview*," she said. "I'm in it." When I called back, Lyda said, "I can't talk. Robbers have broken in the building and the police are chasing them now." The following day Lyda phoned with a more coherent account. Frank had let into the apartment two men claiming to be painters, who then asked for change for fifty dollars. "Since they appeared to be Greek I told them I knew Melina Mercouri," she said, "and sang them a Greek song. Mind you I was naked in the bathtub at the time." All the while Frank had screamed at them to go. Eventually they did leave, without getting any money, but not before they first looked in Frank's bedroom and opened a purse of hers. "We called the police and are only now getting over the excitement." She was going to write Stephen King to ask for his financial help. I gathered she had yet to be interviewed for *Interview*.

Julie answered Lyda's next call. They were having a TV crew in to film their anniversary party. In the meantime, they were getting a refrigerator. A couple of days later Lyda phoned and again spoke to Julie. She wanted us to come for dinner that night, but we had other plans. Julie despaired that she was falling into this old woman's grasp. The next day I called Lyda hoping to escape another outing to the Longs, but in the end I agreed we'd come by that evening, possibly with another couple, who lived in Brooklyn.

Efforts to persuade our friends to accompany us were to no avail. They'd heard too much about the Longs to be enticed. When we arrived, Frank and Lyda said they were glad we'd come alone. Julie gave Lyda flowers and some seashells she'd collected at the beach in Massa-

chusetts, while I presented Frank with a copy of the complete manuscript of my book. They offered the usual spread—vodka and orange
juice and a selection of deli salads. While Lyda talked at Julie, I discussed Lovecraftian matters with Frank. I said Bob was considering
writing a critical study of his work for the same company that had published S. T.'s Lovecraft guide. Frank showed me the prize he'd received
from the Horror Writers of America in June. It was a weighty ceramic
trophy in the form of a "haunted house," with his name inscribed inside
the little front door.

Eventually Lyda began to rant. One senior figure in the field had
driven his wife to suicide or was otherwise responsible for her death.
"Being gay, he only liked her for display," she asserted. When she spoke
highly of another individual, Frank objected, and they were soon engaged in a shouting match. We tried to slip out, but they turned their
attention to us, asking questions about our families. "It's only because
you dedicated your novel to your grandparents that I took an interest in
you in the first place," Lyda yelled. Frank started to boast of his descent
from Lord Mansfield, who freed the slaves in England, and from Edward Doty, the only servant on the *Mayflower*. Lyda then berated her
"idiot" for having taken down the poster of Lenin on the back of the
bathroom door. Apparently, when I'd told him that the friends who
might join us lived in Brooklyn, Frank had assumed they'd be Jewish
and, being Jewish, offended by the poster of Lenin. Frank saw us out,
saying Lyda didn't understand how certain people who'd befriended her
had ulterior motives.

When the phone rang the next morning, I answered it at Julie's in-
sistence. It was indeed Lyda, who said she wished to have lunch sometime soon with Julie alone. After she hung up, Julie and I agreed we'd
gotten into a trap, like the poor guy at the end of Evelyn Waugh's *A
Handful of Dust* who's forced to live out his days reading Dickens to a
lunatic. In addition, we both recognized Frank and Lyda as grotesque
parodies of ourselves, a nightmare vision of how we might turn out at
their age if we weren't careful.

Lyda did not press Julie further for lunch, though she continued to
phone with bits of news through the end of the summer—Frank had
received a big royalty check from Arkham House; Frank's article in
Reign of Fear (an anthology of essays on Stephen King) was the best in

the volume. Then Frank called, to ask for a loan of fifty dollars. He subsequently picked up the money in an envelope I left with our doorman.

Lyda called to thank us for the loan, which she said they were prepared to repay the next time we met. I vowed we'd invite them to dinner soon. First, however, I saw to it that we had some support. Ted, loyal friend that he was, agreed to come and even offered to pick the Longs up in his car. I said that wouldn't be necessary, since Lyda used some sort of service for invalids to drive her places. When I phoned the Longs, Lyda was delighted to accept. She promised to bring us the fifty dollars. Ted later realized we'd chosen to entertain the night of the first presidential debate between Bush and Dukakis. Fortunately, though, he could tape it on his VCR.

The appointed evening Frank arrived at our apartment, like the Longs' a ground-floor rear one, around 7:30. He explained that they'd gotten off at the wrong address and Lyda was up the street, her wheelchair not working too well. Shortly after we retrieved Lyda and her wheelchair, Ted arrived, thank God. We ushered our guests into the living room, where everyone took a seat around the coffee table—Lyda in a chair next to Julie, Ted next to Frank on the couch. When I offered drinks, Lyda asked for straight vodka with a glass of orange juice on the side. (She never touched the orange juice.) Frank ordered Scotch. He refused the hors d'oeuvres. As Ted told me after the party, he was sure Frank deliberately got drunk.

First, Lyda did her show-and-tell routine—photos that Giles had taken at Frank's birthday, a collage or two, old newspaper clippings, mementos of the Yiddish theater, the lot. Frank told me he'd gone through most of my manuscript and had a few corrections to suggest; I said a friend of mine was reading his *Autobiographical Memoir* and enjoying it. "I'm contemplating writing a real, full-scale memoir in which I'll talk about all the famous people in the science fiction world I've known," he said. "This will be my big book, which will take care of all our financial needs for the rest of our days."

Lyda complimented us on our apartment, which as an artist Julie had spruced up considerably since our wedding, in large part through the addition of some of her own paintings. At one point, when I led Frank to the bathroom, he praised Julie's decorating taste. He was also impressed by our built-in bookshelves, and admitted he had few books in his own library. True to form, Lyda started to hold forth on her pet peeves. Having consumed his Scotch, Frank fell into a stupor. Once or twice he roused himself to take exception to his better half's wackier pronouncements. We heard all the familiar tales again—Frank's resemblance to Dostoevsky's "idiot," their courtship and marriage, the world's failure to appreciate her Frankele.

Shortly before we served dinner, Ted excused himself to go turn on his VCR. Since he lived only a few blocks away, he was back in time for the first course. The party moved into the dining room. Julie, as fine a cook as she was a decorator, had prepared a feast, which Frank proceeded to gobble up without comment, course after course, while the company endured Lyda's criticisms of Tom, of Kirby, of de Camp, of conventions, of horror writers in general. At moments Frank did dispute Lyda's more malicious slanders, but clearly he cared more about polishing his plate than arguing. After dessert the men returned to the living room, while Julie remained stuck at the table in a tête-à-tête with Lyda. (Julie later reported Lyda had revealed that she and Frank had had sex for three months after their wedding, then stopped. She'd wanted a divorce, but Frank refused to give it to her.)

Back on the couch Frank complained to Ted about the fast pace of modern life.

"You seem to have escaped the drudgery most people have to go through in their careers," said Ted, rather disingenuously, I thought. "How have you done it?"

Frank ignored the question. "We may be blown up in a nuclear war," he replied, "so nothing matters anyway."

Around 11:30, Julie and I decided the party was over. We helped our older guests, who seemed to be unaware of the time, with their coats and baggage. (Later we saw that we'd overlooked some of Lyda's photos.) Ted and I found a friendly cab driver, gave him fifteen bucks and instructions on taking the Longs home. As the cab sped off downtown, I turned to Ted in exasperation. What could we do to rid ourselves of these emotional parasites?

"Get them nice and comfortable," Ted said, "and tell them about the rabbits . . ."

XI
October 1988–February 1989

When Lyda phoned the next day to thank us, I felt a little less like shooting the Longs. "Your apartment is like a gallery," she said. "It's like the Louvre." Two days later when Lyda called, I told her Julie wasn't home when in fact she was. "Frank was wondering if Julie might be Jewish," she said. Three days later Lyda phoned to say she had a girl to introduce to Ted. "Please have Julie call me back." A month later Lyda left a message on our machine accusing me of not giving Julie her calls. A week after that she succeeded in reaching Julie and told her she considered her "one of my best friends." Julie gritted her teeth and promised they'd get together soon.

Early in December Frank spoke to Julie. He wished to see me. When I called back, Frank said Lyda had been in the hospital for blood tests. I said Julie had been ill. "I've been under a lot of pressure," he said, "but I wanted to give you some background on Alfred Galpin and Clark Ashton Smith pertaining to slips you made in your study." Galpin and Smith had been friends of Lovecraft's. On the whole my manuscript had impressed Frank. "Did Mosig write the first part?" he asked, Mosig having been one of those under contract who had not delivered. No, I said, I wrote the entire thing. "I'll pay back the money I owe you when we next get together," he said. Apparently he hadn't been able to get down to the shop in the Village where he sometimes sold his more valuable books. I promised I'd call him again in a couple of weeks.

The following day Frank left a message on our machine. Lyda was worried about Julie's health, given what I had told him. In fact, Julie's ailment had been minor. Lyda later left a message expressing her concern. Two days later Lyda called again, wanting to talk to Julie. I said she was asleep. She got through to Julie a few days before Christmas, to invite us to dinner. A subsequent message on our machine the same day reneged on the invitation. We thanked our lucky stars. The final day of the year Lyda called and again spoke to Julie. Frank had woken up in the night and didn't know where he was. She was very worried.

Early in January Lyda phoned. "Guess what?" she said. "A Providence TV station wants to interview Frank, but they won't get very far unless they pay." I asked to speak to Frank. "I'm expecting to get a check soon so I can repay you," he said. I said I'd forget the debt if he'd agree to write a jacket blurb for my Lovecraft study. A sentence or two was all I required. "I'll give you a paragraph," he replied. He had the usual fifteen or sixteen things to deal with, but would do it soon.

A week or so later Lyda called back. "I've been after Frank to write a blurb for your book," she said. Kirby's sister had just sent them a hundred dollars in cash, but she was sure it was some sort of ploy.

Thinking I'd waited long enough, I called Frank to arrange to pick up the blurb. (I didn't trust him to dictate it over the phone.) Within seconds he launched into a tirade—about the value of his time, his early letters selling for hundreds of dollars and his getting nothing, and other outrages. On my lunch hour the following day, I went over to their place, only to discover that the "blurb"—it had expanded to two pages—wasn't ready. The trip wasn't a total waste, however. I returned the photographs they'd left behind at our apartment, and I saw that at last they had a working refrigerator. The kitchen was painted and cleaned up. Perhaps life was getting better for them after all. Before I left, Lyda showed me a black-and-blue mark on her leg where she said Frank had kicked her.

I scheduled another gathering at the Longs'. Julie begged off and S. T. in effect went in her place. Frank met us at the door. "Having spent the afternoon with Kirby, I would've preferred to call the evening off," he said, "but Lyda had everything set." Again, I was struck by how tidy the apartment looked. In the living room Lyda was lying on her bed. A tray of liquor bottles and paper cups rested on the floor. S. T. and I helped ourselves to peach schnapps. I poured a cup of vodka for Lyda. She proceeded to hold forth on India and famous Indians she had known, while Frank retired to his room. When he returned, after some fifteen minutes, Lyda was telling us Kirby was in bad shape. "Everything's fine with Kirby," Frank said, though I later heard from Ted that Kirby had lost Stephen King as a client. Lyda praised Kay, Kirby's sister, for her generosity. Frank showed us the French edition of *Dreamer*, which S. T. said he'd mention in the next issue of *Lovecraft Studies*.

It proved to be one of the easier visits with the Longs. Frank was not his usual agitated or gloomy self—he seemed actually relaxed and even smiled. The banter between him and Lyda was almost good-natured. Frank spoke of earning hundreds of thousands from his prospective memoir about all the science fiction greats he had known over the years. A TV crew was coming down from Providence to interview him about Lovecraft. It was Poe's birthday that day, we remembered, his 180th.

After about an hour I finally asked Frank if he was ready to give me his "review." He said he'd finished his "introduction," though he still had some marginal notes to make on the manuscript. I said the marginal notes could wait. Frank disappeared and came back with two handwritten sheets of typewriter bond. "I cut it down from four," he said. "It's titled 'Introductory Comment.'" When I explained that the series editor had already written a foreword to the book, hence I had no need of another introductory piece, Frank seemed a trifle miffed. It was a good moment for S. T. and me to make our escape.

The first sentence of "Introductory Comment" was quintessential Long: "In appraising a biography of someone who played as important a role in my life as H. P. Lovecraft my first and immediate reaction is likely to be of a generalized nature." Ho hum—but to my joy the text went uphill from there, impeded only by the occasional awkward phrase or infelicitous word choice. It was both highly complimentary and insightful. I derived from it the jacket blurb I'd requested in the first place, while the complete text ran as a prepublication review in the spring issue of *Lovecraft Studies.*

In the days that followed I typed up a transcript of Frank's text, correcting minor errors, and sent a copy to my editor at Twayne. Lyda called asking for Julie. I lied and said she wasn't home. I mailed Frank a postcard thanking him for his review. Lyda phoned again. "The TV crew caused a great stir yesterday," she said. "They spent nearly four hours with Frank interviewing him for a documentary in honor of the centenary." I knew plans to celebrate Lovecraft's centennial year were already in the works. Brett Rutherford, a friend of theirs who'd recently moved to New Jersey from Providence, had been present. Brett was a talented poet.

On Valentine's Day we arrived home late to find a frantic message from Lyda on our machine. Frank had been having seizures and was in a bad way. I called back and spoke to someone who I assumed was a paramedic. He reported that Frank refused to go to the hospital. Half an hour later Lyda phoned again, sounding extremely upset. Frank had been taken to St. Vincent's.

XII
February 1989–June 1989

Three days later Julie phoned Lyda, who told her Frank had pneumonia and phlebitis. The cause of his seizures was unknown. When I next spoke to Lyda, she said I should go visit Frank the following day. He had a correction for me. I promised to stop at the hospital after work.

When I arrived at St. Vincent's, Frank was asleep. He was hooked up to an IV and assorted monitoring equipment. A nurse was in the room. A delivery man arrived with flowers, which turned out to be from Kirby and Kay. After a minute Frank woke up. "Everyone's gone," he muttered. "Fifteen or so." I moved closer to his bedside. As soon as he gained full consciousness, he started to tell me about an error I'd have to fix in my book. "You got Loveman's age wrong," he said. "You called him a young protégé when he was nearly Lovecraft's own age." I later checked. Frank was right.

I asked him how he was doing. He said the doctors would be testing him to find out why his vision was distorted. He had to keep lying horizontally. "I hope to get out in a week," he said, "though it could be a lot longer." The nurse picked up the phone when it rang. It was Lyda. Frank got on the line and told her he was okay. When I got on, she asked me to call her later. "She has several friends to come in and look after her needs," Frank said. "I don't want her going into my room. I have everything arranged just so." I said I'd do what I could to help her. After about twenty minutes I left, promising to return soon. When I got home, I called Lyda. She was worried that the doctors didn't know what was wrong. "Please stay in touch," she said.

I called my editor, who said there was time in production to change Loveman from a "young protégé" to an "early amateur associate." Two days later I spent an hour and a half with Frank, who seemed less with it than before. It was hard to understand his words, but mostly he seemed to be complaining about the agony he'd been going through. A nurse gave him some pills and he drowsed off. Frank coughed now and then, but the nurse said that was good. Kay called. She said she spoke to Lyda daily. I gathered she was looking after things in general. Since

Frank wanted his condition kept quiet, she hadn't informed the science fiction community at large. As for Frank's illness, she pointed out that only a relative could find out what was really going on. Frank raised his hand in a feeble wave when I left. I phoned Lyda to give her an update. That he seemed unchanged didn't strike her as good.

About a week later, on my next hospital visit, Frank was sleeping. He looked better—and actually cleaner than he'd probably been in years. The IV was gone. A set of slippers by his bedside suggested he could walk. Soon after I got home that evening, Lyda phoned. She was feeling terrible and needed help getting to the hospital. Despite the imminent arrival of dinner guests, I agreed to go down to their apartment. Julie could cope on her own. The subway got me there as fast as a cab would have by eight o'clock. Lyda was evidently suffering a spell of depression. She'd tried phoning all her friends, but only I was around. She apologized for pulling me away from my party.

"I don't want to go to St. Vincent's," she said. Her voice was subdued. "I'll just have to wait up all night in the emergency ward and possibly not even be admitted, since there's nothing physically wrong with me." Her doctor, who was Frank's doctor, couldn't be reached until the morning because he was at a party. "Please let me come stay with you," she pleaded. I explained the situation, how it would be awkward with guests at our place, how we simply couldn't put her up for the night. I phoned Julie, who was of a like mind. Lyda asked to speak to her, but Julie was off the line before Lyda took the receiver. We discussed alternatives. In the end she agreed that the best thing was for her to stay at home. At her request I went out and got her two cups of black coffee. "I'm terribly sorry," she kept repeating. "I must let you go." I was home by ten, in time to catch the end of dinner.

At a gang gathering the second week of March, I heard about Frank from others. Bob, who'd recently moved back to New Jersey from North Carolina, said the publisher he'd approached wasn't interested in doing an entire book on Frank—maybe a chapter in a volume covering several writers. Brett said the people from Providence who interviewed Frank were amateurs who hoped a television station might buy their film. Frank had been quite cranky during the interview, but after an hour had settled down.

When I next visited Frank, he'd been moved to a double room. He was wearing his glasses and looked healthy, but was still on his back. Lyda was there, and we chatted in the hall while Frank's roommate was X-rayed. "Frank very much needs visitors," she said. "Giles comes by most evenings." I sat alone with Frank, but we didn't have much of a conversation. He complained of pain in his legs, from lying too long in the same position. He rolled briefly on his side. He talked a little about Bush's politics. He'd been taken for a long walk earlier in the day. Both Frank and Lyda said they'd been asked all sorts of questions by social workers. Frank spoke of starving writers—of the Irishman dying in the streets of Dublin while a play of his was a Broadway hit. Since it was a warm day, Frank rested on top of the covers. I noticed that his bare feet were dry, red, scaly, almost reptilian.

A week later, when I stopped by the hospital, Frank was screaming at Lyda because she'd failed to bring a get-well card from home. She said she forgot it. Frank was sure she was hiding something from him. He was mad that his beard had been shaved off. In fact, he had a half-inch left on his chin. At Lyda's prompting, I said he looked fine.

I gave Frank an envelope, marked "from a fan." It was an anony-mous gift of fifty dollars from Bob's parents that Bob had passed on to me. He was thrilled. (Later I told Lyda the source of the cash.) Then he started complaining about the black woman who had given him a shower. "I'm deathly afraid of blacks," he said. (Black people who were strangers, it might be fairer to say, since he betrayed no fear of Giles in my presence.) "Koch is loyal first to Israel," he added, speaking of the city's mayor. Soon he was bragging of his own exalted lineage, as a *Mayflower* and Lord Mansfield descendant. And for the nth time he chastised me for calling his style old-fashioned. And for the nth time I confessed and bewailed my manifold sin. "Joshi gets things right four-fifths of the time," he said, "but the rest of the time . . ."

I conferred with Lyda in the hall. The problem was that the hospi-tal wanted to discharge Frank, which probably meant his going into a nursing home. "He can't get around by himself," she said. "What are we to do?"

On my next visit I brought, at Lyda's suggestion, a copy of the Sunday *Daily News*. Frank was glad to have the tabloid, since the *New York Times* wouldn't have been as entertaining. On the whole he seemed in good spirits. He had no complaints—except about a new error he'd spotted in my Lovecraft study. In the bibliography I'd accidentally cited Necronomicon Press instead of Arkham House as the publisher of *Dreamer on the Nightside.* I was wrong again. . . . Frank acted more alert, less drugged than before, and his voice was stronger. He had plenty of magazines to read. He gave me a page from the *Times,* an article about a literary tour, illustrated by a cartoon sketch of Poe, Whitman, and Melville walking together. He wanted me to get the picture copied so he could send it to a couple of his correspondents. When dinner arrived, two nurses helped him sit up. I read the paper while he ate. An operation on his prostate a few days earlier had gone well—the next day the doctors would deal with his hernia. Before I left, Frank said he was grateful I'd come to see him.

That night I spoke to Lyda. Frank had had a stroke and could no longer walk unaided, though he didn't know it yet. "His personality has changed too," she said. "He's now less shy, much more assertive." She'd been putting off the social worker who wanted to see their apartment. They'd need someone to stay with them full-time. She didn't trust Kay anymore, since Kay hadn't been so helpful of late.

On my next trip to the hospital I encountered Lyda in the hall outside Frank's room. The hernia operation was a success, but now he'd caught double pneumonia. Frank was obviously not as well as when I'd seen him last. He was back on the IV. I passed on a copy of the latest *Lovecraft Studies,* courtesy of S. T. He read it for a little while with interest, but it was clear he was in discomfort if not actual pain. He was in no state to hold a conversation.

I visited Frank again the day before his birthday and gave him back the picture of Poe, Whitman, and Melville, with photocopies. Both Frank and Lyda commented that the one magazine to be taken from his bedside collection was *Lovecraft Studies.* They said they'd like another copy at some point.

A week later Lyda phoned. "Guess what?" she said. "Ray Bradbury has sent Frank a check for five hundred dollars!" An appeal had gone out and the money would soon be rolling in. Even better, she reported there was a good chance Frank would be able to walk with rehabilitation. A subsequent call from Lyda was a mistake. "I thought I was dialing Ben," she said. Ben, she made clear, was the one who was spreading the word about Frank to the big shots in the horror world. The social worker had told her they could set up a hospital bed for Frank at home. Lyda sounded optimistic, like her old grandiose self again.

When I next saw Frank, he confirmed that Lyda had come out of her depression. He himself was in good form, grousing about the black attendants. He needed to be repositioned for physical therapy, but we decided it was best for the nurse to do it, not me. I brought him a box of Kleenex from the neighboring bed, which was unoccupied, for his cough. He was off the IV. A woman screamed from the next room. "She does it all day," said Frank, implying it was no big deal.

A week later I rescued Julie from another one of Lyda's pestering calls. "I'm expecting ten thousand dollars from Stephen King!" she proclaimed when I got on the line. Frank would be home in two weeks. But Frank would remain in the hospital at least another month, and my visits to him there continued.

In mid-May when I saw him, Frank commented in awe on how strong his black nurse was. When Brett arrived, the three of us discussed Poe, Sarah Helen Whitman, and "The Bells." Frank corrected Brett on some detail in a poem of his about Poe and Mrs. Whitman. Lyda appeared, bedecked in green turban and matching earrings. When Frank started to complain that he was choking and Lyda was ignoring him, I decided it was time to leave.

The first week of June, Lyda called to vent her anger at L. Sprague de Camp, with whom it appeared she had spoken. "He claimed he was broke because he'd just moved to Texas and his wife was in the hospital," she said. "I let him have it. I told him how vulgar I thought he was, the way he behaved at conventions." Somehow I couldn't imagine that dignified gentleman carrying on as some younger immature attendees did at conventions. Lyda was sure he was rich from all the books he'd published. When I visited Frank the next day, he was worried that Lyda hadn't shown up or called. "Probably out shopping," he muttered.

The first day of summer Lyda phoned and spoke to Julie—Frank was coming home at last and we were invited to come celebrate.

XIII
June 1989–September 1989

Julie declined to join the celebration, but bought some flowers for me to bring to Frank. Despite being unable to reach the Longs by phone earlier in the day to confirm, I decided to show up at the hour originally set. S. T. was free to join me. Though we arrived on the early side, our hosts didn't seem to mind. At the door we had to be careful not to let their new pet, a friendly little mongrel named Drushka, escape. Lyda had told Julie she didn't want S. T. to come because he hadn't visited Frank in the hospital, but her manner toward him was entirely cordial.

Frank was lying in a hospital bed set up in the living room. I raised the head of it for him. Lyda provided drinks. She and I each had a beer, while S. T. had a glass of wine. I handed Frank a glass of orange juice—and his copy of *H. P. Lovecraft*, my critical study, which had just been published. Mumbling that he was disgusted with the whole situation, Frank didn't respond, other than to berate me for attributing *Dreamer on the Nightside* to Necronomicon Press instead of Arkham House. "You didn't even read it!" he yelled.

Iris arrived, the Jamaican nurse who had the night shift. Lyda told her how much she liked Jamaican rum. In French she confided to us that Frank, like Lovecraft, detested blacks. I hoped that Iris, like Frank, didn't understand French. I left after less than an hour, since I had to go meet Julie. S. T. stayed. Brett was due to show at any moment. A few days later Lyda phoned to say that Brett and Giles had dropped in after my departure. "What an intellectual conversation they had!" she gushed.

In July, Lyda roped us into attending a party in honor of their new dog. Since she said there'd be seven other guests, we decided it wouldn't be too bad. Brett greeted Julie and me at the door. We gave Drushka a chew toy, a rubber bird, in which he showed almost no interest. Frank was stretched out in the hospital bed, looking well, though he didn't at first recognize Julie. Julie accepted a glass of wine, I a beer. Frank drank orange juice. As usual Lyda held forth, but this time it was largely in praise of Brett. She read a poem from one of his collections that he'd given the Longs. In addition, she shared the same letters, collages, and photocopied materials we'd seen so often in the past.

Frank contributed little to the conversation, other than to worry that Lyda had invited too many people. "Fifteen you told me," he said to her. Then he was disappointed when no one else appeared. We three were in fact the only guests. In the kitchen Brett heated up some turkey and stuffing and a baked potato for Frank. After about two hours the three of us left, agreeing that the evening could have been a lot worse.

Through the rest of the summer Lyda phoned, leaving messages when we were out: "Kay has sent us a check for reprint rights to one of Frank's stories. . . . Columbia University has invited Frank to speak. . . . A French organization wants Frank to join a group of horror writers gathering in honor of Lovecraft's hundredth. . . . Frank's now using a walker, but he needs intellectual stimulation. You should round up Joshi and the others and visit. . . . I want to introduce Ted to a couple of available women."

In September I finally succumbed and organized yet another expedition to the Longs, but this time we had a small group, including Brett, S. T., and his fiancée, Leslie Boba. When the four of us arrived, Lyda complained that they had no home attendant that day. In any event, she tended to dismiss them early because they never did much. I helped Frank sit in his wheelchair and change his shirt. Lyda offered refreshments—beer, orange juice, which Brett brought, cheese and salami. As at the start of every such occasion, Lyda did all the talking. When she announced that she was going to stop, Frank piped up, "I hope so."

Brett tried to explain that there was no reason for her to feel miffed because Frank hadn't been included in a breakfast where three science fiction writers would be speaking over the weekend as part of the annual New York Is Book Country fair. Nor should she be put out because Frank's books weren't being sold at the festivities. Lyda said Ted never called her back when she left a message about setting him up. She complimented Leslie on her appearance and remarked what a bad dresser she thought Brett was when she first knew him. Since S. T. was sitting in a corner behind Frank's wheelchair, it took Frank an hour to realize he was present. Julie arrived late, having missed nothing.

On the Longs' living room wall was a pencil portrait of Lovecraft, an excellent likeness, by an artist fan who had recently sent it as a gift. This same fan had mailed S. T. his copy of *Dreamer on the Nightside*, and S. T. now took the opportunity to get it signed. Frank, however, misunderstood and inscribed the book "For Joshie" [*sic*]. When this error was brought to his attention, Frank told S. T., "If you want to, you can write his name over yours." Frank's handwriting was pretty shaky. "Maybe he won't notice the difference." The artist's name was Steve.

Giles appeared, shortly before Frank started to squirm in his wheelchair. I was close enough to hear Lyda whisper "Is it one or two?" and to hear his reply—"b.m." At Lyda's direction we younger guests retired to the hall while she and Giles attended to Frank. When we returned Frank was in bed, looking more comfortable. It seemed the moment to leave, but Lyda insisted we stay another fifteen minutes. When we finally did get away, she said how important it was for Frank that we had all come.

XIV
November 1989–February 1990

The week before Thanksgiving, Lyda called and spoke to Julie. She never wanted to see us again. When we returned from Thanksgiving in Massachusetts, there was a message on our machine from Lyda forgiving me. "I never forget a kindness," she said, "your staying up with me that night." Another message was from S. T. about getting together with the representative for an Italian publishing house who was in town and wanted to meet Frank. Julie insisted that this time I avoid the Longs. I phoned S. T. and gave him what I believed was their current number to pass on to Giuseppe Lippi, the Italian visitor. When Lyda called a few days later to invite us to a party for Giuseppe the following evening, I said I was sorry, we couldn't make it. The next week Lyda reported that the evening didn't come off because their phone had been out of order.

A week later I spoke again with Lyda. "I'm planning a party for Frank and I want the names of Lovecraftians I don't know to invite," she said. She was going to bring to New York Brett's play about HPL and his wife Sonia. (It had been staged in Providence, I knew.) Returning from a weekend in Connecticut, we found several messages from Lyda on our machine, including one that lasted minutes because she'd failed to hang up the receiver properly. After she stopped talking we could hear the TV humming and Frank quietly griping.

I decided to pay the Longs a surprise visit the next day. As it turned out, they had guests that evening. Kay, whom I was pleased to meet finally face to face, had brought over an old friend of Frank's, Julius Schwartz, who was famous among Lovecraftians for having agented as a teenager one of HPL's major tales the year before his death. "It was at a party in the Village," he said. "I just went up to Lovecraft and introduced myself and asked if he had any unplaced stories." For once I was truly annoyed by Lyda's dominating the conversation, since I had little chance to talk with "Julie," who was obviously a charming and witty man. He referred to Frank as "Belknap," the name people called him in his youth to distinguish him from his father, Frank, Sr. I showed him Frank's copy of my new book, though I was a bit embarrassed when he couldn't find himself in the index. (Later I saw that I'd mentioned him but not by name.)

When Julie started to tell me about how he and Belknap used to meet with other writers once a week in the Village in the forties, Lyda interrupted with a rant about how Frank had been exploited. "I haven't been exploited!" screamed Frank from his wheelchair, hitherto all but silent. Then Lyda started attacking Kirby—which didn't go over well with Kay. In the background the Hispanic home attendant giggled.

Finally, probably sensing nobody really cared to listen to her, Lyda delivered her showstopper. She turned to Schwartz and asked, "Do you want to fuck?" Julie hadn't been afraid to talk back to Lyda earlier, but even he was at a loss for a snappy reply to this one. Lyda repeated her request. While he and Kay didn't leave immediately, a pall settled over the party from which it never recovered. Frank summoned enough energy to criticize me for not including *The Early Long* in my bibliography. I said I'd listed it in *Pulptime*. Lyda said Joseph Papp was going to produce Brett's Lovecraft play. "I'm playing Sonia!"

When it came my turn to depart, Lyda gave me a present for my Julie—a shell necklace with matching purse. She assured me it was worth two hundred dollars.

For the rest of the month Lyda bombarded us with messages. "Julius Schwartz called to say he'd like me to be his mistress," she initially reported, though he evidently hadn't left his number, for in trying to reach him through information she'd talked to some other Schwartz, a Russian immigrant, who in the end offered to translate Frank's books. She phoned Kay to tell her the great news, but Kay was too busy to listen. "You call Kay and tell her," she said. Frank translated into Russian, the ultimate triumph, but I ignored her. One message told us to go to hell for not giving her presents—another that Frank had broken from Kirby. "I'm Frank's agent now!" As for her propositioning Julius Schwartz, she said she'd done it to liven things up.

In January the tune changed. She told Julie she was going into the hospital. When I called back she sounded calm. She was concerned about Frank being left alone. Later she informed us that she was too anemic to be operated on—for what she didn't say. Near the end of the month we received a letter stating "I have gifted you royally" and accusing us of giving her nothing in return. Under her signature she had written "Grâce à Dieu I am not a Lousecraftian." Julie and I seriously discussed severing all ties with the Longs.

When Lyda next called, I angrily told her we had our own lives and to stop bugging us. Her tone was conciliatory. She urged me to come visit Frank. When I phoned a few days later, she said because she had the flu I would have to postpone my visit. She was grateful I'd called. The following week she phoned again. Frank had fallen and was in the hospital, but fortunately he'd broken no bones. The first anniversary of his seizure loomed. Julie took her next call. Frank was coming home, and she expected us to bring over a bottle of champagne to celebrate on Valentine's. On the 14th we were occupied with a personal crisis of our own. The following day Julie listened as Lyda left an irate message on our machine. With my approval Julie wrote Lyda a letter saying we wanted nothing more to do with her, but leaving the door open for me to see Frank.

The last weekend of the month there was a gang gathering in the Village. After the usual bookstore sweep, Bob and I dropped by the Longs'. Frank was stretched out on the living room couch. The hospital bed was gone. While Bob chatted with Frank, Lyda apologized to me. They were desperate. Since Brett had moved back to Providence, there was no one around to visit on a regular basis. I promised to bring over a larger contingent of Lovecraftians the next time. Frank speculated on the relative intelligence of whites and blacks. At Lyda's request I walked the dog.

XV
March 1990–May 1990

On March 23rd, the afternoon of Julie's birthday, I visited the Longs. I had called in advance and they were expecting me. The home attendant opened the door. In the living room Frank was in his wheelchair watching a soap opera on TV, while Lyda was sitting in a corner with the dog. Frank didn't greet me until Lyda made a point of calling my presence to his attention. Lyda praised the home attendant, Elizabeth, who had now been with them three months.

"She washes Frank everywhere," she said, "even his tiny penis." Elizabeth, a Puerto Rican woman, had her post in the alcove outside the kitchen, where she sat watching a mini-TV. From the way she handled the Longs that afternoon I could tell Elizabeth was a loving person with a good sense of humor—they were indeed lucky to have her. "She kisses Frank when she bathes him," Lyda added. "Like a baby."

Lyda took a couple of pictures with her new Polaroid camera—one of me talking to Frank, the other of me holding Drushka with Frank to the side. She gave me the first photo, as well as a hardcover copy of Stephen King's novel *The Dark Half,* which she said she'd bought on the street for $1.50. (After reading it I got about the same price for it from a used-book buyer.) Her old cheap camera, she explained, had been stolen by someone who'd offered to get her a cab.

Lyda complained that her teeth couldn't be fixed (she was missing her front two) because she was too anemic. She'd recently received a legacy of eight hundred dollars, from a friend who'd died in 1978, so they were better off financially than they'd been. She asked if Julie had gotten over her anger. She clearly valued Julie's good opinion. Frank looked reasonably well. He'd been walking a little with his walker. "I find it astonishing," he said, "that a person could win two big lotteries. A math professor says the odds are only about one in thirty of such an event happening." Maybe the math professor meant thirty thousand— or thirty million. Frank smiled at the dog, even laughed, as the animal played at his feet. It was the only time I saw Frank laughing aloud.

Lyda chided Frank on their sex life. "You said you had a big erection last night," she said. "I want you to fuck me"—when you're well enough to do so, she seemed to be suggesting.

"Don't use such language," Frank replied.

This exchange led Frank to comment on what a gentleman Lovecraft was. "His grandfather's library of nineteenth-century books made all the difference," he said. Actually, it was his grandfather's eighteenth-century books that HPL regarded as a strong formative influence. "Only once did Howard ever revise my poetry," Frank continued, "changing a line because it disparaged a career in business." After all, Whipple Phillips, Lovecraft's maternal grandfather, had been both a cultured man and a man of affairs. Frank's grandfather Doty had been a bigwig connected with the Waldorf Hotel.

"Lovecraft was a homosexual!" Lyda proclaimed.

"No, he wasn't!" Frank retorted.

"That's why Sonia left him!"

"You have it all wrong. Howard was not a homosexual!"

"Well, maybe a quarter or an eighth."

Frank changed the subject—to my failing to list *The Early Long* in my Lovecraft study. "You misattributed it to Arkham House instead of Doubleday," he whined. It appeared he was confusing my sin of omission, neglecting to cite *The Early Long*, with my sin of commission, crediting *Dreamer on the Nightside* to Necronomicon Press instead of Arkham House.

Lyda said Frank had a trunk full of papers he wanted to go through, but he couldn't do it alone. Brett was going to help, before he moved. I offered to assist instead, though I doubted he'd preserved any real treasures. Lyda was aware that the forthcoming HPL centennial in Providence was an important event. She wondered why Joshi was such a big shot. I said S. T. was universally acknowledged as the world's leading Lovecraft scholar. (She wasn't surprised when I told her he was no longer engaged.) In June the Horror Writers of America would be holding their annual meeting in Providence in honor of the centenary. Lyda planned to get on a panel and tell everyone off for neglecting Frank. Frank remembered how the young Isaac Asimov once came up to him and told him that he, Frank, was one of his heroes.

Lyda in her turn waxed nostalgic. "I remember how I first saw Frank in his Brooklyn apartment," she said, "with his cat walking on the ceiling. So innocent, so unassuming."

"No, I'm not unassuming!" Frank protested. "What do you mean unassuming?" That she'd claimed his cat had been "walking on the ceiling" didn't seem to be an issue for dispute.

Lyda moved next to Frank. "He needs to be with intellectuals," she said, stroking his hair. "I'm not one." She asked Frank to recite some of his poetry. On cue he declaimed "Sonnet" ("The gods are dead . . .") and a stanza from "In Mayan Splendor." A few tears rolled down Lyda's cheek.

"Frank's family has a plot in Woodlawn in the Bronx," she said gently. "One day he'll be buried there."

"Well, it won't be long now," Frank muttered.

The tenderness didn't last. Soon they were back on Lovecraft. "Lovecraft hated blacks and Jews and so does Frank!" Lyda roared. "This one black hospital attendant was especially frightening to Frank. You should have heard him. If only we had a tape-recorder!" How I wished I'd brought a tape-recorder!

So passed perhaps the most outrageous, certainly the most affecting, visit with the Longs since they entertained me and Julie in their hall. Again, emotions had run high, but this time there'd been a redeeming element—a real display of love, at least on Lyda's part. One had to give her credit for that, as I later told Julie over her birthday dinner.

Almost two months went by before we heard again from Lyda. She was depressed. She was afraid she'd have to go into the hospital, where she'd soon die. Then Frank would have to go into a home, which he'd never survive. "You've been our one constant friend," she said. I promised to keep in touch.

Three days later, after consulting Lyda, I stopped in for an hour. Frank looked well. He said Mondadori, the Italian publisher, was reprinting *Rim of the Unknown,* his second Arkham House story collection, and paying him four thousand dollars. If true, he had good reason to be cheerful. He showed me a batch of recent fan mail. One fan had written a complimentary letter that asked nothing for himself. Another wanted Frank to autograph some gummed labels he'd enclosed. Lyda was subdued, letting Frank do the talking. It was in the depth of her depression that she was the most considerate of others. Frank said he worried about her in her current condition. Nonetheless, he was optimistic he would make it to the Lovecraft Centennial Conference that summer.

XVI
May 1990–August 1990

When I spoke with Lyda in May, she said she thought she'd put Frank on a bus to Providence for the conference, accompanied by a home attendant. I was sure we could do better than that. On my next visit I told them Bob would be driving from New Jersey and might be able to give them a ride. They showed me a letter from the librarian in charge of coordinating speakers for the weekend, which was sponsored by Brown University's John Hay Library, home to a vast collection of Lovecraft's papers, and supported in part by a grant from the state of Rhode Island arts council. The organizers were aware that Frank was among the more distinguished Lovecraft authorities to be invited (certainly the most venerable), and had offered him a room at the university's guest house.

Lyda said she'd been corresponding with relatives in Russia who hoped to emigrate to Israel. Frank burbled about his illustrious ancestors. Lyda asked me to go through Frank's manuscript trunk sometime after the conference. The radio was turned on to the Saturday afternoon opera. Frank said he liked classical music but not opera, a preference I said I shared.

Frank could now walk outside, though he was quite unsteady when he got up and grabbed his walker in the living room. "When I first knew Lovecraft he looked ten years older than his actual age," Frank remarked. "You look ten years younger." Lyda questioned me more about myself than usual. She admitted she'd just come out of a three-month depression. Before I left, she gave me a copy of the *Chelsea Clinton News,* a neighborhood paper. She wanted me to prepare a piece for it on Frank and the conference.

When later that day I proposed to Bob that he drive the Long entourage up to Providence, he declined the honor. He had other passengers, driving into the city was a hassle, the luggage might not all fit. And, while Bob didn't say so, he could imagine as well as I could that traveling eight hours to Providence and back with the aged couple would be no picnic. I had my own excellent excuse: Julie and I would be vacationing in Little Compton, Rhode Island, the week immediately beforehand. Nonetheless, I knew that if Frank was to make it to the Lovecraft Centennial Conference, I had to be the one to ensure that it happened.

Lyda called several times over the next few days. Once she reached Julie while Julie was on the other line and refused to get off. She liked the idea of being driven to Providence. She would pay me to sort through Frank's papers. Frank had received a check for $36,000. Frank had seen a doctor who told him he was too thin at a hundred pounds. In the meantime, I spoke to Jenny Lee, the Brown librarian, who promised to look into providing wheelchairs at their end. It would be better for the Longs to stay at a motel, since the guest house had stairs.

As word spread of the Longs' situation, more than one Lovecraftian came forward to offer his help in paying for the rental of a van to transport them to Providence. This seemed the most sensible solution. Now all we needed was a chauffeur. There was one obvious candidate—Stefan Dziemianowicz. Stefan, a relative newcomer to our local Lovecraft circle, had never met the Longs. Like a Boy Scout, he was, I sensed, brave and trustworthy. Assuming the role of the commanding officer forced to select a "volunteer" for the hazardous if not suicidal mission, I asked Stefan if he would get the job done. He accepted without hesitation.

When Lyda next called, I told her I'd lined up Stefan to drive them to Providence. I'd arrange a meeting with him soon. When I asked whether a home attendant was free to go with them, Lyda said they'd be taking along a "secretary." It was impossible to get a straight answer from her, now that she was in her latest manic phase. "I've just won a trip to China and Russia," she said when she phoned two days later. "I'll have to leave Frank in Brett's care in Providence."

The last day of July, Stefan and I met after work and walked over to the Longs'. On the way I filled Stefan in on what to expect. Frank and Lyda were waiting for us on the sidewalk in front of 421, in their wheelchairs. Standing beside them was a home attendant, a young Nigerian woman, who seemed friendly and kind. Frank was wearing a striped shirt with flowing cravat. Someone had obviously decided he should be looking his best for the occasion. Frank got up and walked in a circle using his walker, with a confidence and strength not evident my previous visit. A cloudburst drove us inside. We regrouped in the lobby.

Lyda took drink orders. The home attendant brought me a Cherry Coke from the apartment, then went to fetch beers for Frank and Stefan from the corner store. She said she was willing to accompany her charges to Providence, and seemed relieved when I told her it would only be for a weekend. I discussed logistics with Lyda. She thought the vehicle that had recently delivered Frank to the hospital for his checkup could take them to Providence. I said this was an unlikely option. Frank, as I later heard from Stefan, complained to him about a new anthology of Cthulhu Mythos fiction. The order of the stories made it appear as if Clark Ashton Smith had written the first non-Lovecraft tale in this vein, when in fact he Frank had done so, with "The Space-Eaters."

After about forty-five minutes of this, Stefan and I were ready to go. I gave Lyda a paragraph I'd written about Frank and the conference for the *Chelsea Clinton News*, where as far as I know it never ran. Frank had one last thing on his mind. "That story of yours in *Crypt*," he said, speaking of "The Appreciative Puritan," a tale of mine with a Lovecraft-like protagonist, a lame attempt at women's magazine fiction, fit only for Bob's zine. "You got Howard's character all wrong. He never would've said and done the things you have him say and do." I suppose I should have been grateful Frank was willing to share his critical comments.

The following day I phoned Lyda to tell her to expect Stefan on Friday the 17th for the drive up to Rhode Island. She subsequently left a string of short, incoherent messages—great things were happening, she was going to be on TV. In her present state I realized Lyda could make a real nuisance of herself at the conference. This wasn't just another "con" (convention) but a serious academic tribute to Lovecraft. A number of foreign scholars would be coming, from France, Germany, and Italy, countries where, in contrast to the United States, HPL had a reputation outside the genre as an important author. Would they want their weekend marred by Lyda's antics? Why, for that matter, should she spoil the weekend for anyone? One Lovecraftian in Providence, a psychiatric doctor who treated psychotics, offered half in jest to have her committed on arrival.

I conferred with Kay. She said she'd never set foot in the Longs' place again after that evening Lyda insulted Julius Schwartz—who would never go back either. Frank's friends all avoided him when they came to town on her account. In the past Lyda had checked into hotels, including the Plaza and the Chelsea, and racked up huge bills. (They'd thrown her permanently out of the Chelsea, the landmark hotel on West 23rd that traditionally welcomed struggling writers and artists.) For now, thanks to the two hundred dollars or so Kirby gave them every month on top of their Social Security, the Longs had enough to live on. Kay was in touch with their doctors (Lyda had medication but refused to take it) and the home-care people. I described the suffering Lyda had caused Julie.

After talking with Kay I decided that ideally Lyda should remain in New York while Frank and the home attendant made the journey to Providence. I called Kay back to tell her so. As long as Stefan had one or two other able-bodied persons along to restrain her, he could haul Frank off and leave her behind. On the other hand, such strong-arm tactics might upset Frank. Better would be to give them some advance notice, to prepare them for the idea. Kay agreed it was worth a try, though if Lyda insisted, Stefan would have to bring her too.

I felt better when Stefan told me he'd recruited Scott Briggs, another one of our local group, for the drive. The day Julie and I left for Little Compton, I mailed Lyda a letter politely but firmly suggesting that everyone, herself included, would be happier if she stayed home.

XVII
August 1990–January 1991

Friday evening of the conference, at the welcoming reception at the John Hay Library, I heard that both Frank and Lyda were coming. My letter had succeeded only in angering Lyda. Was she going to remain quietly at home when she had a chance to bask in Frank's reflected glory and have her say before a large audience? I'd been a fool to think there'd been the remotest possibility. At least I wasn't the one in charge of coping with her that weekend. Other Lovecraftians could have their turn.

I ran into Stefan and Scott at the registration desk after the reception. They both looked shellshocked. They'd just come from dropping off the Longs at the Days Inn. The trip had been a nightmare. When they arrived at ten that morning Frank was still in bed. It took Lyda two and a half hours to pack—virtually her entire wardrobe it would seem, a dozen bags and suitcases. She brought her guitar because she said she'd arranged with Jenny to sing as part of the program. Whether any home attendant had been present wasn't clear. At any rate, none accompanied them. With the delayed departure they encountered terrible traffic on the Interstate.

The program of panel discussions commenced Saturday morning, at Brown's Sayles Hall. Julie left just as we spotted Stefan pulling up in the rented van with the Longs. She was to visit her parents overnight outside Boston and return the next day. Frank was scheduled to appear on the second panel, moderated by Marc, on Lovecraft's "Life and Times." After the other participants had spoken, Marc introduced Frank, who'd been parked in his wheelchair at the back of the auditorium. Stefan and Bob pushed him to the stage, followed closely by Lyda. While Frank and his chair were hauled into place, Lyda hoisted herself on the edge of the stage. "I am Lyda Arco Long," she announced, "Frank's attendant." She described his hospitalization the previous year—then proclaimed she was going to present a check for five hundred dollars to her great friend Brett. (I don't think Brett regretted having made a point of being out of town that weekend.) In the ensuing silence Marc turned the microphone over to Frank.

Frank had little to say other than to apologize for not being better prepared. "I'll do better next time," he said. "I'll now recite three poems." He didn't identify them, but I think one of the maybe two he did repeat was by Clark Ashton Smith. The audience clapped and cheered, at one point giving him a standing ovation. Afterwards, feeling bad about the distress my letter had caused Lyda, I went over to tell her how fitting I'd thought her remarks on Frank's health had been. She ignored me.

That evening Frank took part in one more panel, on the craft of the horror fiction writer, moderated by Bob and including a weary-looking Stefan. This time Frank brought a tattered page of notes that more than once he paused to consult with the aid of a magnifying glass. Unable to hear questions from the audience, he had to have Stefan repeat them in his ear. Again, he received a big hand from the crowd, less for the content of his remarks than for his valiant effort to say anything at all half coherent. For those of us watching, especially the young for whom it was their first and probably last glimpse of the man, his very presence was enough. In response to a fellow panelist's request that he recite one of his own poems, Frank launched into "The gods are dead . . ." Lyda was absent, decoyed by the promise of an interview.

Sunday morning I attended the panel of foreign experts. Julie pulled me out toward the end of it, saying Stefan wished to speak to me in the lobby. Lyda had gone berserk, Stefan reported. When he arrived to pick them up, he found that she'd barricaded herself and Frank in their motel room and was screaming for their doctor. Frank was dying. She'd asked for me. I told Stefan there was probably nothing wrong, she was just being hysterical. Stefan rounded up some able bodies and returned to the motel. Julie said she'd learned that the night before, despite Lyda's failure to be interviewed (the "interviewer" couldn't find the Days Inn), Lyda had accepted the situation calmly.

I returned to the auditorium for the final panel of the program, as a participant. My mother was in the audience, as were Julie and her parents. The last one to speak, I shared some thoughts on the current state of Lovecraft studies, which for all the achievements of recent years I said remained largely the province of amateur scholars, such as myself, and needed to attract more professionals, such as English professors, if Lovecraft was to gain wider recognition as a serious author. In his closing remarks, in an aside, S. T. said my call for more attention in the academy might do Lovecraft more harm than good. (Indeed, to let loose the deconstructionists and the multiculturalists on HPL would be no advance, yet in the long run I was confident he could only benefit if read and appreciated by literate people with more power and influence than ourselves.) During the question period, Julie rose from her seat and challenged S. T.'s dismissal of my argument. I was touched. Even after the end of the ceremonies she went up to S. T. and continued the debate.

When we got home to New York that evening, we found an abusive message from Lyda on our machine. Julie exploded. At first she wanted to write the Longs a letter signed by me, then decided it was better simply to cease communication altogether. I had to agree. This was a step I'd been contemplating myself. We'd put up with their nonsense for far too long. I'd prided myself on my tolerance and patience. Where others had abandoned Frank when Lyda became too much to bear, I'd stuck it out. But now I was ready to leave Frank to his fate. After what I was sure had been his last hurrah, I was tired. . . . One evening, while on our honeymoon in Sicily, Julie and I had dined at a restaurant with an outdoor garden. Suddenly the stillness was broken by the sound of broken crockery and a man shouting *"Basta!"* Enough. We stopped eating. We couldn't tell the source of the noise, but it had to be coming from one of the houses overlooking the garden. Seconds later there was another crash of crockery and again a masculine voice (that of a long-suffering husband who'd reached his limit?) shouted *"Basta!"* Smarting from Lyda's latest insult, I felt like that man. I'd had enough.

As it happened, Julie and I were moving at the end of August across the Hudson to Hoboken, New Jersey. With any luck the Longs would never find us there. Someone else could rummage through Frank's papers.

The next day Lyda phoned. She'd changed her tune—and was now offering me the check for five hundred dollars she originally announced she was giving Brett. As proof of my new determination, I hung up on her. I later spoke to Stefan, who told a harrowing tale of the drive home that Sunday morning. After managing to coax Lyda into unlocking the door to their motel room, he decided to get them back to New York as soon as possible. As a result of his self-sacrifice, Stefan had missed much of the conference and had scarcely enjoyed the part of it he did attend.

Later in the week Bob informed me that the Longs had been threatening to sue me because I hadn't hired a limousine to take them to Providence. They were puzzled they hadn't heard from Stefan since Sunday. Stefan was no doubt grateful they knew neither his phone number nor his last name. Bob also passed on the story that Frank had been proposing to a lot of women around the time he met Lyda. The wrong one just happened to accept. I told Bob and Stefan we'd severed relations with the Longs.

In September Stefan reported Lyda had written Kay that she and Frank were going to tour the Soviet Union with Gorbachev. In December Kay told me Lyda was back in one of her deep depressions. In January Lyda finally got our number in Hoboken. Julie listened long enough to hear her say Stephen King was giving them twenty-five thousand dollars and she was going to sue all us Lovecraftians. Or maybe she said Lousecraftians. A note from Kay said that Lyda couldn't understand why the Lovecraftians had dropped them. One day when I came home Julie said Lyda had called persistently. We considered getting an unlisted number.

XVIII
Fall 1993–Fall 1994

In the fall of '93, I spoke with Ted about ensuring Frank received an obituary in the *New York Times*. Ted had likewise concluded this final honor was due him and wrote a letter to the *Times* obituary editor making the case. Though I hadn't seen Frank for more than three years, I did on occasion hear reports of his condition. Ben and Stefan had visited him recently in the hospital. The end had to be near. I unearthed a copy of Les Daniels's tribute, which Ted sent to the *Times* editor. In the months following the centennial conference I'd picked up the paper every day half expecting to read of Frank's death. But he'd continued to live on, ever weaker in body, mind, and spirit. Despite her having left me two years earlier for a fellow artist, I kept my word to Julie. Recovering from her loss was emotional trial enough without the added burden of resuming relations with the Longs. I was once again living in my old neighborhood on the Upper West Side—and had, as of that October, remarried.

The first Monday of the new year, Ted called to say that Frank was dead. He'd died the day before, January 2, at St. Vincent's. Ted had heard the news from Kirby—he had no further details. Two days later the *New York Times* ran an obituary headed "Frank Belknap Long, an Author of Science Fiction, Is Dead at 90," accompanied by a photo dated 1949. Frank had been almost chubby in middle-age. The text clearly derived from Les Daniels's article. Ben phoned to say Lyda was okay. I wrote her a condolence letter.

The day after I mailed it I received a call from a woman with a Spanish accent, presumably a home attendant. Lyda was wondering how I'd found out about Frank. I wondered at the speed of the mail, and said I was available to visit anytime. Later Lyda herself left a message, a friendly one. When I stopped in that Saturday, I found all was forgiven. She remembered the time I'd left my own party in order to come stay with her. She never forgot a kindness.

I heard about Frank's last months. After a fall in which he broke three ribs, he went into the hospital where he ended up spending five weeks in the ward for, as she put, "the mildly psychotic." When he came home, he wouldn't let anyone touch him and yelled obscenities. He complained that he was lonely, unable to understand why no one came to see him. Lyda apparently didn't know what if any arrangements had been made for his funeral. She gave me a letter from an official at Woodlawn Cemetery, dated the previous September, verifying that Frank was entitled to be buried in the Long family plot.

Later I spoke to Ted, Bob, and Stefan. No one seemed to know what was happening. I suggested we hold a memorial service at the grave in the spring. For the moment, Stefan told me, the hospital was willing to hold Frank's body in the morgue. At the end of January, I received from Lyda what I later realized was a copy of the last page of a memorial tribute to Frank that Stefan had written for *Locus,* a magazine devoted to the science fiction and fantasy fields. On one side she'd penned, "Come All Ye Faithful—I miss him so"; on the other, "Recall—Peter—one night I asked you to stay—and you did—and how is the spouse—my best."

In February I wrote a short story called "The Letters of Halpin Chalmers," a sequel to "The Hound of Tindalos," that conveyed my ambivalent feelings about Frank and Lyda far better perhaps (certainly more succinctly) than any lengthy memoir. Though it only marginally fit the genre, Stefan was kind enough to accept the tale for one of the Barnes & Noble anthologies he'd been coediting, *100 Crooked Little Crime Stories.* In March, while doing some freelance work at the New York Public Library, I looked up Frank's birthdate on microfilm. The records showed a Frank B. Long had been born in Manhattan on April 27, 1901, two years earlier than the usual date in the reference books.

In June I spoke to Kay. She and Kirby weren't taking the lead on arranging a funeral or memorial service, though they'd be glad to chip in if someone else did. I said I'd consider assuming the responsibility. Lyda continued to be abusive toward them. Since they'd sent out an appeal for money when Frank was in his last illness, donations for his burial were slow in coming from those in the science fiction world. Later in the month I spoke to Mark Berman, to whom the letter from Woodlawn Cemetery had been addressed. Though we'd never crossed paths, I gathered he'd looked after the Longs' day-to-day needs for years, buying food and running errands. His late mother had been Lyda's best friend.

Mark had some startling news: Frank had been buried months before in Potter's Field, where the city's indigent are unceremoniously laid to rest. "Don't tell Lyda I told you," he said. I should have known St. Vincent's wouldn't have held his body indefinitely. Happily, having read a *New Yorker* article on Potter's Field, I knew the process wasn't irreversible. Mark said he'd received an estimate of $2,100 to have Frank exhumed and reburied. (By keeping him on ice, Lyda had been hoping to continue receiving his Social Security payments.) I told Mark I thought this sum could be raised within the larger Lovecraftian community.

On a hot day in early summer, Ben and I paid Lyda a call. As Mark had warned, she was in one of her manic phases. "Wait a minute!" she shouted from behind the door. "I'm naked!" Lyda herself greeted us, wrapped in a sheet. "Ben and Peter, my two favorite people!" she exclaimed. "Thank God, thank God." We followed her into the living room, where she sat on the bed, cooled by two small electric fans. We saw no home attendant. In response to some ribald comment from Lyda, Ben joked about his sex life after a prostate operation. He knew exactly how to handle her—by being playful, by refusing to take offense at any of her more personal remarks. Lyda loved it. For my part I was concerned to avert my eyes as her casually draped sheet didn't always preserve modesty. Attempts to discuss retrieving Frank from Potter's Field were unavailing.

In July Mara Kirk Hart, daughter of George Kirk, one of the original Kalems, came to town. A librarian, she'd run across *Pulptime* (in which her father has a bit part) and written me early in '91 inquiring about other members of the Kalem Club. I'd replied that Frank was to the best of my knowledge the group's only survivor. We'd met the summer of '93 in New York, and now she was back for another visit, with her grown daughter. One evening, as I later heard, the two of them spent five hours with Lyda. They ordered take-out food, they gossiped, they had a hilarious time. Mara mentioned Nan Hawley, my new wife, whose existence I'd been keeping a secret from Lyda. Now that we were back in touch, I feared the prospect of her becoming fixated on Nan, as well as her probing me about a painful recent past.

Nonetheless, I was glad that Mara had been the one to inform her of this dramatic change in my own life.

In August Lyda mailed me photocopy blow-ups of two pictures—one of the Polaroid shot of me and their dog with Frank to the side, the other of a long-ago party in their living room, filled with smartly dressed men and women. In the surrounding white space she'd written the names of a few of the guests—Paul Destinée, George Reavey, Yvette Chantilly—everyone a musician or an artist. In September she sent me a Jewish New Year's card, or to be precise, a photocopy of Tenniel's white rabbit from *Alice in Wonderland* bearing a banner with "best of years" wishes from "Lydash and Frankele."

As part of his fall Necronomicon Press catalogue, Marc included an appeal for funds to pay for Frank's burial in Woodlawn Cemetery. He discreetly didn't mention that Frank, for the moment at least, was planted in Potter's Field. The fans on Marc's mailing list were quick to respond. Stephen King gave most generously. By the end of the month Marc had received enough money for us to proceed.

When I visited the funeral home on West 23rd where Mark had gotten the original estimate, I discovered that complete costs would run to more than three thousand dollars. Annoying, but an amount still within the capacity of Necronomicon Press to raise. Bob agreed to come in from New Jersey to officiate at a memorial service, which we set for three in the afternoon of November 3, a Thursday. That Frank might not be in Woodlawn by that date I decided didn't matter, as long as we knew he was on his way. I brought the papers to authorize the transfer over to Lyda, who for once was in a mood to cooperate. Indeed, she was humbly grateful for our efforts. Since she hadn't been feeling well, she told me to go as soon as she'd signed the papers. Marc sent the funeral home a $2,100 check, the rest to be paid on delivery.

I ordered a map from Woodlawn that turned out to include a history with a list of famous occupants. Founded in 1863, the Woodlawn Cemetery billed itself as the second oldest organization in the Bronx. Under the "Hall of Fame" category labeled "Famous Writers, Poets, etc." were, among other illustrious names, Herman Melville and Countee Cullen. Frank would be in good company. Perhaps one day an updated version would mention the author of "The Space-Eaters" and "The Hounds of Tindalos."

I spoke to Kay, who promised to provide champagne and flowers for the reception tentatively scheduled after the ceremony. Before the end of October, however, both Mark and Ben informed me that Lyda was too ill either to attend the service or receive visitors at home—she might even have to check into the hospital. A pity she couldn't make an event where she deserved to be center stage, but then her absence meant less trouble for others.

The afternoon of November 3, I drove Ted up to the Bronx and promptly got lost. We arrived at Woodlawn ten minutes after the hour to find that those ahead of us had yet to locate the Long family plot. From the cemetery map, though, we knew we had to be close. After some assiduous hunting I discovered the tall granite obelisk that I knew had to be nearby, marked on one of its four sides with the names of Frank's grandparents. We reassembled by this monument, fifteen or so of us, including Stefan, Scott, and S. T.

Under a low, bright autumn sun, dressed in full clerical garb, Bob conducted an informal service as befit Frank's agnostic beliefs, reading poems by both the deceased and his friend HPL. When Bob called for people to step forward and share their thoughts, three did so. One was Joe Wrzos, former editor of *Amazing,* a magazine that had published Frank back in the days when his stories still had a professional market. Another was Ben. The third was Perry Grayson, not yet twenty-one, who'd flown from California just for the occasion. Perry regarded Frank as his literary idol. I took photographs. The group broke up around four. I drove a carful of passengers back to Manhattan via the teeming streets of the South Bronx, having somehow missed the turn-off for the highway.

The following week Mark called to tell me that Lyda was in the hospital, with liver and pancreatic cancer. She might have only months or weeks to live. As it turned out, when I stopped by St. Vincent's the next evening, she had less time than that. When I first entered her room I mistook another old woman for her. In fact, Lyda was in the bed opposite, heavily sedated, almost unrecognizable with an oxygen mask over her nose and mouth. She may have turned her head slightly toward me when I spoke, but I doubted she recognized me. In the hall I found a nurse, who explained that that morning Lyda had made a fuss—torn at her IV, screamed and cursed the doctor. I could imagine.

So instead of the hospice route, she ended up on a morphine drip. Instead of a couple more weeks of life, she now had only a couple more days. Relieved of her suffering, she would never regain consciousness.

Outside the hospital, as I walked the few blocks east to the restaurant where I was meeting Nan for dinner, I shed a few tears. I was sad in a way I simply hadn't been when I heard the news of Frank's death. For Frank I'd felt mainly relief that he was at last out of his misery. For Lyda I felt genuine sorrow. I regretted that I hadn't told her of my doings during the years of my silence—for in the end I realized that, as mean and selfish and crazy as she could be, she'd appreciated who I was and what I had done for them and, unlike Frank, had told me so. And with her passing, too, I was mourning a part of my life forever gone yet from which I was hurrying with a sense of renewed hope and joy.

XIX
November 1994

Early in the afternoon, two days later, four of us met on the stoop of 421 West 21st Street—myself, Ben, Mark, and a stranger named Brad Verter. Ben and I decided later that Mark must have alerted Brad that the moment had come to check the Longs' apartment for valuables. Brad said he was an old friend of Frank's. A graduate student in theology at Princeton, this young man admitted he was also a book collector and dealer.

Mark let us into the building and the apartment with his keys. I made a point of telling Mark that we regarded him as Lyda's heir, that anything of hers after her death belonged to him. Since Lyda was sure to have no will, I was of course acting outside the law. In the circumstances, however, both Ben and I felt this was a morally justified gesture, one worthy of Sherlock Holmes himself. Mark thanked me.

Once inside Brad announced that Lyda had promised he could have Frank's Life Achievement Award. A cast-metal effigy of H. P. Lovecraft designed by the cartoonist Gahan Wilson, the "Howard" was the horror world's equivalent of the Oscar. Neither Ben nor I objected. What did we know? Mark, not being an aficionado of the genre, was in no position to judge. Brad secured his trophy in the living room.

The living room looked almost abandoned—dustier and more paper-strewn than it had been my last visit. From a desk Mark pulled out Lyda's passport, which he said he'd used in repeated and fruitless efforts to get her on Medicaid. From the same desk Mark retrieved some old snapshots. One tattered print, dated February 1958, showed a red-haired, red-lipped Lyda before a fireplace in a golden, off-the-shoulder gown. Between the fingers of one red-nailed hand lifted to the mantel was an aperitif glass half filled with red liquid. On the back she'd written "The Jade of Jades (the mask of sophistication)" and "Lyda not Lydasha." Mark confirmed that the apartment had been hers at the time she and Frank were married. She'd probably been living there since the forties. Despite her claims of multiple husbands, she'd had only one. As for her singing career, she had once sung a solo as part of a program at Carnegie Recital Hall.

The next stop was Frank's bedroom, the last mystery. For years I'd wondered what it contained, though I wasn't expecting to find much of interest. In the event, I was in for a pleasant surprise. There was a bureau, a desk, a single bed beneath the lone security-fenced window—and dozens and dozens of books, heaped here and there. Frank's horror library occupied a set of shelves at the head of his bed. While he'd long before sold such rarities as *The Outsider*, Lovecraft's first Arkham House collection, he still had plenty of books that fans would want, including battered paperback copies of the Gothics he'd penned under Lyda's name and such later novels as *Monster from Out of Time* and *The Night of the Wolf*. There was a stack of his chapbook, *Rehearsal Night*. Brad, who knew his way around the bedroom from past visits, encouraged Ben and me to help ourselves.

And help myself I did, like the proverbial kid let loose in the candy store. Chief among my acquisitions for my own library were a jacketless copy of *The Early Long* and a beat-up Arkham House edition of *The Hounds of Tindalos*. Greedy I may have been, but given the poor condition of virtually every volume I was hardly enriching myself. Frank, I liked to think, would have wanted me to have a book or two or three of his, had he for a moment thought to stop his nitpicking and show me some gratitude. Furthermore, others not present who'd been true friends to the Longs deserved some tangible reward. Certain items I set aside in my mind for these selfless souls.

Brad suggested I might like to take Frank's typewriter (there was only one), but I didn't need a bulky old manual typewriter. Another relic Brad brought to my attention, however, did catch my fancy—the manuscript of what must have been the novel Frank said for years he was working on and never completed, *Cottage Tenant*. It could in fact be a scarce example of a Long manuscript, for the trunk full of Frank's papers Lyda had asked me to go through was nowhere to be found. Brad had seen it in recent years, but it wasn't in its accustomed spot.

We inspected another trunk, which contained ordinary books—contemporary thrillers, a bestseller or two—nonetheless reflecting some literary taste. One title caught my eye, an old paperback of Dostoevsky's *The Idiot*. There were boxes too. One held a collection of old vinyl records, 78s—classical, heavy on opera. Another was filled with Yiddish theater memorabilia. Brad promised to take this material to the Yivo Center for Jewish Research. On the floor were a couple of scraps of paper of personal relevance—a postal card I'd sent Frank thanking him for his introductory comments on my Lovecraft study; a royalty statement from Paul Ganley for one or two dollars, Frank's annual share of *Pulptime.*

A home attendant arrived. She looked sad, no doubt aware that Lyda wouldn't be coming home. We told her to take anything she wanted from the living room and kitchen. As for the books, Ben and I were fast formulating a plan. Even with the cream skimmed off the top, Frank's library could, we reckoned, bring hundreds of dollars. More money was needed to pay the total cost of his reburial. Having his name engraved on the family monument in Woodlawn would be an additional expense. Ben suggested we take the books to a dealer he knew upstate. I had a better idea: why not ship them to Marc in Rhode Island? He could prepare a catalogue and offer the collection to the patrons of Necronomicon Press. They after all had been among Frank's more loyal supporters in his last years, buying his *Autobiographical Memoir* and issues of *Crypt* featuring his fiction. They deserved first crack at a souvenir from the library of Frank Belknap Long.

With Mark's approval, Ben and I relayed armfuls of books into his capacious station wagon parked on the street. We had no time to waste finding boxes to pack them in first. By mid-afternoon we'd finished loading every book we figured Frank's fans would consider significant. We were ready to leave but not so Brad, who was in a panic. He couldn't find the Howard. Ben and I were perplexed. What could have happened to it? After a few minutes we discovered the home attendant was the unwitting culprit. From the bottom of a garbage bag she'd been packing full of old clothes and costume jewelry, she produced the statuette. Brad's relief at recovering his prize was palpable.

Ben and I drove over to St. Vincent's, where we found Lyda still in a coma. We tried to discover what would happen to her when she died, but no one could answer us, since in theory only a family member could deal with the matter. Ben had already learned that the cost of having her cremated would be around four hundred dollars. Back home I found a message on my machine from the undertaker handling Frank's reburial that it was set for Wednesday, two days hence. That evening I phoned Marc Michaud. He said he'd be glad to handle the disposal of Frank's library through Necronomicon Press. Later that night Mark Berman called to tell me he'd heard from the hospital—Lyda was dead.

XX
November 1994–April 1995

The next day I brought Ted up to date. I was confident no one would challenge our removing Frank's books—the stakes were too small. His literary estate was highly unlikely to generate the kind of money to provoke legal wrangling.

"I guess you haven't heard," said Ted. "Steven Spielberg has just announced plans to film 'The Hounds of Tindalos.'"

I laughed, but not for long. The following morning I heard from the funeral home that we had to reschedule for Thursday. Because of unrest on Riker's Island the prisoners were locked up in their cells that day and couldn't do any digging in Potter's Field. Then Ben phoned with worse news. Mark had just learned that, since Lyda died intestate, we had no right to clean out the apartment. The contents belonged to the city. Not wanting to break the law, Ben was prepared to give all the books back.

I spoke to Mark. He was seeing somebody downtown about the matter that afternoon. He was hopeful that we wouldn't have to turn over everything we'd collected on Monday to the authorities. He agreed not to make a point of admitting we'd taken books that were of some value. He would, however, be honest. Like Ben, he was inclined to stick to the letter of the law. When I said he was the one who stood to lose the most, he said he'd have to accept that. (Of course, the other big losers would be the collectors of Longiana.)

While I didn't say so to my fellow thieves, I for my part wasn't about to surrender any of my Long goodies to the city, especially not the manuscript of *Cottage Tenant*, which I now took the time to examine more closely. It consisted of two partial drafts, mostly photocopied pages. The first couple of paragraphs afforded a unique glimpse of Frank as wordsmith, starting with the first, handwritten draft.

Chapter one opened on a lyrical note: "Of all American shorelines the Coast of New England appears to have been the most mysteriously haunted. Dreamers, visionaries, poets and prophets have made of it a time-dissolving portal into the unknown close to without precedent."

My editorial eye halted at that final prepositional phrase. How about "close to unprecedented" or "almost unprecedented"—or better yet, why not end the sentence after the word "unknown"? Well, that would have spoiled the rhythm. The phrase "close to without precedent," after all, did sound poetic. Hence it remained in the second, typed draft.

The second paragraph of the first draft resumed: "Thoreau, the most legendary of hermits, spent a lengthy period attached to the blowing sands of Cape Cod's desolate wasteland, Hawthorne described its periph[er]ies as a magnet for witches, and Melville in a miraculous display of genius, hovered over a captain and crew that went white whaling in a several-times-repeated screen dramatization." Huh? It must have taken a miraculous display of genius to make those screen dramatizations seaworthy, particularly the several-times-repeated variety.

In the second draft, no doubt mindful of the need to revise, Frank had let Melville hover "over a captain and crew that went white whaling in a famous screen dramatization by Ray Bradbury." Well, this was an improvement. As far as I knew *Moby-Dick* had been made into a movie only once. Sensing perhaps that he still didn't have it right, Frank had crossed out the end of the sentence so that in the final version the captain and crew go "white whaling in a Moby Dicksonian legend that transcends its creator." Were those echoes of Emily Dickinson and Transcendentalism deliberate, I wondered? A perusal of *Cottage Tenant* after the first page confirmed that Frank's failure to complete his last novel was no tragedy.

That evening I spoke to Mark again. All was well. The city bureaucrats weren't about to insist we return what we took from the Longs' apartment. Ben was willing to proceed as originally planned with shipping Frank's books to Marc in Rhode Island.

The next day, before meeting S. T. for the drive up to the Bronx, I went by the apartment for a final sweep. Mark had given me his set of keys on Monday. The place looked all the more desolate, ransacked. I didn't envy the landlord. It might be a while before the premises were cleaned up and available for rental. I looked in vain for Frank's HWA award and had to presume Brad had taken it as well as the Howard. And what of the painting of Lyda and the swan? Would whoever finally unscrewed it from the wall bother to save it? I salvaged a few more paperbacks, in particular the copy of *The Idiot* I'd spotted in the trunk.

It turned out to be inscribed: "To my Beloved 'Idiot'! Lyda Long." Perhaps she'd given it to Frank as a wedding present. (Dostoevsky's "idiot" is Prince Myshkin, a naively open, childlike man too good for the corrupt society that eventually destroys him, I later discovered on reading the novel.)

I stopped at the funeral home on West 23rd, where I made sure the prisoners at Riker's were cooperating that day and I had proper directions. I delivered a check for the balance. After rendezvousing with S. T., we bought sandwiches at a deli and headed up to Woodlawn. There, at one o'clock by the main entrance, we met Fred, the funeral director I'd been dealing with, in his station wagon. I could have ordered a hearse to transport the body—no doubt Frank and Lyda would have preferred him to travel in style on his final earthly journey—but as neither was in a position to object I had as usual chosen to go economy.

A car supplied by the cemetery led our little procession to the gravesite, where Ben was waiting. The sky was gray and overcast, the temperature more fall-like than it had been two weeks before at the memorial service. Under Fred's supervision a work crew unloaded the metallic bronze casket (in theory the cheapest model) and placed it on the bier, while I took pictures. Did that casket really contain Frank's remains? What if it was the wrong body—say, that of a poor anonymous black person? Maybe earlier I should have asked to verify the identity of the corpse in its wooden box when it was delivered to the funeral home, but my taste for the ghoulish didn't extend beyond the printed page. I was content to trust the *New Yorker* article's assertion that those in charge kept excellent records at Potter's Field.

I photographed Ben and S. T. by the casket, then handed my camera to Ben for him to take my picture at the same spot. At last Fred suggested it would be appropriate for one of us to say a few words. Addressing myself mainly to the solemn workmen standing at a respectful distance, I explained that we'd already had a service for Frank and that he was finally where he belonged. The three of us continued to chat among ourselves, until I realized we were keeping the workmen from finishing their job. We moved on, in search of Lovecraft's grandparents' grave. We found the headstone, almost hidden by an overgrown bush. I snapped a picture of Ben and S. T. holding back the branches so as to reveal the name "Lovecraft."

The next day I spoke to Brett, who'd moved back to New York. He said he'd persuaded Lyda not to throw out a cache of Frank's papers, though it appeared at some point she did so, perhaps when Frank was in the hospital during his final illness. I mailed the *Cottage Tenant* manuscript to Marc, who listed it in his catalogue of the Frank Belknap Long library. At $250 it was more than ten times the price of the average item offered. Sales from the catalogue paid for all funeral-related expenses, including Lyda's cremation, which occurred the same day as Frank's reburial.

In January I received a letter, dated November 17, from Brad, who'd originally mailed it to my old, pre-Hoboken address. Among other evidence of his efforts on Lyda's behalf, Brad enclosed a copy of the cover letter he'd sent to an individual at the Yivo Center along with Lyda's vital papers on her family and the Yiddish theater. He suggested that they call Mark Berman to arrange for the removal of the painting in the Longs' hall. He identified the artist as Haile Hendrix, a cartoonist, and two of the other figures in the painting as the author Bel Kaufman and the actress Bette Davis. Perhaps within her own realm, I fleetingly thought, Lyda had left a greater legacy than Frank had in his field.

Also in the new year Perry invited me to contribute to a booklet of articles he was editing about Frank's life and work. Perry would indeed found his own small press devoted largely to publishing work by and about Lovecraft's best friend. At the Lunacon in March I bought a copy of Frank's story-cycle-turned-novel, *John Carstairs: Space Detective.* I was becoming a casual Long collector. I contracted with a stonecutter to have his full name and dates inscribed on the family obelisk. This would fill the available space. When asked, I said Frank's widow would not be joining him in Woodlawn. I wasn't quite telling the truth.

By what would have been Frank's ninety-fourth birthday, when Ben and I returned to Woodlawn, the engraving was finished. Ben supplied yarmulkes and recited the Kaddish. I read the translation of the Hebrew in phonetic English as best I could. Over Frank's sunken, not yet grass-covered grave we took turns sprinkling Lyda's ashes—half of them at any rate. Mark had reserved the other half for casting into the waters off Sea Gate, in Brooklyn. (In her last days, according to Mark, Lyda had expressed the wish at one point to be with her beloved husband, at another to become one with the ocean opposite her favorite part of Brooklyn.) That ceremony, however, I wasn't planning to attend. I'd performed my last service for those "old, dear, exasperating, maddening but unique friends," to borrow Ben's phrase from the affectionate memoir of the Longs he would prepare for his EOD zine. I was free—free to begin contemplating writing my own memoir of that immortal couple.

Afterword

Ramsey Campbell

I have frequently discovered myself to be of the opinion, which I have not been shy of expressing aloud even if there was nobody else to hear—though I'm assuming, of course, the total absence on these occasions of invisible spectres and of any other presences not discernible to ordinary eyes—that an account of the last years of Frank and Lyda Long ought to be set down for the record by somebody who not only knew them but who is in possession of sufficient talent for prose to do them justice—a writer, in other words, unless some tentacled denizen of another planet in orbit around, let us say, distant Betelgeuse could be found to have observed them in the apartment where they ultimately lived and was able to share the experience. Such a one (I leave my readers to decide on his humanity or otherwise) is Peter Cannon. In case anybody who has read up to this point is wondering whether his memoir is exaggerated, let me say that my experience suggests it couldn't be. Jenny and I often reminisce about the evening we spent with the Longs.

It was in 1976, after the World Fantasy Convention in New York. The Longs were at the convention, Frank pottering about for all the world like a Brooklyn version of the Walter Brennan character in *Rio Bravo*. Lyda summoned us to their table in the hotel lounge and greeted me as (apparently Frank's phrase) a brilliant young writer. She invited us to dine at their apartment, promising that we would eat as we had never eaten before. Indeed, our first stay in New York was to be marked by unforgettable meals—this was the convention at which the banquet proved to be a buffet delivered in meagre servings at yawning intervals, all of which maddened the famished fans, who swooped on it like vultures onto carrion. Eventually one dissatisfied banqueter went out and bought a portion of Kentucky Fried Chicken to fling at the convention committee. At the time we saw none of this as an omen of dinner with the Longs.

Kirby McCauley was invited, but pleaded a previous engagement. I'm not sure whether it was on his recommendation that we took a litre of white wine with us—a wise move, at any rate. We arrived on time, to find `that for some reason nobody else had. Frank ushered us past a bicycle into the bedroom Peter has already immortalised, then took refuge in the bathroom. "Frank, you bastard," Lyda screeched to make him vacate it. "Where have you put my tiara? He's being a prima donna in there." She continued to assure us how uniquely we would eat. Eventually some of our fellow guests ventured to appear—Ben and Janet Indick, H. Warner Munn and his young companion Brenda, who had been thoughtful enough to bring a joint we young folks duly smoked next to the bicycle. I can't remember the names of the other guests, but the place soon took on all the qualities of a party in the heyday of the Beat generation, or perhaps a version of one dreamed up by Hollywood. A stringy fellow sang or intoned—even at the time it was impossible to judge—poems while accompanying himself on a guitar. A later arrival than most, a spectacularly neurotic young woman, said nothing for several hours before without any visible preamble she downed most of a bottle of vodka and passed out on the bed. Perhaps she had been overcome by the tardy spectacle of the promised dinner: half a baked potato per guest, to accompany their portion of the *pièce de resistance,* a silver salver bearing an artistic arrangement of four hot dogs surrounding segments of not as many more. It did tempt Frank out of the bathroom. Presumably he spoke to the guests, but it's Lyda we recall. Attired not in a tiara but a kaftan, she told Jenny how, having been brought up in India, she spoke proper English like us but unlike Frank.

You can take all this as being horribly funny or horribly sad—more likely both. I just wish I could offer more to balance it, but I don't think it helped Frank that his early work became legendary in his lifetime. Certainly *The Hounds of Tindalos* used to be a favourite book of mine, so that when he sent me a story for *New Tales of the Cthulhu Mythos* I could hardly wait to read it—not, at least, until I saw the first line: "It was just the right place for an encounter with an enchantress." I imagine Lovecraft's reaction, had he been able to read that, might have been similar to mine—a sinking sense that Frank had lost his feeling for the tale of terror to the romances he'd written under his wife's name. The story tells how the narrator meets an attractive widow and her children on a beach, and talks to her about childrearing and poetry. Eventually, maybe before the reader despairs, a Cthulhoid item floats up and sinks again. I waited for a punch line but found none, and so suggested a final paragraph to Frank, which he said I should add to the story myself. He did, however, assure me that it was one of his strongest stories.

It wasn't, and that, more than the encounter with him and Lyda, is why Frank haunts me. Just as Peter and his first wife saw their own potential future in the Longs, I often wonder if I'm as wrong as Frank to feel that my work is improving. Sometimes only the fact that I'm able to imagine the dread possibility is a reassurance. Poor Frank! Poor Lyda! At least they've entertained us in their way, and Frank left us images that enrich the imagination. I shall continue to remember the long hand the space-eaters reached into the forest, a glimpse worthy of Lovecraft and his praise, and try not to be too hard on the shakier passages of the tale. The pulps would have been poorer without Frank, and so would my waking dreams. If I can see no point in telling less than the truth as I know it, certainly part of that truth is that I was enthralled by his work when I was learning the tradition of my field, and was privileged to meet him.

Wallasey, Merseyside
July 1997

Afterword to
Autobiographical Memoir

Frank Belknap Long is a modest man. If he is too reticent to do no more than hint at his accomplishments in this memoir, let me begin by pointing out just a few of the current highlights of a writing career that has lasted over six decades. Author of many works of imaginative literature—horror, fantasy, science fiction—including those classics "The Hounds of Tindalos" and "The Space-Eaters," he continues at present to produce stories as good as any from his earlier days. *Crypt of Cthulhu* magazine recently published his poignant new tale, "Discovery Time," and will soon be doing a special Frank Belknap Long issue. His friend Tom Collins interviewed him for the January 1982 *Twilight Zone,* and last year *Pulpsmith* magazine did him the honor of running both an interview and "The Hounds of Tindalos." Other recent recognition include his winning the Edna St. Vincent Millay poetry prize, and his appearance as a character in Richard Lupoff's *Lovecraft's Book* and my own *Pulptime,* two pseudo-historical novels featuring his old friend H. P. Lovecraft.

Of all the distinguished literary figures that Frank Long has encountered in his life, Lovecraft is of course preeminent. Frank has chronicled his relationship with the master of *Weird Tales* in a number of places, most notably his book *Dreamer on the Nightside,* but there's an overlooked aspect or two of that extraordinary friendship that I think deserves some comment. At the time they became acquainted in the early 1920s, first through correspondence followed later by meetings in New York City, HPL most certainly saw in the precocious, aspiring writer a younger version of himself. An only child, the son of parents of English stock (or "old American" as HPL would have put it), Frank

Long Jr. was sensitive, bookish, unworldly, and poetic in a way that the Providence Gentleman could easily identify with. Too, he had suffered some serious medical problems, and his parents did coddle him, in particular his mother—a situation very familiar to HPL in the liberating wake of his own overprotective mother's death. The young Frank Long may have been more progressive politically than the arch-conservative Lovecraft of the period, but the older man seemed not to have minded; indeed, he was inclined to view the leftist leanings of his immature friend with a smile. What mainly mattered in establishing their bond was their affinity of background and family experience.

"Belknapius" was really more a kid brother than a "grandson" to Lovecraft, who in his vanity falsely assumed that his young protégé thought and felt just as he did on certain vital matters. As the decade passed, Frank developed a writing style and approach increasingly removed from that favored by his best friend. Eventually, HPL would come to accept that "Sonny" was not inclined to the same strict art-for-art's sake attitude as himself.

Whatever their differences in aesthetic theory and practice, Frank Long has always appreciated Lovecraft as a pure artist who wrote to satisfy his own high standard without any conscious concession to popular taste or the commercial market. He has astutely pointed to the great failing in *Lovecraft: A Biography:* L. Sprague de Camp's inability to understand that often geniuses tend to be impractical, perverse, and self-defeating, and had HPL been more "normal" (like de Camp), he probably would not have been capable of writing the immortal horror fiction he did. Frank also appreciates the cosmic side of Lovecraft (he laments its complete lack of mention by de Camp), while freely admitting that this quality is missing from his own psychological makeup. For all his classical inclinations, H. P. Lovecraft was a species of romantic (if a rather peculiar one), and so was and is Frank B. Long.

Over the years no doubt other differences emerged. In fact, Frank Long has always cared more for conventional "manly" pursuits than his austere mentor. As he indicates in passing in this memoir, he likes pretty girls and enjoys a drink now and then and isn't ashamed to admit it. One of the more hilarious letters from the *Selected Letters* has to be the one in which HPL, with the air of a prim, slightly nervous schoolteacher, admonishes Frank to defer sexual experience until marriage. Here was a subject, FBL must have realized, upon which the all-wise but prudishly Victorian older man was not to be relied in his counsel. Frank's insightful description of his first meeting with Lovecraft at Sonia Greene's Brooklyn apartment, where he gathers that something is up between them, is one of the finest parts of *Dreamer on the Nightside*. Ever tactful and discreet, he casts himself in a preferred role: that of observer of the curious behavior of the unusual people he's had the good fortune to know. Thus this present memoir, with its emphasis on others, is quite in keeping with the reticent Long tradition.

Given all these features of his character, Frank struck me as the perfect choice for narrator of my apocryphal tale about Lovecraft and Sherlock Holmes, *Pulptime*. He seemed ideal for the Watson-like role of staunch and loyal companion to the brilliant horror writer (who in turn plays a kind of Watson to the great fictional detective); providing the limited and innocent point-of-view appropriate to such fiction. I did not mean the character to be obtuse, however; if anything, I believe he shows more commonsense than either HPL or Holmes. At heart the story is as much his as it is theirs. Along with all the detective work, Frank gets exposed to the adult issues of sex and marriage, seeing firsthand how some men choose to deal or not deal with women. What Frank may have learned from these adventures I have left unsaid, for it would not have been in character for him to speak of his personal feelings in such circumstances.

In using a living person in this manner, I was aware I was being highly presumptuous. I had first set eyes on Frank Belknap Long at the First World Fantasy Convention in the fall of 1975, when we both registered late, about noon Saturday (a case of coincidence—or synchronicity?). I had called upon him briefly the following spring at the urging of Dirk Mosig, and had gotten together a few times later in New York in the company of other fans. Since I didn't know him well, it was with some real trepidation in the spring of 1982 that I sent him the finished manuscript, uncertain how he would react to the sometimes satirical and perhaps unflattering portrait of Lovecraft. Of course, if I had any hope of publication, I had to secure his approval.

The account of his response that Frank gives in his introduction to *Pulptime* is true enough in spirit. If he was put out by the unauthorized use of his name, he betrayed no annoyance to me. In fact, the first con-

cern he expressed when he called me after reading it was that author-
ship not be attributed to him; there should be no question but that I
was sole author. I assured him that I had no intention of deceiving anyone of that score. I wasn't planning to pass off *Pulptime* as a hoax.
Frank then went on to say I'd gotten a few details wrong—facts only he
could have known about. It had been chiefly his mother who worried
about his health, not so much his father. (I made appropriate changes.)
The Kalem Club members all spoke proper English, and never the
slang I'd attributed to them. (Here I made no changes.) Lovecraft as
well always used formal language when he talked: those wonderful
jaunty passages in dialect I'd lifted from the letters were characteristic
only of HPL's letters at that period. On the whole, however, Frank
agreed that these inaccuracies scarcely mattered—some distortion of
"reality" was okay for the sake of a lively story. In sum, he graciously
allowed me to use him as a character (I may have reminded him that he
had put HPL into "The Space-Eaters" back in the twenties), and in
addition was kind enough to supply a foreword. (I find a certain poetic
justice in returning the favor after a fashion by writing this afterword!)

Today Frank Long and his wife, Lyda, live in Chelsea, a district of
Manhattan that has traditionally been home to writers, artists, and other Bohemians. A devoted and loving husband, he will on occasion slip
out for an hour or two with "the boys," joining us fans at a local eatery
for a bite and a drink and some congenial conversation, in between
puffs on his ubiquitous pipe. A slight, soft-spoken man, he can be quite
outspoken. Not content simply to dwell on former days, he takes an active interest in current developments in the horror-fantasy field and in
the world at large. He regards the rise of Stephen King and the prolif-
eration of pornography with bemused astonishment. Who could have
imagined just a short time ago that a horror writer could make millions
a year—or that full genital nudity could be obtained for a couple of
bucks at the neighborhood newsstand?

A shy man, possessed of an old-fashioned reserve, he can be candid
with friends (and here again he's akin to HPL). He has lived in New
York City all his life, but he prefers the countryside and the seashore,
where he and his family evidently spent many vacations. (Two recent
tales, "The Autumn Visitors" in *Twilight Zone* and "Dark Awakening"

in *New Tales of the Cthulhu Mythos,* have beach settings.) Like HPL, he has a special affection for New England.

Frank takes a quiet pride in his achievements, and it seems as if every visit he has some new foreign translation of his work to show. He corresponds regularly with scholars and fans, though is careful not to "fall into the trap" of too much letter writing, as did that compulsive scribbler who was his closest friend.

Champion of the florid, extravagant poetry and prose that flourished in the decadent era just before his birth, senior presiding genius of the genre, revered and beloved figure to colleagues and fans alike—in short, Frank Belknap Long is a true American original, as unique any of the illustrious names he's so fond of reminiscing about in deference to his own.

Substitute Paragraph

Winner of the World Science Fiction Convention's first Fandom Hall of Fame Award, recipient of the World Fantasy Convention's Life Achievement Award, in the company of such giants as Borges, Ray Bradbury, Italo Calvino, and Fritz Leiber—Frank Belknap Long stands as a true American original, as unique as any of the illustrious names he is so fond of reminiscing about in deference to his own.

Review of
Autobiographical Memoir

Frank Belknap Long. *Autobiographical Memoir*. West Warwick, RI: Necronomicon Press, 1985. 32pp. $4.95. (Reviewed by Dabney Hoskins.)

Fans of Frank Belknap Long will welcome this genial new "autobiographical memoir" by one of the most distinguished figures in the field of imaginative literature. Anecdotal and impressionistic, it is written in the form of a "fireside chat." Long provides glimpses of his childhood and of such legendary friends as HPL, Sam Loveman, H. Warner Munn, and James F. Morton; some theoretical analysis of the SF genre; a delightfully fanciful conversation with Lovecraft on an "astral phone communicator"; and some striking examples of synchronicity in his life. Readers expecting basic biographical facts may be disappointed. For information on such subjects as Long's family, his education, and his own writing career, they should turn to his introduction in *The Early Long* and to *Dreamer on the Nightside*. In Peter Cannon's self-serving afterword (much of it amounts to a plug for his novella *Pulptime*), Cannon explains Long's reticence as modesty, and underlines the great importance of friendship to him, which is what this warm memoir is mainly about.

Like the complete Sonia Davis memoir also published by Necronomicon Press, this in essence is a kind of original document. The editor has shown good judgment in preserving all Long's stylistic charm, including his asides on space limitations. Less to the editor's credit is the annoying typo "dome" for "come," and it would be nice to know whether the name of Otis Adelbert Kline's beach house was *The Midge* or *The Madge*. These and other minor errors, however, can be corrected readily enough in a second printing.

Lovecraft on Long

Among the more charmingly amusing passages in H. P. Lovecraft's *Selected Letters* are those concerning his young protégé Frank Belknap Long. One is tempted, like August Derleth in pieces such as his "Addenda to 'H.P.L.: A Memoir,'" simply to string together extended quotations from the letters and, with minimal commentary, let Lovecraft speak for himself. Since the letters were not yet published, Derleth had the excuse he was presenting fresh material, however superficial his approach. I have no such excuse, other than perhaps a wish to defer a deeper analysis until I am ready to write a full account of my own years with Frank Long. At any rate, in surveying the relations between HPL and FBL as revealed in the five volumes of *Selected Letters* (Arkham House, 1965–1976), one cannot help noticing certain recurring themes—Lovecraft's more eloquent expressions of which, under Derleth-like headings, I offer below. All quotations are from the *Selected Letters*, except for those from R. H. Barlow's Florida journal, reproduced in *On Lovecraft and Life* (Necronomicon Press, 1992).

FBL's Boyishness

In April 1922, during his first visit to New York City, Lovecraft finally met the prodigy he had been addressing since 1920 in his correspondence as "My dear Mr. Long." In a lengthy letter dated May 18, 1922, describing their first encounter, which occurred in the company of Sam Loveman in Brooklyn's Prospect Park, he writes: "there dawned upon us the new infant celebrity who was to form our principal focus of interest during the entire residue of the sojourn—

FRANK BELKNAP LONG, JR."

(Next to the announcement of his marriage nearly two years later, few events in Lovecraft's letters get such heralded fanfare.)

"Long," he continues, "is an exquisite boy of twenty who hardly looks fifteen. He is dark and slight, with a bushy wealth of almost black hair and a delicate, beautiful face still a stranger to the gillette. I think he likes the tiny collection of lip-hairs—about six on one side and five on the other—which may with assiduous care some day help to enhance his genuine resemblance to his chief idol—Edgar Allan Poe. . . . A scholar; a fantaisiste; a prose-poet; a sincere and intelligent disciple of Poe, Baudelaire, and the French decadents. He is as modest as Loveman himself. . . . He attends N. Y. University, but is now out because of his convalescence from last winter's appendicitis operation. His life was despaired of, and he is still in bandages. He cannot walk swiftly yet, and has to retire each night at nine."

Here, in addition to the archetypal image of Long as handsome juvenile aesthete, is a portrait of him as semi-invalid. Later in the decade, because of a weak heart, Long would not be among those to share his mentor's miles-long, afterhours pedestrian tours of New York City. In 1933, in remarking on a decline in his usual energy level, HPL could claim: "Ordinarily I have about 50 times the vigour and endurance of young Belknap." Little could he have imagined that his delicate friend would survive to ninety-two!

After this initial meeting, Lovecraft's letters to Long take on an increasingly playful tone. They begin "My dear F. Belknap" or "My dear F. B. L." or "My dear Frank Belknap." After a second extended New York visit five months later, the greetings become positively effusive. The first published letter to follow this second sojourn, dated April 6, 1923, opens "H'lo Grandpa's Nice Boy!" Others of this period start "Hello, Sonny!" or "'Lo Sonny!" By the end of the decade HPL would settle into the somewhat less jaunty "Young Man," with occasional variations such as "Flaming Youth."

Like many a child wise beyond his years, "Sonny" would eventually ask about what his older (but not necessarily more experienced) friend viewed as "bawdry and nastiness." In a response to an apparent query about sex in literature, from January 1924, Lovecraft in effect tells the lad to assume the same prudish attitude as himself: "There is no more true sense and artistick discrimination in a modern coxcomb's praise of

Jurgen or *Ulysses*—or Swift at his worst—than there is in a small boy's praise of the dirty words which a bigger boy has dared to chalk up on the back wall of the stable." A month later he admonishes him further on the subject: "As to pornography—no Child, I don't believe you enjoy it! You've heard all the big boys praising it, and you think it's awfully grown-up and everything . . . but I don't believe you like it for yourself any more than I used to like the tobacco I so assiduously smoked for effect before I put on long trousers." Again, in addressing the youngster, Lovecraft cannot help couching his counsel in boyish imagery.

Strongly opposed to facial hair, Lovecraft would never approve of Long's efforts to grow a moustache. An apparent mention of possibly raising a beard drew the following predictable response, dating to February 1928: "Beard? Thou little rascal. If you want to do anything toward looking half-respectable—as respectable, at any rate, as a Bohemian decadent can look—you'll delete that infamously Neronic upper-lip down and be a decent, clean-shaven Roman nobleman of equestrian rank and consular dignity." In the journal Robert Barlow kept during Lovecraft's 1934 Florida visit, Barlow records, "he frequently expressed a desire to remove Long's abortive moustache." (Here HPL takes the same attitude as P. G. Wodehouse's Jeeves toward Bertie Wooster's pathetic attempts at cultivating "the lip fungus"; Jeeves, of course, had better luck in the end in getting his young charge to remove the offending growth.)

In February 1929, evidently in answer to a correspondent's curiosity about his friends, Lovecraft asserts: "Long is my favourite 'adopted grandson'—a brilliant, bookish small boy of nearly 27 who will never grow up if he lives to be 127. He has the pure aesthete temperament to a phenomenal degree, & shews a freshness & vitality of the most delightful sort; even though—like others of our circle—he tends to have a wider experience in literature than in life." A month later he further explains:

> it was because of a very genuine mental family resemblance that I 'adopted' the little imp as an aesthetic grandson & heir a decade ago, when I first noted the nature of his work & saw my own youth repeated in him. We are very different on the surface, however; for 'Sonny' pretends to like modern ways & professes a vast boredom anent his old

'Grandpa Theobald's' perennial Georgian antiquarianism. At other times, though, he claims to be a greater antiquarian than the old gentleman; & to hark back to the Renaissance for his intellectual and emotional sources. He likes to link himself up with the Mediterranean tradition, & to consider himself the reincarnation of some cinquecento Florentine nobleman or Castilian Hidalgo. A great boy—& he'll never grow up!

At this date, despite their being "very different on the surface," it appears Lovecraft still regards Long as more of a soulmate than anyone else of his acquaintance. His friend's perennial boyishness remains a source of delight.

Frank's Family

One area where Lovecraft recognized strong kinship with "Kid Long" was family background. Like himself, Frank was an only child, of "old American," i.e., English stock. Counting a *Mayflower* passenger among other distinguished predecessors, he was just as ancestor proud as HPL. Furthermore, he enjoyed the kind of comfortable upper middle-class life, with two sane parents, that HPL could only envy. If "Sonny" became an "adopted grandson," then Lovecraft was soon welcomed by Frank Sr., a prosperous dental surgeon, and his wife, May, as a sort of second son at the "House of Long" (presumably an echo of Poe's "House of Usher"), as Lovecraft calls the Longs' Upper West Side Manhattan apartment in his thank you letter of April 18, 1922.

"It is needless to say how delighted I was to meet you in person, or how keenly I enjoyed and appreciated the delightful hospitality extended by your household. Indeed, I may truthfully say that no other single incident forms so pleasing a memory of my unexpected and inspiring first trip to the metropolis," he writes to his host. Elsewhere he states, "We were given the most agreeable hospitality by all the local amateurs, and took infinite pleasure in meeting that young wonder Frank Belknap Long, Jr." He adds, "We dined twice at his house—his parents are delightful."

By the end of August, Lovecraft is back in New York, where the Long family all but adopts him, as he reports to his Aunt Lillian Clark: "The Longs are all splendid—their home is upset with painters and decorators, so they dine out at an expensive uptown café, the St.

George, on Broadway. Each meal-time they insist on my going with them, and likewise insist on paying all expenses. . . . Really, I never knew the world held so many generous people till I started on my travels!" When he considers returning home to Providence, he says that "small Belknap entreats me to be as slow as possible in leaving him to his accustomed desolation—he told Mrs. Greene over the telephone that 'he can't see enough of me'!" No doubt credit is mainly due to "Mrs. Greene," the future Mrs. H. P. Lovecraft, for luring him back to New York and keeping him there through the month of September, but the Longs remain at least as great an attraction: "Wednesday found me at Belknap's again—sometimes I fear I impose on the Longs by being with them at dinner practically every day, but they protest so violently that I don't impose, that I cannot but believe them!" He continues, "One day when I thought I had another engagement . . . but later found I hadn't, and telephoned Belknap that I was coming to see him; Mrs. Long said his face positively lighted up with pleasure when he heard the news of my coming."

After Lovecraft moved to New York in March 1924, and especially after his bride left the city to find work at the end of the year, he took even more advantage of the hospitality the senior Longs were so pleased to offer him, the man who brought such joy to their sensitive son. A case in point is the lavish Christmas festivities chez Long, described in a letter from December 1925, from which I shall resist quoting. (As FBL would put it in 1944 in his reminiscence for *Marginalia*, "I should like to quote at length from his letters, but if I succumbed to that temptation, I should have little space left in this briefest of memoirs for the memories of the man himself.") It is no surprise to find Lovecraft in September 1927, more than a year after his departure from New York, lamenting the impending demolition of 823 West End Avenue to its one-time tenant. "I note your household removal with a certain species of gentle melancholy, for to me good old 823 was the one oasis in all the metropolitan desert which really seemed like home."

In July 1927, Lovecraft joined the Longs for part of a motoring tour of New England, whose quaint sights did not appeal to every member of the family. "Through all the sightseeing poor philistine Dr. Long was atrociously bored, and I was at my wits' end devising means to palliate his patient misery. At length, in the evening, the Fates intervened in my favour—in the form of an electric-appliance shop from whose broad doorway the Dempsey-Sharkey returns were in process of broadcasting. Doc was happy at last." After remarking that their protracted motor trip will extend to the end of August, he adds, "It's a gay life—but they deserve the outing; for Dr. Long works like a slave when he works, whilst both Belknap and his mamma are in such poor health—cardiac trouble—that they can never take walks or outings in the ordinary way." Here is another capsule portrait of the Longs—the hardworking father, with the semi-invalid mother and son, able to afford the sort of leisurely vacation, by private car, beyond the means of the penurious writer reliant on public transportation.

As much as the Longs may have represented the ideal family in his eyes, Lovecraft was too acute not to notice how their closeness had its unhealthy aspects. In a letter dating to August 1931, he says: "Old age tells—you can't be flexible & expansive when the chill of the thirties gets into your bones. That's why I hope Sonny Belknap will break from mamma's apron-strings before it's too late for him to enjoy a sense of freedom." In Mrs. Long he surely must have seen the shade of his own smothering mother, whose debilitating emotional influence he had escaped only with her death.

In any event, "the chill of the thirties" seems not to have made young Frank any less dependent on his parents. In December 1932, Lovecraft finds the home scene essentially the same as it was a decade earlier: "Just before Christmas I received an invitation from Papa and Mamma Long to drop around for the holidays and surprise little Sonny out of a whole year's moustachelet-growth." Leaving Providence the day after Christmas at two in the morning, he is "set down squarely at Belknap's door at eight-thirty a.m. . . . The Child was still abed, but Pa and Ma smuggled the old gentleman into the dining room. When at length Sonny did toddle drowsily out to breakfast he was properly electrified to see his Grandpa nodding over the morning *Tribune*—and then and there began a session of arguments on everything from bolshevism to the Iroquois Indians, which lasted till eleven-thirty p.m., Jany. 2."

Belknap's Bolshevism

What spurred the two to argue over the Iroquois Indians is impossible to determine now, but it is easy to understand their debate over bolshevism. In the early 1930s, as Lovecraft began to shift from conservative elitist to New Deal Democrat, he was increasingly at political odds with his far more radical friends. In letters from his last years he speaks dismissively of "wild-eyed bolsheviki like Long" or "Sonny Belknap and other dupes of European ideas." In this realm Lovecraft realized that their differences were very real—and that Long's left-wing zeal was yet another manifestation of a romantic and unworldly nature that could get him into trouble in later life.

With the chill of the forties getting into his bones, and with his income dwindling, HPL complains more and more to his correspondents about his inability to make a living. He sees Long falling into the same trap as himself: failing to learn a practical trade. In June 1933, he says of his financial plight: "No one had less instinctive aptitude or experience in the cryptic and devious ways of money-making . . . unless it be Little Belknap." In "The Thing on the Doorstep," written in August 1933, the fate of the "boyish" Edward Derby, whose "attempts to raise a moustache were discernible only with difficulty," underscores the folly of not growing up.

Lovecraft was too much of a gentleman to judge his friends harshly in letters. In person, however, he could more candid in expressing his opinions, as R. H. Barlow records: "He remarked also [that] Long was a Bolshevist *poseur*, and has even been so mercenary as to sell letters of famous men to him; and his grandfather's cane. … Long's sale of his rather miscellaneous library was caused by his radical activities—he was in need of money and his eye lit upon books as a saleable commodity—an attitude not accepted before." To be fair, selling his books was something he was doing as early as September 1922, as evidenced by HPL's comment on a prospective bookshop expedition: "Belknap is going to take along a suitcase full of old books which he wishes to get rid of either by sale or by trade."

In 1934, Lovecraft says of his conversion to socialism: "with me, the process has not been any wild emotional jump like Sonny Belknap's plunge into Russian bolshevism. I have gone almost reluctantly . . . and am still quite as remote from Belknap's naïve Marxism as I am from the equally naïve Republican orthodoxy I have left behind." As seriously misguided as he considered his friend to be, to the end of his life Lovecraft could not hide his fondness, even as he was being utterly damning. In June 1936, for example, he states he has been able to resist orthodox communism, despite "the shrill thunderings of my little grandchild Belknapovitch Longievsky (a true young Trotsky who loves the proletariat, except when the maid burns the sirloin or is slow in answering the bell!)."

Sonny's Stories

It was a promising Poe-like story, "The Eye Above the Mantel," that first drew Long to Lovecraft's attention. Shortly after their initial meeting, HPL predicted that the "young wonder" would be "one of the literary giants of the next amateur generation." Frank, however, seems not to have cared to dwell in the amateur world, and within a couple of years would be publishing professionally alongside his mentor in *Weird Tales*.

The *Selected Letters* contain little comment on individual tales, though no doubt HPL was fulsome in his praise of such early efforts as "Death Waters" and "The Ocean Leech." The first significant mention of FBL's fiction, or potential fiction, occurs in a letter dated January 26, 1924, in connection with a tale in H. G. Wells's *Thirty Strange Stories*: "I do not think 'Æpyornis Island' anticipates your dinosaur egg story, and advise you to write the latter. Think of the difference—the dinosaur belongs to aeons immemorially remote and unconnected with anything in human experience, whilst the museum-cellar hatching can be handled with a creepiness wholly alien to anything in Wells. Your story is far the stronger, and Grandpa will spank you if you don't write your story like a good boy!"

Frank was not a good boy. Six years later, after a "miserable hash" of a dinosaur's egg story appeared in *Weird Tales*, Lovecraft laments that neither he nor Belknap had followed up on the idea. He had urged him to write the tale, "but just about that time he read Wells' 'Æpyornis Island,' & thought that any prehistoric-egg story would constitute a plagiarism. I told him that such an idea was nonsense—& just then the news came of the finding of the first actual dinosaur eggs by an expedi-

tion from Belknap's own pet museum!" If there is a note of exasperation here, Lovecraft yet believed at this date, October 1930, that his
cohort was capable of writing "a *real* story on the theme!"

Long's caricature of Lovecraft in "The Space-Eaters" clearly tickled
the old gentleman. After reading a draft of the story, in September
1927, Lovecraft writes: "As for your new novelette—look here, young
man, you'd better be mighty careful how you treat your aged and dignified Grandpa as here! You mustn't make me do anything cheerful or
wholesome, and remember that only the direst of damnations can befit
so inveterate a daemon of the cosmick abysses. And, young man, don't
forget that I am prodigiously lean, *I am lean*—LEAN, I tell you! *Lean!*
And if you're afraid that my leanness will make the horror get you instead, why just reduce like your Grandpa and escape as well!" (In the
published story, which ran in the July 1928 issue of *Weird Tales,* the
Howard character is described as "slim.") Lovecraft goes on in the next
paragraph to chide him for tearing a map out of a book: "Hasn't your
Grandpa told you not to deface all your nice books? For shame, Sir! To
think that a grandchild of mine shou'd so little appreciate literature!"

Long's cavalier treatment of books was not Lovecraft's only literary
bone to pick with him. Just as HPL started to disapprove of his politics
in the early Depression years, so he had increasing cause for dismay
with his fiction. In March 1930, he whines, "This is my constant quarrel with Belknap and Loveman—both splendid poets, yet each with
characteristic limitations in prose which proceed from a one hundred
percent and lifelong use of the machine." This may say more about
Lovecraft's prejudice against the typewriter than about Long's writing
skills, but certainly by this period he was aware of basic philosophical
differences in their respective approaches to their work. Speaking of the
rarity of cosmicism among contemporary weird authors, he says:
"Loveman's sense of the unreal is a strictly human, classical, & traditional one—albeit exquisitely developed—& Long's is precisely the
same at an earlier stage of development."

Another side of Sonny's "story-telling" to provoke Lovecraft was
his tendency to exaggerate, or simply to confuse the facts. In April
1931, after Long apparently spread the word that Putnam's had accepted a collection of HPL's stories for publication, he complains to a correspondent: "Confound the exaggeratory tendencies of that little

Belknap rascal! All Putnam acceptance dope originated within that bushy young head, for his old Grandpa told him exactly what you were told and nothing more!" In a letter from September 1933, he further expounds on his friend's tendency to err: "But Belknap slipped up on one thing—for he was absolutely and unqualifiedly wrong in believing that I have published non-weird fiction under a pseudonym. I not only have never done so, but have certainly never said anything from which such a mistaken inference could legitimately be made. That's the kid's one trouble—his imagination flies off on a tangent, and now and then goes beyond the plain facts. . . . In the present case I think Sonny got two separate things mixed up and exaggerated both."

But it is primarily Frank's faults as a writer that concern him in his later letters. In November 1932, he admits August Derleth can create characters in a way he cannot: "I can't—and recognising my limitations, I soft-pedal the elaborate delineation of dissimilar characters. Long can't either—and not recognising his limitations he reels off page after page of alleged characterisation in which all the figures, from savants and demigods to bootblacks and charwomen, think and feel and act and talk exactly like little duplicate Belknaps!" In July 1933, he points to a reason for FBL's weakness in this department: "Regarding experience in life—certainly a writer can use all he can get, & a good amount of *general experience* (i.e., firsthand familiarity with the way in which average people react to average situations) is really essential to any realist. The trouble with Long is that he lacks this general experience."

Still, Lovecraft does not lose all faith in his friend as a writer. On the subject of contributors to *Weird Tales*, he says in a letter from January 1932: "only a few are likely to break into real literature. . . . Long very possibly may." Given his own self-doubts at this period, HPL is perhaps too hard on both himself and others. At any rate, he is more inclined in his disillusionment to point out flaws than extol virtues. Writing in August 1934, he gives himself credit for at least recognizing his limitations: "I lack the natural faculty of imagination which gives the genuine innate author the instinctive power to understand and portray what different sorts of people would feel and say and do in various given situations. Long also lacks this faculty, but he won't admit it. All his characters are little duplicate Belknaps in thought, manner, and speech."

No, Lovecraft does not lose all faith until the very end of his life. In October 1936, railing against the commercialism that has driven literature out of the weird-fiction marketplace, he says, "The literary ruin of brilliant figures like Long, Quinn, Merritt, and Wandrei speaks for itself." Finally, in a February 1937 letter to Catherine L. Moore defending his art-for-art's-sake stance, he declares: "I disagree totally & violently with your belief in making concessions in writing. One concession leads to another—& he who takes the easiest way never comes back. They all say they *mean* to come back some day—but they never do. Belknap is gone."

Not to end on too cynical a note, it is fair to point out that, scarcely two weeks before his death, in a letter dated February 28, 1937, Lovecraft could yet wish his no longer so young friend well: "Hope Belknap's magnum opus will be one of the sensations of 1937. His confidence is at least in his favour."

Frank Belknap Long: When Was He Born, and Why Was Lovecraft Wrong?

In his introduction to his story collection *The Early Long* (1975), Frank Belknap Long says, with calculated imprecision, "I was born in the early years of the century." While April 27, the month and day of Long's birth, has never been in question, the actual year is another matter. Most sources, such as the biographical blurbs of *Sleep No More* (1944) and *The Hounds of Tindalos* (1946), identify it as 1903. The *New York Times* obituary, which appeared January 5, 1994, proclaimed him "Dead at 90." Evidently, H. P. Lovecraft, his best friend, believed he was born in 1902. According to New York City birth records, however, a Frank Long was born in Manhattan on April 27, 1901. (When I examined these at the New York Public Library, I found no Frank Long born in New York City on April 27 in either 1902 or 1903.) Vanity might account for his shaving a couple of years off his age as he grew older, but how and why did Long deceive his mentor on this most basic of biographical facts from the very outset of their relationship?

In a letter dated January 23, 1920, Lovecraft says of his youthful correspondent, "I fancy he is anywhere betwixt 18 and 20 in age." In the spring of 1922 he would have the opportunity to learn his protégé's age from the man himself. In a letter dated May 3, 1922, written in the wake of his first visit to New York City "April 6–12," he mentions meeting "that young wonder Frank Belknap Long Jr. . . . a slight, dark, exceedingly handsome, and altogether poetic lad of twenty." Quite likely Long told Lovecraft his real age when they met in early April, but not that he soon had a birthday. A year later, by then aware that Long was born on April 27 and remembering him as having been "twenty,"

HPL composed a poem in honor of his pal's twenty-first birthday—one year too late. In a letter dating to May 3, 1923, he writes "lamp the enclosed panegyrick delivered on the coming-of-age of our tiny pal Belknapius!" Overwhelmed by the tribute, Long refrained from correcting his friend in order to spare him embarrassment.

In 1927, in perhaps an indirect nod to his favorite "adopted grandson," Lovecraft has the eponymous hero of *The Case of Charles Dexter Ward* come of age in April 1923. In February 1929, he describes Long as "a brilliant, bookish small boy of nearly 27 who will never grow up if he lives to be 127." In August 1931, in a letter written the day after his forty-first birthday, Lovecraft says of "Sonny Belknap": "To think the little rascal will be thirty next April." And again in September 1932 (though the letter is dated "1732"), among that ecstatic catalogue of events from the turn of the century, he lists "Harlem note in the *New York Tribune* for 1902—'Dr. and Mrs. Frank Belknap Long are receiving congratulations on the birth of a son, Frank Belknap Jr., on April 27th'."

Long must have worried at times about being caught in this deception, but it appears his fellow weird-tale author went to the grave ignorant of his true age. Indeed, if he could fool the great HPL, however inadvertently, why not others? At any rate, after Lovecraft's death in 1937, he could subtract another year from his age with little fear of being challenged—as he did in "Some Random Memories of H.P.L.," published in *Marginalia* (1944), where he explicitly states, "I was thirteen years Howard's junior." On the back flap of *John Carstairs: Space Detective* (1949), he takes the coy approach: "Born in New York City (would be just as well satisfied if the exact date could be left a little nebulous in this jacket blurb)."

Not everyone, however, was misled by the 1903 birth year that began to appear on dustjackets and in reference books from the 1940s on. For example, in a letter written to Long dated May 3, 1989, Robert Bloch writes: "Hard to realize you've attained your 88th birthday—I've got a ways to go before matching that!"

Only a birth certificate will provide final and conclusive evidence when Frank Belknap Long was born. In the meantime, those who propose to have the dates 1901–1994 engraved beneath his name on the Long family monument in the Bronx's Woodlawn Cemetery can, I believe, do so with complete confidence.

Fiction

Pulptime

Being the Singular Adventure of Sherlock Holmes,
H. P. Lovecraft, and the Kalem Club
As if Narrated by Frank Belknap Long, Jr.

For my grandparents,
Lillian R. Cannon and Charles P. Harper

Acknowledgments

Most heartfelt thanks to Frank Belknap Long for so graciously permitting the persona of his younger self to serve as narrator of this tale.
—P. C.

Foreword

Frank Belknap Long

I've often thought that Sherlock Holmes and H. P. Lovecraft were more closely akin, in almost every aspect of their approach to the problems of daily living, and the realities of their age, than might ordinarily be suspected.

Both were *originals*, in the best and most defiant sense of that greatly abused, and often misunderstood, term. Both were *strong-willed*, and would have laughed to scorn the charge of eccentricity, if only because the adoption of certain so-called poses helped them to express some aspects of their personalities which were of vital emotional importance to them. Let others mock what was as natural to them as breathing, and let all such carpers be damned!

The resemblances become even more striking when we break them down, and consider them one by one. Both men were hermitlike in many ways, preferring a bachelor life of their own choosing, where originality of thought could be pursued in some measure remote from the whirlwind distractions of big city life (even though London dwarfed Providence in that respect, the latter was not exactly a village). The fact that Lovecraft was married for a brief period, and traveled quite a bit in his later years, does not alter the basic resemblance here. Holmes traveled even more extensively, and took an active part in many of the investigations he set in motion. But always he returned to his Baker Street lodgings, to create about himself the legend that has become familiar to us all.

The creation of such a legend, never a simple or less than inspiration-inspiring thing, no matter how much it may be in accord with a man's strongest impulses, brings up another point of resemblance of major importance.

Whatever pursuits may have fascinated Holmes to an extreme degree, enabling him to deal with the criminal mind in both a coldly scientific and miraculously intuitive way, he remained primarily, as did HPL, an artist to his fingertips. To combine such a legend with a body of work that is outstanding in itself can never be less than a work of art.

Although HPL liked to pretend that he was far more interested in things apart from his writing, such as his New England heritage in general, and ancient, gambrel-roofed houses in the sunset's glow, and the sweep of cosmic immensities which made all human striving seem ultimately meaningless when viewed in the light of exploding suns, it was the *combination* of his stories and poems, and that other, legendary aspect of himself which provided him with the kind of fame that will endure—and this I have never doubted—well into the twenty-first century. And that is just as true of Holmes (always remembering, of course, that there may not be a twenty-first century for Man).

I was pondering all of this when, a short while ago, Peter Cannon placed before me a manuscript bearing the byline of a long-vanished young writer who had yielded to no one in his respect and admiration for Holmes, and who had accompanied HPL on many walks in his now legendary New York days and shared with him the enchanted vistas of those far-off realms which his pen turned wholly magical across the years.

The wonder of it, I must confess, left me totally stunned. "How did this ever come into your possession?" I finally managed to gasp.

"Well, you see, I—" Peter's voice trailed off for a moment, as if he were marshalling all of his defenses to justify what he'd done.

"I wrote it myself, of course," he said at last. "I took the liberty of attaching your name to it as the author because I felt you wouldn't really mind."

My name! I thought. Of all the gall—

It is always disturbing to be forced, right out of the blue, to ask yourself an often-quoted question: "Oh say, could that boy have been I?" But when I remembered what a dedicated Lovecraftian Peter had been for more than a decade my momentary pique was gone.

Just in the past seven or eight years books about HPL have increased so greatly in number—including, of course, my Arkham House memoir, *Dreamer on the Nightside*—that to discuss them in a critical way, however briefly, would exceed the space limitations I've set myself here. But Peter's achievement can be summarized quite simply. Without some recent and direct source material to guide him at the time, Peter secured an M.A. at Brown University through his early interest in the Lovecraftian supernatural horror story Mythos, and since then, as an editor in a major publishing house in New York—located at the very core of the Big Apple, so to speak—he has brought a vanished era to life in so imaginatively splendid a way that I have no wish to challenge a word of it, beyond one small matter which a reading of HPL's letters probably led him to exaggerate. My health at that period was far from good, and *I had recently suffered a heart attack.* Whenever I returned at a late hour from the wilds of Brooklyn—there were a few lethal muggings even in those days—my mother stayed awake, and worried. And her own health at that time had me worried, since her physician had warned her not to lift anything heavy, and avoid all housework of a strenuous nature. To HPL she appeared over-solicitous and she undoubtedly was, to some extent, but not nearly as much so as was HPL's mother when he went rambling about Providence in the small hours. My father's concern was just as genuine, but he had the good sense to realize that if you don't take risks, even grave ones at times, you curtail independence.

Oh yes—just one thing more, which Peter couldn't possibly have known about. In my last and final conversation with Holmes he made a surprising revelation. "This fellow Doyle," he said, "meant well—he always did. But it was Watson who had the wit and wisdom to truly understand me. He was a man of superb intellectual perceptiveness. He downplayed all of that deliberately, pretending to be just the opposite. It pleased him to put on a mask, pretending to be a naïve and credulous dolt because—well, because he was an artist to his fingertips. He was somewhat like Boswell in that respect, and we all know now, from the many volumes of Boswell's letters, that he was Johnson's peer, and perhaps more than his peer, in the position he occupies in the hierarchy of the immortals."

"But the Lovecraft cult, I fear, is on even a more infantile level than the Baker Street Irregulars and the cult of Sherlock Holmes."

—Edmund Wilson

I

One dreary spring afternoon, in April of '25, I was immersed in a volume of Swinburne, when my mother knocked on my bedroom door and announced that Howard was on the 'phone. So absorbed had I been in the floral excesses of that extravagant poet, that I hadn't noticed the ring. I immediately set aside my book, and rushed into the hallway to grab the receiver.

"Howard, you're back from the South!" I exclaimed.

"Indeed I am, Belknapius," said my friend. "It was truly an aesthetically satisfying trip for the Old Gentleman. The neo-Greek and -Roman architecture of the Federal City really brought home a vivid sense of the Periclean or Augustan Age, as I wrote you."

"Yes, I got your postcards. Thanks." I didn't bother to mention that, out of the half dozen cards he'd sent, so crammed had they been with his minuscule script declaiming playfully about our nation's capital "named for that traitor against his lawful majesty, King George III," two had been charged an extra cent each postage due.

"Some forty-eight hours I believe it's been since I returned to this Babylonish burg—most of it spent sawing the proverbial log. Right now, though, I'm feeling in the mood to blow a buck on a reg'lar feed. Any chance you could pop out to Brooklyn and join me for a bite at the local Italian eatery?"

"I'm sure Mother and Dad won't mind. I can easily meet you there by six."

My parents consented to my outing, though my mother insisted that I wear my raincoat, in spite of every sign that the sky was clearing. An hour later I had left the Upper West Side of Manhattan and was riding the IRT train, crowded with businessmen and secretaries headed home at the end of the work day, across the East River into Brooklyn. I brought along my Swinburne, to keep me company during the journey. I disembarked at Borough Hall, and walked the few blocks east to Willoughby Street, the site of John's Spaghetti Place. While the many fine houses of nineteenth-century vintage along my route revealed that this had once been a prosperous district, the area now retained at best an air of shabby respectability—a far cry from the lovely Parkside address Howard had had to give up after Sonia's departure for a job in the Midwest at New Year's.

I had a while to wait outside the diner, Howard being notoriously unpunctual, before I spotted the distinctive form of my mentor approaching me with quick, jerky strides from the other side of the street.

"Good ole Sonny!" cried Howard Lovecraft, as he seized my hand. "I'll be damned! You haven't changed a bit in my absence. Still sporting those hairs on your upper lip, I see—four on one side, five on the other."

I ignored Howard's little joke about my moustache, but I may well have winced slightly at "Sonny"—a nickname, as I've noted elsewhere, that I've never cared for. Would that he'd stick to the dignified, Latinate "Belknapius" when addressing me, his favorite "grandson."

For my part, I was pleased to find Howard in good spirits, which had been all too rare in recent months with his continuing failure to secure a job. Though he never discussed his financial situation with me, I knew his revision work couldn't be bringing in much of an income, and he hadn't sold an original story in over a year. Nor had he written one since "The Shunned House" in October.

I was pleased, too, to note that my friend appeared to have lost even more weight during his travels. After his marriage to Sonia in March of last year, he'd positively ballooned out under her solicitous care and steady feeding. From first-hand experience I knew what an excellent cook she was. Now he was close to resembling again the lean figure I'd first met in person in April of '22, while he'd been courting his future wife in Brooklyn.

Over a plateful of spaghetti and meatballs HPL held forth on the architectural delights of Washington, D.C., which he and George Kirk, a friend who occupied the room above him at his boarding house on Clinton Street, had been shown by E. L. Sechrist, a correspondent who was an anthropologist at the Smithsonian. He explained that Mrs. Renshaw, a revision client, had driven them about in her motor-car, but more memorable really had been the exploring on foot.

"At last," said Howard, "after traversing a delectable bit of Park, Kirk and I reached the Capitol on its commanding elevation, and began to circumnavigate it till we reached that central and original portion whose corner-stone was laid by General Washington, with

Masonic ceremonies, in 1793. The original Capitol building—central portion with dome, and the two wings—was finished in 1827; the two extensions being added during the 'fifties. As I gazed upon this gigantic construction, I could not but compare it with other similar buildings I had seen; and I will confess that some of its rivals did not suffer by the estimate. For perfect artistry of form, delicacy of detail, and purity of material, it cannot compete with the modern Rhode Island State House."

With the monologue now round to Providence, to home, Howard grew grim, his long jaw slackened. He began to speak wistfully of his native city, or at least of certain geographic regions within it—Exchange Place, Market Square, Narragansett Bay, Quinsnicket Park, the "Antient Hill."

I'd been finished some time before Howard finally ate his last bite of vanilla ice cream (washed down with the dregs of a cup of sugar-laden coffee), and we left John's Spaghetti Place. This nostalgic talk of Providence led my comrade to remark upon his present less than ideal circumstances. As we strolled leisurely back toward the boarding house at 169 Clinton, he had a lot to say about one of his fellow lodgers.

"That Syrian with the room next to mine still plays eldritch and whining monotones on a strange bagpipe. Just last night it made me dream ghoulish and indescribable things of crypts under Bagdad and limitless corridors of Eblis beneath the moon-cursed ruins of Istakhar. I have yet to see this man—in my imagination he wears a turban and long robe of figured silk—so I can picture him in any shape that lends glamour to his weird pneumatic cacophonies."

For a moment Howard seemed to brood on this exotic image. Then he continued.

"On the brighter side, since my return I've discovered a new tenant—an honest-to-God white man—living on the floor above me. An elderly fellow, he apparently keeps as odd hours as Grandpa; for I encountered him in the front hall quite early this morning. He was sneaking about in the most outlandish garb, yet I detected a certain nobility in his wrinkled visage. He introduced himself—in a flat, twangy voice—as 'Mr. Altamont of Chicago.'"

Chicago, home of *Weird Tales*, I thought. Where Howard might have been at this moment had he cared to accept the editorship of "The

Unique Magazine" when the owner, J. C. Henneberger, offered it to him last March. Alas, that he had had to turn it down, because Chicago has no Georgian buildings!

As we neared Howard's boarding house, from about a block's distance, we spied a knot of three people gathered in conversation on the stoop of 169 Clinton. In the fading light it wasn't easy to tell, but one appeared to be a tall, older man with a bushy white beard, while the other two had all the earmarks of young street toughs. Abruptly one of the latter shoved the bearded fellow, who in reaction put up his dukes in John L. Sullivan fashion and began to return the blows. Howard and I glanced at one another, then started to run toward the scuffle, no one else being in the vicinity.

As we charged down the sidewalk, we could see that the toughs were getting the better of their older adversary, who nonetheless kept fighting in a spirited way, until a solid shot to the head felled him to the ground. Noticing our rapid approach, the two youths abandoned their victim and fled up the street into the gloom.

"Good God, Frank," said Howard as we bent over the sprawled figure, trying to raise himself on his elbows. "It's that new lodger I was just telling you about. Are you all right, Mr. Altamont?"

"I'm okay, mister," gasped the man. "Those guys didn't break nothin', I guess."

"Filthy, rat-faced Asiatic slime," muttered Howard, looking in the direction of the by now vanished assailants.

We carefully helped Mr. Altamont to his feet, and despite his protests led him, breathing heavily and making feeble motions to brush the dust off his checked suit, inside the boarding house and into Howard's ground-floor room. There we insisted that he lie down on the fold-out couch that served as HPL's bed. For someone his age, Mr. Altamont clearly had a strong, sinewy physique, however unsteady his movements. After a minute or two of resting in a seeming daze, deaf to our entreaties, he sat up on the couch, his gray eyes alert above his ample whiskers. He drank a glass of water Howard had drawn for him from the tiny corner sink and began to speak:

"Pardon me, gents, but at seventy-one an old duffer such as myself ain't the one for fisticuffs like I used to be. Otherwise I'd 've shown those hooligans a thing or two. I'm much obliged to you—Mr. Lovecraft, ain't it?—and to your young pal here for the timely rescue."

We murmured that it was no matter, that we only regretted not having arrived a few seconds sooner. And then, ever mindful of the formalities, Howard said, "This is my good friend, Frank Belknap Long, Junior."

"You're a bit on the bookish side, I bet," said the man, turning his keen eye on me. "You've got that dreamy look too." I was taken aback by the old codger's perceptiveness, then realized he must have spotted the Swinburne verses clutched in my hand—though this was an unlikely remark, it struck me, coming from someone of apparently little education.

"Ho, ho, a regular Sherlock Holmes, eh what, Sonny?"

"Precisely," said Mr. Altamont.

"Precisely?" said Howard.

"I am Sherlock Holmes," he said, suddenly speaking in a decidedly cultivated British accent. A trace of a smile showed on his lips, and a twinkle glinted in his eye.

"Are you indeed, my dear sir," answered HPL in his haughtiest of upper-class New England tones. He exchanged a knowing glance with me, as if to say let's humor the fellow. "Very well then. Would you mind giving us a demonstration of your renowned powers of deduction to prove your identity? Anyone can see that Belknap here is a delicate dreamer, but what can you deduce about myself?"

"As for yourself, Mr. Lovecraft," he said, nodding toward Howard's extensive bookshelf, "you are even more erudite than your young friend; but rather squeamish for a writer of tales of such monstrous mayhem. A pity that your career as an author of the supernatural has not proven as lucrative as one might wish."

Howard flushed visibly at this personal observation.

"Pray forgive me," he continued, "but every evidence from your threadbare (albeit neatly patched) suit to your Spartan larder points to a frugal existence."

Howard looked furtively over at the shelf stocked with cans of spaghetti and baked beans, packages of crackers, and packets of sugar scrounged from cafeterias which constituted his food supply.

"And, I venture, you have an abnormal sensitivity to cold weather."

"What, how . . ."

"My dear Lovecraft, your kerosene heater, judging from the odor in this room, has obviously been much in use lately. Now the weather, as unsettled and cool as it has been, has not been unusually cold. Your average American, especially one of limited means like yourself, would not be apt to use such a device, unless warmth were a prime consideration. And yes, I realize our landlady is British, and hence prone to keep the furnace at low heat."

"But, but how did you know about my . . . my 'squeamishness' as you put it?" Howard's lantern jaw had sagged almost a foot by this fpoint in the demonstration.

"In the course of our encounter early this morning in the hallway, I observed that you were headed for the community rubbish bin, carrying a couple of used mousetraps at arm's length. Now only a man of at least moderate circumstances could afford to dispose of two perfectly good mousetraps, as these clearly were—or else a man who did not care to handle small animal carcasses."

Although Howard wasn't altogether pleased by our visitor's amazing deductions about himself, a certain startled look of wonder on my friend's face indicated to me that any doubts as to the veracity of the old gentleman's claim were fast receding. As for myself, I had in the course of this dialogue come to accept the man's assertion as to his identity, and now stood gaping like a yokel in speechless awe.

"Sherlock Holmes!" exclaimed Howard, persuaded at last. "Why, I used to be infatuated with you! I read every one of Dr. Watson's stofries,[1] and even organized a detective agency at thirteen, arrogating to myself the proud name of S. H."

"My blushes," replied the great detective, "but if you will allow me to repay the compliment, you should realize that you are not entirely unknown in England, Mr. H. P. Lovecraft. Copies of *Weird Tales* do reach us across the Atlantic—where, I might add, many readers of discrimination, myself included, consider your 'Rats in the Walls' the finest tale of supernatural horror to come out of America since the work of your countryman, Mr. Poe."

To these handsome words of praise, which undoubtedly put to rest

---

1. But perhaps not *His Last Bow*, else HPL might have caught on to the Mr. Altamont guise right away. [Editor's note]

any remaining ill-feelings, Howard responded with characteristic modesty: "You mustn't take us *Weird Tales* hacks seriously, Mr. Holmes. Arthur Machen, M. R. James, Blackwood, Lord Dunsany—your native English and Celtic authors—they are your modern masters of the tale of supernatural horror."

"Only later generations can determine who will hold the most exalted rank in the genre, Mr. Lovecraft. In the meantime, I advise you not to let your natural humility cause you to undervalue your own talents, to the detriment of your original fiction writing."

How much longer this mutual admiration would have gone on I can't say, but by this juncture I couldf restrain my curiosity no longer. With all the impetuousness of my twenty-two years, I abruptly asked the obvious question: "But Mr. Holmes, what are you doing in the United States? And in Brooklyn, in a boarding house, of all places? I thought you'd retired to the English countryside and were raising bees."

"Quite to the point, young man," he replied. "Please forgive me if I do not explain everything at once. For the moment suffice it to say that an extremely important case—a case involving one of Britain's most respected figures—has brought me to your hospitable shores." His lined face grew grim, as if memories of some dark deed weighed heavily upon him.

"In any event," he continued, brightening, "the quiet life on the Sussex Downs, with all its agreeable features, has been too often dull. I was in need of a voyage, and wanted to see your grand country one final time before age forces an end to any extensive traveling."

"We're infinitely honored by your presence," said Howard.

"I must confess, Mr. Lovecraft," said the venerable detective, "that my conclusions about your living habits were not drawn solely from my own observations, since you so kindly brought me to your rooms. A mutual friend has told me a good deal about you. Furthermore, my taking lodgings at 169 Clinton Street was no accident. I would have disclosed my true identity to you soon enough, had not this evening's little mishap provoked the revelation. Perhaps it is all for the best."

"A mutual friend, you say?" said Howard.

"Yes, the celebrated conjuror and escape artist, Harry Houdini. When I communicated with him prior to my sailing for New York and asked as to suitable allies outside the official forces that might aid me in this matter of utmost delicacy, he recommended you. Soon after my arrival, disguised as a retired English squire, I met with Houdini, who supplied me with more details as to your qualifications. I was persuaded that you were my man—a gentleman whose good sense and discretion I could trust. With delight I learned that you are an indefatigable walker, and are quite familiar with the more obscure byways and alleys of Manhattan and Brooklyn."

"Only in certain older districts, where there are still survivals of an earlier, more gracious age than the current decadent era," said HPL.

"And you do engage in free-lance 'literary' work, Houdini tells me. Might you consider a job of a non-literary nature, but which would make use of your skills as a guide? I daresay you might find the pay somewhat more remunerative."

"I'm terribly flattered, Mr. Holmes, though I scarcely imagine that I'd be equal to the task."

"Well, you may not be required to act as my sole lieutenant. But enough for now. Events have happened so quickly, with surprises for us all. You need time to think matters over—I shall say no more tonight. I am rather fatigued, and also have this bruise to nurse." So saying, Mr. Holmes rose slowly and deliberately from the couch and tottered to the door, with one hand at his temple and the other waving aside any proffered assistance.

"One final word before I retire to my own room. I must have the assurance of you both that you will keep my identity—and of course my presence here—a secret. It is essential to my effectiveness that I remain incognito."

We readily gave him our assent.

"Do not even hint of this in your letters to your aunts, Mr. Lovecraft," said the detective, shaking a slim hand toward Howard's desk, where lay the start of one of his lengthy epistles describing the minutiae of his daily existence to his Aunt Lillian Clark in Providence. "There will be time enough tomorrow to discuss matters in detail and make decisions. Until then I bid you good-night, gentlemen, with heartfelt thanks again for appearing 'in the nick of time,' as they say.

"No, please, I can make it up the stairs on my own steam," he said, exiting with a short bow.

After the departure of our extraordinary guest, Howard and I looked at each other in stunned silence. To be honored by the confidence of no less a personage than Sherlock Holmes! The implications were overwhelming. All we could manage at last to say was that we'd talk the next day. The hour was getting on, and I didn't want to be riding the subway too late. At parting, Howard promised to call me as soon as he and Mr. Holmes had had a chance to confer—and we both vowed to keep this wonderful secret of Great Britain's foremost private consulting detective to ourselves.

II

I waited at home the next day, too excited to concentrate on either reading or writing, for Howard to 'phone, which he finally did in the early evening. He apologized for not getting in touch sooner, but he and Mr. Holmes had been engaged in intense conversation all through the afternoon.

"The man's no less remarkable in person than in Dr. Watson's accounts, Belknap," said Howard. "Age seems to have little affected his keen intelligence. The good doctor's assertions to the contrary in *A Study in Scarlet*, he has a wide and brilliant knowledge of many subjects. The only disturbing sign is a certain air of abstraction, a shortness of his attention span at times, perhaps a result of the blow he received from those hoodlums yesterday."

"Where is he now?"

"Taking a nap. He does seem to need his rest." Howard paused a moment, then continued. "I must say I'm immensely gratified that he seeks my help in this 'case' and yours, too, Belknapius. We discussed it, and we agreed there was every advantage in bringing you in on it. We old gentlemen could use a fresh, energetic kid like yourself ."

How my friend, less than half the age of Sherlock Holmes, could persist in his "old man" conceit in the circumstances was beyond me, but I held my tongue.

"As for the particulars of the case and what Mr. Holmes specifically desires of us, you'll learn soon enough. Two days from now we'll be coming into Manhattan to pay a call on Houdini, who'll give us the straight dope. By all means you must join us for the meeting."

"Why don't you first stop by here with Mr. Holmes," I said. "Then we could go on to Houdini's place—he lives nearby."

"That's an excellent idea, Sonny. Swell. Unless Mr. Holmes has any objections, we'll plan on swinging by the House of Long earlier that afternoon."

"And he does plan to pay you?"

"Indeed, yes. He repeated his promise to pay Grandpa—and you—actual long green; you know, kale, jake, berries, details yet to be worked out. Boy, if this detective business doesn't beat David V. Bush revisionism all to hell!"

"What shall we tell my parents?"

"I suppose we could tell them that he's an amateur press associate of mine from Great Britain—or some such. Before our rendezvous I'm sure he and I can work out some plausible explanation for our acquaintance.

"By the way, I've persuaded our distinguished friend to drop that corny accent and ridiculous slang—he'll blow his cover if he keeps it up." Howard himself, of course, from time to time among those he knew well indulged in the use of slang, aware of the humorous contrast it made with his naturally formal and precise, almost archaic manner of speech.

In closing Howard said that he had to go shortly to wake up the detective, to take him on a walking tour of the Clinton Street neighborhood.

My parents wondered at my agitated behavior over the next two days, my mother fearing it might be the onset of some nervous affliction, but I assured her I was quite all right, just anxious for them to meet Howard's "English colleague," on vacation in America.

When HPL and Sherlock Holmes showed up at our apartment at 823 West End Avenue (well before the hour of our appointment with Houdini), Howard introduced his companion to my parents as "John Altamont, Esquire—of Devon" (not Chicago). My mother insisted that our visitors have some tea, while my father returned to his dental surgery offices next door.

Once settled comfortably in the parlor, our foreign guest explained in his normal British voice that amateur journalism had become his chief hobby in retirement.

"While his natural modesty precludes him from saying so," put in Howard, "Mr. Altamont is in truth one of the leading lights in the Transatlantic Circulator. He and I have engaged in a most lively correspondence through that organization since its inception in 1921."

"Perhaps the pleasantest aspect of my American holiday so far," responded the detective, "has been my meeting in person one so celebrated in the circles of the National Amateur Press Association along with his delightful friends." He repeated this last phrase with a wink toward my mother.

"Are you married, Mr. Altamont?" asked my mother, as she poured out the fragrant Oolong tea.

"I am not, madam, nor have I ever been," answered Sherlock Holmes. "To have admitted the intrusion of the softer passions into my own delicate and finely adjusted temperament would have introduced a distracting factor which might have thrown doubt upon all my mental results. For the man of highly developed intellect, they have no place."

Since my parents were used to my associating with all manner of eccentric persons, with all manner of eccentric views, my mother betrayed no particular surprise at this statement.

"Oh, Mr. Altamont, you can hardly expect me to take you seriously," she said. "Why. look at Howard here. He's certainly a man of 'highly developed intellect,' yet he's found it in his heart to take a wife. How is Sonia, might I ask? Has she had any success in finding a job in the Midwest?"

"She's well, thank you, Mrs. Long," said Howard. "She's not as bothered by nerve trouble as she was. She has a number of leads in the job hunt. I believe she'll be back to New York for another visit next month."

Conversation fell into something of an awkward lull after this, and we had barely finished our first cup of tea before Howard suggested that it was time to head over to Houdini's. "The sprightly wizard has an extremely busy schedule, and I wouldn't want to keep him waiting for an instant," he announced.

As we took our leave, Sherlock Holmes thanked my mother with much show of gallantry, which appeared to make a great hit with her. Since there was a little time yet before our appointment, we determined to follow a roundabout route through Riverside Park. There, on the embankment by Grant's Tomb overlooking the Hudson, all golden and shimmery in the late afternoon light, we paused to admire the view. Howard began to wax in characteristic fashion about the sunset and architectural vistas which so potently provoked his fancy and so on—all very familiar to me from repeated hearings but of course new to the detective.

"Coming for the first time upon the town," began Howard, "I had seen it in the sunset from a bridge, majestic above its waters, its incredible peaks and pyramids rising flowerlike and delicate from pools of violet mist to play with the flaming clouds and the first stars of evening."

As HPL continued to rhapsodize in this vein, I noticed a certain glazed look come over the eyes of Sherlock Holmes. Truly Howard's speech was having a hypnotic, one might almost say soporific, effect on him. At last Howard stopped, and the spell was broken. "Most poetic, most poetic," mumbled the detective, abruptly coming back to life.

We moved on, back along the picturesque, winding paths of the park, the older men walking briskly in long strides ahead, while I trotted to keep up a few feet behind. I sensed that a strong rapport already existed between my two companions—a real sympathy of character and temperament. And, as fragments of talk of complicated chemistry experiments reached me to the rear, I'll admit I felt a sharp twinge of inadequacy, for being so obviously not nearly the equal of either of these two geniuses.

At 278 West 113th Street, a solid building with elaborate stonework in the Romanesque style, we rode the plush elevator up to the Houdinis' tenth-floor apartment. Mrs. Houdini greeted us warmly at the door, then ushered us down an ornately carpeted hallway, lavishly furnished with Victorian pieces and knickknacks (not at all to Howard's taste, I knew), to the library of the greatest magician and escape artist of the age. A large mahogany desk, littered with papers, dominated the center of the high-ceilinged room, but our attention was immediately drawn to the walls of bookshelves on every side of us. No doubt here we were face to face with the conjuror's fabled and vast collection of books on magic, occultism, and arcane lore of every description.

After a minute or two (which we put to good use studying the contents of the shelves), Harry Houdini himself entered the room, clutching a copy of a western adventure magazine. A short, broad-shouldered man, with wiry dark hair shot with gray, and a head like an "idealized bust of a Roman general or consul" (to quote an esteemed American critic), our host shook hands with each of us in turn, with a grip, needless to say, of iron.

"Gentlemen, gentlemen, please sit down," he said, as he moved around the desk, gesturing toward the Gothic Revival armchairs arrayed before it. He took his own seat, and tossed the magazine among the debris atop the desk. "I suppose none of you is keen on cowboy yarns, but I do recommend 'Lightning Kid's Debut' by Phillip Roberts in this issue of *Ace-High.*"

He was right. Neither HPL nor I had ever been a fan of the western pulps. On the other hand, given his involvement in a number of cases with roots in the American West, Mr. Holmes may have been more receptive to such tales.

"Speaking of fine stories," continued Houdini, "let me tell you again, Lovecraft, how pleased I was with 'Imprisoned with the Pharaohs.' A year after its appearance in *Weird Tales* it still gives me the creeps to think of it. The bit at the end where the five shaggy-headed monsters turn out to be the fingers of an enormous *paw* came as a real shocker."

"You are too kind, Houdini," said HPL, "though if I do say so myself I went the limit in descriptive realism in the first part, then when I buckled down to the under-the-pyramid stuff I let myself loose and coughed up some of the most nameless, slithering, unmentionable *horror* that ever stalked cloven-hoofed through the tenebrous and necrophagous abysses of elder night."

While Howard had been pleased with the story he had ghostwritten for Houdini, it had been a rush job and had brought on one of his more severe headaches. In fact, HPL had spent much of his honeymoon in Philadelphia retyping the manuscript, having lost the original typed copy on the journey from Providence to New York to marry Sonia.

"Now, my dear Holmes," said Houdini, clasping his mighty hands together and leaning forward, "on to the matter at hand. To begin with, how much do our young friends know of this business?"

"I have given Lovecraft a brief account of the background," said the detective after a moment, "but for the benefit of Frank I believe we ought to go over everything from the start. Pray, Houdini, please tell your end of the tale first."

"Very well, Holmes," said Houdini, turning his stern but kindly gaze on me. "Frank, have you ever heard of Jan Martense?"

I answered that I hadn't.

"Yes, I suspect you don't often follow the society columns of our metropolitan newspapers where the name now and then appears. Martense is a wealthy man, yet unobtrusively so, living quietly for the most part at his mansion on Suydam Street in one of Brooklyn's more fashionable old neighborhoods. He is a man of refinement, a collector of rare books and manuscripts, a patron of the arts. He served his country as a captain of infantry during the World War, and was wounded at Belleau Wood. He is the scion of one of New York's ancient Dutch families—and he is one of the most clever criminal minds operating on the Eastern Seaboard today."

"Astounding that a man—a gentleman—of such distinguished lineage should turn to crime," interjected HPL.

"What exactly has he done in the criminal line?" I asked.

"Among his nefarious activities," resumed the magician, "is bootlegging. He owns and runs a chain of profitable speakeasies in Brooklyn. Indeed, he keeps an office at one, at Richard and Wolcott Streets. You may know the area, Lovecraft—it's not far from you.

"Along with the liquor trade, he also traffics in the smuggling of illegal aliens into this country. He maintains a number of seedy buildings, including a run-down Roman Catholic church, as holding stations for these people near the waterfront in the notorious Red Hook district—the same section as where his speakeasies are located, as it happens. I gather most of these wretches originate from the Middle East or the Orient."

"Unclassified Asian dregs wisely turned back by Ellis Island, in fact, Houdini," said Howard.

"As serious as these crimes are, Martense has managed to keep his own hands clean. The authorities have never been able to connect him directly with these goings-on. Besides, he is on good terms with the Brooklyn police force, who tend to look the other way at the bootlegging and speakeasy operations, and have little desire to probe too deeply into those sinister buildings with their teeming alien hordes by the waterfront. More men are seen to enter than to leave them, I might add. He is a powerful man.

"But, however heinous these activities, they are of little concern to me. He has, though, gotten into a new racket of late that very much does concern me. Does the name Cordelia Garrison sound at all familiar to you, Frank?"

"Yes, it does," I said, "but I can't place it."

"Miss Cordelia Garrison has made something of a sensation among certain circles of New York society—as a spiritualistic medium. She's received no small degree of attention in the papers. Not since the medium Margery created such a fuss in the matter of the *Scientific American* prize contest last year have I encountered such a wily—and charming—opponent. I have several times challenged Miss Garrison to give a demonstration of her spiritualist powers under my supervision, but she refuses to set a date and manages to put me off short of an outright refusal." Houdini shrugged his massive shoulders, as if in annoyance that a mere woman should frustrate him.

"In any case, I haven't the time to pursue her, as I'm soon leaving on a cross-country tour. At some point I may even have to go to Washington, to testify before Congress concerning pending legislation to outlaw fortune telling in the District of Columbia. Well, you may be wondering what connection all this has with you, gentlemen. Miss Garrison is known to be a very close friend of Jan Martense, who I have every good reason to think has been orchestrating her career. At more than one séance he has appeared as her companion. Here's where you pick up the thread, Holmes . . . Holmes?"

The great detective had been leaning back in his chair, fingertips pressed together, eyes closed, seemingly in deep concentration.

"Eh, I say, how's that?" he said at last.

"Holmes, if you will, please tell Howard and Frank a bit more of this link between Miss Garrison and Jan Martense," said Houdini, a trifle testily, I thought.

"Yes, quite so. Thank you, Houdini," said Sherlock Holmes, opening his eyes. "Mr. Martense has lately spent some time in England—to negotiate with his suppliers in the liquor trade. Whilst in my native land, he succeeded by devious means (I won't bore you with the details) in gaining possession of some extremely sensitive documents—documents whose rightful owner would pay any price to have recovered discreetly. This is where I come into the case. The reputation of one of Britain's most illustrious figures hangs in the balance. Confidence requires that I not disclose my client's identity even to present company—at least not at this time."

"Miss Garrison has the support of some very prominent people, I fear," began Houdini, as I wondered to myself who this esteemed personage could be of whom the detective spoke with such solemn secretiveness. "One of them is no less than your celebrated English author, and my friend, Sir Arthur Conan Doyle. Only the other week he told reporters that he believed her to be genuine. An endorsement from so eminent a figure only makes our cause the more difficult."

"A pity that such a man should be so woefully deluded," remarked Howard, whose philosophy of mechanistic materialism had made him a foe of spiritualism from his earliest years. "He's contributed so much that's enduring in literature—his history of the Boer War, *Micah Clarke*, *The White Company* . . . Ah, the foibles of old age!"

"Yes, he's a brilliant man, a deep thinker, well versed in every respect, and comes of a gifted family. And he's extremely genial and kind-hearted," added Houdini.

"Let me tell you a story," continued the magician, a certain tenseness evident in his tone. "Despite our differences over spiritualism, we'd always managed to maintain our friendship. Then, three years ago, we met by chance on the beach at Atlantic City. June 17, 1922—the date is burned into my memory. That afternoon Sir Arthur and Lady Doyle offered to give me a demonstration of spirit writing, which out of politeness I consented to. Spirit writing is Lady Doyle's specialty in the mediumistic field.

"We retired to their hotel room, where Lady Doyle settled herself in a chair before a small table, poised with pen in hand. Soon after entering a trance state, she commenced to write furiously, in a short time covering several sheets of paper with a large, scrawling script. The result was a message to me—a message supposedly dictated by my late, sainted mother!" Houdini paused, for the moment no longer master of his emotions. In embarrassment I looked away, toward Howard—whose grave expression betrayed his sincerest sympathy. The loss of his own beloved mother, as recently as 1921, had been a terrific blow.

"The highly-colored 'letter' consisted of vague generalities and sentimental balderdash that anyone might spew out in haste," said Houdini, his poised restored. "But most damning of all was the fact that it was written in English—a language my dear mother spoke at best brokenly and never learned to write. You can understand why since this incident a coolness has entered my relations with Sir Arthur."

A heavy silence followed the conclusion of this story. Finally, Sherlock Holmes spoke: "Spiritualism has never had a more sincere champion. But to return to the main point, Houdini. We are agreed, then, that we have goals of mutual interest. You wish to have an end put to Miss Garrison's fraudulent career. I am most willing to approach her and discover her methods, for in so doing I stand to gain a strong card in my effort to recover what I seek, if played at just the right time.

"Winning Miss Garrison's confidence will require my moving out of Brooklyn at some not too distant point, and establishing myself in one of Manhattan's finer hotels; representing myself as a well-to-do Englishman who wishes to establish contact with the spirit of his late son, lost with millions of other noble souls in the Great War." Howard's countenance clouded at this revelation.

"Do not worry, my dear Lovecraft, I shall maintain my Clinton Street quarters as well, and I have a good deal of leg work yet ahead of us in Brooklyn. We must pay a visit soon to Mr. Martense's Suydam Street mansion (preferably when he is not at home), and see what we can find there. We should also call in at one of his speakeasies. This will necessitate a little undercover work, which I trust, Frank, you will be game for." I felt a palpable thrill of excitement at this last remark.

"I wish I could join you in this adventure, gentlemen," said Houdini, gesturing with an unspoken "Oy-vay" expression at the heaps of papers on his desk, "but my work . . . I will have to content myself with observing your progress from the gallery." With another gesture he indicated that our interview was over.

"The best of luck to you, Holmes," said the magician, as he showed us out, shaking hands again firmly with each of us. "Oh, and Lovecraft, speaking of all this spiritualist business, do let me know what your Providence protégé Eddy thinks of my proposed anti-spiritualism book. Perhaps after this is cleared up you'll have the time to set down to a collaborative effort. *The Cancer of Superstition* I think would be a good working title."

"Well, my dear fellows," said Sherlock Holmes in high good humor once we'd reached the street, "you should now at least have an inkling of what we are up against. I admit my plan is somewhat of an indefinite one; we shall have to play certain things intuitively as the action develops. If either of you has any doubts at this stage, please speak up. You are still free to bow out, but I shall consider you committed for the duration of the case, whatever the vicissitudes of our fortunes, if you choose to continue."

"I think I speak for Frank as well as myself, Mr. Holmes," said Howard, "when I say that you have our wholehearted support."

"Splendid, splendid," replied the venerable detective, rubbing his thin hands together. "With two such stalwart allies a successful outcome is all but assured."

I said farewell to my two comrades at the 110th Street subway stop, where they planned to catch a train for Greenwich Village. Despite his contempt for the Bohemian and pseudo-artistic elements of that antique district, Howard was eager to show our famous friend some of its more obscure, Colonial thoroughfares, which appeared to particular advantage in the moonlight.

III

The following week, after our visit to Houdini, Howard 'phoned to say that Mr. Holmes wished to attend the next meeting of the Kalem Club, our informal literary group that gathered as a rule every other Wednesday, more often than not at my parents' apartment, to discuss books, art, politics—the burning issues of the day. The Kalem Club, or simply "the Gang" as Howard preferred to call it, was so designated because the last names of the original members all began with K, L, or M. Once again my parents had generously offered our apartment for the use of the Kalems.

"As before, Mr. Holmes will present himself as Mr. John Altamont, of Devon, England," said Howard. (Devonshire, as HPL had proudly informed me on more than one occasion, was the ancestral home of the Lovecrafts.) "We'll tell the Gang the same story that we told your mother. No one besides myself knows anything about the activities or membership of the Transatlantic Circulator."

"What have you and Mr. Holmes been up to?" I asked.

"Oh, we've made some real progress, Sonny. In the course of less than a week our renowned colleague, posing as a delivery 'boy,' succeeded in befriending the cook at the Martense mansion—an elderly widow. I must say, he can act quite the ladies' man when circumstances require it of him! From her he learned all the details he needed of the house's floor plan, and the hours her master customarily keeps.

"Then, just last night, I joined the detective in a *bona fide* second-story job, with jimmy and everythin'! (Mind you, we were careful to leave no signs of our uninvited entrance.) You couldn't have told ole Grandpa from a reg'lar cracksman, had you seen me decked out in all the proper felonious fittings. We thoroughly searched Mr. Martense's vast, high-ceilinged study, but found no trace of that which Mr. Holmes is looking for. In any event, he is now persuaded that it's sequestered at other than the Suydam Street premises, so we must seek elsewhere."

Any disappointment I may have felt at having been left out of this escapade was somewhat made up for by the fact that its results had been successful only in a negative sense. I expressed none of this to Howard, though, and merely said I'd look especially forward to the forthcoming gathering.

That Wednesday evening, the 29th, my parents left around 7:00, before the arrival of the first Kalem, as they had tickets to the latest Broadway hit comedy, *The Grand Duchess and the Waiter*, with Basil Rathbone. My mother, as she invariably did before one of our meetings, had set out a tray of cookies and prepared a pot of strong black coffee, which she had left to simmer on the stove. Because Mr. Altamont's presence would make this a special occasion, she'd also baked a cake. My father, true to form, had grumbled a little, saying he was glad they were going out for the night, and thus wouldn't have to hide in the bedroom and listen to the hum of "all that gab" coming from the living room, as they had to do whenever the gang was over and they were home.

The guests for this particular meeting included Sam Loveman, the poet and boyhood friend in Cleveland of Hart Crane; Rheinhart Kleiner, a retired accountant and justice of the peace; kindly, white-haired Everett McNeil, an author of boys' books in his day; George Kirk, owner and proprietor of the Chelsea Book Shop on 8th Avenue; Arthur Leeds, a writer of adventure stories; Wheeler Dryden, Charlie Chaplin's half-brother; and James F. Morton, mineralogist, liberal arts essayist, and Negro rights advocate. HPL appeared last of all accompanied by the detective, dressed in a suit of worn but stylish tweeds, as would befit "John Altamont of Devon, a retired gentleman of property" (as introduced to the company by Howard).

In deference to his age, I offered our foreign visitor the most comfortable chair, the one habitually reserved for Howard, but he declined, choosing instead a less conspicuous seat on the divan. My mentor winked at me, as if to say this was all right—Sherlock Holmes preferred to observe from the wings rather than place himself at the center of attention.

Howard sat down in his accustomed spot, which commanded the whole room, and commenced the proceedings with, for no especial reason (unless perhaps it had formed a subject of discussion on the ride over from Brooklyn), a tirade against modern poetry. Reared as he'd been on Pope, Dryden, Samuel Johnson—in short, the eighteenth-century English school that had regarded the heroic couplet as the epitome of the verse form—he had no sympathy for the radical poetry of the present era. T. S. Eliot's *The Waste Land*, in particular, had been anathema to him ever since its sensational appearance in *The Dial* earlier in the decade.

"*The Waste Land* is a practically meaningless collection of phrases, learned allusions, quotations, slang, and scraps in general; offered to the public as something justified by our modern mind with its recent comprehension of its own chaotic triviality and disorganization," began Howard, warming to the attack.

"Yes, Howard, yes," interjected Sam Loveman, after HPL had spontaneously recited a passage from his parody, "Waste Paper," "the form may be off-putting, but the poem's message seems to be that the past is far superior to the present—an idea I'm sure you have no quarrel with. What's your opinion, Mr. Altamont?"

After a few moments, the detective, who'd been in his meditative pose, fingers tented, replied, "I beg your pardon?"

"Sam's curious to know what you think of T. S. Eliot's epic poem, *The Waste Land*," said Howard.

"I am afraid I have not read it," said Sherlock Holmes. "I am too old to take much of an interest in current high-brow literature. I suspect, however, that I would agree with Lovecraft's assessment of Mr. Eliot and his work." No one troubled our guest with any further questions about twentieth-century art and literature.

As frequently happened, the talk broke down among smaller groups. Sitting next to Ev McNeil, Sherlock Holmes nodded in interested fashion as the venerable boys' writer prattled on about his youthful exploits. Loveman told me that he had been in touch with the littérateur Vincent Starrett, who had expressed an interest in seeing some of Howard's stories. HPL and Morton exchanged a few heated words on the issue of Negro rights.

When music came up as a topic, our British friend admitted that he used to play the violin as a hobby, but had in his retirement virtually given it up. "A touch of rheumatism has stiffened my fingers such that I am no longer as nimble on the strings as I once was," he said.

Howard said that he'd studied the violin as a boy, but couldn't stand the long hours of practice. "It pleased my mother and solicitous older relatives to imagine they were fostering a musical prodigy; though they relented when they saw how close I was coming to actual nervous collapse."

"A shame you were unable to continue," remarked the detective, "for I am sure you would have found ultimate mastery of the instrument more than ample reward for those many painful hours of learning."

"After I abandoned the violin I did play a zobo with two other boys," added Howard. "We called ourselves the Blackstone Military Band."

Later I overheard Sherlock Holmes and Wheeler Dryden discussing the English music hall theatre and the prominent London stage figures of the gay nineties. "I once considered a career on the stage," confided the detective. "Friends used to flatter me on my powers as an actor."

The gang broke up on the early side, just as my parents returned (they greeted everyone, then retired down the hallway). It wasn't uncommon for a meeting to last far into the small hours, but Ev McNeil was looking droopy-eyed, and Kirk and Leeds had ceased trying to hide their yawns.

Howard and Mr. Holmes lingered, after the rest departed. "A capital set of associates you have, my dear Lovecraft. All sharp and keen—good men indeed. They may well prove useful in case we require extra hands in this business. For now, however, we three will suffice.

"I trust, Frank, that you will be available Saturday for our next move—a visit to Mr. Martense's Wolcott Street speakeasy. Here it is that he maintains an office from which, I understand, he carries on his business in the bootlegging trade. We have scouted the vicinity on more than one occasion, and locals have told us that his handsome French touring car is frequently seen parked before it. I imagine this excursion might be even more interesting, and let us hope more fruitful, than last week's house-breaking adventure. Do you think your parents will object?"

"No, no, I don't think there'd be any problem," I said. Then I asked a question that had been preying on my mind since our first acquaintance. "I'm sorry if I'm being too inquisitive, Mr. Holmes, but why isn't Dr. Watson here in America on this case with you?"

"Oh, I'm afraid Watson has seen fit to take yet another wife of late, his fourth or fifth, I believe. He is evermore the staid, family man in his declining years. No more gallivanting about for him."

And so, my curiosity satisfied at least on this minor point if still somewhat befuddled by the larger mystery of what I was getting involved in, I wished my two older friends a safe journey back to Brooklyn.

IV

That weekend following the meeting of the Kalems, I found myself once again on the car to Brooklyn, anxiously anticipating the evening's stake-out of Martense's Wolcott Street speakeasy. I'd told my parents that I was going to attend an impromptu gathering of some of the gang at Sam Loveman's apartment in Columbia Heights. I knew full well that they'd have forbidden my attendance had they been informed of my true purpose and destination. A speakeasy was not a place they'd allow any son of theirs to patronize.

I wore my two-toned sports jacket, since Howard had said that Mr. Holmes wished us to dress casually. "According to the esteemed detective, the clientele who frequent the speakeasy adhere to a standard of dress far removed from our own Anglo-Saxon tastes," my friend had said. "We must not make ourselves conspicuous, but blend in with the local yokelry."

I'd never worn this jacket in Howard's presence, for fear of inciting his ridicule. Indeed, when he greeted me at the door to his room he let out a laugh and exclaimed: "My God, Belknapius, aren't you the flashy boob. Your getup's perfect!"

Since HPL's wardrobe consisted principally of a few dark suits (he was now wearing the pants to one of his older suits and a white shirt), he was relying on Sherlock Holmes to supply him with the necessary costume. We mounted the creaky stairs up to the second floor, where we waited outside the detective's room a minute or so after knocking before he let us in. His quarters turned out to be even more Spartanly furnished than Howard's, a huge steamer trunk at the base of the bed dominating the room. There was a strong scent of stale pipe tobacco. (Pipe smoking had of late become one of my own more pleasurable habits.)

"How fortunate we are, my dear Lovecraft, that you and I are of the same approximate build," said Sherlock Holmes, as he rummaged through the giant trunk. "This spiffy number ought to fit you to a tee." The detective held up in both hands a badly pressed sports coat of a green and pink hue that made my own by comparison seem like a formal dinner jacket. Howard blanched at the sight of such a monstrosity, but quickly recovered his poise and gamely slipped it on.

"And here's a neck-tie to match," said our British friend, proffering a strip of cloth which appeared to be decorated with scrambled eggs.

"Gad," said Howard, eyeing the thing as if about to be sick to his stomach, "it even has a pattern!" For someone who shunned even striped regimental ties as too gaudy, to wear such a garment was a colossal concession. But HPL's mood for adventure soon mastered his natural repugnance. "Ugh. Well, if one's to pass for a zippy moron, one has to dress the part!" he said, adjusting the knot.

The detective's clothes tended also to the garish, but were much more muted than Howard's and showed some trace of style. He rather resembled my image of an English racetrack tout.

The detective slipped Howard a few dollar bills to cover our expenses, then departed with a final word of instruction: "Remember, lads, your job is simply to keep a sharp eye on me whilst I attempt to learn what information I can from the patrons. They are chiefly locals who are apt to be wary of any trouble from strangers."

We followed fifteen minutes later, walking south on Clinton into the shabby Red Hook neighborhood. We'd calculated that we'd reach our destination by foot in less than half an hour, though Howard slumped along, I noted, in a dispirited fashion the very opposite of his usual rapid gait. I guessed this was due to more than just insuring that we gave our elderly friend sufficient lead time.

"Are you bothered appearing in that ghastly jacket, Howard?" I asked.

"What? No, no, I'm quite willing to play my part in the disguise end of things. In fact, there's another consideration far more disturbing to my sensibility. Although I've informed Holmes that I detest drink, I didn't have the heart to confess that I've *never* touched the nauseous stuff—and don't intend to start now. I hope you won't mind doing the booze guzzling for us both, Belknap."

Around nine o'clock Howard and I found ourselves standing in front of a nondescript "candy" store, the windows of which were filled with posters and bills advertising fights and other local events. Across the upper panes was the name O'Connell's. Parked in front was a fancy foreign car, a four- or maybe even six-cylinder Renault, that had to belong to Martense.

As Sherlock Holmes had instructed us, we sauntered down the block and turned down the alley dividing O'Connell's from the next building. We picked our way carefully along its shadowy length, Howard pausing more than once to mew affectionately at a stray cat, before coming to an imposing wooden door flanked by garbage cans. At our knock the door shortly opened, just enough to permit the head of a beefy-looking Irishman to peer out.

We must have passed the initial inspection, for the man said in a not unfriendly manner: "Strangers, eh? Hope you don't object to a search." We submitted to being frisked without protest, then having proved clean were allowed to enter.

"The local flatfoots are okay, but you can never tell when the feds might drop in," he said as we followed him down a flight of steps to the basement. We proceeded along a well-lit, whitewashed corridor to another heavy door, at which stood an only slightly less burly sentry. This sentinel gave us the scrutiny also, but declined to search us. He opened the door and waved us inside.

Through the thick cigarette smoke that clouded the large, low-ceilinged room, we could discern little at first. We sat down at a small, rough oak table by the entrance, which afforded a good view of the whole premises. The room held a jumbled array of similar small tables, and along one wall an old-fashioned saloon bar with brass fittings. There we soon spotted Sherlock Holmes—with glass in hand chatting amiably, it appeared, with a couple of other customers.

The crowd consisted of solid working-class folk, mostly male. Perhaps a few could be described as tough characters, but many were decently dressed in coat and tie. I'm sure it crossed Howard's mind as it did mine that our flamboyant attire may not have been precisely necessary. For a moment an elegant figure stepped out from behind a curtained area in one corner, surveyed the scene, then slipped back out of sight. "Martense," said Howard.

We ordered two beers from a hearty, blonde waitress, who returned in a minute with two frothy mugs and collected a few coins from HPL. Howard picked his up gingerly, as if it were one of his used mousetraps, his long face registering complete disgust.

"Here, Sonny," he said, after a perfunctory sniff at the brew, "I simply cannot bring myself to drink this revolting liquid." He pushed the mug in my direction. "No one's apt to notice your drinking my share as well in this joint."

Now my parents weren't Puritans, and we did enjoy an occasional, precious bottle of wine left over from pre-Prohibition days, but I was far from accustomed to imbibing more than moderate quantities of alcohol. I'd been still in my teens when the Volstead Act was passed. But I was thirsty, and quickly despatched my own beer. At intervals Howard furtively poured the contents of his mug into mine, and once or twice, with nose wrinkled, brought his mug to his lips, feigning to sip.

As soon as I was done, the buxom barmaid removed the empties and deposited another round.

"Pardon me, Miss," said Howard, "but my friend and I didn't order these beverages."

She gave him a hard look and answered rather abruptly: "Listen, pal, you're here to drink, ain't ya?" Then winking and in a softer tone she said, "Come on, have a good time. Don't be such a sourpuss!"

There was no arguing with this. Howard's natural courtesy prevented him from protesting further to the lady, and he handed her some more change.

I for one was beginning to "have a good time." I swallowed my third and fourth beers in short order, while Howard concentrated on keeping an eye on Sherlock Holmes at the bar. The ancient detective was talking animatedly with his companions, with much convivial raising and clinking of glasses. Howard expressed the wish that he would finish up his business soon so we could leave, but our British friend showed no sign of moving on at any time soon.

Inevitably I had to excuse myself, and scuffled my way among the clusters of tables, across the sawdust floor, toward the Gents sign. When I returned to my chair a few minutes later, still feeling very happy, I was mildly startled to hear someone shouting close at my ear through the general din.

"I don't believe it! It really is Howard P. Lovecraft, the teetotaling, human walking machine, in O'Connell's saloon!"

I turned around with some deliberation, and found myself gazing directly into the beaming red face of the distinguished modernist poet, Hart Crane. I'd seen him in person only once before, but there was no mistaking those boyish good looks, as yet showing no trace of the ravages of alcohol.

"Why hello, Hart. Good to see you," said Howard, in a tone, however, that belied the sincerity of his greeting.

As I've written elsewhere, HPL had met Crane in Cleveland while visiting Sam Loveman in 1922, and they had run across one another since then in New York City. One couldn't have imagined two men more opposite in taste and temperament, though a certain grudging mutual respect, if not full cordiality, existed between them. Here, I vaguely realized, was another momentous encounter; a replay, of sorts, of a chance meeting in a Greenwich Village cafeteria the year before. Again I was privileged to witness perhaps the foremost American poet of the postwar generation accosting the twentieth-century master of the supernatural horror tale on whom had fallen the mantle of Edgar Allan Poe. I knew Crane had been working on his masterpiece, *The Bridge*, inspired by the view of the Brooklyn Bridge from his rooming-house window, and a snatch of it came suddenly to mind: "And when they dragged your weary flesh through Baltimore—did you betray the ticket, Poe?" No greater single line has ever been written about Poe—or so I thought at the time (though now I can't figure out what on earth I meant by this judgment!). Surely, in any event, I like to think, the shade of Poe, more than a little tipsy, presided over the scene.

"Here, you don't mind if I draw up a chair and join you boys. Hey, that's some outfit you've got on, Howard. You must've paid some Lower East Side shyster all of five dollars for it!"

"Please, Hart," said HPL, "keep it down. Frank and I would prefer it, in fact, if you left us alone."

"I bet you would," said Crane, giving me a funny leering look. "I've been watching you guys. How many rounds have you bought for your young friend here? Five? Six? Now don't tell me he's your nephew, or grandson, or something!" The poet patted me benevolently on the head.

"You've met Belknap . . . er, Frank, before, Hart," said Howard.

"At first I couldn't believe it," said Crane, his joviality unaffected by Howard's terseness. "Prissy Howard Lovecraft entertaining a young gentleman friend in a speak. Wait till Loveman hears about this!"

"Christ, Hart, don't tell Sam. Dammit, I can't explain."

"Oh, there's no need to explain, Howard. I understand. Jesus, I always wondered about you and Sonia Greene—and that piping voice of yours, hah!"

No doubt Crane's remarks must have been provoking to HPL, but he kept his temper. A Rhode Island Yankee has to maintain his dignity.

"Say, come on, don't take this romance stuff too seriously," continued Crane. "You ought to adopt a more lighthearted approach. Which reminds me, you've gotta meet *my* friend. We met on the wharf not more than two hours ago a case of love at first sight if there ever was one." He turned and waved somewhere in the distance of the room. Whether Sherlock Holmes had observed the advent of a third party to our table I was unable to tell.

"Hey, sailor . . . yeah, you, come on. . . . Don't be shy, these are buddies of mine."

Out of the smoke emerged a chunky, coarse-looking youth, yet handsome in a dark, Mediterranean way, dressed in foreign naval garb. He seemed reluctant to join us, but Crane cajoled him into a chair, and swung a comradely arm around his shoulder.

"Manuel doesn't speak English so hot, so you'll have to excuse him if he doesn't contribute much to the conversation."

Crane motioned to our waitress—whose bosom I frankly admired as she leaned over—and ordered another round of beers. She eyed Crane and his sailor friend with disapproval, I thought, acknowledging the order without speaking.

Perhaps realizing that our uninvited table companions were planning to stay for a while, Howard tried to make the best of it by turning the conversation to other topics.

"Sam tells me that you're thinking of leaving the city, giving up your apartment. It's in the same building, by the way, Frank, from which the crippled Washington Roebling supervised the construction of the Brooklyn Bridge." The poet didn't interrupt the historio-architectural disquisition that ensued, as he paid ever increasing attention to his nautical pal, who was now smiling a little but still dumb.

"Yeah, I gotta get out of the city for the summer," said Crane suddenly. "Sweet's Catalogues pays me a lousy thirty-five bucks a week. Say, Howard, you found a job yet? And where are our drinks?"

How Howard would have replied to the first question will remain forever a mystery, but to the second question we did receive something of an answer.

"Excuse me, 'fellas,'" said a large-bull-necked man who'd come up to our table, "are you through yet with the tea-party?"

None of us deigned to reply to this rude question.

"You are pansies, ain't you?" he continued.

"Who, sir, are you calling a pansy?" said Crane.

"Listen, we don't like your kind coming to a place for decent people, so why don't you and your chums shove off quietly? Or to put it another way, go on, beat it! Scram!" He started to pull Crane's chair back.

"All right then, if you insist," said Crane, slowly rising from the seat slipping from under him. Abruptly he wheeled about, and made a roundhouse swing at the bouncer. Unfortunately, the blow missed by a long shot, and the momentum carried him almost gracefully over onto the neighboring table, which exploded in a spray of foam and liquid.

"Okay, buddy, out you go the hard way," muttered the man, seizing the form of the sodden poet by the pants.

Howard and I sat transfixed, incapable in this instance to rush to the rescue. Manuel, however, did not remain passive. He rose up with a roar, the first sound he'd emitted in our presence all night, and leapt on the back of the bouncer, in the process knocking over a second table, much to the horror of its occupants. We could see other husky employees approaching what was clearly developing into a general fray. How long Crane and Manuel would be able to resist the uneven fight Howard and I did not wait to find out. Forgotten for the moment, we seized the opportunity to duck out the now unguarded door, its sentinel already committed to the growing battle. Our last glimpse was of the trim, well-dressed gentleman we'd seen earlier emerging from behind the curtain.

Outside, pausing under a lamp post, we caught our breath. "Gad, we would have to run into that ———," said Howard. "What a case the man is!" Then, taking a more pitying tone: "Poor Crane! A real poet and a man of taste, descendant of an ancient Connecticut family, and a gentleman to his fingertips, but the slave of dissipated habits."

"I wonder how Mr. Holmes is getting along," I said.

"A fine pair of undercover agents we've turned out to be, Belknapius. I fear we've failed Holmes this time out."

As Howard expounded on how unconstitutionally fitted he was for this work, a lithe figure slipped into the light.

"Capital, capital," said the detective, rubbing his long hands together. "You've done excellent work tonight, my boys, excellent work."

"What!?" exclaimed Howard.

"Come, let us remove ourselves from the precincts of O'Connell's speakeasy and proceed briskly back to Clinton Street. Some fresh air will especially do you a terrific lot of good, Frank, I believe."

"Did you discover any useful information, Holmes?" asked Howard, as if he were still incredulous that our outing had been anything less than an utter disaster.

"Indeed, I did, my dear fellow—thanks to that brilliant diversion you created. It drew Mr. Martense from his office just long enough for me to steal in unnoticed and make a rapid survey of its contents. In his haste he left exposed on his desk a most revealing document—a schedule of ships due to dock in the East River over the next two months. One date in particular was circled in red. If I am not mistaken, I daresay he shall be unloading a shipment of illegal aliens into his Red Hook way-stations that same night. Yes, we now hold an extremely valuable card by making the most of a lucky break thrown our way. My companions at the bar, as congenial as they were, had little to tell me of Mr. Martense and his activities.

"Incidentally, that handsome friend of yours is possessed of a great deal of charm. Soon after you departed he calmed down considerably, apologized to Martense, even offered to pay for damages. An extraordinary fellow. When I left he and Martense were standing at the bar, chatting about poetry, oddly enough. Do tell me who he is, and how you came to know him."

Given this invitation, Howard outlined the history and accomplishments of Hart Crane for the rest of the time back to 169 Clinton, relieved, I suspect, that the detective had not asked for a detailed account of the circumstances leading up to Crane's outburst on the present occasion.

I went home to Manhattan, perhaps feeling not quite as well as I had earlier, but still in a cheerful mood as I reflected on my own role in the night's adventure.

V

A couple of rather uneventful weeks passed, uneventful compared to the previous two at least for me. Howard checked in by 'phone once to say that Sherlock Holmes had established himself at the exclusive Gotham Hotel in Manhattan. Posing as a wealthy British widower, he had already made contact with Miss Cordelia Garrison. In the meantime, Sonia had returned from the Midwest on one of her periodic visits to New York. It was just as well that the detective only showed up occasionally at 169 Clinton, where he still maintained his room, and required no services of HPL during this period. At the Kalem Club meeting on the 13th, Howard appeared listless, and failed to dominate the proceedings in his usual fashion. "Mr. Altamont" did not attend.

The following weekend, however, I received a call from Howard, his voice filled with all the enthusiasm he'd shown in the first days of his association with Sherlock Holmes. "Holmes has succeeded in arranging a séance with Miss Garrison at her apartment on lower Fifth for this coming Tuesday evening. It's all settled that you and I will accompany him as seconds. By Azathoth, I won't let the intrepid sleuth down this time!" he vowed.

Shortly after six o'clock on the appointed day, Howard and I, dressed in our best suits, met Sherlock Holmes at his hotel suite, which in its lavish splendor formed a real contrast to his Clinton Street digs. The detective as well fit the part of the worldly retired manufacturer, "John Altamont, Esquire," attired in spotless evening clothes. His wild white beard was now neatly trimmed in a fashionable George V spade. He looked remarkably relaxed, as he lounged in a fancy Empire chair, pipe in hand, as if he were quite accustomed to such comfortable surroundings.

Howard, too, seemed in good form, his cheerfulness a result no doubt in part from having found earlier that day a volume of Bulwer-Lytton in a second-hand bin for just 10¢. Both he and I listened attentively as Sherlock Holmes outlined the plot for this night's excursion.

"I have had a number of preliminary interviews with Miss Garrison, as she is extremely careful in whom she selects. Had she known of my connection with Houdini, she surely would have refused my request for a séance. The amount of money I have agreed to pay is large, but not excessively so. By acting not overly eager, I think I have allayed any suspicions rather than the opposite.

"From studying the newspaper accounts of her demonstrations—here, have a look at these cuttings—I believe I have an excellent idea of her methods, and am tonight prepared to counter them. You will note that a 'spirit box' is her preferred mode of communication with the 'outer spheres.'"

Howard and I glanced at the newspaper articles describing her sensational successes. A somewhat fuzzy photograph revealed Miss Garrison to be a comely blonde.

"I have told her that you, Howard," continued the detective, "were a friend through correspondence of my late son, an active member in the British amateur press. She raised no objection to my bringing two American companions to the session to act as 'controls.' She seemed particularly impressed when I said that both of you were professional writers; and all the more so that you were writers of tales of the supernatural. When I mentioned *Weird Tales*, she admitted that the names of Lovecraft and Long were indeed familiar to her from those pages. Because you write about ghostly manifestations and what not, I suspect she assumes you are likely to believe in such things in actuality. Pray do not disappoint her by betraying your fervent mechanistic materialist philosophies." The detective chuckled, then took a long draw on his shag.

"Mr. Martense is almost certain to be present, I might add," said Sherlock Holmes as he rose languidly from his chair. "And now, gentlemen, if you are ready, the game's afoot. Let us grab our hats and be off."

In the taxi riding down Fifth Avenue the detective gave us some final words of advice on conducting ourselves. "Be sharp, lads. I need hardly say that Miss Garrison is a most attractive young woman. We must not allow a pretty face to affect our judgment adversely."

The building at 55 Fifth was a fine brick structure with stone facing, some twenty stories high, located across the street from the bookseller Dauber & Pine (where, as chance would have it, Howard would do part-time work the following spring, just before moving back to Providence). A uniformed doorman directed us to a private elevator, which carried us up to Miss Garrison's penthouse apartment.

A Negro maid showed us into a marble-floored foyer, took our hats, and led us down a short hallway into an airy living room, furnished with white and cream-colored chairs and sofas and piano as well in the ultra-modern, art-deco style. Even Howard, who could abide this mode no more than he could the Victorian, appeared struck by the aesthetics of the scene. *"Certe, nullas bananas hodie habemus,"* he quipped, feigning a chord at the keyboard.

Beyond the piano our attention was drawn to a pair of French doors, opening on to a terrace. While we waited we couldn't resist going outside for a look. The three of us stood entranced at the railing, gazing beyond the Italianate clocktower of the Edison Building toward the East River and Brooklyn. Howard very possibly was on the verge of launching into a spiel on the outspread cityscape, but a soft voice behind us broke the spell before he could begin.

"Yes, gentlemen, it is a magnificent view."

We turned, and there, silhouetted in the doorway to the terrace, was one of the most ravishing women I'd seen in my life—a vision worthy of Shelley or Keats. The newspaper photo had scarcely done her justice. She had curly blonde hair, set off by dark eyebrows in pleasing contrast, and wore a simple evening dress of some gauzy, diaphanous material; on her feet were what appeared to be ballet slippers. That her arms and neck were bare of jewelry served only to highlight her natural beauty.

"Miss Garrison," said Sherlock Holmes, bowing, "may I introduce to you my friends, Howard Lovecraft and Frank Long, Junior."

"My pleasure, Mr. Altamont," replied our hostess. She smiled and extended an exquisite long-fingered hand.

Howard and I took her hand in turn, each of us mumbling a few banal words of greeting. I was jittery, and clearly Howard was not insensible before such glamorousness. Only the detective retained his outward composure—but then he was an older man and seemingly indifferent to women, if one took his pronouncements at face value.

"You know, Mr. Lovecraft, I'm a regular reader of *Weird Tales*," she said, joining us at the rail. "'The White Ape' truly made me shudder." She shivered, which may have been caused as much by the thinness of her dress as by the memory of HPL's story.

"I am gratified that you liked that particular tale, Miss Garrison," said Howard. "I only regret that it was published with such an obvious title. Were I to employ such a title by choice, I can assure you that it would have nothing whatsoever to do with a white ape. Properly it should have been 'Facts concerning the Late Arthur Jermyn and His Family.' Ah, the vagaries of editors!"

"And you too, Mr. Long, you also possess great talent. 'The Desert Lich,' 'Death Waters,' and 'The Ocean Leech' all show promise of a bright future in one so young." She lightly placed a hand on my shoulder as she delivered these compliments. Too overwhelmed to reply, I kept staring out at the lights of the city, thankful that darkness hid my flushed cheeks.

After a few more moments, Miss Garrison observed that it was getting cold on the terrace, and we returned to the living room, where the colored maid waited respectfully.

"Shall we have a drink, gentlemen, before we commence? I always find the spirits more receptive when all participants are at their ease."

Sherlock Holmes and I each asked for a glass of wine, while Howard ordered a ginger ale. At that moment the door buzzer sounded.

"Never you mind the door, Dinah," said Miss Garrison. "I'll answer it while you take care of the drinks." She excused herself and with a light step disappeared down the hallway.

Though we couldn't see this new visitor as he entered, I could tell from the delighted murmurs we heard that this person was a welcome and familiar guest to the apartment. Miss Garrison shortly returned on the arm of the man we'd spotted in O'Connell's—Jan Martense, impeccably dressed as before in evening clothes. He was a smart-looking fellow of about thirty-five, inclining to the corpulent, with slicked-back hair, graying at the temples, and a pencil moustache. As he shook hands with each of us in turn, it seemed he hardly noticed either Howard or myself, but did study Sherlock Holmes with some intensity.

Dinah brought us our drinks, along with a plate of sliced cheese (one of Howard's favorite foods, as it happened). When Miss Garrison sat down in one of the deco chairs, we likewise made ourselves at home.

Martense led off the conversation, talking about the world of sophistication and society, travel abroad—all topics beyond the mundane experiences of Howard and myself. HPL did attempt to join in with an account of his maternal grandfather's Italian journeys, but only the detective was capable of holding his own with the man. He matched Martense's stories of this or that high-class hotel or restaurant with anecdotes concerning foreign capitals, French wines, the best London tailors, and so on—without being too personal or particular. Soon the two of them became wholly absorbed in their two-way exchange, with the pleasant result that Howard and I were left with Miss Garrison to ourselves.

Miss Garrison queried us further about *Weird Tales* and the amateur press movement in America, Mr. Altamont's late son and his amateur activities in Britain, and gently probed us on our views toward spiritualism. Without overplaying our parts, I think HPL and I managed to convey an open-mindedness, even enthusiasm, toward spiritualistic experimentation. We admitted that this would be the first time for both of us.

"Astral planes and auras, isn't that what it's all about?" I said, deliberately pointing up my naïveté on the subject. I also stated my belief in telepathy, which of course ironically is a real phenomenon.[2] This helped give her the right impression.

After about a half-hour of this agreeable getting acquainted, Miss Garrison said that it was time we moved on to the library for the business of the evening. Mr. Martense directed us down the hallway to a door just off the foyer. This opened onto a considerably less modern room than the one we'd been sitting in, the windows covered with heavy maroon draperies, the walls lined with built-in bookshelves (one I noticed was filled with the shopgirl romances of R. W. Chambers). A dim overhead light barely illuminated the only furniture of the room, a card table and three chairs. Underneath the table was a solid wooden box, about a foot square and several inches deep, with a spring hinge on top.

"This then I take it, Miss Garrison, is the celebrated spirit box?" asked Sherlock Holmes. "As I understand it, the spirits will communicate with us by depressing the flap, which completes a circuit powered by dry cell batteries, thus ringing a bell?"

"That's correct, Mr. Altamont," said Miss Garrison.

"You have no objection to my taking a look at the apparatus and making a quick inspection of the room?"

"None at all."

"I appreciate your indulgence, for I have been fooled too often in the past," said the detective, as he sauntered around the room, cursorily examined the rug, the drapes and windows, and the bookshelves. "I must be absolutely certain in my own mind that the spirit phenomena are genuine—that there is no chance for trickery. Yes, no wires here, I see," he added, picking up the box. "In this regard I also appreciate your allowing me to bring along my young friends."

"You have my assurance, Mr. Altamont, that Miss Garrison is entirely sincere," said Jan Martense.

---

2. The ESP experiments of J. B. Rhine and others would verify it in the thirties. [Editor's note]

"We're ready to proceed," said Miss Garrison, taking a chair.

"Capital, capital," said Sherlock Holmes, sitting down in the chair to her left. He rolled up his right pants leg, exposing sock and garter and a stretch of white leg, just below the knee.

"This is the correct procedure, then?" said the detective, taking her left hand in his right, and pressing his right ankle against her left calf.

"That's satisfactory," she said.

"Here, I say, Howard, Belknap—would one of you be so kind as to sit on Miss Garrison's right and assume an identical posture?"

I was eager for the honor, but shyness prevented me from speaking up. Happily, Howard demurred.

"I think Frank would do a better job than I," he said.

Accordingly I sat down next to Miss Garrison, and imitated Sherlock Holmes' position, taking her right hand in my left and pressing my left leg against her right calf (though I wasn't bold enough to roll up my pants leg). Thus was Miss Garrison "controlled"—that is, she could not move without one of us detecting it.

We determined that Mr. Martense and Howard would wait just outside the door, while this phase of the séance was conducted. Later perhaps HPL would have his turn. Martense extinguished the light as they left, leaving those of us remaining in blackness.

After a minute of silence, Miss Garrison began her invocation, in a soft but emotion-laden voice, calling upon the spirit of the "late Jack Altamont, of His Majesty's Royal Fusiliers." She went on in this manner for maybe a quarter of an hour, pausing now and then as if waiting for a response. It was an eerie experience, I'll admit, though on the whole an entertaining one. The opportunities of holding hands with a beautiful girl in the dark were rare enough for me in those days, and I was savoring every moment.

"Oh, spirit from the great gulf beyond the great gulf beyond, manifest thyself, show that you favor this gathering of sincere believers now before you," intoned Miss Garrison. "One ring for yes, and two rings for no. Oh, spirit, do you hear us?"

There was a single ring. I jumped, but kept my grip on her hand.

"Mr. Altamont? Are you listening, Mr. Altamont? You may now speak to the spirit of your late son."

Suddenly Sherlock Holmes came to life and launched into a sentimental spiel about how pleased he was to be at last in communication with his own dear boy, and how grateful he was to Miss Garrison for providing the opportunity. His thin voice cracked with emotion—it was a very persuasive performance.

"Are you happy, Jack?" asked the detective finally.

One ring.

"Are you with your dear mother?"

One ring.

"Is she happy?"

One ring.

He went on in this vein for some time, and I would have rapidly lost interest if it weren't for the proximity of Miss Garrison.

Mr. Holmes eventually wound down, and our hostess asked me if I cared to put a question to the spirit before he rejoined the great void.

"I sure would," I said. "Can it be about the future?"

"Certainly," she said, giving my hand a squeeze. "Proceed."

"All right. If I were to predict, spirit, that you will answer this question with two rings, would I be telling the truth?"

This was followed by a long silence.

"I think, Mr. Long, that we have lost the spirit with that question of yours," said Miss Garrison at last with a trace of asperity. "Not every question about the future can be answered simply yes or no." She released my hand and announced in a loud voice that the session was over.

Almost immediately the door opened, and the overhead light came on. Blinking, I could make out Howard and Martense standing in the foyer—and behind them, Dinah, holding our hats. Evidently Mr. Martense had decided it was time for us to go. Sherlock Holmes asked about the possibility of holding another séance, but Miss Garrison declined to set anything definite. We all thanked her for a most enlightening demonstration, bade Mr. Martense adieu, and departed.

We said little in the cab back up Madison Avenue, though Howard did lament his failure to draw Martense into a discussion of his host's ancient Dutch ancestry, which the man appeared curiously uninterested in. On the other hand, Martense's attempt to sound out Howard on his tastes in contemporary literature did reveal their mutual appreciation of Herman Melville's masterpiece, *Moby-Dick,* a copy of which Kirk had recently given Howard. When we pressed the detective for his thoughts on the séance, he waved aside our pleas, saying we would have an explanation soon enough when we got back to the Gotham. Only an enigmatic smile gave any clue that he had been satisfied with the evening's proceedings.

Howard and I waited with growing impatience in the sitting room of the suite, while our friend changed into his dressing gown. In time he joined us, and began assiduously to fill his pipe, tamp it, light it, and so on. Clearly he was enjoying keeping us in suspense.

"Well, Holmes," said Howard, no longer able to restrain his curiosity, "did you detect the fraud? I kept a close watch on Martense while we waited outside, and I'm certain he couldn't have caused the box to ring."

"I'm baffled," I said. "As far as I can tell, Miss Garrison never moved an inch. Did she have a hidden buzzer under her foot?"

"No, Frank, there was no hidden buzzer. I saw to that when I studied the area of carpet immediately under and before her chair. There was nothing."

"How did she do it then?" persisted Howard. "Surely you aren't suggesting the action of a supernatural agency."

"You may have noticed, my dear fellows," said the detective, "that in addition to having a finely shaped body, Miss Garrison also possesses a very athletic build. By means of small, subtle movements of her right leg she was able in the course of her preliminary speech to shift her foot within range of the box. These movements would have been imperceptible to ordinary skin.

"You ask how I was able to sense this motion? For several hours earlier today I wore a silk rubber bandage just below my right knee. By this evening my calf had become swollen and extremely tender. The heightened sense of feeling permitted me to notice the slightest sliding of Miss Garrison's ankle or flexing of muscle. Did you not observe, Frank, before the lights were put out, that Miss Garrison wore silk stockings and that her skirts were pulled well above her knees?"

I certainly had. "But what if she had moved her right leg, the one I was touching?"

"An excellent point, Frank. After picking up and examining the box I took the precaution of setting it down a bit to the left, in my direction, making it an awkward proposition to effect the ringing with her other foot . . ."

Howard and I gaped in astonishment at the man's ingenuity. "That sensitizing the leg business is an old trick," continued Sherlock Holmes. He chuckled softly. "I taught it to Houdini himself years ago when we crossed paths during one of his European tours. Well, now that we know Miss Garrison's method, we hold a very powerful trump in our hands. The threat of its play—the exposure of Miss Garrison— should contribute a great deal toward obtaining from Mr. Martense what we seek.

"The hour is getting on, my friends, and an old man needs his rest. So I must say good-night—till tomorrow when the Kalem Club convenes. At Sam Loveman's Columbia Heights apartment, is it not? In Brooklyn. Very well. Soon the Kalems may play their part, a troop of loyal retainers, in what will surely be the final act of our little drama. Farewell."

"What's this about the Kalems getting into the act?" I asked HPL as we strode out onto Fifth Avenue, into the fresh spring night air.

"I'm not apprised fully of the wily private eye's intentions for them myself. But undoubtedly we will learn all we need to know tomorrow."

VI

The Kalem Club meeting for this particular Wednesday, the 20th, had originally been scheduled to be held at Ev McNeil's. Howard, however, had thought it judicious to switch it to Sam Loveman's, since Ev tended to be even more tedious in his own surroundings and some members might be apt to avoid a McNeil gathering. According to Howard, the detective wanted to be sure there was a good turnout. Howard had also hinted to the others that this was to be more than just the usual literary gab session.

When I arrived I was asked if I knew what was on HPL's mind, but I pleaded ignorance. Sherlock Holmes and Howard were the last to appear. With the exception of the "dainty" (as Howard referred to him in private) Wheeler Dryden, who had returned to England, all the original gang were on hand who had met "Mr. Altamont" before—Leeds, Kleiner, Morton, Kirk, McNeil, and Loveman.

"Fellow Kalems," began Howard, addressing the gang assembled in Loveman's one-room apartment, "may I have your attention."

"What's going on, Howard?" asked Morton. "Are you about to announce you've sold a collection of your stories to a book publisher?"

"Before I say anything further," continued Howard, not deigning to answer Morton, "I must request of you all that what you'll shortly hear not go beyond this room. It is vitally important, for reasons I'll soon make clear. Do I have the assurances of every one of you to keep silent, upon your word as gentlemen?"

After a little hesitation, we all, including myself, murmured our assent.

"I have to confess," said HPL, "that I've been guilty of a deception. Mr. Altamont here is not merely a retired professional man of fine old Anglo-Saxon stock . . ."

I noticed Loveman roll his eyes at this remark. He'd never been one to tolerate Howard's harping on the superiority of the Nordic race and culture-stream. Indeed, in later years he would break from Howard on this account.

"No, Mr. Altamont happens to be very much in business at this moment—in his capacity as a private consulting detective."

This revelation prompted a few exclamations of surprise and wholesale muttering from the Kalems.

"He has been engaged on a case requiring the utmost delicacy and discretion, on the behalf of a prominent English client, who wishes to remain anonymous. His investigation has brought him to America, where lies the ultimate solution to the case. He is requesting your help, as it is a matter too sensitive to confide to the official police forces. I think we should consider it the highest compliment that he deems us equal to the task. He himself will now explain the details."

Sherlock Holmes, who'd been listening calmly to Howard's introduction, rose slowly from his easy chair. His keen gray eyes darted from one face to the next, as if to measure each man's mettle with a single piercing look.

"Thank you," said the detective. "I believe everyone here knows of the notorious Red Hook section of Brooklyn, with its seedy waterfront and dilapidated warehouses? For the benefit of those who have not seen it for themselves, pray, my dear Lovecraft, could you give us a description—in just a few sentences—of this unsavory district?"

"Yes, certainly," said Howard. "Red Hook is a maze of hybrid squalor near the ancient waterfront opposite Governor's Island, with dirty highways climbing the hill from the wharves to that higher ground where the decayed lengths of Clinton and Court Streets lead off toward the Borough Hall."

You couldn't accuse HPL of whitewashing his own neighborhood, I thought.

"Some of the obscure alleys and byways have that alluring antique flavor which conventional reading leads us to call Dickensian. The population is a hopeless tangle and enigma; Syrian, Spanish, Italian, and Negro elements impinging on one another, and fragments of Scandinavian and American belts lying not far distant."

"Thank you, that will be sufficient," broke in the detective. "To speak plainly, I seek a certain master criminal who has in his possession a valuable item that rightfully belongs to my client. This man has his headquarters in a building in Parker Place in Red Hook. I have every good reason to suppose he is holding this item there, and I intend to confront him in his den, as it were, and secure its safe return—this Saturday night the twenty-third.

"With Lovecraft's guidance, I have learned a good deal about the area in the few weeks since I arrived in New York. Through unostentatious rambles, carefully casual conversations, and well-timed offers of hip pocket liquor, I have succeeded in soliciting all the background knowledge I need."

"Who is this guy you're after, if you don't mind my asking," said Leeds.

"He is Jan Martense, elegant man-about-town. Besides being a thief, he is a smuggler of illegal aliens and engages in the bootlegging trade. He also promotes a little mediumistic charlatanry on the side."

From the confused buzzing that followed this statement, I gathered no one was familiar with the name, let alone had heard of his nefarious activities.

"Much of Red Hook, houses and waterfront," continued the detective, "is underlain by a system of subterranean passages—tunnels with exits at various strategic locations. I need men to watch these potential escape routes."

For nearly a minute the group sat in stunned silence. Morton looked at Leeds; Leeds looked at Kleiner; Kleiner looked at Kirk; and Kirk looked at Loveman. (I avoided all glances.) For these men, whose most thrilling exploits consisted of browsing through second-hand bookshops and dawdling in cafeterias, this call to action must have hit hard. Here was a chance to partake in a real adventure—not just read about it in a pulp magazine or book. Had I not been already involved, I know I would have leapt at the opportunity.

"Is there any danger?" piped up old Ev McNeil.

"There might be some danger," said Sherlock Holmes. "To be fair, I cannot deny the possibility."

This admission sparked off another round of muttering.

"Weapons will not be necessary, I daresay," he continued. "I shall carry a sidearm, but I cannot recommend that any of you do so. I have gotten the goods on this chap Martense—information that should persuade him to hand over what I want without argument in exchange for my silence concerning certain criminal pursuits of his. I realize it is not easy to make a quick decision on this, and I would be more than happy to withdraw from the room while you discuss it amongst yourselves.

"I might add that I am willing to pay each man ten dollars for his services for one night's work."

The detective beckoned to Howard, and the two of them retired outside in the hall. The rest of us huddled together. Despite expressions of nervousness from some quarters, we soon reached a decision and called our companions back into the apartment.

"We're with you, Mr. Altamont, one hundred per cent," said Kleiner, speaking for the gang, "even though for some of us it will mean missing the Blue Pencil Club meeting scheduled for this Saturday. Just give us the low-down on what you want us to do."

Sherlock Holmes declared his satisfaction at our unanimous support, and then proceeded to outline the specifics of his plan:

"I have determined to pay our call on Mr. Martense in three days' time, because he will then be occupied with the transferring of a large number of aliens from a tramp steamer which recently docked in the East River—a period when he will be especially vulnerable."

The detective spread a large scale street map of Brooklyn out on Loveman's coffee table, then commenced with a red pencil to mark the positions we were to take in the vicinity of the Parker Place headquarters. Operating in pairs, each pair of Kalems would be at their respective posts by ten o'clock. Our job would be to watch for any suspicious disturbances, and if need be provide help to the team that would be descending into the underground passages. On the map Sherlock Holmes also drew in a rough network of tunnels, based on what he'd gleaned from loquacious locals. When Kleiner volunteered to provide his motor-car, which could be used for a quick getaway, our British friend readily assented.

"Very well, then," concluded the detective. "We shall all gather at my Clinton Street room early Saturday evening. Please take care to wear your oldest, cheapest clothes."

After this there was no question of settling down and resuming the usual sort of Kalem Club discussion of abstract matters—the whole gang was clearly too excited at the prospect of the forthcoming "raid." Just before breaking up, Kleiner offered to take those who were free Friday afternoon on a scouting excursion in his Ford through Red Hook. Mr. Altamont said he thought such a trip would be wise, but cautioned discretion, not to journey too far off the better-traveled streets.

I accompanied Howard and Mr. Holmes as far as my subway stop. The detective's mood definitely seemed to be sanguine.

"I have appreciated more than I can say the role you two have played so gamely," he said. "Your help has been inestimable. I cannot guarantee the success of our endeavors, but I do feel on the whole confident—confident enough to have gone ahead and booked passage back to England for late next week."

Neither Howard nor I said anything in response to this surprising news, but I'm sure he must have felt the same dismay in the light of the detective's near departure as I did.

"To speak frankly," said Sherlock Holmes in a graver tone, "I have not been wholly candid with you about the real nature of this case; but I promise you a full explanation once this is all over.

"Much yet remains ahead of us, and until then I strongly urge, Sonny, that you get plenty of rest in preparation for Saturday. We want your ardent youthful spirit to be an inspiration to us all in the coming trial. Farewell."

VII

I anticipated our expedition into Martense's Red Hook lair with a keen sense of what could only be called adventurous expectancy. When I arrived at Clinton Street that Saturday night, I found the rest of the gang all gathered in the detective's room—every Kalem suitably attired in old working clothes. In order to avoid any pointed questions from my parents (who were assuming I was attending the Blue Pencil Club meeting), I had worn my customary jacket and tie. Howard had said Mr. Holmes would once again provide whatever was required in the costume line.

The detective did in fact pull from his voluminous trunk two pairs of grubby mechanic's trousers with suspenders and two greasy plaid shirts, which Howard and I quickly donned. Thus were we transformed such that our own mothers would have been unable to distinguish us from the toughest of dockside louts. As a final touch, Sherlock Holmes applied dark make-up to the faces of all of us, to lend a swarthy cast to our white and pink skins.

"Gad, we've been turned into veritable Syrians!" exclaimed Howard.

"Our being able to pass for 'natives' may be essential to our success tonight," said our English friend.

Before the gang departed, we reviewed our instructions. Morton and Loveman would take their post outside the dance-hall church; McNeil and Kirk would cover the wharves; and Leeds and Kleiner, in Kleiner's car, would wait in an alley near Parker Place.

"Yesterday's scouting of salient landmarks was a big help," said Kleiner. "We all know where we're supposed to go."

Sherlock Holmes wished our six comrades well, and slipped each a ten-dollar bill as they left. Kleiner would drive the entire group as far as the vicinity of Parker Place, whence each twosome would walk to their respective destinations. We waited another minute while the detective finished his preparations. He slipped a pocket compass into his leather jacket, along with a flashlight, and what appeared to be a small bundle of envelopes. Finally he drew a small-caliber revolver from a bureau drawer.

"I trust we shall have no need of this, lads," he said, as he loaded the chambers, "but we must be careful to take every precaution."

The sight of the gun didn't reassure me especially, but I wasn't about to admit that I felt any fear. I was grateful enough that my older colleagues were permitting me to accompany them in the first place. On Friday Howard had called, evidently because Sherlock Holmes had had second thoughts about my role, to try to persuade me to take a lesser, safer part with the rest of the Kalems. He was worried for my parents, in case anything should happen to me. But I was adamant. Having participated in every action of consequence so far, I wasn't about to miss the climax to our efforts. All my life, owing to a congenitally weak heart, I'd been coddled. A nearly fatal acute appendicitis while at N.Y.U. a few years earlier (which had cut short my academic career) had only increased this over-solicitousness of others. For once to expose myself deliberately to some sort of physical danger—for me, with my frail health, this had an irresistible appeal.

Shortly after ten o'clock Sherlock Holmes, Howard, and I were heading south along the derelict length of Columbia Street, toward the center of Red Hook. Soon we were making our way through a cluster of monotonous squalid streets, lined with brick houses dating from the first quarter to the middle of the nineteenth century. HPL commented now and then on a particularly notable architectural feature, but for the most part we proceeded in silence.

Sherlock Holmes led us past the tumbledown stone church, where we saw Morton and Loveman loitering near the steps, among a crowd of foreigners jabbering away in some strange patois. We could hear the strains of jazz coming from the open door at the top of the steps, indicating that a dance was getting under way. We of course did not acknowledge our two friends as we passed, but I couldn't refrain from turning around for a last glimpse just before rounding the next corner—and caught them conversing with a couple of girls in gaily colored dresses.

"The church is nominally Catholic," remarked Howard, "but priests throughout Brooklyn deny the place all standing and authenticity."

After another two blocks we came to Parker Place, a dingy square of dilapidated brownstones, then walked by a side street, where we spotted Leeds and Kleiner standing next to Kleiner's Model-A. If a speedy exit from this dismal locale should prove necessary at any point, they were ready to drive off in only the time it took to turn the crank.

Presently we entered a dim, dirty alley, filled with evil-smelling garbage cans whose contents must have been ripening for weeks. The detective motioned us to stop by a pile of discarded crates, which suspiciously looked as if they had once contained liquor bottles. At Sherlock Holmes' bidding, Howard and I dismantled this heap, revealing an ancient manhole cover. Again our British comrade signaled with a bony hand, and Howard and I lifted the heavy metal disk away from the opening. The detective shined the thin beam of his flashlight into the hole, but Stygian darkness hid the bottom.

"This entrance should serve us as well as any other," he whispered. "I discovered it on one of my earlier rambles in the district."

Sherlock Holmes gingerly slipped into the hole first, followed by myself, and then Howard, who succeeded in pulling the manhole cover back into place. We didn't want to leave any trace of our entry from the inside if at all possible. The three of us climbed down perhaps a good fifteen or twenty feet, carefully clutching onto slippery iron rungs, the only illumination from the detective's feeble light.

With relief we reached a solid surface, the concrete floor of a tunnel with an arched ceiling maybe eight feet high at its apex. In the light Mr. Holmes guardedly swept about us, we could make out nitrous brick walls and stretches of rusty pipe. A rank smell left no doubt that we were in a sewer.

The detective consulted his compass, and we proceeded in Indian fashion in the same order in which we descended in a southwesterly direction. The only noises were the dripping of water and the soft scurrying of small creatures that seemed to be all around us, yet mercifully never strayed into our yellow beam.

We met with a number of intersecting passageways, and each time the detective chose without hesitation one path or another, glancing on occasion at his compass. An increasingly vile fishy odor pervaded the fetid atmosphere, suggesting we were nearing the waterfront. Behind me Howard stifled a gagging sound, and I recalled his strong aversion to seafood.

As we continued through the clammy labyrinth, we could hear the sound of human voices and footsteps—but these were very faint, as if coming from an infinite distance ahead of us. The rough brick work gave way to plastered walls, and light bulbs in overhead sockets began to appear at regular intervals, obviating the need for our artificial light. We were soon traversing a proper corridor, with open archways on either side leading to what seemed to be storage rooms. We briefly investigated two of these rooms, and found one to be an extensive wine cellar with racks filled with bottles to the ceiling and the other to contain wooden boxes stamped with Scotch whiskey labels.

The noises of human activity we had heard earlier were louder and more distinct now, and all at once it sounded as if a group of several gruff-speaking men were about to round the corner a few yards in front of us. We quickly stepped into the nearest room, which proved to be a sort of dormitory with lines of crude wooden bunk beds against the walls. Happily, this gang passed beyond our hiding place, and we remained undetected.

We resumed our progress at a more cautious pace, and took the time to explore two other rooms farther down the corridor. The first contained a printing press and a large assortment of printing paraphernalia. Stacked in neat piles on a table were cards that Sherlock Holmes identified as United States Immigration Authority health forms. The second room was furnished with desks and a blackboard, and was clearly meant to serve as a classroom. Howard picked up one of the textbooks that were scattered about—it had the title *Well Bred Speech* (if I recall correctly). What Jan Martense was up to here couldn't have been plainer.

By some miracle we encountered no one, until at last the corridor we were following opened out into a vast cavernous space and we abruptly found ourselves among a crowd of milling foreigners with dark complexions on a kind of pier or dock. Before us was an oily canal lit by flaming torches—a marvelously spectral scene that would have done justice to any tale of supernatural horror. Amazingly, we were not challenged by any of these people grunting softly among themselves in alien dialect—it was as if they were all anxiously awaiting some event, and too distracted to take notice of strangers. Or perhaps in the gloom, with our dusky faces, we weren't recognized as such.

Suddenly a ray of strong light shot through this scene of phantasms, and we heard the sound of oars amidst the low babbling. From a bend in the canal a boat with a lantern in its prow darted into sight, followed closely by a second, and then finally a third. Each made fast to an iron ring in the slimy stone pier, then poured forth its occupants—huddled masses of humanity, many of them women and children. Those on the pier helped the newcomers out—some with low shouts or exclamations of joy, as if they'd discovered a relative or friend. As soon as their living cargo were all unloaded, the row boats untied and set out again into the darkness of the canal.

Amidst the general confusion, we observed a few authoritative-looking individuals herding people into small groups, then leading them off into one or another of the side passageways. Then at once there appeared a well-dressed, debonair figure, who contrasted sharply with those in humble garb around him. He surveyed the operations for about a minute, barking an occasional order to his lieutenants (in an unintelligible tongue), and finally, seemingly satisfied, retreated towards an exit at the far end of the pier.

Sherlock Holmes nodded grimly at us both, and we immediately made bold to follow Mr. Martense; Howard and the detective instinctively adopting a kind of forward, slumping gait, in order I realized to minimize their height among the swarms of sawed-off Levantines.

We pursued Martense at a discreet distance through a series of passages. He appeared too preoccupied to notice our trailing him. In any event, parties of men were rushing about all over the place, so we were not especially conspicuous.

Plaster walls soon gave way to actual wooden panels and wainscoting, with electric-light sconces. Paintings hung on the walls, and there was carpeting on the floor. Surely we had crossed into the area of Martense's own personal apartments—the nerve center of the complex. "We must be directly beneath Parker Place," murmured Mr. Holmes, glancing at his compass.

We succeeded in following Martense into a room decorated tastefully with modern drawings and photographs that may have been an office before he turned and acknowledged us. At first he gibbered at us in a queer language that was wholly incomprehensible. When we failed to react, he frowned, then spoke in English in a genial enough tone.

"Yes, may I help you? Are you by any chance lost?"

"No, sir," said Sherlock Holmes, as he closed the door, an ancient one with antique panels, behind us. "Chance is not a factor. My friends and I have some very important business to conduct with you, Mr. Martense."

If our adversary showed any initial surprise at hearing such a rude-looking fellow speak the King's English, he quickly recovered.

"How's that? Do I detect the unmistakable voice of Mr. John Altamont? Or would you prefer that I address you by your real name, Mr. Sherlock Holmes?"

If our companion was surprised in his turn, he betrayed no sign. For a moment we all stood somewhat awkwardly, Mr. Martense stroking his moustache absentmindedly as he regarded us—three clearly by no means welcome guests—with a puzzled air.

"Shall we drop all pretenses, then?" replied the detective. "I believe you know why I am here and for what purpose."

"Yes, I do. The letters."

"Are you willing to hand them over?"

"And if I refuse?"

"I am on to your game, Martense, or rather I should say games. To begin, my colleagues and I have tonight witnessed your smuggling operations in full swing. I admit I am impressed by their scale and organization."

Martense bowed.

"Secondly—and of more immediately personal concern to you—are the mediumistic practices of Miss Cordelia Garrison. It should come as no surprise to you that in the course of the séance in which all present participated I detected the method of her cheat. An exposure in the press would be most damaging to her reputation. My associate Harry Houdini is fully prepared to join me in a campaign against her—if required."

"You appear to know a great deal about me, Mr. Holmes," said Martense. "A great deal. Perhaps too much."

"Granted these crimes, sir, I am willing to leave you alone, the law being certain to bring you to justice in the long run, if only you will return to me what rightfully belongs to another."

"Ah, sir, you can hardly expect me to produce the letters at such sudden notice."

"I think I can make such a demand," said Sherlock Holmes evenly. "I have thoroughly searched your Suydam Street mansion, which you seem to spend very little time at these days, and found nothing. Nor did I uncover anything at your Wolcott Street speakeasy. Nor would a man of your independence rely on a safe deposit box in a commercial bank. No, it has to be here—in this unlikely spot—that a secretive collector such as yourself keeps the cream of his magnificent collection."

During this exchange, I'd had the chance to study more closely the decorations and furnishings in the room. The photographs I now saw were all of famous authors—Wells, Verne, Conrad, Hardy, Kipling, Tennyson, Dickens—with autographs beneath each. A row of cases with glass tops, just like a museum, contained further manuscript and pictorial materials. Mr. Holmes' conclusion that here was where Martense kept the pride of his collection must not have been difficult to arrive at.

"Very clever, Mr. Holmes," said Martense, in a voice lacking its earlier good humor. "Yes, you stand now in my private sanctum. Here I maintain the bulk of my literary collection—almost solely for my own viewing, I might add. I assure you that fewer than a handful of educated men have entered this room besides yourselves. Perhaps eight know of its existence. I'm a very private man—much like you, my dear sir.

"I admire, too, your boldness in attempting to beard me in my own den. Don't you worry that I could have dozens of armed men in here at the touch of a buzzer? You'd have no prayer of escape."

"I have taken the precaution, Martense," answered the detective, "of placing a sizeable number of my own men at key points in the immediate district. They have orders to call in the official forces, if I and my two friends have not emerged from these burrows by midnight. A raid at this juncture could have very unfortunate results for you and your operations."

This was sheerest bluff on the part of the detective, but thankfully Martense didn't challenge it.

"Yes, I'd gotten a report that two suspicious characters were at the church. How characteristic of you, Mr. Holmes, to rely on amateurs rather than professionals."

"I have no desire to have to resort to force," said the detective. "I firmly believe we can come to terms through reasonable discussion. I judge you to be a reasonable man."

"Very kind of you to say so, sir," said Martense, and then with a certain tone of resignation: "Well, then, let's discuss this business like gentlemen. As you've observed for yourselves, tonight I have many things to attend to, but perhaps we can come to some sort of accommodation in short order. I'm sorry I can't offer you each a chair, but would any of you care for a cigar?"

Martense proffered a box of Dutch Masters, but we all declined. He took one for himself and sat down in the one chair in the room, situated behind a modern glass-topped desk. He settled back, cut off the end of the cigar with a pocket knife, lit it, and drew a couple of puffs. By this nonchalant act of taking his ease, Martense succeeded in cutting the tension somewhat.

"I wish you'd heeded my warning when you first arrived in this country, Mr. Holmes," began our reluctant host. "Oh yes, my agents got wind of your intended American voyage in London. I knew you could be crossing the Atlantic for only one purpose."

Martense sighed, petted his moustache and resumed.

"At first I meant to frighten you, so I sent a couple of my boys around to Clinton Street—to dissuade you from your quest. It appears that they didn't make the message clear—or else they were interrupted by the fortuitous appearance of Messrs. Lovecraft and Long before they could convey it properly."

Perhaps, I thought, Mr. Holmes had been in one of his distracted moods when accosted by those ruffians.

"Then I changed my mind," continued Martense. "I don't care to use violence when I don't have to—especially against such an eminent personage as yourself. I decided to wait and see how you would proceed. Let me compliment you on how well you've done in figuring out my game in these past weeks. You've done remarkably for a man of your years."

Throughout this discourse Sherlock Holmes had remained expressionless. If he was feeling any discomfiture, he didn't show it.

"You should realize, Mr. Holmes, that I'm one of your greatest admirers. A most devoted fan of your adventures. Possessing these letters of yours to the late Irene Adler 'of dubious and questionable memory,' so revealing of that passionate side of your nature that your loyal biographer has so brilliantly concealed, gives me supreme satisfaction. They are the crown jewels of my collection."

My mouth nearly dropped a foot at this stunning revelation. I began to feel acutely embarrassed, and dared not look at Howard.

"Rest assured that I would never in a thousand years reveal the existence, let alone the contents, of these most sensitive epistles. It is in the mere possession of them, the fact that I am one of the very few persons in the world who is privy to their secret—in this lies my joy. To share the knowledge would only diminish the pleasure. What the world would give to know! But the world will never know. Please believe me when I say that I have no wish to tarnish that austere image of the cold, perfect reasoner for posterity."

Sherlock Holmes had gone quite pale, and a slight tremor may have seized his limbs, but with a sudden effort he steadied himself and spoke.

"Yes, yes, that's all very well," he said huskily. "I appreciate your gesture of discretion. But, to get back to the main point, will you return the letters? Their sentimental value to me is incalculable."

"I understand your impatience, Mr. Holmes. I confess your threat of exposure does present problems. If it were a matter of me alone, it might not matter so much. But someone else is involved—my bride, Miss Garrison."

For an instant I considered offering my congratulations, but I kept quiet.

"Cordelia and I are to be married in a quiet ceremony tomorrow afternoon at my family's old Dutch church in Flatbush. Thence we will depart on a Cunard Liner for our honeymoon. As my wife, she will no longer practice her arts as a medium. She's retiring entirely from the business, so you'll have nothing to fear on that score.

"As for the liquor trade, I don't plan to wind it down at any time soon. If that tribe of bluenoses, prigs, and old women hadn't snuck the Volstead Act through Congress while we red-blooded men were in France fighting the Hun ... Well, maybe someday this country will come to its senses and repeal this crazy law and I'll be out of business."

I wondered what HPL was thinking of Martense's pronouncements on Prohibition and the World War. His attempt to enlist in the army in 1917 had been thwarted by his mother, who had gotten him disqualified from the Rhode Island National Guard on the grounds of his chronic ill health. This was an episode that my friend didn't care to talk about.

"At least you have to give me credit," continued Martense, "for importing the genuine article. That's real Scotch whiskey in those crates. You can't accuse me of cooking up and poisoning people with home brew."

Home Brew, the magazine that ran Howard's "Herbert West—Reanimator" and "The Lurking Fear" before he discovered *Weird Tales.* Funny how such idle thoughts hit one in the most dire circumstances.

"As for the human cargo you've no doubt beheld during your tour, neither is my traffic in this commodity easily ended. Until our lawmakers relent on this ridiculous quota system set up by the Johnson Act . . . In this department, gentlemen, you must grant that I've done some good. Can you blame me for trying to help these poor souls, driven by prejudice and poverty from their native lands, only to run up against our discriminatory racial quotas? The Statue of Liberty should cover her face and lower her torch in shame!"

This reference struck a personal chord. My grandfather, Charles O. Long, had been the building contractor to construct the pedestal of the Statue of Liberty. He'd served as its superintendent for many years.

"Here in this underground way-station," said Martense, waxing grandiloquent, "I see to it that they receive some medical care, the rudiments of an education—in particular instruction in English—in short, the basics to get a fair start in this country. Our church building serves as a social center. Need I remind you, sirs, that we are a nation of immigrants, and it behooves us whose ancestors were among the first settlers (as mine were in this city) not to begrudge a chance to those who've come later, whatever their race or color or religion.

"Of course, there's a bit of profit to be made in all this, but it's been off lately and it's unlikely that I'll continue in this line indefinitely."

Howard may have been on the verge of responding with his opinions on these matters, judging from the almost apoplectic expression on his face, but Sherlock Holmes held up a restraining hand. He was evidently fast losing patience with Martense, though for other reasons.

"Yes, come, come, Mr. Martense, these are commendable sentiments," said the detective, "but are you going to give me the letters or not?" He moved his hand toward the pocket with the revolver.

"Ah, well," said Martense. He sighed again. "I concede. I'll freely give you what you want. If you can hold on a second longer, I'll get them for you."

He put down the butt of his cigar, got up from his chair, and went over to one of the museum cases. He opened the door of the cabinet beneath, revealing the door of a safe. After a few deft turns of the tumbler, the door swung open and Martense withdrew a thick packet of yellowed envelopes, secured with a faded violet ribbon.

"Here you are, Mr. Holmes," he said, handing them over. The detective quickly riffled through the pack, seeming to count, then pulled one letter from its envelope as if to verify the contents. He shook his head with a satisfied nod.

"Thank you, Mr. Martense, for your cooperation," said Sherlock Holmes. "I am much touched by your magnanimity." While this last remark had its grudging edge, I sensed an underlying tone of sincerity.

"Now, gentlemen, if you'll pardon me, but I have a little more work here to see to before I go home. Must be fresh for one's wedding day, after all."

Martense rose, ushered us out into the corridor, through a door that opened into a basement, and then up a flight of what one might describe as "evilly worn" stairs to a shabby parlor room. There a couple of seedy-looking fellows, stationed by the front door, eyed us with ill-concealed disdain. Martense grunted a few foreign syllables at them, as if to explain our unexpected presence. Most non-alien guests, it would seem, entered the premises through this dingy room.

"I imagine you'll be able to locate your friends somewhere nearby," said Martense as he held open the door for us. "Good night." He didn't wait for our acknowledgment, but turned away and abruptly shut the door behind us.

"Come, let us not waste any time, in case Mr. Martense should have a change of heart," said Sherlock Holmes. The three of us scurried across the dismal stretch of Parker Place, proceeding in the gloom until we emerged into some slightly less oppressive thoroughfare. We paused to catch our breath in the damp spring night air, so welcome after the fetid vapors of the unwholesome Tartarus we'd lately quitted.

"Pray, my dear friends, please keep to yourselves the nature of the highly personal revelations you have heard tonight," said the detective. "I do not feel the other Kalems need be informed of the identity of my 'client'—only of our success in retrieving what we set out for."

Howard and I swore we'd never tell a soul. We resumed our rapid pace, and shortly we entered the street where Leeds and Kleiner were waiting by the Ford. Our comrades greeted us heartily, and we assured them that all had gone well as we scrambled into the car. Kleiner gave the crank a couple of turns and we were off. First we drove to the wharf region where we picked up McNeil and Kirk, who reported having seen rowboats plying from a freighter moored about a quarter-mile away in the channel to the wharves—and disappearing underneath them! We filled in the gang on the course of our adventures, leaving out only certain details of our interview with Jan Martense. As we approached the area of the dance-hall church, our last stop in Red Hook, I realized that we were going to have a tight fit. Kleiner's Ford would resemble, with all of us stuffed in, one of those crazy vehicles out of the comedies of the Keystone Kops. The "Keystone Kalems," I thought, in the jubilation of the moment.

But as we coasted to a halt near the dance-hall church, Morton and Loveman were nowhere in sight. "Where the deuce could they be?" muttered Sherlock Holmes. With some difficulty he opened the car door and clambered out onto the sidewalk.

"Want one of us to go inside with you and get them, Mr. Altamont?" asked Kirk, leaning out the window.

At that moment, however, our two missing comrades sauntered out from the entrance to the church, each with a pretty girl on his arm. The girls were giggling.

"Hello there!" cried Morton, waving in cheery fashion. "Is it time to go? The band's just starting up again. Give us another minute."

"Good Lord, are they fool enough—" sputtered the detective. What further he might have said about Morton and Loveman's laxity on the job will never be known, because suddenly a mob of toughs swept out from around the far side of the church, headed straight for our car. Mr. Holmes swiftly drew out his revolver—but his grip wasn't secure (we watched for agonizing seconds while he fumbled with the weapon) and the horde was upon him before he or any of us could react.

The efforts of Leeds, Kleiner, Kirk, McNeil, Howard, and myself to struggle out of the cramped confines of the vehicle to rush to our British friend's aid proved in the event futile, for we were almost immediately surrounded by a bevy of ruffians who blocked our exit at both doors and shook menacing fists through the windows. Fortunately, they made no attempt to force the doors or break the windows, evidently content to keep us penned in while their fellows dealt with Mr. Holmes. A surging mass of bodies, glimpsed in patches near the hood of the Model-A, gave us hope that the detective was putting up some sort of valiant fight, despite the overwhelming odds. Loveman and Morton and their companions had disappeared from the top of the church steps, but whether they had joined in the fray outside or fled inside the church no one could tell.

Suddenly, a shot went off close at hand, then a whole series of shots in quick succession—at some indeterminate distance.

"This is the police. Put down your arms!" yelled a commanding voice.

At this welcome cry the gang of toughs scattered, apparently unarmed and unwilling to confront this new and formidable adversary. Perhaps also, I thought with a sickening feeling, they had reclaimed their prize from Sherlock Holmes. We all tumbled out of the Ford, now that the siege was lifted, anxious to attend to our fallen friend.

"My God, Mr. Altamont's been hit!" croaked Leeds, who was the first to reach the crumpled form of the detective, lying unconscious on the pavement. "He's bleeding from the head!"

As we huddled over Mr. Holmes, a tall, heavily built man with a smoking pistol cocked warily in his hand came around the front of the car. Morton and Loveman, bereft of their lady friends, appeared from the direction of the church. "What's going on here? Everyone all right?" asked the man, who was dressed in nondescript civilian clothes.

"Our buddy's been shot, mister," quaked Ev McNeil.

Our deliverer regarded us closely and hesitated, as if unsure whether to trust us or not. Our pleading looks must have persuaded him we weren't about to jump him, because he tucked his pistol inside his coat and crouched down to examine the detective. We waited anxiously for his verdict.

"He'll be okay—it's only a flesh wound—though he'll have a nasty bump and a killing headache when he comes to," said the man. "I suggest you get him to a hospital without delay in any case. You can't be too careful, an old geezer like him with a concussion."

Under this authoritative man's direction, Leeds, Kirk, Loveman, and I gently hoisted the limp frame of Sherlock Holmes off the street and into the backseat of the Model-A.

"Say, what's this?" exclaimed the heavily built man, who'd been poking around the gutter and now held up by the end of the barrel a familiar-looking revolver. He sniffed at it. "This .38's just been fired. Is this your friend's?"

None of us denied it. With a sad heart I realized Mr. Holmes had been wounded by his own gun.

"Wait, there's something else down here, too," he continued. He picked up what at first appeared to be a small bundle of papers, but when revealed in the light of the Ford's headlamp turned out to be—to my inexpressible joy—a packet of letters tied with a dirty violet ribbon.

"Ahem, I'll look after those, if you don't mind," said HPL, almost snatching the packet out of the man's grasp. He gave Howard a hard look, then simply shrugged.

"Okay, buddy," he said, "but I think I'll hold on to the .38 for the time being. Take it easy, I'm acting unofficially here—I'm not out to make trouble for you boys. But I would be curious to hear what happened, if you'd be kind enough to give me a ride out of Red Hook—on the way to the hospital. I can show you the way to the nearest one."

Again, we didn't argue with the man's request. Somehow we all squeezed into the Model-A, which Kleiner had gotten started while we had settled "Mr. Altamont" in the back. With relief we were at last on our way out of Red Hook.

"I appreciate the lift," said our new friend, who soon showed himself to be entirely agreeable. "I've spent more than enough time hanging around this Godforsaken slum for one night." In this sentiment I heartily concurred.

"But tell me, purely off the record understand, what were you guys doing outside Red Hook's infamous dance-hall church, dressed up like foreigners? At first I figured you were rum-runners, run afoul of a rival gang—but from talking to you I know you aren't. You all speak regular American, and I bet that's greasepaint smeared on your faces. What gives?"

Credit must go to Loveman for thinking up a halfway credible story in reply. He explained that we had disguised ourselves in order to crash the dance at the church. As white men, we would have been unwelcome outsiders. As it was, regrettably, some of the males at the dance had seen through our deception, and because they didn't like us messing with their women had been trying to persuade us to leave when our deliverer had arrived on the scene.

"Lower-class gals, especially if they're of Latin or Mediterranean or some other dark-skinned type, can be very attractive," commented Morton. "I've heard a lot of the swells like to hang out at the dime-a-dance dives and meet the tarts. One of our most noted young critics, in fact, makes it a habit—"

"Please, Morton," interrupted Howard, "this sort of sordid talk we can do without. We haven't yet found out what our rescuer was doing tonight—indeed, sir, we don't even know your name."

"The name's Mahoney," the man replied. "Detective Thomas F. Mahoney. I'm an undercover cop from out of state—on special assignment. I can tell you no more than that I'm investigating certain criminal activities centered in the Red Hook district."

*

Without incident we reached Brooklyn Hospital, guided also by Howard, who'd gotten to know the place well from his frequent visits there the year before when Sonia was hospitalized with her nervous trouble. We checked in the still unconscious Sherlock Holmes under the name of John Altamont. Detective Mahoney flashed his badge and assured the on-duty nurse that our patient had injured himself accidentally while cleaning his gun. There would be no legal complications. Howard thanked him for covering for us, and Detective Mahoney said he would keep in touch and gave Howard his card, marked with a Brooklyn address.

Howard and I elected to wait until we received definite word on Sherlock Holmes' condition, while the rest of the Kalems and our new detective friend left for their respective homes in Kleiner's motor-car. In less than an hour of restless waiting we heard that all was well—the patient was in a state approaching normal sleep.

"I'm afraid you'll have to pick up your own clothes another time," said HPL at the entrance to the subway station near Borough Hall where he was leaving me off. "I don't have a key to Holmes' room."

"My parents will have been long in bed by the time I sneak in," I said. "I'll be able to change and wash up before they see me."

"As for bed, I feel as if I could sleep a week! At least I can retire with the satisfaction of our ultimate victory, however near-run a thing it was. Gawdelpus, what a night! You know, Belknapius, I'd hate to see any of the letters I wrote to Sonia fall into the wrong hands.[3] I'll call you when and if I ever wake up. So long, Kidlet!"

For a few moments before descending to the platform I watched the lean figure of my friend hasten in jerky strides toward Clinton Street. His energy was truly extraordinary. I myself was exhausted, both physically and emotionally—there'd been many shocks in the past several hours. And yet I, too, felt cause to be pleased by the results of our labors. Little could I imagine as I rattled back to Manhattan on an empty IRT car how short-lived our triumph would prove.

VIII

I stayed in bed most of Sunday, taking my meals on a tray while propped up with pillows. Confused and uncomfortable thoughts troubled me as I could not help but reflecting on last night's astonishing revelation regarding the private life of Sherlock Holmes. My parents concluded that the Blue Pencil meeting must have been especially heated, their son a victim to strain brought on by too intense debate.

Monday I felt much improved both in body and spirit—well enough to read some Swinburne and even attempt to write a poem myself. Late in the morning the 'phone rang, and my mother called from the hall to say that Howard was on the line and did I feel well enough to speak with him. Of course, I sprang out from under the bedclothes and rushed to seize the receiver, eager to hear how my friend was faring in the wake of our adventure.

"Frank, I've got some bad news," choked Howard, his agitation evident in every syllable. "While I slept my dressing-room alcove was entered, either through the door to the next room or through the door by someone having a key; and all my suits except the thin blue, my Flatbush overcoat, a wicker suitcase of Sonia's and Loveman's radio material have been stolen! This would be devastating enough, but whoever it was also

---

3. After their divorce in 1929, Sonia destroyed HPL's letters to her—a trunkful. [Editor's note]

took the old jacket of Holmes' I was wearing—with the packet of letters still in the pocket. Heaven alone knows what I'm going to tell him!"

HPL's description of this catastrophe hit me like a bucket of cold water in the face. What a blow! All I could get out in response were a few strangled words of general sympathy.

"Maybe they were petty thieves who didn't realize the value of what they inadvertently took," I offered lamely.

"Let's hope so, Sonny, and not the long arm of Jan Martense at work; but I fear the worst. Though what he could want with my wardrobe Nyarlathotep only knows."

To clothe his arriving aliens? I wondered—but didn't voice the opinion.

"And to top it all off," continued Howard, "I read a notice in this morning's Brooklyn *Eagle* of Martense's wedding. He was leaving today on his honeymoon—three months in South America."

I couldn't think what to say to this.

"Well, I was going to walk over to the hospital now to visit Holmes anyway. If he's in any kind of shape to bear the shock, I'll have to tell him. To Hades with everything. I'm so sick I could curse the atmosphere blue!"

Four days later I saw the great fictional detective for the final time, in the company of Howard on the Cunard pier shortly before embarkation for the return voyage to England. Our small party, though not as demonstrative in our farewells as other groups of well-wishers, was no less emotionally charged. Sherlock Holmes was dressed in a smart herringbone suit, which hung loosely on his gaunt and stooped frame. He seemed almost to have aged another decade since my last view of him, and yet the spark in his gray eyes remained undimmed. A cloth cap covered much of the bandage at the side of his head. The wound was healing nicely, and the doctor had given his consent to travel.

"Once again, Holmes, I apologize," said Howard. "If only I had taken more care . . ."

"Please, my dear fellow, please," protested the detective, raising a narrow, claw-like hand. "You must not blame yourself. You did your best on the behalf of a vain old man. Indeed, you have done better than you know. I may have been humbled by a few physical knocks, but I have not—not, I say —been defeated."

So saying, Sherlock Holmes smiled and withdrew from his suitcoat a packet of letters a packet of letters tied with a violet ribbon!

"O, Gawd, O Montreal!" cried Howard.

"Are those . . . are those *the* letters, Mr. Holmes?" I stammered.

"Yes, these are the letters—the real letters," said our friend, as he slipped them back out of sight, with a furtive glance at the surrounding crowd. "I have after all collected the final and decisive trick. Game and match are mine."

"But how . . . what?" said HPL, clearly still as much at a loss as I was.

"Pray accept once more my apologies, but I did warn you that I had not informed you of every detail of my plot. Before departing England, I took the precaution of preparing a counterfeit set of the purloined epistles, in case opportunity should present itself for effecting a discreet switch with the genuine letters. Hence they were among the items I brought with me the evening of our Red Hook jaunt.

"In the event, as you witnessed, I never had to make recourse to this ruse. I was carrying both packets on my person at the time I so foolishly was drawn into that scuffle outside the dance-hall church; and it was only by the sheerest good fortune that the bogus bundle fell into the street and not the other with it. (You can imagine my relief when upon regaining consciousness in hospital I was able to search my clothes and ascertain that at least the real letters were in my possession.) I daresay, Lovecraft, that Martense's henchmen observed you retrieve the letters, and accordingly Martense arranged for their uninvited visit to your rooms the following night.

"I like to think that he had no time to examine the letters carefully after their 'return' to him. Perhaps, preoccupied as he surely was with his imminent honeymoon, he gave them no more than a cursory look. Still and all, as the immortal Capablanca has said, the good player is always lucky."

If Sherlock Holmes seemed pleased with himself, Howard's long expression indicated that he was in no mood to rejoice.

"Forgive me, Lovecraft, for not telling you before this moment, but I had to assume Martense's agents continued to have us all under close surveillance; even now on this teeming dockside his men may be watching. Had I revealed the happy fate of the actual letters to you, I daresay you would have been hard pressed to maintain a suitably downcast countenance until such time as I had recovered. Any hint of the true state of affairs may have aroused suspicion, and I simply lacked the strength to do battle from my sickbed in case they elected to call upon me.

"And, too, you must allow an old showman the pleasure of one final, grand deception. It is usual that the audience comes away all the more satisfied for having been so thoroughly mystified."

Howard declined to comment on this remark. Possibly sensing HPL's discomfiture, Mr. Holmes made haste to change the subject.

"As for the deeper issue of how I came to write these letters, I believe I owe you at least a general explanation. Again forgive me if I am not too specific. Some memories are painful, and time grows short. As a young man, just about your age, Frank, I was a dashing rake; and it is only thanks to Dr. Watson's discretion and concern for my image before the public that this phase of my career has been suppressed. After the fire of my youthful ardor burnt itself out, I led a life of exemplary moral virtue—with only an occasional lapse into licentiousness. Once on a previous American assignment, I admit to you with no little shame but few regrets, I seduced a pretty young married woman, a Yankee of old New England stock, she assured me. This was late in 1889, as I recall. She said her husband was a traveling salesman away a great deal from home—whom she suspected of consorting with the basest sorts of her sex. I think she was swayed to submit as much by a desire for revenge as by my manly charms. But that is another story, and I ramble on."

From his jacket the detective withdrew two envelopes, and gave one to each of us. "Here, some small compensation for your services. Perhaps not quite as generous as I would like to be, but then I had not anticipated hospital expenses. If nothing else, I imagine this episode might provide material for a new story for *Weird Tales*."

"I have to say I've been giving it some thought—'The Red Hook Horror,' or some such," said Howard, perking up slightly.

"But, mind you, do not make it too closely autobiographical. Pray leave out the character of the ridiculous old detective, if you please."

Sherlock Holmes shook our hands for the last time, said good-bye, and tottered up the gangway. When he reached the top he turned and lifted his cap, a last bow before disappearing inside the giant vessel. A whistle sounded; remaining passengers hurried to board. The boat would soon be easing out of its berth.

We opened our envelopes. The sum of money in mine was not overly generous, just as the detective had confessed. From Howard's long face and slackened jaw I could tell his share was not going to cover the cost of replacing his suits.

"Eheu, fugaces" said Howard with stoic resignation. "Kirk has offered me a temporary job addressing envelopes; he's letting me have his entire stock of envelopes with his old address. And maybe that assistant curator job with Morton will come through, the gods of Pegāna willing."

"Did you by chance get Mr. Holmes to investigate your robbery?" I asked, as we wandered away from the pier.

"Ah, Belknap, I didn't have the heart to trouble the old gent about it, occupied as he was as soon as he was released from the hospital with packing up both his Manhattan and Brooklyn abodes. I did, however, get in touch with Detective Mahoney, who's been by for a look—though he could discover no clues. He's a bright fellow for a Mick, a Dublin University man."

Reminded of his recent grievous loss, Howard began to speak of his plans for the culprit.

"If I ever catch the —— —— thief, why by ——, I'll smash his —— —— —— with one fist whilst I pulverize his —— —— —— —— with the other, meanwhile kicking him posteriorly with both feet in their most pointed shoes and manner!—i.e. if I catch him."

"Do you think you'll actually write a story based on our adventures with Mr. Holmes?" I asked, to deflect my friend from these painful ruminations on revenge.

"Yes, I think I might. I've been reading an article on witch cults and devil worship in the *Encyclopaedia Britannica* which could provide a potent background. I suppose I could change a few names, make up a real 'hero' for the thing, throw in some lurid supernatural colouring . . .

"But I'm not ready to hit ole Farnie with a hell-raiser of mine just yet. For now I must persist with more mundane grubbing to keep this wreck animated. I promised Kirk I'd show up at his shop an hour ago. Well, back to the —— —— envelope addressing!"

Afterword

Robert Bloch

It's always pleasant to read about old friends, and surely Frank Long, H. P. Lovecraft, and Sherlock Holmes are friends of mine—even though I've only met Long on a few occasions, knew HPL solely through correspondence, and haven't set eyes on Sherlock Holmes in years.

But I'm glad to learn of their exploits together, and further gratified by how accurately the author has succeeded in capturing the individual essence of their diverse and complex personalities.

I'm further intrigued by the introduction of the late Harry Houdini in this account, though if you'll permit a small cavil, I'm inclined to question the rendition of his speech.

From two people who knew him personally—the late Buster Keaton, whose acquaintance extended back to his babyhood in vaudeville and medicine-shows, and my own mother, who visited with him in Milwaukee at the home of mutual friends during the 1905–1916 period—I learned that Houdini was not a polished or erudite speaker. His stage dialogue was memorized and his writing (as in the case of "Imprisoned with the Pharaohs") was almost invariably ghosted or "touched-up" by editorial hands. He did read extensively and his library of magic is, of course, famous in prestidigitous circles. But Houdini himself was a man of limited formal education. Like many of his "show biz" contemporaries, he picked up and used—or misused—any number of scholarly phrases and developed an impressive professional *persona*, reflecting his keen intellect. Nonetheless, he frequently fell victim to the grammatical lapses of one whose childhood had been spent in a household where a foreign language was spoken. One recalls the famous anecdote of his attendance at a séance where the medium obligingly summoned up the spirit of his dead mother, who conversed with Houdini for some time. Asked if he had any questions for her he said, "Yes, only one. When did you learn to speak English?"

Houdini himself did speak English; it's just that his ordinary mode of communication sometimes betrayed his lack of schooling. Of course most people judge him by "his" writings and "his" stage pronounce-ments and lectures, so in that sense he is accurately portrayed here.

And this—like the story itself—is part of the magic.

Discarded Prologue

As a devotee of H. P. Lovecraft, the greatest American fantasy and horror writer since Edgar Allan Poe, I knew within a few months of settling in New York City that I had to meet Frank Belknap Long and get the real lowdown on what it had been like to be the Providence master's best friend. I have to admit that when I moved from my parents' home in New England to Manhattan's Upper West Side early in the summer of 1975, I had no notion that Frank Long was still around, let alone living just a few dozen blocks south of my apartment at 89th Street and West End Avenue. In fact, I'd largely forgotten the question of his existence until the historic First World Fantasy Convention, which I'd decided to attend quite on impulse after seeing mention of it later that fall in a letter to the *New York Times* travel section. While checking in at the registration desk at noon that Saturday, November 1, at the Holiday Inn in Providence, Rhode Island, I chanced to notice that the slight, white-haired old gentleman with wispy goatee registering beside me was pinning to his gabardine lapel a name tag marked . . . Frank B. Long.

I was too diffident that memorable weekend to introduce myself to this living legend, perhaps rather as HPL declined to approach Lord Dunsany after hearing him lecture in Boston in 1919; but on several occasions, including his interview by French radio, I hovered nearby in the milling crowds of fans and observed with awe as he hobnobbed with other luminaries of the fantasy field—tall, spade-bearded L. Sprague de Camp; jovial Robert Bloch; folksy Manly Wade Wellman; and self-effacing Joseph Payne Brennan. The formidable red-haired woman, who seemed to be in constant attendance, I eventually learned, was his wife.

I listened enthralled to the "Lovecraft the Man" panel Sunday morning—especially to Frank's reminiscences of the friend he had known probably better than anybody for the final fifteen years of HPL's life. More than any event during that magic weekend this panel brought home to me the sense of my literary idol as a real man, as someone who had passed on not all that long ago and whose spirit so poignantly pervaded the proceedings. Garnering the fact somewhere along the line that Frank still lived in his native New York, I resolved to seek him out soon after returning to the city. I also made a point of buying in the Huckster Room the Panther paperback edition of *The Hounds of Tindalos,* containing such classic Long tales as the title story, "The Space-Eaters," and "A Visitor from Egypt."

I did not, as it turned out, try to make contact with FBL immediately after the convention. Then I received my copy of Frank's memoir, *Howard Phillips Lovecraft: Dreamer on the Nightside* (which sadly hadn't been available in time for the convention). I read eagerly such delightful anecdotes as his first meeting with HPL at Sonia Greene's in Brooklyn, HPL's buying a hat, buying a pen, visiting the Cloisters, visiting the Woods Hole Oceanographic Institute, where HPL signed his name in the guest book "Edgar Poe," and many more tantalizing tidbits. I gained especially an appreciation for the very neighborhood I was now living in. The Long family had had their apartment at 100th and West End, where HPL had frequently been a visitor. He and Frank had roamed lovely Riverside Park, had sat on its benches and gazed at sunsets over the Hudson, just as I was doing. The site of the farmhouse where Poe worked on "The Raven" (as described in HPL's "Homes and Shrines of Poe") was at the corner of 84th Street and Broadway. I toured the Nicholas Roerich Museum, a favorite landmark of Lovecraft's near the Longs', though it had been moved since his time to a building a few blocks away from its original location. In my walks along West End Avenue and Riverside Drive, little changed I'm sure from earlier days, I think I succeeded in capturing a heady sense of the mood of that halcyon era fifty years ago, when HPL and his young protégé strode these same streets. My resolve to get in touch with FBL was once more strong.

Since the convention I had been corresponding with renowned Lovecraft scholar Dirk Mosig, whom I had not been shy to approach, and in one letter he said he'd written Frank Long about me. All I had to do was give him a call and arrange a rendezvous. I flattered myself that he would be almost as pleased to meet me as I would be to meet him. After all, with a senior honors essay from Stanford and an M.A. thesis from Brown both on HPL, I was certainly a cut above the average fan. When, however, I tried the phone number Dirk had supplied me, I got a recording saying the number had been disconnected. Since no new one was given, I was temporarily thwarted.

About two weeks later I made a trip to the Science Fiction Shop on Eighth Avenue in the Village, to buy a copy of *Marginalia* that I'd spotted on a previous visit for $80. This early Arkham House edition of secondary Lovecraftiana wasn't in the best of condition, but it was a rarity that I had felt I'd better grab while I had the chance. As I left the store, it occurred to me that I was probably only a ten-minute walk or so from Frank's address in the West Twenties. Why not pay a surprise call on the venerable author? It was a beautiful spring morning, and I was in an impulsive mood.

In response to my ring of the Long buzzer at his building on West 21st Street, there appeared after a minute on the stoop the frail figure of Frank Belknap Long, dressed in threadbare bathrobe and ratty slippers. As we shook hands, I introduced myself and reminded him of Dirk's writing about me. Frank nodded. As a conversation starter, I showed him my recent purchase. "Oh, yes," he said, perking up, "one of Howard's first books published by Arkham House." (He quaintly pronounced it "Awkum.") "I paid $3.50 or thereabouts for it when it came out. Now I'd say a copy without the jacket like yours would fetch as high as thirty-five or forty dollars." After a pause Frank explained that he was halfway through writing a novel to order for a paperback house, and since it was due in thirty-six hours he had to get back to it. In any case, his wife wasn't feeling well. We parted with assurances that we'd get together soon.

A month after this auspicious introduction, I managed to set up our first dinner engagement, which took some doing since we were communicating by postcard. I had made it clear that it would be my treat. Though I extended the invitation to include his wife, Lyda, she declined to join us—nor did she ever on any future occasion. Over a period of almost a year Frank and I must have met nearly a half-dozen times, usually at one of the unpretentious little restaurants along Eighth or Ninth Avenues. We were especially fond of Italian places. While FBL was prone to long spells of silence, during which fiddling with his pipe might be his only sign of consciousness, he could, with sufficient prodding and frequent refills of his wine glass (no teetotaler he like his pal HPL), become quite garrulous. Whenever he spoke of HPL and their times together I'd listen utterly entranced.

One evening, having lured FBL to my apartment with the promise of a succulent spaghetti dinner (with my own special homemade sauce), I was bold enough to tell him that I'd been a bit disappointed by *Dreamer on the Nightside* (which, incidentally, he'd been kind enough to inscribe for me during our last get-together). As much as I'd enjoyed the assorted anecdotes concerning his adventures with HPL, I felt certain there had to be more to it; he had to be holding something back. I'll admit that I came close to bullying the old boy as I ushered him into my most comfortable living-room chair and poured him another glass of Chianti. For a moment I feared that the blank expression coming over his face (to which by now I was well accustomed) indicated that his mind was soaring Randolph Carter–like in spheres beyond the mundane waking world we know.

"Young man," said Frank at last, returned to earth, "you aren't the only one who has accused me of not divulging all that I might have. At the time some critics complained that much of what I wrote wasn't really to the point. You have to understand that I didn't intend to write a comprehensive biography, like Sprague in his book, you see. I was only recording certain, selected impressions of Howard, best as I could recall—trying to get across my unique view of him, particularly during his so-called 'New York exile' period. I wasn't taking a conventional approach."

Frank stopped to tamp his pipe, and again I thought I was losing him to dreamland. I repeated my query for him to reveal some hitherto unknown anecdote. Eventually, a smile animated his face, and he resumed.

"Now that you mention it, there is one incident that springs to mind from that long ago era which I'd almost forgotten. You may find it of interest. It sheds light on the genesis of 'The Horror at Red Hook'—not one of HPL's best tales, I'll grant you, not a masterpiece like 'The Shunned House,' but important nonetheless for its autobiographical implications. It puts those dark days for the dreamer on the nightside in a somewhat different perspective.

"Of course, at the time, you see, all of us involved were sworn to secrecy. But as I grow older, I feel more and more like getting it off my chest. Everyone's gone now anyway who had any part in it, and I believe a certain fifty-year copyright is about due to expire, so I guess there'd be no harm in telling you."

At this enticing statement, I drew my chair nearer and put the Chianti bottle at the ready in case my guest showed any signs of faltering.

"Yes, it's really a very interesting tale, and it involves some famous names of the day, people I'm sure even you'd have heard of. It would have made a pretty good fictional story, but I just never had the energy to get around to putting it on paper. Never mind that now at my age . . . Here, let me have another half glass, young fella. Not too much thanks, I have to be alert on the subway ride home."

And so with not overly many interruptions to refill pipe and try to light it, Frank Belknap Long proceeded to narrate the following extraordinary tale concerning HPL and the Lovecraft circle and events in New York City more than fifty years before. As soon as he'd concluded, around midnight, and I'd whisked him out the door, I sat down at my desk and rapidly wrote out a rough transcription of all the wonders I had heard. I finished towards dawn.

In the final version I have made no attempt to retain FBL's inimitable style of speech, nor mimic his distinctive prose style. The language is my own; the substance is his. Any lapses of literary competence or errors of fact are mine.

As for whether he'll grant me permission to publish this account—well, that's an issue to take up with him another evening, perhaps over another spaghetti dinner and bottle of wine.

Episode of *Pulptime*

Since the publication in 1984 of *Pulptime,* that *Singular Adventure of Sherlock Holmes, H. P. Lovecraft, and the Kalem Club, as if Narrated by Frank B. Long, Jr.,* more than one fan has asked about a sequel. At last I have further news of the old gang—though in all fairness it is not a full-length follow-up but only a pendant, as it were, to *Pulptime.* Recently, while preparing a personal memoir of the late Frank Belknap Long (who I like to think regarded me in his dotage as his favorite "adopted grandson"), I came across some notes from a meeting we had in 1985 or '86 that show I succeeded in coaxing the venerable pulp-meister into adding to his earlier tale. While I may have had some idea of writing them up at the time, I must have gotten distracted by other projects and eventually forgot their existence. I fear my memory is not what it used to be now that I am almost as advanced in years as the Old Gent himself when his shade shambled off to join Holmes and Watson in "some fantastic limbo for the children of the imagination—or for imaginative child-like authors," to paraphrase Conan Doyle.

As my forthcoming memoir will reveal, getting together with Frank Long at this period was a challenge. He had no phone and with diminished health could not escape from his cave-like apartment as readily as when I first cultivated his acquaintance. When visiting him at home, one had to brave the invective-breathing dragon that demanded attention in the form of full, undivided attention to herself before granting access to her "Frankele." On this particular occasion I had the foresight to bring along a magic potion—a bottle of vodka—that served to speed me past the threshold into the far den, where the Lord of Partridgeville presided over his treasure horde, a lifetime's accumulation of clunky statuettes and parchment-like testimonials, on his wheelchair throne.

We exchanged the usual pleasantries—about sex, religion, and politics—before I dared broach the sensitive subject that was uppermost on my mind.

"You know, Frank," I said, "readers of my novella have been wondering whether you and Howard and the other Kalems had any more adventures with Sherlock Holmes."

"They can keep wondering—we only had the one adventure."

"Maybe Howard went to Quebec in 1933 to rendezvous with Holmes, who was on a secret mission."

"No, I tell you! Sherlock Holmes returned to England in 1925. He never saw America again. And Howard never went overseas."

"Are you sure?"

"Of course I'm sure! What do you take me for, an idiot?" Then, in a softer tone: "On the other hand, if Howard did go to Quebec on a secret mission, he might not have said anything. He never invited me to join him on his travels, you see. Probably thought I wasn't energetic enough to keep up. I was recovering from a near-fatal heart attack or appendicitis or whatever it was that gave me an excuse to stay home and not work for a living."

"Getting back to *Pulptime* . . ."

"Look here, about your book," Frank declared. "I've found a few more errors. In the first chapter you make it sound as if I was telling the tale soon after the events I was describing, then in another chapter you make it sound as it was long afterwards."

"Well, you know if you hadn't been so kind as to write a foreword, I might've used my original prologue, which would've made clear that you were looking back from the present."

"You said 'last year' when you should've said 'the year before' or 'a year earlier.'"

"Yeah, you're right. I myself noticed only the other day how I'd screwed up the time frame, thereby confusing my editor. In the séance chapter he turned your comment about J. B. Rhine's thirties E.S.P. experiments into a footnote, so I sound like the credulous one, not you."

"You can always correct it in the second printing."

"Uh, the second printing just came out."

"Say, what do you mean I'm the credulous one?"

This seemed like a good moment to offer Frank some vodka. I excused myself and went in search of the guardian of the House of Long, whom I found snoring in her bathtub. Without disturbing her, I was able to retrieve the half-empty bottle clutched in her claws and pour my host a modest dose of the potent potion, cut with orange juice—just enough to loosen his tongue.

"Thank you, young fella," said Frank, taking a sip. "Phew, that's a bit strong! How about some more orange juice?"

I obliged him. From past experience I knew I had to be careful not to overdo it or the oracle would soon fall fast asleep. In the event I must have gotten the proportions right, for by the time he had drained his glass he was in a talkative, expansive mood. Some gentle prodding was all it took before he started to reminisce about those halcyon days of yore.

"Come to think of it, there may be something else worth telling about. I didn't mention it earlier, you see, because it had no direct bearing on the case we were helping Mr. Holmes with. It was only a minor incident, an episode if you will . . ."

*

At some point soon after the séance at Miss Garrison's Fifth Avenue apartment, I received a 'phone call from, to my astonishment, Sherlock Holmes himself!

"Pray excuse the short notice, Frank, but I have just received a note from Mr. Jan Martense inviting me to join him at four o'clock this afternoon at his club, the Racquet & Temperance. He hopes both you and Lovecraft are also available to attend what promises to be, in contrast to the other evening, a purely social outing   an international tennis tournament."

"Will Miss Garrison be there?"

"I fear not, Frank. The Racquet & Temperance is a men's club."

"Oh well, that's all right," I said, trying not to sound too disappointed.

"I have already spoken to Lovecraft, who expressed enthusiasm at the prospect. I am not surprised to find the fellow, indefatigable walker that he is, keen on sport."

Mr. Holmes may not have been surprised, but I was, though I didn't say so. For as long as I had known him my friend had never shown the slightest interest in games, whether physical or mental.

When Sonia was in the hospital the previous year with her nerve trouble, they used to play chess together, but he later complained to me that he kept forgetting the moves and lost every time. He had made the effort only to please the old ball-and-chain.

A moment after I got off the line, the 'phone rang again. It was Howard, who was relieved to hear that I had promised to join Mr. Holmes at Jan Martense's club.

"Ah, Belknap, I'm afraid I'm once again guilty of misleading our distinguished British visitor. You may recall his skill as a pugilist and all-around athleticism from Dr. Watson's accounts. Well, when the subject of boxing and other sporting contests came up the other day, I failed to make clear my own aversion to such pointless physical exertion. Indeed, I even went so far as to praise that classic bare-knuckle thriller, *Rodney Stone*. Misleading too may be mentions of prize-fighting in certain stories of mine—the Houdini job, one of the *Home Brew* herd pleasers, and "Art Jermyn." Just because I refer to professional fisticuffs in my fiction doesn't make me a ringside regular!"

As Howard held forth on how deception played a part in each of his imagined boxing matches, I thought it a pity that during his visit to my parents' Mr. Holmes had had no chance to chat with my father. Dad was an avid follower of the sports page in the newspaper as well as the title bouts on the radio that were at the time beginning to be broadcast. He took a fishing holiday every summer, with me as dutiful bait boy. Even before my illness, I have to say that I care almost as little for such activities as Howard. In my experience, sons can have quite different tastes and interests from fathers.

"At any rate, as no doubt the sagacious sleuth informed you, Sonny, tennis not boxing is in the offing this afternoon at the R & T. Far be it from me to disparage our humble gang, but I do look forward to setting foot for a change inside a genuine gentlemen's club!"

I have always thought of Howard as a natural aristocrat, someone who by virtue of birth and breeding ought to have been a prominent member of a proper club. The Kalems may have been the center of his social universe in New York, but even I in my youth and inexperience recognized that the gang was light years away from the real thing, from the life of wealth and privilege enjoyed by the elite. Of course, there are grades in between. I remember Howard telling me that his mother had encouraged him after he came of age to join a Providence men's club, but since it was associated with a church, he could not as a strict materialist do so in good conscience. When asked, however, to pen an occasional verse for this club, he cheerfully obliged with a typical Georgian effusion, "The Members of the Men's Club of the First Universalist Church of Providence, R.I., to Its President, About to Leave for Florida on Account of His Health."

The Racquet & Temperance Club proved easy to find, since it occupied an entire block on Lexington Avenue. I must have walked past its impressive Palladian façade a dozen times before, assuming it to be another grand hotel in the tradition of the nearby Waldorf. My maternal grandfather, descendant of Edward Doty, the only servant on the *Mayflower,* served for many years as the Waldorf's manager. Above the entrance of what I now knew to be a private club hung a blue and pink flag, which was emblazoned with a crossed "racquet" (a warped-looking tennis racket) and hatchet (possibly the type Carrie Nation favored in her anti-saloon crusades).

The front door led into a large hall reminiscent of a hotel lobby. Behind a mahogany desk stood a dignified butler kind of chap in gray uniform who asked me my business. When I said I was a guest of Mr. Jan Martense, he produced an open ledger and asked me to sign my name. I saw that "John Altamont, Esq." and "H. P. Lovecraft" had already inscribed their John Hancocks. For a moment I was tempted to write "Edgar A. Poe," as years later I would witness Howard do in the official visitors' book of the Woods Hole Oceanographic Institute (in the thirties my family summered on Cape Cod), but I contented myself with a simple "Frank B. Long, Jr." Another uniformed fellow took my hat and directed me to the waiting room opposite the front desk. There I found Mr. Holmes and Howard seated in leather armchairs—the detective dressed in casual tweeds, a copy of *Country Life* on his lap, my friend in his best dark suit, his lantern jaw slackened, his brown eyes bulging, in a state of respectful awe.

We had barely time to exchange greetings before our host appeared, sporting a navy blazer and a blue-and-pink bow tie dotted with little racquets and hatchets. As we shook hands, I noticed that his cufflinks and blazer buttons bore the same motif.

"I'm glad you were free at the last minute to swing by my club, Mr.

Altamont," said Jan Martense. "And you too, Lovecraft, Frank."

"We literary types keep rather flexible hours," I offered.

Howard muttered something about a welcome break from letter writing.

"Since the match doesn't start for another hour, we have plenty of time for a tour and a spot of tea. That okay with you gents?"

"Your suggested program sounds most agreeable," answered the detective. "We are entirely at your disposal, sir."

Mr. Martense took our British friend by the elbow and guided him out of the waiting room and through the hall to a broad staircase. Howard and I followed.

"If you'd like to avoid the stairs, Mr. Altamont, there's always the elevator." The man gestured toward a recessed mahogany door to the side of the staircase.

"Please, sir," said Mr. Holmes with a dismissive wave of this hand. "You need not defer to my age."

"Remind me, Mr. Altamont, the other evening—did you say you belonged to Queen's or to Hatfield House?"

The detective launched into a lengthy disquisition on London clubs without exactly answering the question, though I confessed I soon stopped listening, my attention diverted by the handsome hunting prints hung at intervals along the stairway. Mr. Holmes set a slow enough pace for us to linger over these. "Early nineteenth century, Belknap, judging from the scarcity of periwigs," Howard said under his breath.

At the top of the stairs we found ourselves facing a magnificent high-ceilinged room filled with overstuffed couches and armchairs, empty but for a couple of napping graybeards. Mr. Martense said tea was served in the lounge every weekday afternoon at four-thirty. We didn't enter the lounge but continued on to our right, past a cigar stand, then through a door leading to a dark-paneled room with two or three writing desks, a long table covered with magazines and newspapers, and built-in shelves loaded with hundreds of books, both old and new. Howard and I didn't need an invitation to start scrutinizing this trove. We shortly realized that the volumes were arranged by category—baseball, boxing, fishing, football, hockey, hopscotch, soccer, swimming, tennis, tetherball—you name it, every sport known to civilized man seemed to be represented.

"The largest, most complete library of its kind in the country," said Jan Martense with quiet pride. "There's even a section on cricket and rugby, Mr. Altamont."

Both Howard and I murmured appreciatively, but I know he was as dismayed as I was that not a single book in the room was worth a second glance. I did, however, get an idea or two from the fishing section for Dad's next birthday.

From the library we moved on to the "temperance hall." There members gathered for evening lectures on the evils of alcohol, according to our host. To me it looked suspiciously like a bar. With its counter running the length of the room, clusters of tables and chairs, mirrors and murals, it resembled a high-class version of the Red Hook speakeasy where we'd done our first important undercover job for Mr. Holmes. A fellow in a red jacket standing behind the counter hailed Mr. Martense like an old friend.

"Your shipment of 'Earl Grey' has just reached the dock, Jimmy," he replied. "Six cases will be delivered Monday."

I caught Howard raising an eyebrow at this exchange, while there was a definite twinkle in Mr. Holmes's eye. Perhaps sensing the prevailing skeptical mood, Mr. Martense announced, "Speaking of the real McCoy, you boys ready for some tea?"

We returned to the lounge. By now there'd been wheeled into the middle of the room a cart topped by a silver tea urn, along with cups and saucers, toasted muffins, and a dish of cookies. The antique specimens had disappeared, their places taken by a handful of men in business suits who'd presumably left the office early. A couple were playing backgammon, while another pair smoked cigars by the fireplace.

"Help yourselves, gents," said Jan Martense. "Don't be shy. We've got English muffins, the nearest thing to crumpets to be found in Manhattan . . ."

I began to load up a plate.

". . . and Lorna Doones, the nearest thing to Scottish shortbread."

"Gosh, Mr. Martense," I said, "if you can import all that tea from England, why can't you include some crumpets and shortbread cookies as well?"

"And of course we have marmalade and strawberry jam."

"My compliments to the management, Mr. Martense, for making

an Englishman feel so at home."

"Thanks, Mr. Altamont. The R & T does its best to uphold the traditions of the Mother Country."

"God Save the King!" croaked Howard, seemingly overcome by so much English elegance and good taste.

Jan Martense led our little party to a pair of facing couches in a vacant corner. We set our cups and saucers down on the low table in between. I hadn't brought my pipe, but I was careful to remove from an ashtray and slip into my pocket a matchbook bearing the club racquet-and-hatchet emblem.

While we sipped our tea and nibbled at our muffins and cookies, our host gave us a brief history of the club, until interrupted by the arrival of a round-faced fellow about Howard's age carrying an athletic bag and a couple of funny-looking tennis rackets.

"Good to see you, Jay," said Mr. Martense, rising to clasp the man's hand. "Let me introduce you to some new friends of mine. Mr. Altamont, Lovecraft, Frank, may I present Mr. Jay Gould, the world's number one amateur tennis player. He'll be taking on the English challenger in, oh, about twenty minutes I see." A giant gold clock over the fireplace showed the time to be nearly a quarter to five.

"Sorry I can't join you for a quick cup of tea, Jan, though I'm not sure it would really do to make myself too comfortable here." Mr. Gould glanced toward the men playing backgammon. They had paused in their game and were staring in our direction.

"We'll be cheering you on, Jay, not that you really need our support. Good luck."

After the champion departed for the changing rooms on the third floor, Mr. Martense leaned over and said, "In nearly twenty years of competition, Jay's lost only one match—and that was two years ago, soon after his father's death." Then our host leaned even closer and whispered, "I should also explain that, even though he's the finest damn player in the whole history of tennis, he doesn't belong to this club."

"Why not?" I asked.

"Let us just say that certain members of the R & T have kept him blackballed on account of his . . . religious antecedents."

"Infamous!" hissed Sherlock Holmes.

"Or purported religious antecedents. The thing of it is, it's only a rumor. Not that it's any less silly or shameful."

"A pity, that for all your claims to classlessness, you of the New World have not been spared the pernicious snobbery of the Old," added the detective.

Howard was silent, but from his pursed lips I could tell he was pained.

"Back in the last century his father, the celebrated robber baron, built his own court in Lakewood, New Jersey. It was there that Jay, starting as a boy under the tutelage of one of the best English pros, developed his mastery of the game."

"I wouldn't think building your own tennis court would be so unusual," I said, "especially if you were a robber baron."

"Ah, Frank, forgive me. I should've said something sooner. I'm not talking about lawn tennis, that parvenu pastime. No, no, I'm talking about the grand old game of 'court tennis,' what the Brits call 'real tennis.' Right, Mr. Altamont?"

Sherlock Holmes bowed in acknowledgment.

"Court tennis," continued our host, "the glorious game of kings! Henry the Eighth was a devotee, you know."

"So Mr. Gould was carrying not tennis rackets, but—"

"Yes, Frank, those were court tennis racquets or bats. You'll have noticed the smaller, lobe-shaped head and the heavier rim, which helps impart cut on the ball."

"And the racquet on the flag, and on the matchbooks, and on your, uh——"

"You're beginning to get the picture. It'll be easier to explain once we get upstairs and I can show you an actual court. There are only about a dozen in active use in the entire United States. Hardly more than that in Europe. Why at the peak of the game's popularity in the seventeenth century, there used to be hundreds in Paris alone!"

"What happened to them all?"

"Sad to say excessive gambling and all the corruption that brings ensured the game's downfall in the eighteenth century. For long periods it was actually banned."

After draining the last of our tea, we rode the elevator up to the fourth floor, where we found ourselves amid a bunch of smart-looking chaps, some with British accents, chatting at top volume, glasses and cigars in hand. We followed Mr. Martense through the crowd into a low, dimly lighted room, containing several rows of folding chairs. On the walls were wooden plaques listing the winners of various tournaments: Crane, Sands, Pell, Cutting, Stockton.

"I've reserved us seats in the dedans, gents," said Jan Martense.

"The what?" I said.

"The dedans. It's a French term. Tennis is first mentioned in the historical record as played in twelfth-century French monasteries. A ball hit into the dedans from the receiver's end is an outright winner."

Running most of the length of one wall was a net-covered opening through which we could see a lofty enclosed space that resembled nothing so much as a medieval courtyard. The Middle Ages were of especial interest to me, as you might have guessed if you've read such poems of mine as "Sir Guy de Mandeville." A sagging net divided it in the center, but unlike a lawn tennis court this court was asymmetric.

"Note the weird geometry, Belknap," said Howard. "Why it's practically non-Euclidean!"

Along the far end and left side and apparently above us, about eight feet off the floor, ran a sloping roof, like that over a cow shed. Below the roof on the left side was a row of rectangular, netted openings. The right-hand wall ran straight until, toward the far end, it went off at forty-five degrees for two or three feet before running straight again.

"You see that little window in the right-hand corner of the receiver's end?" said our host. "That's called the grille. A ball hit into it wins the point, as does one hit into that last window on the left, which is called the winning gallery. That jog in the wall near the grille is called the tambour. Balls that strike it can go off at all sorts of strange angles."

"What are those lines on the floor, Mr. Martense?" The floor on our side of the net somewhat resembled a football gridiron, though the surface was dark stone instead of grass. On the side walls, just above the floor, were numbers that could've been yard markers.

"Those lines are used to determine chases, Frank."

"What are chases?"

"Ah, the divine chase, the very heart and soul of the game!" Jan Martense paused, a look of rapture on his face such as I had not seen him wear even in the presence of Miss Garrison.

"Let me first say that court tennis is scored like lawn tennis, fifteen-thirty-forty, game and set, but with one vital difference. Here's an example. If the player on the server's side—you always serve from this side—fails to hit the ball before it has touched the floor twice, then he makes note of the spot where it lands on the second bounce. Let's say it lands on the line marked five. Then it's 'chase five.' If it lands a little closer to the back wall, then it would be called 'better than chase five.' A little beyond, 'worse than chase five.' A chase is a kind of point in abeyance. You follow me?"

"Sure," I said, though I was still lost among the grilles and tambours.

"One can also establish a chase on the receiver's side, though there they are called hazard chases."

I glanced at Howard, for whom I suspected this was even more incomprehensible than the moves of chess. His mouth may have twitched a bit at this last mention, though "Chase" was the middle name of his beloved uncle, his aunt Lillian Clark's late husband, while "Hazard" was an old Rhode Island family name on his mother's side.

"When two chases are established, or if there's one chase and a player reaches forty, then the players switch sides. On the next point they play off the chase, or if there are two chases, the next two points. The player who is now the receiver, to win the point, tries to return the ball such that it lands closer to the back wall on the second bounce than the ball his opponent hit that first established the chase. Thus a ball that hits the floor on the second bounce at chase four would beat chase five. If it falls, say, at chase six, then it loses. The other player doesn't even have to return the ball to win the point."

"What if it lands on the same spot?" I asked.

"Then it's chase off and no one wins the point."

At this stage I was too confused to ask any more questions. In any case, the seats were beginning to fill up with spectators. Jay Gould and his opponent had come on the court, dressed in whites. Supervised by a referee similarly attired, they spun a racquet to decide who got to serve first. Mr. Gould won. The referee took his post in a doorway just under the roof by the net. Mr. Martense explained that this official was called the marker and would keep track of the score. He added that this was a special exhibition match, pitting his friend against a young, upcoming challenger, from the Drones Club in London, named Bertram

Mannering-Phipps. Those English voices we'd heard on the way in be-longed to some of his pals who'd come across the Atlantic to cheer him on.

"Frankly, I don't think Mannering-Phipps has a ghost of a chance, especially against Jay's railroad serve."

The two men commenced to hit the ball back and forth across the net in a manner not so different from that of lawn tennis. Occasionally, the ball would strike a wall, or a combination of walls, but the players always seemed to know where to stand to return it with ease. They actually had dozens of balls at their disposal, stored in a shallow trough that ran the length of the window behind which we were sitting. Dead balls rolled into a gutter below the net.

After a few minutes of warm-up, the match began. Mr. Martense, who was sitting between me and Howard, said the champion had to serve along the penthouse, as the sloping roof was called, such that the ball dropped into the fair area on the receiver's side. Standing next to the penthouse around chase two, Mr. Gould whacked an overhead shot that flew like a bullet right on the edge of the roof until falling off and hitting the back wall a foot or so above the floor. Mannering-Phipps swung and smashed his return into the net. The marker called "fifteen-love."

Though he had won the point, Mr. Gould looked a little hesitant, almost puzzled. He served again, a shot almost identical to the first. The Englishman hit a whizzing cross-court return that landed somewhere in the right-hand corner, untouched by the American.

"Chase better than a yard!" cried the marker.

This time Mr. Gould looked positively confounded by what had just transpired, though he didn't dispute the call. He served again, this time a slower ball which took a funny skip at the receiver's end of the penthouse, rolled along the back, and dropped on the floor near the grille.

"Fault!"

Mr. Gould looked toward the official, clearly exasperated in some fashion. Then he walked up to the net. The two of them started to confer, the champion gesticulating toward the penthouse on the receiver's side. After a bit, they went around to the far side to join the challenger, a tall, willowy fresh-faced fellow, who appeared equally perplexed.

Then Mr. Gould reached up and ran his fingers along the edge of the penthouse.

"Do you know anything about this?" I could hear him say as he looked sternly at Mannering-Phipps. A buzz arose from the spectators, notably the contingent of visiting Englishmen.

From our position in the dedans, it was hard to tell what was going on, but evidently Mr. Gould was refusing to continue until some problem was cleared up. People began to stand and mill around. Mr. Holmes, hitherto a model of gentlemanly calm, paced like a cage bloodhound that's caught a powerful scent. Minutes went by, until at last a few souls made bold to join the group on the court to see for themselves what was holding up the match. Sherlock Holmes hesitated a moment, no doubt fighting his natural investigative instincts, but in the next instant he was out the dedans door and after the others. Howard and I and Mr. Martense followed.

On the court the detective quickly took charge, questioning both players and marker. Then, with a leg up from Mr. Gould, he climbed on the penthouse, where he proceeded to crawl around the receiver's end, his nose to his trusty magnifying glass.

Jan Martense, I noticed, observed this show of activity from his elderly guest with a bemused smile.

*

"Is that it?" I finally asked. Frank's eyes were closed, and his head had started to loll forward. Maybe I'd made his drink too strong after all.

"What? Did you say something, young fella?"

"I said is that the end of your story?"

"Pretty much. Mr. Holmes figured out that someone had put furniture polish on the penthouse, to sabotage Mr. Gould's so-called railroad serve. Play resumed shortly afterwards, and the champion beat the challenger anyhow with no trouble."

"Did Sherlock Holmes catch who did it?"

"No, he was too eager to retrieve the stolen documents he was after to have time for solving more frivolous crimes. He couldn't pursue both, you see. Then of course he got shot with his own gun and wound up in the hospital. As soon as he recovered, he went back to England."

"Too bad he sort of blew his cover by acting like a detective."

"It didn't matter anyway. As you might recall, Jan Martense had known 'Mr. Altamont' was Sherlock Holmes and was on his trail even before he left England. Least that's what the gangster told us in his underground hideout."

"I'm not sure my readers are going to be satisfied with this."

"Hold no, I meant to say Sherlock Holmes didn't catch the culprit in New York, or rather culprits. Sometime later Howard received a letter from him in England saying he'd learned that some heavy bets had been riding on the match between Mr. Gould and Mannering-Phipps, not that anyone believed the challenger could win of course. It was all on the point spread. It seems some of the lads from the Drones Club conspired to try to beat the bookmakers' odds. Since they gained nothing by their tampering, Mr. Holmes decided there was no point in bringing the miscreants to justice."

"Sounds a bit unconvincing to me. Are you sure Jan Martense wasn't behind it all? Maybe he wasn't positive that Altamont was really Holmes, and he rigged an elaborate trick to get him to show his hand."

"I don't think so. Martense may have been a bootlegger and a promoter of fake mediums, but he obviously loved court tennis too much to stoop to such a crooked stunt."

"What happened to Mr. Gould?"

"He resigned the championship the following year. Ill health eventually brought him to an early grave, at forty-six, the same age as Howard."

"That reminds me, Frank. What year did you tell me you were born? I've seen conflicting—"

"Don't push your luck, young fella! You got your story. Don't you have something better to do than pestering an old man?"

And so, without further ado, I bade my host farewell and dashed for the exit, taking care to dodge the insults hurled by the raging dragon in my wake.

The Letters of Halpin Chalmers

"I'm glad you've come," said Ida Carstairs. She was sitting by the window beneath the pagoda-shaped bird cage, her face nuzzled by Max, her pet conure. Little had changed in the three years since I had last stopped in, to pick them up for the drive to the Halpin Chalmers centennial conference. About the cluttered living room, displayed on walls or tables, were the dusty souvenirs and tattered testimonials I had come to know over countless visits, the tokens of a long career that had brought its share of recognition but limited financial gain. If anything the place looked tidier and neater than in the past, thanks to the current services of a series of home attendants—and of course emptier. When earlier in the month I had seen the obituary in the *Partridgeville Gazette*, I had decided that it was time to put aside our differences, that I should pay my respects to the widow.

And then there were the letters, the letters of Halpin Chalmers to his best friend, Fred Carstairs, to whom he wrote almost daily during his prolific Brooklyn period. Having recently received the contract for the first critical biography (provisionally titled *Secret Watcher: The Life and Strange Death of Halpin Chalmers*), I was determined at long last to lay my hands on these priceless epistles from the pen of America's foremost author of the occult.

"I knew you'd come, Peter," said Ida Carstairs. "Please sit down." She gestured at Fred's old wheelchair.

For a woman in her late eighties Ida was in remarkably good shape, as strong in body as her husband had been frail. With no sign of strain she rose and lifted Max off her shoulder and into his cage.

"Fred's last months were very difficult," she said. "After he got out of the hospital he wouldn't let anyone touch him. And his language! Such words I had never head out of his mouth before. He was no longer my sweet little Fredela."

I had known that Fred had been hospitalized, that for a time he had even been placed in the psycho ward.

"His pain wasn't just physical, Peter. 'Why doesn't anyone come see me?' he'd cry. 'I'm so lonely.'"

Why indeed? Why didn't the fans—and certainly Fred had his own followers, apart from those who cared only about his connection with his more illustrious friend—line up at his bedside to comfort him in his final days? Partridgeville may be off the beaten track, but I believed it when she said no one came. The sad truth is they stayed away, we all stayed away, because of her.

"He was so unworldly, my beloved," she said, mercifully not mentioning my own neglect of Fred, "like Prince Myshkin in Dostoyevsky's *The Idiot.*"

As fond as she genuinely was of her late husband, in my experience she could never stand him getting all the attention, even if that attention was motivated out of a regard more for the occult tales of Halpin Chalmers than for the occult tales of Fred Carstairs. I alone of the Chalmersians recognized that the key to Fred lay through Ida. I alone knew of the existence of the Chalmers letters, secreted in a musty old trunk I had managed to inspect in Fred's bedroom while pretending to go the bathroom during one of my earlier visits. So over the years I listened for hours to her wild and fantastic stories of her glamorous youth on the stage and to her grandiose dreams of future travels and triumphs, if only to gain a few minutes with Fred—who might if I was lucky drop a fresh, precious nugget or two concerning Halpin Chalmers all those decades ago.

But I could take only so much. My patience ran out in 1991, the year of the Chalmers centennial. I had written Ida a letter politely suggesting that she stay home while I drove Fred to Brooklyn to be the guest of honor at the hundredth-birthday celebration weekend. But she didn't take the hint. She had insisted on going too—with her parrot. Those who attended need not be reminded how her antics (and those of her bird) on more than one occasion disrupted the proceedings. She defied me. She had to pay the price. As a consequence, I ceased my visits to Fred. I refused to return her phone calls.

"You know, Peter, Fred and I were not all that well matched. My friends, people in the theater, wondered what I saw in him. He was so shy. At parties he hardly said anything."

As a matter of fact, he hadn't said a whole lot at the centenary either, apart from parroting the same tired anecdotes about Chalmers he'd been repeating for more than sixty years, ever since his fellow author's premature death in 1928. His semi-senile performance there should have been Fred's last bow. No one expected the venerable occultist to reach his own century or beyond. (While the obituary had reported he died at 100, he was really 101, having shaved a year off his age at some point in his career. To one correspondent Chalmers clearly states that his boyhood pal was born in 1893, not 1894.) But he astonished everyone by surviving another three years. In the meantime, I concentrated on producing shorter critical works for *Chalmers Studies* and other learned journals, knowing that sooner or later I would get my chance at the letters in Fred Carstairs's trunk.

The Chalmers letters to Carstairs! What a trove! A few teasing extracts, a mere fraction of the total, had been published in the *Collected Letters of Halpin Chalmers*. Literally hundreds of virgin pages had yet to meet the feasting eyes of the Chalmers scholar. Why hadn't their recipient sold them? In his declining years, before he fell and couldn't leave their Central Square apartment, Fred had consigned other items in his occult collection to a local second-hand bookdealer, including his copy of *The Secret Watcher,* inscribed by Chalmers himself. I know, I was the one who had picked up this treasure at a price so enviable I forbear from citing the figure. Had he tried to sell off the letters, whether piecemeal or as a lot, my informant, the proprietor of the Angell Hill Bookshop, would have alerted me immediately.

As much as he could have used the money, did Fred deliberately keep the Chalmers letters to himself out of spite? Whenever I hinted at their existence, he pretended not to understand. In face of such coyness, I decided early on not to push the matter, instead to adopt a waiting policy, hoping to gain his confidence and eventually the prize that would secure my own name as the world's leading authority on Halpin Chalmers.

"Nobody knew he was a writer. He certainly didn't dress like one. Let me tell you, Peter, before he broke his hip he used to go out in that shabby coat of his and do the shopping. When he sat down to rest, strangers would put a dollar in his hand, thinking he was a homeless person! Can you imagine, Fred Carstairs, the great occult author, mistaken for a homeless person!"

If it can be said that Chalmers died before his time, then Carstairs lived beyond his time—long after his time. At his death Chalmers was at the peak of his powers. His posthumously published work established his reputation as the supreme practitioner of the genre. His heirs are rich today from the royalties generated by the millions of copies of his books still in print. On the other hand, Carstairs in his prime never achieved more than a workmanlike competence. In his old age he was honored more for his longevity than for any lasting contributions to the field. During the occult resurgence of the late 1960s and 1970s, he enjoyed a revival of sorts, but by the 1980s and early 1990s he could expect only the rare anthology appearance, or possibly a foreign rights sale, to supplement the monthly Social Security checks that supported him and his wife and their bird in their golden years.

To be fair to Fred, he could be perfectly candid about his own lack of genius relative to his best friend's. One has only to read that sketchy, rambling, error-riddled, if often charming memoir of his, written in his dotage, *Halpin Chalmers: Voyager of Other and Many Dimensions*, to appreciate the man's modesty. And yet, and yet, there must have been times when he deeply resented his old friend—when the interviewers, their indifference to Fred Carstairs only too evident, asked him just one question too many about Halpin Chalmers.

"He lived in this dump of a town all his life and they completely ignored him. But Fred's big-shot celebrity-author friend, that turd, they named for him that fancy housing development in Mulligan Wood!"

Both writers had grown up in Partridgeville, but Chalmers had left that provincial New England city and settled in Brooklyn, to compose the masterpieces on which his fame rests today. As for Carstairs, he had remained in Partridgeville, where nothing newsworthy had occurred since the death of Halpin Chalmers at age thirty-seven during a short homecoming sojourn. Fred, in fact, had been the last person to see him alive, though he had apparently been no more illuminating when questioned by the police at the time than in 1976 when I first queried him on the subject. (To another correspondent, Chalmers records his frustration over his friend's tendency to mix things up—a tendency that did not improve with age.) This was soon after I moved to Partridgeville, where I had been quite fortunate to find a one-bedroom condo in the new newly-erected Halpin Chalmers Estates.

"Occult writers, bah! Such people—no class, no culture," Ida continued. "But what did I know? It was only a month after we met that we decided to elope."

Fred and Ida had married late in life, after a brief courtship in New York, he for the first time, she for the fourth or fifth (she was always vague about how many husbands she'd had). Fred had brought his bride back to Partridgeville, a place that she grew to despise and that she loved to abuse almost as much as occult writers. But I had heard the story of their tragi-comic marriage a thousand times before. I couldn't care less, especially now. All that mattered was obtaining the letters. At the next pause in the monologue I excused myself and headed down the hall.

Proceeding past the bathroom door I entered Frank's dank, curtained bedroom, hoping to find it unchanged since my last snooping expedition. It was in one essential: the ancient trunk still rested at the foot of the bed. While feigning to listen to Ida, I had conceived a plan: to remove the letters a bundle at a time and slip them into my jacket or the book bag I habitually carried. In the coming weeks and months I would visit Ida regularly. I was forgiven; we were, after all, friends again. I wished I had thought of this expedient long before and wondered at my past scruples. But time had not seemed of the essence, until I received permission from the Chalmers estate for the biography—which would be a lesser thing without ample quotations from the Chalmers letters to Carstairs. I didn't want to disappoint the heirs.

From the living room I could hear Ida conferring heatedly, in French, with the Haitian home attendant. The moment had come to act. My heart in my mouth, I raised the lid. There was the same stale, musty odor I remembered, though somewhat less pungent than previously. I could dimly see— I could see nothing! Or rather, almost nothing. On the bottom lay a few scattered sheets. I seized an envelope and, as I peered closely at the handwritten scrawl, behind me I heard a squawk.

I turned and saw Ida in the doorway, her pet parrot on her shoulder.

"We knew you wanted those letters, Peter. Fred and I often talked about it. It was so obvious. My little 'idiot' said he was going to reward you for your kindness by leaving you the letters after he died. It was to be a surprise. But then, for no good reason, after that horrible trip to Brooklyn, you stopped coming. Then Fredela got ill, and I tried to call you and you still wouldn't come. You, the most faithful and loyal of all the Chal*merde*sians!"

I made no apologies. All I could do was stammer something about the letters and their value.

"Oh, yes, I knew we could sell for a pretty penny such dreck. Fools! But at our age, what did we need for cash? Because Fred was a fighter he protested at first when I said I had a better use for them. From his wheelchair, though, he couldn't really go against my will. In the end he went along."

I followed her back into the living room, hoping against hope that she had simply removed the letters of Halpin Chalmers to elsewhere in the apartment.

"The supply has nearly run out, so I'll have to go back to using old newspapers." She placed the conure inside the pagoda-shaped cage and shut the door. "There, I bet you didn't realize Max was also a critic!"

Last Fight

At Partridgeville General that gray November morning I found Ida in a coma. I'd known the old witch was ill, but not that ill. Pancreatic cancer, painful and always fatal. A fighter to the last, she hadn't gone quietly, the nurse told me. Tearing at her IV and cursing Dr. Smith had ensured the morphine drip route, not the hospice. It was now only a matter of time—twenty-four hours, maybe.

That afternoon, under a drizzly sky, Ken Corey and I met outside the apartment house in Central Square. Like me, Ken was one of the few locals who appreciated Ida, whose combative outbursts we'd suffered, eventually with good humor, for the sake of her late husband, the occult writer Fred Carstairs. We were soon joined by Sid Buzzby, who for much of his fifty-odd years had been Ida's surrogate son, looking after things, great and small, with little thanks. He had the key. With Buzzby was a young guy, Henry Wells, who introduced himself as a Carstairs fan. He'd driven all the way from Brewster as soon as he'd heard the news from Sid. I had no reason to doubt his claim he'd been a frequent visitor in recent years. After a falling out with Ida in '91, I didn't get back in touch until after Fred's death from pneumonia in January. (But that's another story.)

We had to act fast. Fred had left no will, and Sid was pretty sure Ida hadn't either. We had to remove all valuables—before she died, before the authorities realized she was intestate and sealed the apartment. Frankly, I wasn't expecting to find much, but I was in for a surprise.

Inside Wells led us straight to the bedroom, a sanctum I'd never before entered. Heaped on the floor were dozens and dozens of dusty, dog-eared occult books, some Fred's own, others by the master himself, Halpin Chalmers. No rare first editions, which Fred must've cashed in long ago at the nearby Angell Hill Bookshop, but even the dross might be worth hundreds.

"You know," I said, addressing the group, "I think Sid deserves any proceeds we might receive from the sale of Fred's library. Agreed?"

"Fine by me," said Ken.

"That's really kind of you," said Sid.

"Speaking of dividing the spoils," said Henry, "Ida promised me Fred's Halpin."

"Fred's what?"

"His Halpin Chalmers Life Achievement Award, from the Occult Writers Guild. It's in the living room. I'll go get it."

Ken and I exchanged glances. Maybe we were overly trusting, but if Wells had indeed gotten chummy with Fred and Ida, such generosity wasn't wholly out of character. Ida could always recognize a true friend.

The kid returned with the Halpin, a faux pewter statuette of this century's finest occult author, who incidentally had been Fred's best boyhood pal. It was a fair likeness, ugly and unsmiling, of the Partridgeville Puritan.

"Sure, go ahead take it," said Ken, ever the gentleman.

"I don't mind," said Sid, who not being an occult fan was in no position to judge.

We started to load the books, armful after armful, into Ken's hatchback. At some point we noticed Henry Wells had disappeared.

Next stop was the Angell Hill Bookshop, where the proprietor offered us mid three figures for the lot. When I casually asked what he would pay for Fred Carstairs' Halpin, talking theoretically of course, the man replied: "Well, now. Halpins almost never come on the market. But given the special relationship between Carstairs and Chalmers, I'd hazard, oh, $1,000."

A blinding fog descended on Partridgeville that night. About eight Ken phoned. Sid had just learned Ida was gone. *In pace requiescat*, old girl.

Next morning I picked up the *Gazette*, expecting to see Passing of Widow of Famed Occult Author on the front page, but it wasn't. A tragic car crash was the top local news item: "Mulligan Wood. Nov. 14. Henry Wells, book dealer of Brewster, died around 7:45 p.m. when he lost control of his two-door sedan and ran off the road into a tree. A witness said the victim, 25, swerved to avoid an elderly woman in a white gown who suddenly emerged from the dense fog shouting insults. Wells was wearing his seatbelt. Partridgeville General's Dr. Smith attributed his fatal injury to a blow to the skull from a cheap metal figurine found in the front seat."

As I said, a fighter to the last.

It Was the
Day of the Deep One

The Legacy in Green

Life is full of funny connections, coincidences you might say. As a practicing accountant and *Skeptical Inquirer* subscriber, I take a jaundiced view of what Jung calls synchronicity or what surrealists prefer to think of as "objective chance," yet I am convinced that the laws of probability can produce highly unusual results more frequently than is commonly assumed. Take the matter of an unexpected legacy—from, on the face of it, a most unlikely family source. It is no exaggeration to claim that I owe my present philosophical outlook to what amounts to an off-hand gift of fate.

My knowledge of the thing began in 1983 with the death of my grand uncle, John C. Dunn, chaplain emeritus at Mercy Hill Hospital, Brichester, Ohio. An ardent advocate of Irish independence in his youth, this relative, then a plumber by trade, was convicted of treason for refusing to register for the draft in World War I and served two years of a twenty-year sentence in Atlanta Federal Prison, so his passing at the age of ninety-four may be recalled by at most a few other ancient Fenian fanatics. In his dotage he was an unapologetic supporter of the I.R.A. and proudly displayed a "Brits Out of Eire" bumper sticker on his '67 Pontiac GTO.

I was by no means my grand-uncle's only heir, for his survivors included dozens of nephews and nieces, the children of those of his late brothers and sisters who elected not to take holy orders, as well as hundreds of their offspring, who promise to keep the Dunn line increasing exponentially for at least another generation. In his last years, though, I was his closest kin, both geographically and emotionally. Soon after I entered college at nearby Oberlin, my mother urged me to call on "Uncle Johnnie," then the most venerable member of our clan, at the home for retired priests where he had a room. I did so, via the intercity Brichester bus line, and was delighted to discover that we shared a common interest—not in religion or politics, mind you, but in amateur journalism.

In his mid-twenties, my grand-uncle had been active in the Partridgeville Amateur Press Club, whose ranks happened to include the future occult authors Halpin Chalmers and Fred Carstairs. Father Dunn (the name by which I addressed him) had no taste for genre fiction, though he was aware in his own way of the modern reputations of these two Partridgeville natives. Having devoured their works in my early teens, I was amazed at my good fortune to find a blood link to my literary heroes. At our first meeting I was able to coax my relative into telling me all he could remember of the pair—which admittedly wasn't a whole lot after more than six decades. Still, I gathered enough material to fill one issue of my fanzine, *Drowsing Cortex*, for the Order of the Secret Watcher, the a.p.a. devoted to Halpin Chalmers and his circle.

Thereafter I visited Father Dunn on average once a semester, since without a car I had to rely on not always convenient public transportation while he avoided all highway driving. We kept in touch through a correspondence largely concerned with superstition and the supernatural. ("I have never actually seen a ghost or had what is commonly referred to as an 'occult experience,'" he wrote when I prodded him on his beliefs, "though I suspect there is something behind the old legends of the 'wee folk.'") An unobservant Catholic, I was deliberately vague where I stood on religion. On the other hand, my relative made it clear that he'd never suffered any doubts about the faith or our forefathers. As for his time in the "big house," I gathered he'd found his fellow cons less contentious, more open to a gentlemanly exchange of views, than his colleagues in the Partridgeville Amateur Press Club.

At what was to prove our last meeting, the spring of my senior year, Father Dunn started off by denouncing the occupation of Northern Ireland with his usual vehemence, then settled down to hear me recount my latest exploits in the amateur press world, as had become our custom. At parting I gave him a copy of the current *Drowsing Cortex*, which he said he looked forward to reading. Alas, I'll never know what he thought of the issue, with its rare reprints of some early Carstairs poems. A week later the charwoman discovered my grand-uncle slumped over his desk, where lay a half-completed letter to the *Brichester Herald* attacking the Irish policies of the Thatcher government. A true son of Erin to the finish!

After the memorial service, attended by some half-dozen inmates from the retirement home, the presiding priest drew me aside as the sole relative present. Father Dunn's only asset, the Pontiac GTO, would soon go on the auction block, the man confided, and the proceeds per his final wishes donated to the Tommy Sands defense fund. In the meantime, his meager personal effects were mine to dispose of as I pleased.

Back in my late grand-uncle's room there was little enough to sort through. Above his desk was a bookshelf, whose predictable contents had never piqued my curiosity—a couple of Bibles, several biblical commentaries, a life of St. Patrick, a biography of Michael Collins, an illustrated history of the Emerald Isle. These I now removed from the shelf and examined for the first time. All were indeed entirely ordinary books, except for one slim volume. With its plain green wrapper it appeared to be another work of Irish interest. It wasn't, being some sort of diary written in a hand not my relative's. Tucked inside was a typed note on paper so fragile that it tore along the crease when I unfolded it. At the top was the seal of the U.S. Navy Department, with the inscription "Chaplain, R.C.: Portsmouth Naval Station." This is what I read:

My dear father:—

Among the belongings of those seized in the February raids was the enclosed. I don't know what became of its author, but I think you'll agree after reading that his (was?) a first-class mind, despite his heretical notions. I was reminded of certain matters you and I used to discuss in seminary. Don't hesitate to correct me (as if my old roomie wouldn't!) should you think otherwise.

No rush to return.

Yrs. in Christ,

Fr. Iwanicki

P.S. Unlike in your case, the feds aren't apt to release any of the prisoners here ever. Rest assured, their reasons for this precaution are excellent. The ways of the Lord are merciful.

This letter was undated, but I guessed from the age of the paper and the art deco-ish–looking Navy seal that it was pre–World War II vintage. Here, if I was to have any keepsake of my grand-uncle, was the obvious souvenir to take home. Though I might have been able to sell some of the other books, especially the oversize illustrated history of Ireland, I decided none of them was worthy lugging with me. The diary fit snugly into my jacket pocket.

On the bus to Oberlin I inspected the diary page by page. Printed in bold blue letters inside the front cover were the words "Property of Percy Babcock, E.O.D., Innsmouth, Mass." The body of the text, written in a cramped cursive script, was not so easy to decipher, though it seemed to be mainly concerned with spiritual matters, the record of its author's sometimes rocky progress towards enlightenment. The total wordage was not great. The first entry dated to 1924, the last to 1927.

Why my grand-uncle had never bothered to return this odd volume to his friend, why he had hung on to it so long, was unclear. Perhaps he was moved by Babcock's fervor, despite the diarist's patently alien faith. Or maybe he merely liked how it looked on his shelf, with its "emerald"-colored cover. The more I reflected on its contents, however, as well as on its physical form, the more certain I became that the modest volume I struggled to read as the bus bumped along the highway represented a mystery beyond any ultimate understanding. Was it even authentic? Might it be a hoax, I wondered, a practical joke left behind by my deceptively simple relative to puzzle posterity?

Certain anomalies troubled me. First, I had the feeling the diary was transcribed from an earlier, cruder state. The handwriting was too neat, too regular, with no crossing out of words, to be spontaneous, although to give him credit, Babcock may have written as naturally and fluidly as he spoke—but in a language other than English. Some sixth sense told me this was a *translation*. On returning to my dorm room, I performed an experiment with a variety of pens, pencils, and markers, to confirm or deny another aspect of the diary that struck me as very peculiar. Binding and pages had a waxy almost plastic sheen, like a deck of expensive playing cards. Neither ink nor graphite left an impression. After further trial in the men's shower that evening I could only conclude—the diary was waterproof!

II

Extracts from the Diary of Deacon Babcock

1924

Sept. 15: Took the Fourth Oath of Dagon before Rev. Eliot and congregation at ten o'clock baptismal service off breakwater—can no assume full duties of deacon. Glorious day! Father Dagon be praised! Hail Mother Hydra!

Oct. 19: Rev. Eliot reassuring on the Trinity—Great Cthulhu of course supreme, with Father Dagon on His right facial feelers and Mother Hydra on His left. These two equal but not always so. Worship of Mother Hydra a relatively modern development.

Nov. 1: Ring cracked chimes calling the faithful from Devil Reef. An honor in my new role. Spectacular sight under midnight moon!

Nov. 20: Point out to Rev. Eliot resemblance of Elder Sigh to symbol of upstart political party in Germany much in news. He says not to worry—NSDAP swastika clockwise, Elder Sign counterclockwise.

Dec. 10: Ponder basic EOD commandments—not obvious why Old Ones should be banished for practicing "black magic." But belief in their ultimate return unshaken.

1925

Jan. 4: Agree to teach fellowship course on Elder Gods. Problem of lack of materials. Only Nodens named. Why? Must ask Rev. Eliot.

Jan. 7: Rev. Eliot reminds me that certain sacred doctrines are not for "self-blinded earth-gazers" to question. Cites gnostic gospel of Har'oldfarnese.

Jan. 22: In sermon Rev. Eliot preaches against Manicheism. Elder Gods rebel only under sufferance of Old Ones. Hence they rarely stir forth from the Great Abyss at or near Betelgeuse.

Mar. 1: Awakened by slight earthquake tremor from fantastic dreams. Elated, as if on verge of new revelation.

Mar. 24: Very bizarre dreams last night. Maybe vision of submarine city R'lyeh. Feel feverish. Am I "psychically sensitive" or just "queer"?

Mar. 28: Dreams persist. Broad impression of vast angles and stone surfaces. Cyclopean architecture?

Apr. 2: He is risen! He is risen! Hallelujah! Hallelujah! The stars are right! Iä, Iä, Cthulhu fhtagn!

Apr. 3: For the first night in what seems like strange aeons sleep without dreaming. Feel reborn. Need time to think, to absorb His revelations.

May 1: Am reluctant to accept the call—why should I, of all His myriads of minions, be chosen to serve as His avatar on earth? Stupendous implications.

May 30: After teens transition class, raise issue of "elementals" with Rev. Eliot. While I don't put it in these terms, I suggest that the notion of Great Cthulhu as a "water elemental" is a bunch of blarney. He only happens to be trapped under the sea, I point out, having originally filtered down from the stars where H_2O is scarce, to say the least. Rev. Eliot patiently explains that our Lord has spent millions of years submersed—plenty of time to assume characteristics of ocean floor. Analogy—after a mere two or three centuries, some Yankees feel they typify soil of New England. Hence Great Cthulhu is the genius loci of sunken R'lyeh, etc. Remain unconvinced.

Aug. 19: Summer doldrums. Many parishioners on vacation in Y'ha-nthlei. Again take opportunity to challenge dogma. Can accept Nyarlathotep in role of messenger as "earth elemental," even Hastur as "air elemental," but Cthugha as "fire elemental"? On whose authority is this hierarchy decreed? Hint darkly that EOD has strayed from true path, like so many lost young of Shub-Niggurath. Rev. Eliot not amused.

Sept. 3: Stern lecture from Rev. Eliot on my recent "blasphemous" notions. Says I'll never be allowed to take Fifth Oath if I continue to challenge authority. Decide to lie low for a while, not make waves. Better perhaps to work quietly from within.

Oct. 31: Demoted to mere acolyte in this year's Devil Reef ceremony. Despite efforts to dissemble, fear permanent loss of Rev. Eliot's trust.

Dec. 2: Establish secret coven of converts, headquartered at old firehouse. We are but three or four (I'll name no names), those open-minded enough to discard a naïve evil vs. good world view and accept instead a more sophisticated faith. Promote what I term a "cosmic" perspective.

Dec. 26: Interdenominational singles supper with Kingsport brethren a roaring success. Doctrinal differences forgotten thanks to Yule spirit and case of bootleg liquor.

1926

Jan. 3: At firehouse gang debates efficacy of Elder Sign. No one willing, however, to take risk of putting to real test, so issue remains unresolved.

Feb. 10: Distinguish between "pessimism" and "indifferentism" at secret coven, now grown to six. Put to rest one member's concern that to take a detached view of the universe amounts to emotional denial.

Apr. 18: We are now ten. Call ourselves Church of the Starry Wisdom, after defunct sect in Partridgeville. Discuss significance of Shining Trapezohedron legend, as revealed in the Book of Dyzan.

May 1: Rev. Eliot informs me that as part of exchange program I'll be spending the summer in Dunwich. Reluctant to go, distance from sea, etc., but don't dare protest overly much.

May 3: Great Cthulhu speaks in a dream—gives go-ahead for Dunwich sojourn.

Jun. 18: Bus trip through some pretty weird countryside. Stone altars atop nearly every dome-shaped hill.

Jun. 20: Dunwich EOD in sad shape. Handful of regular worshipers at most. Fear taint of general indolence and apathy.

Jun. 22: Board with family in semi-renovated farmhouse outside town. A dump. Makes Innsmouth waterfront look like model community. But price is right.

Jun. 25: My hosts a fascinating case study in rural degeneracy. Half-crazed Old Whateley, twisted albino daughter, Lavinia, and uncouth gargoyle grandson, Wilbur—who I sense has Messianic ambitions of his own. Since most of firetrap of a house unusable, must share ground-floor room with Wilbur.

Jun. 30: Attempt to make Wilbur see the light futile. Egregious example of religious fanaticism.

Jul. 5: Pervasive and revolting tarry odor getting to me as the days become hotter. Tempers short. Discreet criticism of housekeeping leads to blow-up with Lavinia. She accuses me of stinking up the joint—"like a week-old mackerel!"

Jul. 14: Complain of loud noises at night from boarded-up upper floors. Old Whateley says giant squirrels in woodwork impossible to get rid of. Lame excuse if ever I heard one.

Jul. 20: Hillside ramble with Wilbur spoiled by pack of dogs that chase us up tree where we spend several hours before local rustic comes to rescue. (Hard to believe a kid seven feet tall is such a chicken.) Truly have sense of trial in the wilderness. The ways of Great Cthulhu are devious.

Jul. 27: Am counting the days before I can leave here.

Aug. 25: Return to Innsmouth to find I've not only been stripped of my deaconate but excommunicated from the EOD! During absence Rev. Eliot assailed me from the pulpit as an apostate. As fronts for EOD, Congregational and Baptist churches provide no refuge. Nothing to do.

Aug. 28: Discover others in secret coven gone, now permanent residents of Y'ha-nthlei. Am close to despair. How can Great Cthulhu have forsaken me, His avatar?

Sept. 15: Consult Necronomicon at Miskatonic U. Find some consolation in the mad Arab's double entendres, though they're not easy to sort from his superstitious misconceptions.

Oct. 20: Decline Whateleys' illiterate invitation to return for "Sabaoth" [sic] festival. What short memories some entities have. As if I'd ever consider setting foot in that pest zone again!

Nov. 1: Resume His work whilst most everybody at sea. This time I'll be even more careful.

Dec. 15: Old firehouse no longer possible as site to meet, so new coven gathers in abandoned railroad cut toward Rowley.

1927

Jan. 22: Less hierarchical, more inclusive approach gaining larger following than before. Original sin precludes no one from joining the saved.

Jan. 31: Revelation—any sincere male believer in Great Cthulhu can become a priest, or even a wizard-priest.

Feb. 15: Formally declare New Church of the Starry Wisdom. We are nearly a score strong. Select "safe" upside-down variation of Elder Sign as our symbol.

Mar. 1: Write Old Whateley and Wilbur a brief condolence note. According to the latest communication, there's little hope after all these months that Lavinia will ever be seen again.

Mar. 10: Suspect Rev. Eliot may have gotten wind of our activities. But we'll soon be too powerful for him and the EOD to oppose.

Apr. 4. Rev. Eliot stigmatizes females for choosing to be masters (mistresses?) of own bodies. Grave offense to Mother Hydra, etc. We of the NCSW pride ourselves, quite justifiably, on right to choose whether or not to remain half-human.

Apr. 14: Females eligible for the priesthood? So Great Cthulhu has decreed in His wisdom, I reveal to flock. Could the wizard-priesthood be far behind?

May 21: Size of NCSW doubled in last month or so since revelations sanctioning female priesthood. Many propose we go public. As leader urge caution, but promise day will soon be at hand when we may do so.

Jun. 9: Newest revelation—divorced Deep Ones may remarry within NCSW. Brethren greet with enthusiasm.

Jun. 15: In vision Great Cthulhu puts His tentacle of approval on right to mate with Fungi from Yuggoth. Decide it best to withhold this revelation for time being. Must introduce slowly idea of intergalactic miscegenation.

Jun. 20: Agree time has come to proclaim His message in the open. Select New Church Green, opposite the Order of Dagon Hall, for late night rally. Can fix date later.

Jun. 22: Plaster every rotting pier and crumbling store front with NCSW posters—"safe" Elder Sign prominently displayed.

Jun. 23: EOD thugs, no doubt on Rev. Eliot's orders, tear down or otherwise deface NCSW posters.

Jul. 2: Run off new posters, with rally date below Elder Sign. Advise church not to shrink from confrontation, verbal or physical, if our opponents make further trouble. Innsmouth awake!

Jul. 8: Scuffle with EODers on Fish St.

Jul. 11: Plans now set irretrievably in motion. Entire population invited, both on shore and off. Nothing can stop His avatar now!

Jul. 16: Disaster. Early this morning, just as folk are beginning to gather in force on New Church Green, word arrives that every able-bodied Deep One has to join hunt for visiting outsider to ensure he doesn't leave town. Am certain a ruse on Rev. Eliot's part to disrupt rally, but can't convince crowd. Circumstances force me to participate. Lead search party down abandoned railroad cut toward Rowley, where (no surprise) we find nothing. Can't say we look all that hard.

Jul. 19: Town full of rumors. Some persist in believing there really was someone staying at Gilman House, that he made a miraculous escape, etc. I object. What person would be fool enough to spend the night in Innsmouth? How did he get away so easily? Such is how legends or myths get started, with no real basis in fact.

Jul. 21: Some in NCSW think this outsider heralds a Second Coming or dawn of a New Age. Do best to disabuse.

Jul. 30: Great Cthulhu silent. General loss of confidence.

Aug. 3: Plan to reschedule rally postponed to fall.

Aug. 15: Revelation regarding mating with Fungi from Yuggoth hooted down by congregation.

Sept. 21: New sect, consisting of malcontents from both EOD and NCSW, takes over Congregationalist church. Mysterious transcendent visitor proclaimed their savior. Too depressing.

Sept. 28: Rally postponed indefinitely.

Oct. 14: Baptist church now in transcendent visitor fold.

Nov. 3: What if, just what if, it's all a delusion? What if there are other, even higher "gods" who are exploiting Cthulhu et al. as dupes and ill-fated stooges? The mind reels, the spirit sags.

Nov. 10: Infinite regress. The end?

III

Peril in Partridgeville

Probably the most intriguing reference in Deacon Babcock's account was to Partridgeville, the hometown of Halpin Chalmers and Fred Carstairs. In the next issue of *Drowsing Cortex* I duly noted this connection, with passing mention of the diary as a legacy from my late grand-uncle. Judging from later mailing comments, or lack thereof, my fellow Secret Watchers weren't terribly impressed. At any rate, around this time my ajay activity all but stopped, what with graduate study and eventual placement with an accounting firm on the West Coast. Only after my professional career was firmly on track, circa 1987, did I resume serious pursuit of Chalmers and Carstairs.

Or perhaps I should say Carstairs and Chalmers. The truth is, after a period of being out of the field, I returned to it free of the received wisdom that Halpin Chalmers was the superior writer of the two. Far from being a mere moth basking in the glow of his friend's flame of fame, Fred Carstairs was a behemoth of the occult in his own erratic flight/divine right—as I poetically put it in "Fred Carstairs: Moth or Behemoth?," the lead article in the first issue of the revived *Drowsing Cortex*. That not everyone in the order agreed with my reevaluation came as no surprise. Championing the unjustly neglected can be a lonely job.

One self-appointed task was unearthing the mountains of unreprinted Carstairs material from the tons of pulp magazines that proliferated in the first half of this century. The same dozen and a half tales from his classic *My Dog Tindalos* had been reprinted endlessly in various editions, mostly cheap paperbacks, and I was sure many gems and kernels if not outright nuggets awaited the diligent fan-collector-prospector's pick ax. (Please excuse the poetic metaphors, but at times it's all I can do to resist lapsing into the master's rhapsodic style.) I haunted garage sales, scouted secondhand book shops, scoured occult catalogues—in short, conducted a treasure hunt never before attempted in the annals of Carstairs research. Collecting these brittle, flaking, yellowed souvenirs of a bygone era's entertainment was, I'll admit, for the most part more exciting than reading their contents. Then, one day at an estate sale near my home in West Hills, I picked up a ratty copy of an obscure pulp magazine from 1940 called *Amazingly Ignorant Planet Stories* (later shortened to *Ignorant Planets*). One tale immediately caught my eye on the contents page—"It Was the Day of the Deep One," by Dana Autosteps—a name I'd come to recognize from my delvings as my hero's preferred pseudonym.

The title was a tip-off that it was set in Innsmouth, and in this respect my hunch proved correct when I settled into my Barcalounger back at my bungalow with my new find. What I soon realized, however, was that this was truly a far more "amazing" (if not astounding or astonishing) tale than I suspect Mr. "Autosteps" let on to the unsuspecting editors of *AIPS*. "It Was the Day of the Deep One" features a protagonist who undergoes a series of spiritual trials uncannily similar to those suffered by the author of the emerald diary I'd inherited from Father Dunn! Coincidence? Synchronicity? "Objective chance"? Sorry, none of the above. No, I could cite page after page of parallel passages, as Martin Gardner has so devastatingly if pedantically done in his recent exposé of that monument to human vanity, the *Urantia Book*—but suffice it to say that the main character is named "Perry Babson," who becomes "assistant curate" of the "EOG" (Esoteric Order of Gorgo), lives briefly in a hick burg called "Dulwich," and so on and so forth. You get the idea. The only important difference is that instead of just petering out like the deacon's diary, "It Was the Day of the Deep One" ends with a deus ex machina twist—"supermortals" rescue Babson from the concentration camp where federal agents have illegally imprisoned him and his followers.

If on first reading I felt Carstairs had barely disguised his models, later I wasn't so sure. Just suppose my initial assumption was wrong. What if, just what if, instead of the diary being the source for the story, the story was the source for the diary? As noted earlier, there was something fishy, pardon the pun, about Babcock's account. Carstairs could have written "Day of the Deep One" (an abbreviation I'll use from here on) years before it was published in 1940. The hoaxer, possibly this Father Iwanicki, could have concocted the diary after reading the tale in manuscript. Or, in a somewhat less contrived scenario, he simply cribbed from the magazine appearance. I doubted Father Iwanicki was still alive, indeed he'd ever existed, but if Poles are at all as fecund as us Irish, I had reason to hope I could track down surviving relatives.

But then fate intervened in my favor. I learned that Fred Carstairs was still alive! Yes, as incredible as it may seem, I was ignorant of this most basic of biographical facts regarding my demigod of occult fiction. He'd been born in Partridgeville in 1893 or 1894, had been the last person to see Halpin Chalmers alive before the author's brutal murder in 1928, and had married for the first time circa 1960—so much was part of the public record but little else. It just so happened that one member of the Order of the Secret Watcher, who was helping to organize the Halpin Chalmers Centennial Conference and was pretty certain the news of Carstairs' death would have reached at least one of us in the O.S.W., decided to try inviting him to Brooklyn as a special guest of honor. Finally, after many months and much networking, the venerable occultist was located—in Partridgeville!

Diffidence kept me from writing the man immediately, though I refrained in part because rumor had it that Carstairs had long ceased answering fan mail, evidently one big reason for his fall into total obscurity. In addition, he appeared to have no phone. In the end, with the Halpin Chalmers Centennial Conference only a few months away, I wrote him a ten-page, single-spaced letter in which, almost as an afterthought, I asked him about the background to the composition of "Day of the Deep One." In closing, I said I was looking forward to chatting with him in Brooklyn. I had not, by the way, shared my extraordinary discovery with others in the O.S.W., since I had resolved to get the scoop from Carstairs himself before making any announcement. I wanted to avoid any premature speculation.

Receiving, as expected, no response, I decided as a tribute to "Li'l Frednik" (Halpin Chalmers' nickname for his friend in their correspondence) to prepare a special all-Carstairs issue of *Drowsing Cortex*, including a reprint of "Day of the Deep One" along with salient entries from Babcock's diary. In my commentary I drew no conclusions. I signed and numbered each by hand. I anticipated presenting copy number one to my idol at the centennial gathering, now only a week away, but in the moment of creation I was too proud of the finished product to wait. The next morning I dispatched the zine via express mail to Partridgeville, suitably inscribed.

The following day at my office I accepted a collect call from none other than the living legend himself!

"Where in tarnation did you dig up that diary?" shrieked a thin piping voice over the line. "You damned fool! No, I'm the damned fool for having written that story in the first place. Iwanicki was a fool too, and he paid the price… At the time I needed the money, you see. I was broke. Do not, I tell you, do not republish it! I forbid it—it's too dangerous! *It's not allowed!*"

How characteristically modest of the man, I mused. His protests notwithstanding, I took the opportunity to query him on "Day of the Deep One." Did he borrow from the deacon's account, or did the deacon (or Father Iwanicki) borrow from the appearance in *Amazingly Ignorant Planet Stories*—or perhaps even from the manuscript itself?

Babcock, er, I mean Babson, stole the idea from me—I swear it!

Iwanicki gave your uncle that diary, you say? My God, never trust a priest. My reputation will be ruined, ruined I tell you, if the least hint of any of this gets out. Even though I'm innocent. As if I didn't have enough troubles already. I've never been under such pressure. My wife . . ."

It was fascinating to listen to Fred Carstairs speak at such length about his current projects—further exclusive material for *Drowsing Cortex!*—but finally I had to ring off, pleading a need to return to my actuarial tables.

"See here, young man, I'm not a plagiarist. I repeat, I'm not a plagiarist!" he said, returning at last to the subject that had prompted his call in the first place. "And if you have any more copies of that rag you sent me, destroy them, destroy them all! *I beg of you, if not for the sake of an old man on death's doorstep, then for your own safety!*"

I ended by saying it would be an honor to meet him in person at the conference. I couldn't take his admonition against reprinting "Day of the Deep One" too seriously, not that I told him that. After all, *Drowsing Cortex* was only a fanzine (though I confess I was hoping to graduate soon to semi-pro status), and I'd put a lot of extra effort into producing this special Carstairs number.

For all of us who attended the Halpin Chalmers Centennial Conference that fall weekend in Brooklyn, it was an event never to be forgotten. Every notable in the world of Chalmers studies—not to mention Carstairs studies—was present. The highlight of the festivities came Saturday evening with Fred's one-man salute at the Brooklyn Academy of Music, before dozens of adoring fans. During the question and answer period, I perked up when he said that around 1917–18, at meetings of the Partridgeville Amateur Press Club, he remembered his old friend used to enjoy sparring with some Irish plumber over U.S. support of the Allies. I stood up, ready to reveal the identity of Chalmers's long-ago antagonist as my grand-uncle, but before I could be recognized Fred's dynamic wife, Ida, saw fit to add her two cents to the discussion. With her pet parrot on her shoulder, she clambered onto the stage, where she promptly seized the microphone from her open-mouthed husband and started to vilify various occult authors and literary agents, several of whom were in the audience. Then the bird chimed in, drowning her tirade with its squawks.

I was later disappointed to hear that both Fred and Ida had been whisked back to Partridgeville shortly after this episode by their chauffeur, for I'd been biding my time for the chance to grab a minute or two alone with Carstairs. In particular, I'd been hoping to pin him down on *when* he wrote "Day of the Deep One." As if to make up for this loss in some fashion, I unburdened myself Sunday morning to a reporter who was covering the conference for the *Partridgeville Gazette*, Doug Linnet. To him I explained the whole business about the diary and my theory about who was the originator and who was the imitator. In a show of sympathy, Linnet promised to try to work this into his article. In gratitude I let him have a complimentary copy of the Carstairs issue of *Drowsing Cortex*.

A few months later, I received advance tear sheets from the *Partridgeville Gazette*, with the by-line Doug Linnet. I scanned the write-up of the centennial fête for references to myself, to no avail, until I noticed a sidebar with the title "Literary Mystery." "Amateur Carstairs buff believes Halpin Chalmers's unsung sidekick may have resorted to forbidden source for this celebrated occult yarn, 'Daze of the Deep Ones,'" began the piece. It went on to give a more or less accurate account of my researches into the matter, with sample quotations (clearly courtesy of *Drowsing Cortex*) from both the Carstairs story and the Babcock diary. I felt flattered, to say the least, to be cited in a mainstream venue.

Sad to say, not everyone involved was thrilled with such exposure. A couple of days after the tear sheets arrived, I took another collect call at my office from Fred. To report that Partridgeville's most esteemed living author was beside himself would be an understatement. Much of high-pitched whine was unintelligible, but the gist was plain enough—since the publication of Linnet's article all manner of people had been knocking at their door, from curiosity seekers to con men. As eager as he and his wife (and their parrot) were for visitors, this was far more than they could handle at their age. Would I please put a stop to it? I said I'd see what I could do.

Well, as the whole world knows, there was nothing I could do at that point to prevent things from snowballing. Some Woodward and Bernstein wannabes based in Washington got hold of Linnet's article, took advantage of the Freedom of Information Act, and in a series of

investigative reports, in print as well as on TV, blew the lid off the government cover-up of the secret Innsmouth raids during the winter of
1927–28. In due course a bipartisan Congressional committee looked
into the affair. A few implicated nonagenarians testified, though not
Fred Carstairs—he'd gone into the hospital as soon as the hearings began and was deemed too ill even to give a deposition. The headlines
said it all: "Ethnic Cleansing in Innsmouth"; "Aquatic Citizens' Religious Rights Violated"; "Shameful Precedent for Internment of Japa-
nese Americans in World War II." Perhaps the most sensational
revelation was that the federal government was still operating a "concentration camp" as an adjunct to its naval base in Portsmouth, New
Hampshire. While some conservative fundamentalist types opposed the
action, President Clinton issued an executive order in January '94 au-
thorizing the immediate release of all remaining prisoners. Cynics accused him of playing politics, of throwing a sop to liberals after his
betrayal of gays in the military, but I don't think he would have invited
the survivors, most of whom had aged very little, to that White House
seafood banquet unless he was sincere. (A pity Father Dunn died before the Clinton era—he would have been green with pride to witness
this son of the old sod promote peace in Ireland.)

Through it all, to my annoyance, the literary niceties were overlooked. Despite my offers to talk, no reporter bothered to call me for
more than an exploratory interview. Nobody outside the occult field
seemed to care whether Fred Carstairs had written "Day of the Deep
One" based on the Babcock diary or not. (And even within the field,
despite all the national publicity, few were that interested in resolving
the question.) Happily, some tantalizing clues did come out in the
Congressional hearings. One Father Iwanicki had in fact served as R.C.
chaplain at the time of the raids, which experience led him to open a
mission in Innsmouth later that year. Unfortunately, within a week of
arriving in the rumor-shadowed seaport he'd drowned after falling off a
rotten wharf. This explains why my grand-uncle never returned the
diary. As for Fred Carstairs, at a date shortly after Halpin Chalmers'
murder (a tragedy that must have shaken him a great deal), he had tak-
en a janitorial job at the Portsmouth concentration camp, a position in
which, it struck me, he could have easily mingled with the prisoners.
Perhaps as a writer he carefully recorded the conversations he overheard

for possible future fictional use!

At last I felt as if I were on the verge of some final answers. I even started to plan another trip east, whose central purpose would be to speak with Fred in the hospital, assuming he was still *compos*. No one in the O.S.W. was quite sure of his current state of health. Then, a week after the presidential pardon, I opened a letter from Doug Linnet and saw the obituary: "Local Occult Author Dead at 100." I was too late. I immediately wrote the widow a condolence letter in which I specifically asked if she could shed any light on her late husband's composition of "Day of the Deep One."

Not long afterwards I was awakened before dawn by a collect call from someone whose name I didn't catch, but in my fog accepted anyway. In the next second a shrill female voice, with no introduction, barreled down the line. I heard a bird screech in the background, and I realized I was talking to Ida Carstairs:

"Thank God, thank God, deliverance has come! My poor little Fredela is free at last! And one of his oldest and best friends has been here to help me through my time of grief. Oh, thank God, thank God. And what a gentleman, too, not like those awful occult fans. Bah! Not one of them ever visited Fred in the hospital, not one! Let me tell you . . ." I listened patiently until she returned to what seemed to be her main point. ". . . yes, he was the only one. Came all the way from Portsmouth or Innsmouth, some coastal town up north. Fred took one look at his old friend and his mouth dropped a foot. I was there! I saw it! He was so touched by his only visitor besides me, his devoted Idasha, he couldn't stand it! He went into convulsions. It was the end. But do you know what? His old friend was a clergyman! It was perfect—he performed the last rites at his bedside—in Latin! Anyhow, it wasn't English. Can you imagine?" As eager as I was to hear the details of Fred's last moments, I was beginning to wonder what on earth all this had to do with me. "He took me home, dealt with the arrangements, went through Fred's papers. When I showed him your letter, he got very excited. He was sure you had some book that used to belong to him. Couldn't wait to call you—had to fly out last night to L.A. His name? Babson, Babcock, something like that. He said just to call him *deacon*."

I was now sufficiently awake to realize I was soon to meet the answer to my prayers.

Gat-Time

Phil Peters had good reason to feel pleased. His best-selling fantasy novel, *Gat-Time: The Zany Adventures of Halpin Chalmers and the Partridgeville Amateur Press Club in Wonderland,* as if Narrated by Fred Carstairs, was going into another printing. With one exception, the notices had ben raves. Critics agreed it was a brilliant conceit to send legendary occult author Halpin Chalmers and his literary circle circa 1925 into Lewis Carroll's Wonderland, where they battle the more evil creatures there in a war pitting black magic against the weapons of the early Prohibition era, chiefly Thompson submachine guns or "gats." Perhaps his most imaginative stroke had been to tell the tale from the viewpoint of the young Fred Carstairs, Chalmers's best friend, who was still living today at nearly a hundred in his hometown of Partridgeville, all but forgotten.

Not just anyone would pay a fellow writer such a tribute—or exploit him in such a low fashion, as the lone dissenting reviewer, a certain Ms. Cohen, had had the temerity to suggest in the *L.A. Gazette.* Frankly, Phil hadn't bothered to obtain the aging hack's permission, figuring he'd be satisfied with the dedication, "For Fred Carstairs, last of the Chalmersians." After publication Fred had sent him a polite thank you letter. Later, however, he'd heard through the occult grapevine that his "narrator" was unhappy with the novel's irreverent portrayal of the late Halpin Chalmers. When in a subsequent missive the old boy asked Phil if he wouldn't mind entertaining a couple of British fans who'd be visiting Hollywood soon, he decided it was the least he could do to soothe any ruffled feathers. They were due any minute for tea.

Turning on the gas for the kettle, Phil couldn't help thinking of the "mad" tea party—and of other charges by his accuser in print regarding Lewis Carroll's creations. "Some may be charmed by this shameless twenties techno-thriller posing as whimsy," Ms. Cohen had written, "while more discerning readers will be outraged. Does Mr. Peters honestly believe he's honoring the spirit of the Alice books by depicting the White Knight as the boss of Looking-Glass Incorporated, the biggest crime syndicate on the chessboard, with the White Rabbit as rum-runner and the Red Queen and Queen of Hearts as gun-toting molls?" Yes, Mr. Peters honestly did believe he was honoring the originals, thank you Miss Smarty-pants reviewer—and so presumably did the masses who'd bought *Gat-Time*. As for the purists, Phil was sure he'd never have been invited to address the Brentwood branch of the Lewis Carroll Society that evening unless he'd done something right.

"No room! No room!" quipped Phil as she showed his guests, two middle-aged, rose-cheeked sisters named Edith and Lorina, into the breakfast nook off the kitchen.

"Next I suppose you'll be offering us wine and then declaring that there isn't any," said Edith, who was thin and prim-looking.

"Yes, and posing riddles with no answers," said Lorina, who was stout with a glowering countenance. Under her arm she carried a bulky oblong package, which Phil assumed was a present.

"Ladies, please be seated while I bring in the teapot."

The conversation round the table went smoothly enough at first. His visitors had had no trouble finding his house at the end of the long canyon road; after rainy Oxford they were enjoying sunny California; they were sorry they hadn't had time en route to stop in Partridgeville.

"I hear Fred's a nice guy, but as a writer . . . he's too naïve."

"When you say naïve," said Edith, "*I* could show you authors in comparison with which you'd call Mr. Carstairs sophisticated."

There was a pause.

"In my own fiction I admit I can be . . . well, too zany," said Phil.

"Yes, we both read your *Gat-Time*," said Lorina.

There was a longer pause.

"Are you planning a sequel?" asked Edith.

"My agent already has the outline."

The sisters dropped their teacups in unison.

"Ladies, you must excuse me," said Phil, rising. "I have to prepare for the Lewis Carroll Society meeting this evening."

"What a coincidence, we're going too."

"I'm the special guest speaker."

"No, Mr. Peters," said Edith severely. "We understand the special guest speak is a Ms. Cohen."

"Off with the lead!" cried Lorina as she lifted her Tommy gun from under the table and leveled it at his tummy.

Phil wondered what magic could obtain a weapon all but impossible for ordinary citizens to possess since the passage of the 1934 National Firearms Act.

The Hound of the Partridgevilles

"The horror fans came to Partridgeville in a psychedelic fog," said the editor of the *Partridgeville Gazette*. "Thirty years ago, anyhow, at the height of the hippie era."

"I wasn't even born then," I said.

"Consider yourself lucky, Linnet."

"You never went through a hippie phase, Mr. Turrow?"

"Well, I did grow my hair long . . . uh, that is, when I had hair."

I chuckled, but stopped as soon as I noticed my boss wasn't smiling.

"You laugh, Linnet, but one day you're going to wonder why on earth you ever wore that godawful ponytail."

"Yes, sir."

"You don't take drugs, do you, Linnet?"

"No, of course not, Mr. Turrow."

"That's good. We all know what happened, uh, to Halpin Chalmers. Now what's this about a special assignment to cover Chalmerscon?"

I didn't wish to antagonize my boss further by being contradictory, but in fact we don't know what happened to Halpin Chalmers, at least not exactly. During the 1980s, one of the more literate Reaganites turned the legendary occult author into a kind of anti-poster boy, an example of how you could wind up—nude, decapitated, smeared with blue pus—if you were so foolish as not to say no to drugs. Chalmers, as stories in the *Gazette* files from 1928 confirmed, had been experimenting with a new drug, one used centuries before by Chinese alchemists. In my view, however, this new-old drug was not the chief cause of

265

Chalmers's brutal slaying. No, there had to be more to it than that, and while you could say the trail had grown a trifle cold, I was confident a solution to Partridgeville's crime of the century was not entirely out of the question seventy years later.

Since 1968, the fortieth anniversary of his death, the town has hosted a biennial convention to celebrate the occultist's life and work, over the weekend nearest to July 3. The conflict this choice of date often presents with the nation's birthday has ensured that only the more fanatical Chalmersians have attended, or at any rate those for whom love of country takes a back seat to their favorite author. Many local residents feel ambivalent at best toward Partridgeville's most illustrious native writer, though not I should say the town's leading citizen, Cosmo Hopper Partridgeville VIII—direct descendant of founding father Cosmo Hopper Partridgeville I—who has tirelessly promoted the event for decades.

In truth, Partridgeville is such a backwater that the original family who settled it still runs the place more than three hundred years later. Elsewhere in New England immigrants have overthrown the old Anglo-Saxon oligarchy—Irish, Italians, Portuguese, French-Canadians—but not in Partridgeville, where every elected official—the mayor, the police chief, the school superintendent, the dogcatcher—can proudly claim the first Cosmo Partridgeville as his ancestor. So adept was the Partridgeville clan at weathering the economic tempests of the past that today, in the person of its principal heir—it owns most of the town and much of the surrounding county. Since the nineteenth century the family's wealth has derived mainly from the Glue Works and the Chemical Laboratories, which between them employ the vast majority of ethnic types—Irish, Italians, Portuguese, French-Canadians—who inhabit the blue-collar neighborhoods below Angel Hill.

Cosmo Hopper Partridgeville VIII and his kin occupy, of course, the fine Federal mansions on the crest of Angel Hill, as well as various country estates. Indeed, "Lord Partridgeville," an honorific title conferred by the press and since come into general use, prefers to spend his leisure hours at his five hundred acre horse farm near Brewster. For many years he served as Master of Fox Hounds of the Brewster Hunt, the last club in the Northeast still to chase the fox with intent to kill—and, if successful, to take the bloody tail or bush as a trophy.

"Drag-hunting is for sissies," Lord Partridgeville has declared more than once on the editorial page of the *Gazette,* which for the record it's only fair to disclose is part of the family conglomerate, Partridgevilleco.

"Linnet, are you daydreaming again? I asked you a question."

"Huh?"

"Don't lie to me, son—you spaced out on, uh, drugs?"

"No, Mr. Turrow, I most certainly am not—unless you consider the intoxicating atmosphere of an antiquarian's paradise like Partridge-ville a drug."

"Linnet, I don't have time for your jokes. I repeat, what's so special about this year's Chalmerscon that you want to cover it?"

"Well, sir, the thing of it is, if you've read Lord Partridgeville's edi-torial in this morning's edition . . ."

"Yeah, yeah, remind me."

". . . he's given permission for a team of psychics to spend the night at the Central Square apartment where Halpin Chalmers was mur-dered. Nobody's been allowed inside since the police removed the body in '28. They hope to recreate the exact conditions of that tragic night and thereby learn who or what did him in."

"Does he name these psychics?"

"No, but they're extremely well qualified, according to Lord Par-tridgeville."

"His lordship's always had a soft spot for the paranormal."

"I'd like to spend the night in Halpin Chalmers's old apartment, too, if it's all right with you, Mr. Turrow."

The editor smoothed back the scattered hairs on his scalp before replying.

"You know, it's one thing for his lordship to sound off in an edito-rial," he said, "but quite another for a reputable paper to lend legitimacy to dubious claims in a feature story. You're not a bad kid, Linnet, and I'd hate to see you wasting your time on tabloid nonsense."

I tried not to look too disappointed.

"But just to show you what a nice guy I can be, I'm prepared to in-dulge you this once. Tell you what, if you can get Lord Partridgeville's approval to participate, you've got the assignment. I'll even help arrange an interview. Maybe you can find out who these psychics are his lord-ship's so keen on."

"Thank you, Mr. Turrow. Thank you very much. I knew you'd understand. I—"

"Say, aren't you on your lunch break, Linnet?"

"Yes, sir."

"Then why don't you do me a favor and go get a haircut."

A few days later, I was on the Brewster road, deep within rolling hunt country, headed for my appointment with Lord Partridgeville at his farm, Tindalos Acres. Thanks to a map sent me by his lordship's secretary, I had no trouble finding the Tudor-style gate house. Above the arch was the Partridgeville coat-of-arms—a partridge in a pear tree. I've never been to Hampton Court, but I've seen pictures of it, and the stone pile that came into view after creeping a mile or so down the gravel driveway might well have been its twin. A man in livery with an English accent greeted me at the drawbridge. I followed him on foot under a portcullis, through a courtyard, down a dim passage, and into a dark oak-paneled room, where he instructed me to wait while he went to retrieve his master. I passed the time admiring the portrait of a Jack Russell terrier above the walk-in fireplace, the silver cups and blue ribbons in the display cases, the leather-bound sets of *Horse and Hound* in the built-in bookshelves, the crystal decanters with fox-head stoppers on the bar cart, among other totems.

Though I had never met Lord Partridgeville, when he waddled into the room I recognized him at once from his photos in the *Sunday Gazette* society section. A stout man in his late sixties with shaggy eyebrows, red-rimmed eyes, and funny elongated ears, he apologized in the plummy tones of a born aristocrat for making me drive so far, but then it was the height of hunting season and wouldn't I like a drink.

"It's Mr. Linnet, isn't it?" he said as he picked up the Scotch bottle.

"Yes, sir."

"We needn't stand on formality, my boy. My friends call me Cozzy."

"Okay, Cozzy. You can call me Doug."

"Okay, Doug. Here's to you. Cheers!"

My host raised his tumbler, gulped down about half the amber liquor, then plopped down in a chintz armchair with a satisfied sigh. I took a polite sip from my glass, and turned on my tape recorder before sitting on the love seat opposite.

"Nice place you have here, Cozzy."

"You like it, do you, Doug?"

"Very homey."

"Not too ostentatious, is it?"

"Not a bit."

"Grand but understated, people tell me. I'll give you a little history. In 1716 my ancestor, the first Cosmo Hopper, hired the greatest English architect of the day. Do you know who that was, Doug?"

I hesitated.

"I'll give you a hint. He also designed the First Baptist Church in Partridgeville."

"Wait a minute. Are you telling me that Christopher Wren—"

"*Sir* Christopher Wren, Doug. He was knighted in 1675."

"Sorry, Cozzy."

"When I tell you that Sir Christopher Wren designed Tindalos Acres, Doug, I mean he came to America to do the job. Other colonial buildings merely copied the Wren originals in England, but this house and the Baptist Church are the only two actually built under the supervision of the genius who conceived St. Paul's Cathedral."

Mention of the First Baptist Church, whose steeple was demolished during the earthquake of '28 that eerily coincided with the death of Halpin Chalmers, brought the conversation round to the nominal subject of the interview.

"Have you read *The Secret Watchers*, Cozzy?"

"Many times. It's one of my favorite books—other than my usual." He gestured toward the bound volumes of *Horse and Hound*. "Has something of the thrill of the chase in it, wouldn't you say, Doug?"

"If you say so, Cozzy."

"Have your read the authorized biography, Doug?"

"Part of it."

"A pity the Chalmers letters to Fred Carstairs were lost."

"A real shame."

"Fred Carstairs should never have married. You're not married, are you, Doug."

"No, Cozzy."

"Good fellow. I've been a bachelor all my life—accounts for my longevity."

"While Lord Partridgeville refilled his glass at the bar, I wondered if he regretted never having sired a Cosmo Hopper Partridgeville IX.

"So tell me, Cozzy, I said, when my host had resumed his seat, "what's this about a team of psychic investigators spending the night at the spot where Halpin Chalmers met his maker?"

"Ah, you read my editorial. Yes, I admit I was a bit coy in not naming names, but I suppose there's no harm now in revealing it's sort of a family affair. My cousin Nigel, head of the Partridgeville Canine Control Department, is working on his mail-order Ph.D. in parapsychology. The Arthur Koestler Institute, of which I'm one of the governors, recently gave him a grant to finish his thesis, on the death of Halpin Chalmers. Being something of a psychic enthusiast myself, I'll be accompanying Nigel—as will be Ken Corey, author of *Spectral Evidence: Who Killed Halpin Chalmers?* Can't have it too much of a family affair."

"Who do you think killed Halpin Chalmers, Cozzy?"

"Haven't the faintest idea, Doug. Ask me again after July 3."

"The apartment at 24 Central Square has been sealed since 1928. Why?"

"Whim of Dad's, I guess. At the time he was managing the realty division of Partridgevilleco, which owns Central Square. Feel free to mention that fact to your readers, Doug."

"Thanks, I will, Cozzy. Say, is there any chance I could join the investigation?"

"What? You want to come along and join the fun, do you, Doug?"

"Yes."

"And report on the results for the *Gazette*, I suppose."

"Hmph."

There was a pregnant pause. At last Lord Partridgeville took a long slug from his glass and declared:

"Well, why not, my boy, why not?" He laughed. "Only understand that I have final editorial say over what goes into your story. Not everything we're apt to learn about the death of Halpin Chalmers may be suitable for a family newspaper."

"That's most considerate of you. I'm sure Mr. Turrow—"

"Never mind that chrome-dome Turrow! You report directly to me on this one, boy!"

After this outburst, to my relief, my host began to reminisce about his parents, in particular his unknown mother, who had died when he was an infant. His father, Cosmo Hopper VII, had never remarried, cherishing his late wife's sacred memory to his dying day some fifty years later. By the time the butler returned to announce lunch we were both in tears. Indeed, his lordship was too overcome to say good-bye. I switched off the tape recorder and, guided by another servant, left the palace. On the drive home I reflected that Lord Partridgeville was remarkably open with his feelings for someone of English heritage.

My article headed "Lord Partridgeville to Lead Psychic Probe" was timed to appear in the *Gazette* for July 3. I had interviewed the other two participants by phone—Nigel Partridgeville and Ken Corey—and was now eager, that Friday of the celebratory weekend, to meet these two gentlemen in the flesh.

My opportunity came late that morning at the official Chalmerscon kick-off ceremony, held at Mayor Reginald Partridgeville's office in the neo-Georgian Carstairs Civic Center, formerly the Adams Civic Center. (The building had been renamed in 1994 in honor of the late Fred Carstairs, Halpin Chalmers's best friend and fellow occult author.) The ceremony included the launch of two new books: a reprint of Ken Corey's *Spectral Evidence: Who Killed Halpin Chalmers?*, billed as a special seventieth-anniversary edition with an added chapter examining the crime in the light of the latest mathematical thinking; and Nigel Partridgeville's *The C Files*, a slick popular account derived from his thesis-in-progress. Both authors cheerfully signed copies for the crowd.

Since the mayor had declared that Friday a local holiday, the lecture halls and conference rooms of the Carstairs Center were free for convention activities. All the important panels would take place the following day, which meant the afternoon was mostly reserved for certain tired Chalmerscon fixtures the organizers didn't have the heart to deny their turn in the spotlight. Chief among them was L. E. Hancock, a sprightly nonagenarian, who repeated for the nth time how on that fateful day, when he opened his door to take in his cat and pick up the morning edition of the Gazette, he had smelt a peculiar odor in the hall of 24 Central Square . . . Receiving almost as much sympathetic applause was Detective Sergeant Douglas's daughter Kim, who spent the bulk of her session flogging tattered copies of her late father's self-published booklet, *Obscure Poisons*. Sad to say, Willie Morton, great-nephew of chemist and bacteriologist James Morton, failed to show. Rumor had it Willy had been arrested for pushing a synthetic version of the drug Liao to an undercover cop he had mistaken for a fan.

The first major event was the cocktail reception that evening, hosted by the school superintendent, Percy Partridgeville, in his private suite. Cosmo Partridgeville appeared, dressed in white-tie and scarlet tails, about fifteen minutes after he was due to speak. More than a hundred devotees of Partridgeville's most distinguished author lowered their glasses and ceased munching their canapés. All eyes turned toward his lordship as he stumbled up the temporary dais beneath the crystal chandelier.

"Mayor Partridgeville, Superintendent Partridgeville, my fellow Chalmersians," he began, a little breathlessly, "it gives me great pleasure to welcome you all to this, the fifteenth—or is it the sixteenth?—annual, biannual, no, no, sorry, biennial weekend…"

"It's the sixteenth, Cozzy, if you count the gathering in '68 as the first," said Ken Corey in a stage whisper.

"Thank you, Ken. Why don't we just call it Chalmerson '98. Okay?"

A chorus of whistles and cheers greeted this suggestion."

"As you've probably all heard, or read in this morning's *Gazette*, this year we're planning something a little different. Ever since that horrible night seventy years ago we Chalmersians have been wondering . . . wondering about the cruel death of our literary hero. At the time most people blamed drugs. But what about booze? After all, it was the depths of Prohibition, and Halpin was known to drink a little hooch now and then, not that there was anything wrong with that. Many thirsty law-abiding citizens did the same. Did he owe money to rum-runners as one theory has it? Maybe—but as the authorized biography tells us, these were only the first of many rumors.

"Then there's Fred Carstairs. Fred was the last person to see Halpin alive, and he had a motive—jealousy. Even back then Fred must have realized that as an occult author he was always going to play second banana to his more talented pal. You only have to compare the sales of Chalmers titles to Carstairs titles to appreciate this point. Frankly, it's too bad Fred wasn't bumped off in '28 instead. A pity, too, that Fred attended only one Chalmerscon. Of course, we did invite him back, but only if he left his beloved wife, Ida, at home. I'm afraid we had to be tough after she— Well, I just hope it's some posthumous consolation that we've renamed the civic center after him.

"Then there are those who believe the federal government iced Chalmers and has been trying to hide the fact ever since. I emphasize the federal government, not the local government. And then there are those who believe the feds didn't do it—it was, ha-ha, if you can believe it, a bungled alien abduction attempt—but the authorities are still trying to cover up the facts. Again, I repeat, our local officials have never been a party to such a conspiracy. Isn't that right, Nigel?"

"That's right, Cozzy," answered the head of the Partridgeville Canine Control Department.

"On the contrary, they've done their darnedest to discover the truth! And that's what we aim to accomplish tonight, my fellow Chalmersians, discover the truth in the matter of the death of Halpin Chalmers!"

The onlookers erupted in more cheers and whistles.

"To that end I will be joined by two outstanding experts in the field, my cousin Nigel Partridgeville, and Mr. Ken Corey, whom some of you were privileged to meet at the kick-off book signing earlier today."

The applause lasted nearly a minute.

"I'll grant you that each of these fine individuals has his own unique theory," resumed Lord Partridgeville. "They can't both be right. Ken here has taken the abstract route, applying the, the, some Jap—"

"Taniyama-Shimura Conjecture, Cozzy," said Ken. "It all ties in with the proof of Fermat's Last Theorem, the idea that elliptical curves—"

"Right, Ken. Let's not spoil the surprise for your fans, shall we? Nigel, on the other hand, is taking a more practical, down-to-earth approach. You can read his excellent book—and be sure to attend the special panel scheduled for tomorrow evening, when we'll announce the results of our vigil and answer any questions you may have. Thank you."

If Lord Partridgeville had neglected to mention what was happening next it didn't much matter, since anyone aware of the limousine and police escort waiting outside the Carstairs Center could guess that the team would be heading directly to Central Square. That morning his lordship's secretary had phoned to say it would be all right for me to go along for the ride, and accordingly I met the others at the car just as the chauffeur was warming up the engine.

It was less than a mile to Central Square, but we had to proceed almost as slowly as I had along the gravel driveway of Tindalos Acres, owing to the swarms of ethnic folk who clogged the streets in the summer twilight. As the intermittent sound of firecrackers indicated, these locals were not convention goers, but their state of restless excitement reinforced the air of adventurous expectancy we Chalmersians were feeling in the limo.

From an oversized picnic hamper, Lord Partridgeville produced a Jeroboam of red wine, which he opened with the corkscrew on his Swiss Army knife. After a glass or two we were all in a convivial mood, though I have to say the banter between Nigel and Ken soon took on a certain edge. Both authors had reproduced the autopsy photos in their books, but Ken suggested that it was inauthentic for Nigel to have colorized the original black-and-white prints, thus highlighting the blue pus. Nigel replied in so many words that he thought the diagrams and formulas in the new chapter of *Spectral Evidence* would be incomprehensible to not only average readers but also the mathematics faculty of Partridgeville State. In all fairness, as his lordship hastened to point out, Partridgeville State, being a divinity and agricultural college, had only a third-rate math department. As a trustee of that institution, he was in a position to know.

At last we arrived at Central Square, which had been shut off to motor traffic and was filling with people, many of whom I recognized from the reception at the Carstairs Center. Obviously, it had been faster to walk. The police chief, Alasdair Partridgeville, greeted us at the protective barrier set up in front of the former Smithwick and Isaacs jewelry store, since converted to a museum and gift shop dedicated to Halpin Chalmers. He confirmed that a large crowd would be supporting our efforts through the night from the vantage point of the square itself. A detachment of Partridgeville's finest, under his personal command, would ensure everyone's safety.

The super let us into the second-floor apartment, what in today's parlance would be called a studio. The single room was empty, apart from a couple of old bowls in one corner—or what would have been a corner had not every junction of floor and wall and ceiling been rounded off with cracked and crumbling plaster of Paris. Judging from the thick coating of dust and plaster fragments on the floor it hadn't been entered in some time. The room was also hot and stuffy, and with his lordship's permission I opened the window, which looked over the square.

"In Dad's will he insisted the place remain unoccupied in perpetuity," said Lord Partridgeville. "Can't imagine why."

I could see those waiting outside were well equipped with tents and sleeping bags, while we psychic investigators had merely a picnic blanket, which could comfortably accommodate three when spread on the floor. I volunteered to stand—at the window, where I could get some air. I later had reason to be grateful for this choice, though at that moment my prime concern was my stomach. Our only refreshment was the Jeroboam of red wine, and I had drunk enough of that. My brain was definitely feeling fuzzy. I wished I had eaten more canapés at the reception.

Ken took some measurements of the room was a small surveyor's tool, then went to work on his pocket calculator. The cousins set up their own apparatus on the blanket, and began what they claimed was a test of remote viewing. When it became dark, his lordship lit a candle he had the foresight to bring. It fit nicely in one of the old bowls. The bare bulb hanging by a cord from the ceiling was evidently burnt out.

For the next hour or so my colleagues focused on their tasks, with no discernible results. Only the sound of the occasional firecracker in the distance broke the silence. Out of boredom, or maybe scientific curiosity, I nonchalantly popped the pill I had purchased from Willy Morton that morning prior to his arrest... Yeah, I know what I said earlier about not taking drugs, but in the circumstances I was prepared to make an exception. In my view there was more than one road to Damascus—or was it Samara?

Nigel and Ken were arguing over the efficacy of curves versus angles when the smoke started to pour from a big gap in the plaster of Paris in one of the ceiling corners. The candle flickered, the bare bulb swung on its cord, the light dimmed in the swirling brown smoke.

Within seconds a terrific explosion shook the room. Had some fool set off a cherry bomb? Then there was a tremendous thud—and a scream!

Mercifully, the candle did not go out, and when the smoke cleared I could see a huge form on top of Lord Partridgeville, prostrate on the picnic blanket, licking his face!

"Your tongue, ahhhh!" groaned his lordship.

It was an enormous hound with short chestnut hair, lop ears, and deep mournful eyes—though it could all have been an extremely clever costume. Seams and zippers would have been invisible in the feeble candle glow. When the animal stood upright on its hind legs and began to speak, in correct and idiomatic English, I was sure someone was playing a prank and yet—"

"Well, I knew we were destined to cross paths one of these days," the creature said. "And you do remind me of your dear father."

"What!?" spluttered Lord Partridgeville, who was now sitting up and moping his jowls with a handkerchief. "Who—or what—are you?"

"When we first met, Cosmo called me the Hound of Tindalos, but later, after we had . . . Well, I just thought it was more respectable to be known as the Hound of the Partridgevilles."

"Confound it, are you telling me you and Dad were friends?"

"Oh yes, though given certain cosmic limitations we could only meet secretly in our little hideaway. No one knew. If it hadn't been for that unfortunate accident to that writer who used to live here, Cosmo and I might never have… He was inspecting the apartment a day or two after the mess was cleaned up. I was still hovering around. He looked so cute I just had to introduce myself. Well, one thing led to another… Of course, Cosmo was already married, but he confessed early on that his wife had this medical condition, but maybe she could be persuaded to go along, and in the end she did, though the poor thing didn't survive the shock. . . . I was very sorry, especially for you . . . son."

"Ma, ma . . ."

"Cosmo and I agreed it was best not to tell you, until you were mature enough to understand—to understand for instance why you yourself can't have children. I'm afraid it's the old story of the horse and the donkey producing a mule."

"That's why when I first . . . I couldn't . . ."

"Alas, your father died before we felt you were ready to handle the truth. I just hope now you have the courage to forgive us both."

"You and Dad, you—"

"He was proud of you, a natural sportsman! And he was so attentive to me. He always saw to it that I had plenty of food and water when I visited the earthly plane."

I cast a furtive glance at the candle, which continued to flicker in the bowl . . . the dog bowl. Lord Partridgeville sat open-mouthed and wide-eyed on the blanket, evidently dumbfounded.

"This family history of yours is all very well," Nigel said finally, in a tone that suggested he didn't believe a word of it. "But did you kill Halpin Chalmers?"

"I refuse to answer such a rude question."

"You would be wise to cooperate," continued Nigel. "In my professional capacity I have the authority to detain you at the town pound."

"Say, what kind of hound are you anyway, a blood hound?" added Ken. "A hound that laps up human blood and processes it into blue pus?"

"I've never heard such insults!"

Despite her size, she appeared to be a rather timid soul. (By this point I was ready to accept that the Hound of the Partridgevilles or Tindalos or whatever was a dam.) The psychic researchers started to move forward, backing her into the gloom. She barked, and her bark was immediately echoed by what sounded like the distant baying of a whole pack of hounds—or was it the noise of the crowd in Central Square, distorted in the rising wind? Leaning out the window, I could hear the hitherto quiet hordes mutter and complain, like a theater audience that has waited too long for the opening curtain. I was reassured to hear the police chief warning the more agitated spectators not to cross the barrier below.

A sudden blast of air behind me extinguished the candle. I turned but could see nothing. Amidst the inhuman baying that had by now swollen to nearly deafening levels, however, I could make out a lone human voice, the plummy, aristocratic voice of Cosmo Hopper Partridgeville VIII.

"Yoicks! Tally-ho! After him, lads! The quarry is nigh!"

Did I then actually hear the silvery peal of a hunting horn? Or was the drug driving my brain to produce even wilder hallucinations? Those thundering paws that grew louder and louder sounded only too real. In a panic I realized my only escape was the window, but as I climbed over the sill I was hit from the rear with the force of a locomotive. For an agonizing eternity I thrashed in midair, a searing pain at the back of my head. A hundred lights flashed, a thousand throats shouted—then I soared free and the entire universe went black.

"You know, you're a lucky kid, Linnet," said the editor. "Lucky the cops broke your fall before you hit the pavement."

"What about the others, Mr. Turrow?" I asked. It was two days after the episode in Central Square, and I had just returned to work from the hospital. No one had told my anything.

"Ken Corey and Nigel Partridgeville are okay, though they seem to have suffered a total memory loss. They can only remember entering the apartment—nothing after that."

"And Lord Partridgeville?"

"His lordship's presenting undergoing a rest cure at that sanatorium upstate where he periodically goes to, uh, dry out. I'm afraid he's instructed me to spike the story you were planning to write about the outcome of your psychic investigation. He's sorry."

"Just as well," I said. "We didn't solve the mystery of Halpin Chalmers's murder anyway. Besides, I'm not sure my memories are all that reliable, given my mental state."

"His lordship's also sorry for, uh . . ."

"For what?"

"I guess you haven't seen the front page of Saturday's *Gazette*." The editor was grinning as he reached under his desk.

"No."

"We put out a special edition. Since so many camera buffs were at the scene we had plenty of high quality photos to choose from. For a night shot the clarity's amazing."

He was positively chortling when he handed me the newspaper. I snatched it open and read the headline: "Lord Partridgeville Bags Big Game." The picture underneath showed me dangling in front of 24 Central Square—held by the ponytail by his lordship, who was sawing at the roots with his Swiss Army knife. You could see the cross, the details were that sharp.

Acknowledgments

Long Memories: Recollections of Frank Belknap Long was first published by the British Fantasy Society in 1997.

Afterword to *Autobiographical Memoir* first appeared in *Autobiographical Memoir* by Frank Belknap Long (Necronomicon Press, 1985).

Review of *Autobiographical Memoir* first appeared in *Crypt of Cthulhu* 34 (Michaelmas, 1985).

"Lovecraft on Long" first appeared in *Studies in Weird Fiction* No. 23 (Summer 1998).

"Frank Belknap Long: When Was He Born, and Why Was Lovecraft Wrong?" first appeared in *Studies in Weird Fiction* No. 17 (Summer 1995).

Pulptime: Being the Singular Adventure of Sherlock Holmes, H. P. Lovecraft, and the Kalem Club, as if Narrated by Frank Belknap Long, Jr. was first published by W. Paul Ganley in 1984.

"Discarded Prologue" first appeared in *Tales of Lovecraftian Horror and Humor: The Early Cannon, Volume Two* (Tsathoggua Press, 1997).

"Episode of *Pulptime*" first appeared in *Episode of Pulptime & One Other* (W. Paul Ganley, 2003).

"The Letters of Halpin Chalmers" first appeared in *100 Crooked Little Crime Stories*, edited by Robert Weinberg, Stefan R. Dziemianowicz, and Martin H. Greenberg (Barnes & Noble, 1994).

"Last Fight" first appeared in *Horrors! 365 Scary Stories*, edited by Stefan R. Dziemianowicz, Martin H. Greenberg, and Robert E. Weinberg (Barnes & Noble, 1998).

"It Was the Day of the Deep One" first appeared in *Midnight Shambler* No. 5 (Eastertide 1997).

"Gat-Time" first appeared in *Yawning Vortex* 3, No. 2 (July–August 1997).

"The Hound of the Partridgevilles" first appeared in *Forever Azathoth and Other Horrors* (Tartarus Press, 1999).

Peter Cannon is the reviews editor at *Publishers Weekly*
who handles the mystery/thriller category.
He and his wife and their three children live in New York City.

www.ingramcontent.com/pod-product-compliance
Lightning Source LLC
Chambersburg PA
CBHW070446030726
47503CB00004B/919